I0817793

-THE LEGEND OF HULLABEE ISLAND-

GENEVA SOMMERS

and the Myth of Lies

-THE LEGEND OF HULLABEE ISLAND-

GENEVA SOMMERS

and the Myth of Lies

C.J. BENJAMIN

For information regarding permission, write to:
Attention: Crown Atlantic Publishing
2000 Mariposa Vista Lane #104
St. Augustine, FL 32084

Published in the United States by Crown Atlantic Publishing

ISBN 978-1-7326123-7-2

Version 1.1
Printed in the United States of America
First edition printed, January 2019

To all the fighters,
Those who bend, but do not break.
Those who cling to the light,
when surrounded by darkness.
Those who pause; then find the strength to
carry on.
You are my heroes.

VOLCANO
RAINFOREST
N

IS LAND
Tower
-of-
Lux
LUX
Troian Center

PROLOGUE

A fire is building. It's fueling my heart, my desires, my rage. My future is alight with flames. Will they destroy me? Strengthen me? Perhaps they will permit me to rebuild something better from the ashes. I am both mesmerized by their beauty and terrorized by their power. Will they heal or wound? Will they bring rebirth or death? Flames are a fickle friend. Tame them, or they will devour you.

1

The anxious knot in my stomach was growing unbearable. Months of preparation had led us to this moment. It seemed like a lifetime ago we'd fought our way out of the Troian Center and found shelter with the Betos in the rainforest. Since then I'd become a new woman. Or at least I was trying to be. I'd embraced my role as the Eva and studied the history of my people. But my education was short lived. It seemed that my destiny would seek me out before I was ready. Brutal attacks lead by the Ravinori, ending in utter devastation for the Betos, had forced my decision to return to the place I had fled. I was in search of the missing Pillars and a way to stop the dark forces from gaining power. We'd fought for every inch we gained on our voyage back to the Troian Center, but now that we were finally here on the precipice of my destiny, I felt stiflingly uneasy.

We marched forward out of the protective tree line of the forest and into the open field; a wall of bodies, hands clasped moving with purpose toward the Troian Center. Even though we had the protection of Remi's invisibility power, I still felt tense and exposed. My heart pounded with uncertainty as a cool wind rushed past and we picked up speed. I could barely feel the strange sensation of lightness that being invisible provided. My skin tingled, but it felt more like nerves than magic. The last time I'd been invisible the sensation had felt much more intense, which had me worried that maybe it wasn't working right. The possibility that Remi wasn't strong enough to stretch his power over all of us made me shudder with fear. This was more people than he'd ever tried to share his power with before.

"Are you sure it's working?" I whispered to Remi.

"Yes."

"How do you know?"

"I just know. Now stop distracting me," he said sounding strained.

Jemma squeezed my hand supportively. Holding her hand was definitely adding to my uncomfortableness.

"It's working," she said. "Can't you feel it?"

"Just barely. It feels less intense this time."

"Maybe having your powers veiled has dulled the sensation for you, but I can feel it pulsing though me. Look, the hairs on my arms are standing up!" she said.

I sighed realizing she was probably right. I was so used to having heightened senses, but they must have been hooked to my powers because I felt desensitized ever since Jemma veiled them. I shook away the uneasiness and instead focused on how quickly we covered ground. The Troian Center was in full view now and I strained my eyes to cover the rest of the ground between the approaching building and us. It looked odd to me, but I couldn't put my finger on what was different about it. Had we been gone so long that the only home I remembered now looked foreign to me? Maybe it seemed darker and more foreboding? Or maybe that was just my nerves.

"Does something look off to you?" Remi asked as we approached.

"So it's not just me?" I asked, the pit in my stomach growing.

"Yeah, look at all the trees and plants. They weren't there before, right?" Jemma asked, seeming as unsure as I was.

"It makes it look... pretty," Sparrow said with uncertainty in her voice.

"There's a fence too! That's new," Nova said.

"You're right," Journey said. "I can barely make it out behind all the plants."

We slowed our advance, cautiously trying to figure out the subtle differences in the Troian Center and the purpose of the fence that loomed up ahead. We'd always entered through the opening in the courtyard wall. It was never fenced off. It was usually guarded loosely by Grifts, but they were easy enough to slip past. But there didn't seem to be any Grifts in sight. I squinted, making the black fence come into focus. It wasn't especially tall or intimidating, but it's what had given me the perception that the Troian Center had a darker exterior. The black fence seemed to wrap around the entire complex, adding an eerie shadow to the coquina walls. In some places the fence was hard to make out, with trees and hedges blocking our view.

"Who would put a fence around the Troian Center?" I asked.

"I think we need to get a closer look," Journey said. "Let's keep going."

We continued moving forward watchfully, taking in the details of the fence. From this distance we couldn't tell what it was made of, only that it was shaped into evenly spaced black bars. I shivered as it conjured images of prison cells in my mind. The fence was about eight feet high, with pointed tips that glimmered in the remaining sunbeams that managed to filter through the clouds.

"That's strange," Journey said. "I can't see a break in the fence anywhere. Shouldn't there be a gate?"

"I don't know. But the good news is I don't see any Grifts," Remi said.

"Yeah, that kind of worries me," added Nova.

"Me too," I whispered.

We were within 100 yards of the fence now. We slowed our walk to a hesitant pace as we tried to figure out how to get inside. This had never been a problem before. The Troian Center had been designed to keep us from getting out, not the other way around. We were in unexplored territory, now that we were trying to find a way in. We crept within the newly manicured lawn as we headed toward the familiar courtyard entrance. There was no solution in sight to the fence securely positioned in front of us. We didn't know what else to do but keep moving forward. We passed lush vegetation and fragrant citrus trees as we approached. Bright hibiscus blooms caught my eye. They seemed a strategic distraction for any who approached. Tall cypress trees and dense hedges loomed around us, cutting off the view to all but the very top spires of the black fence just ahead. The path narrowed, as if funneling us toward something. My anxiety intensified when Jemma and Remi pushed against me as we squeezed together to fit through an impeccably sculpted pair of hedges. Just as we passed through them I heard Remi gasp and the world went dark.

Blackness.

"MASTER, SHE'S HERE!" Kobel exclaimed, barely able to catch his breath.

He ran all the way to Malakai's office the moment he'd seen the words appear in the *Book of Gods.* He'd held his breath while he watched the ink slowly crawl across the pages written by some unseen force. He'd even closed his eyes and counted to twenty, praying the words would still be there when he opened them. They were. He closed the ancient book and then opened it again, just to be sure. Kobel knew he couldn't disappoint his master again. The penalty would be too steep. He'd seen enough of them doled out to know that Malakai didn't make empty threats.

As he slowly opened the delicate pages of the prophecy revealing book, he let out a breath of relief. Sure enough, the elegant script was still there.

The one you have been waiting for has arrived. Shielded by disguise, you will have to seek out what you covet, for it will not reveal itself plainly.

"You're sure, Kobel?" Malakai asked, looking up at the old man from behind his desk.

"Yes, Master. Look, it's right here," Kobel said proffering the *Book of Gods* before him.

A smile cracked the stern face of Malakai Vanir as he rose to his full height.

"So it begins."

2

The moment we'd passed through the hedges, Remi's power failed and we became visible. Instantly, we were tangled in a mess of heavy nets that toppled us to the ground. I never even saw it coming. It was as if they fell from the sky, enfolding us in terror. Before we knew what was happening, dozens of soldiers from Lux descended upon us, shouting and adding to the chaos. We tumbled about as they wrenched the heavy net, pulling us in a mess of twisted limbs and disorder. Pain seared through my body as I panicked to right myself against the ropes. Our struggles only lasted a moment before we were yanked from under the net one by one. I screamed and kicked against the Luxor who'd grabbed me by the back of my neck and hoisted me from under the net. He twisted my arms behind my back to the point of blinding pain.

My eyes searched wildly for my friends. They landed on Nova. He was already out from under the net and was being restrained by two Luxors. I cried out to him and his eyes locked desperately with mine; stormy green meeting ice blue terror.

"Nova!" I screamed.

Nova struggled against our attackers to get to me. He managed to drag them about a foot in my direction, but he was outmatched.

"Get off of her!" he screamed, disregarding the chokehold restraining him.

He was rewarded with a blow to the jaw that spattered blood onto my feet. Tears welled in my eyes as I watched the Luxor kick him in the ribs so hard that he dropped to his knees gasping for breath.

I tried to call his name, but it came out as an incoherent croak when a rough bag was thrown over my head, blocking my view of the terrifying scene.

My mind was reeling. I was beyond shocked to see Luxors at the Troian Center. They were specially trained soldiers who swore a death oath to protect the city of Lux. Normally they were seen in their crisp grey military uniforms, patrolling the city's border. I was baffled as to why they'd be here.

When the bags were finally removed we were inside the courtyard of the Troian Center. The Luxors were certainly living up to their brutal reputation as they gagged and bound us. One grabbed my arm so hard that I was terrified the bone would break. He was beyond strong and I felt my feet leave the ground as he hoisted me away from my terrified friends. He jarred my arms painfully behind my back and tied them together. But he wasn't done yet; he shoved me to my knees and pulled my fists to my ankles, binding me in that uncomfortable position. I felt something cold and hard next to my ear. It seemed to hum for a split second before the soldier grabbed me by the nape of my neck and jerked my head to the side. The hum changed into a sickening shearing sound. I felt pressure and stinging as the cold metal bit my scalp. I could feel soft coifs, piling up around my bound ankles and I gasped when I realized what was happening. A single tear ran down my cheek and into the corner of my mouth. It tasted salty and bitter. I bit my tongue to stop myself from crying as the Luxor savagely sheared off my hair.

The bag had been put over my head again and I focused on taking small breaths, because I was losing feeling in my limbs and I thought I was going to pass out from the pain. I could hear my friends being treated to the same brutal handling. Their muffled yells tore at my heart, but I was helpless to save them without my powers. Sparrow's sad whimpers sent chills down my spine. This was much worse than I had ever anticipated. We thought we would be dealing with the usual Grifts, and suspected a new headmistress, but never anything like this. We were no match for Luxors. I found myself wondering who they'd been expecting. Was it necessary to send soldiers to attack teenagers?

The commotion suddenly ceased and I held my breath and begged my ears to tell me what was going on. Perhaps the soldiers had left us. I cursed myself for veiling my powers. There was nothing I could do to get us out of this situation. I couldn't even telepath to the others. For a moment I thought of Isby coming to our rescue, but then I remembered I didn't trust the grumpy old bird. Plus, I had told him he was not to follow us from the forest; that I would call him if we needed him.

Another bad decision on my part, I scolded myself.

I counted the seconds of silence anxiously. Surely Nova would burn through the ropes with his powers, or Journey would turn them to stone and bust through them. Still, I heard nothing and I was too afraid to utter a sound.

Finally, I heard the soft crunching of gravel followed by a single voice. It cut through the silence like a hot knife through butter and my stomach churned with fear. A twinge of recognition pricked my mind. I knew his voice. I'd heard it before.

"Now what have we here?" purred the voice, as smooth as

silk. "My deepest apologies, children. I hate that you were welcomed under such duress, but we must always be vigilant. I assure you, if I had been made aware of your arrival it would have been a much more glorious entry to our fine institution."

We were still kneeling in the courtyard surrounded by Luxors as his voice addressed us. He finally gave the order to release us and our binds were untied and bags removed. I blinked rapidly adjusting to the sudden brightness.

I caught a glimpse of a tall, hooded man. I couldn't get a good look at him as he stalked behind us droning insincere remarks. I was horrified to see that all of our heads had been viciously hacked at. There were haphazard patches of hair next to raw sections of still damp blood where the blades had cut too close. The ground was covered in an array of severed hair that swirled into tiny cyclones in the soft breeze. Sparrow and Jemma were still shuddering with sobs. They seemed to have gotten the worst of the scalping, making me wonder what my own hair looked like. My fingers itched to reach for my scalp, but I stood tall, refusing to let this monster know he had gotten the best of me. I wasn't buying his apologetic tone at all. Anyone who brought Luxors to an orphanage was definitely not to be trusted.

He walked over to Sparrow, who was trying to stop crying, but every time her slender fingers clutched a strand of hair that pulled free from her head, she started sobbing all over again.

"Why are you crying, child?" he asked.

"Mm...my hair," she whispered.

He pulled a thin black blade from within his robe and my breath caught in my throat. I helplessly watched him press the cold steel up to her scalp. He held it there for a moment and I watched her tremble. But then, as if deciding better of it, he pulled it away and walked on.

"Merely a precaution. It'll grow back I assure you. It's a small price to pay to ensure identity," he said sounding amused with himself. "We must always provide the utmost protection for our own children."

I was so confused. I looked around and from the expressions on my friends' faces they were just as shocked. The hooded man continued down the line and pressed his blade to each of their freshly scalped heads.

My mind was swiftly recounting his words as I watched him. He had said 'our own children.' There had never been any children at the Troian Center other than orphans. Why would a parent send their children to a place like this?

"Now let me guess," he said interrupting my thoughts. "You six are the orphans that Headmistress Greeley lost. We've been looking for you. I couldn't be more delighted that you've shown up of your own accord." He clasped his hands together with exuberance. "You have no idea how worried I've been for your safety. When I heard that you were missing, I sent my best men out looking for you. This island isn't a safe place to run off in alone. Quite truthfully, I'm surprised to find you all still alive."

There was an awful honesty in the way he delivered that last sentence. It confirmed my instant feeling of distrust in him. Who was he, anyway? His voice haunted my mind as I tried to remember where I'd heard it before. He was circling us with his hands clasped behind his back. He paused from time to time to inspect us. He kept shaking his head and making displeased clucking sounds. When he stopped behind me, I felt his cold blade press against my raw scalp and shivered. After a moment he strode in front of me, and then brought his face so close to mine that it took everything in me not to turn away. He smelled like spice and iron. The scent was so strong, my nostrils flared trying to breathe away the burning odor. My eyes watered, but I met his gaze straight on, not wanting to give this man an inch. My heart faltered when I saw the face that hid in the shadows of his hood. I recognized him instantly. I felt my knees knock together, but I was determined not to show my fear.

"Ah, and you must be Geneva, I presume."

So, he knew my real name. I could feel the eyes of the whole group upon me. I did my best to hide my surprise and keep my tone casual.

"I make it a habit not to talk to strangers," I smartly retorted even though I knew exactly who he was.

"Ah!" He rolled his head back in thunderous laughter, letting his hood fall to reveal his long, dark hair pulled back from his perfectly groomed face. "Right, you are! Where are my manners? Let me introduce myself. I am Malakai Vanir, the new Headmaster of the Troian Academy."

There was a rush of anxious murmurs among my friends as they realized that the suspected head of the Ravinori was confronting us.

Malakai smirked at us coyly, studying our subtle reactions.

"I'm very glad you've come back. As I said, I learned of your escape under the past headmistress, and I don't know what might have transpired to cause you to flee this fine institution, but that's neither here nor there. The important thing is that you're back and you're safe. I think you'll find that I run this institution much differently than Headmistress Greeley. I hope you will appreciate my goals to improve the quality of life at the Troian Academy and to turn it into an elite educational conservatory that you will be proud to attend."

"Funny way of showing it," Journey mumbled.

He was so fast I didn't even see him move, but a Luxor was on top of Journey the moment the words crossed his lips. He had him on his knees and was crushing his throat.

"Tisk, tisk. Thank you, soldier; that'll do." Malakai called the lethal Luxor off of Journey, who collapsed clutching his already bruising neck.

"Ah," Malakai sighed dramatically. "Again, I find myself apologizing to you. I should have told you that I must be addressed as Headmaster or Sir, and that backtalk is not tolerated here at the Troian Academy. We are grooming proper, well-rounded, young adults and no other behavior is acceptable. Anyway, it's not your fault. Once you go through orientation you'll know all the rules you must adhere to. But first things first," he said with a grin. "Escort them to the infirmary to have them *cared for*."

3

The way Malakai had dragged out the last words made me shake. I could only imagine what his version of 'cared for' was when he employed a welcoming committee of Luxors. Orientation was definitely in order. My skin crawled, wishing I still had my telepathy to talk to my wide-eyed friends. I didn't know what I'd say, exactly. It's not like I could comfort them by saying, "Don't worry; everything's going to be all right." Clearly it wasn't. But there wasn't time for talking, or anything really. The Luxors hustled us into a trembling line.

As soon as we were escorted into the Troian Center, I felt lost. The orphanage that had been my humble home for as long as I could remember had drastically changed. I was hit with color and richness. The halls were no longer sparse and shabby with cobwebs and dust littering the dimly lit corners. Everything looked bright, shiny and new, perhaps like it looked when it was originally built. There had always been much speculation among the orphans as to what the Troian Center was before it was an orphanage. Some said it was a prison, others a castle. I'd always leaned toward prison, since that's how it felt to me. But now, it looked like the most extravagant place I'd ever seen, making it seem as though it really could have been a castle. There was so much color. Vibrant tapestries hung from ceiling to floor and beautiful paintings cast in ornate gold frames covered the walls. Rich wood ceiling tiles and beams had been added and long woven carpets lined the center of the marble tiled floors. Torches burned in elegant swirling wall sconces. There were even elegantly scrolled signs in neat bronzed frames with arrows spelling out where everything was located.

Suddenly a sharp tone ripped through the air, causing us to jump. The Luxors halted us and the alarm continued to trumpet three sharp notes. It must be the new signal to end lessons, because the Center bustled to life as doors began to open. Everywhere, children in crisp white uniforms marched single file down the halls, led by Luxors. There were so many more students then there had been when we'd left. Many of them were new faces, and if there were any familiar ones, they were almost unrecognizable with their new looks; boys with buzzed hair, girls with severe hairstyles and painted faces – red glossy lips and sparkling eyelids. As we stood pressed against the cool stone walls blocked by a team of Luxors, I watched as each face that passed me look solemnly forward, not even chancing a glance in our direction.

My heart sunk further into the pit of my stomach. How could we have anticipated all of this? There had to be twice as many children at the Troian Center and the new security measures made it seem like it had been nonexistent before. I didn't even see any of our familiar Grifts, only a full-fledged army of Luxor soldiers. I had severely underestimated my opponent. But with Malakai acting as headmaster and all these elaborate changes to the Troian Center, it confirmed that something suspicious was going on. We had to be in the right place to find the Pillars.

The Luxors led us wordlessly to a white door, labeled *Infirmary,* where we were divided; girls to the right, boys to the left.

Jemma, Sparrow and I were ushered into a tiny white room with nothing in it. We all huddled fearfully near each other, waiting for whatever was coming. Both Sparrow and Jemma still shook and stifled sobs. I didn't know what to say to comfort them. All I could do was hold their hands and squeeze reassuringly.

I looked around at the newly painted walls of Miss Breia's former nurse's station. There was nothing familiar about it. The once cozy room looked like it had been whitewashed. It held a glaring difference to the opulent and warm hallway we had been in moments ago. Everything about this room was sterile and uninviting. The floors, walls, ceilings; all white. The lights in the tiny holding room were blinding. I didn't know what was beyond the door in front of us, but I doubted that the familiar yellow and white gingham curtains and comfortable cot bed were waiting for us.

Finally, a woman dressed in an official looking white coat came out of the white door with a clipboard in her hand.

"Sommers, Jemma?"

No one moved.

"Which one of you is Sommers, Jemma?" questioned the woman, looking up over the rim of her glasses.

"Me. I am," Jemma said finally finding her voice.

"Follow me," the woman quipped.

We watched as Jemma timidly followed her through the door, looking back over her shoulder at us nervously.

~

"WHAT'S SHE LIKE, MASTER?" Kobel asked when Malakai had returned to his office.

He'd been instructed to wait there by Malakai even after much protest. Kobel had been anxiously waiting to meet the supposed chosen one for as long as he could remember. But Malakai had forbidden it. This angered Kobel, but he knew better than to challenge his Master. Instead, he clutched the *Book of Gods* hoping it would reveal whatever Malakai was encountering in his absence. The book had remained silent. No new words worked their way across the brittle pages, leaving Kobel as restless as ever.

"She's just like the rest of them; a filthy, scrawny wretch. You'll meet her soon enough. I've sent them all to the Infirmary to be disinfected. Who knows what vermin they carry," Malakai said with disgust.

"Can you confirm her identity?"

Kobel was trailing too closely behind Malakai, hanging on his every word. He stepped on the edge of his black robe and Malakai whirled around, causing Kobel to cower instantly.

Malakai scowled, but didn't raise a hand to the old man. Instead he moved to his desk and sat down, leaning over the open *Book of Gods*. He steepled his fingers and rested his strong chin upon them.

"Yes, but..." He paused. "She's peculiar. Not what I was expecting. I was prepared for her arrogance, but she's so small and powerless. I expected...more."

"We mustn't be fooled by her size like Greeley was," Kobel said cautiously. "I wish you would have let me come with you. I've seen her in my visions. I could have helped you."

"You've shared your visions with me. I recognized her plain enough. And she bares the mark on her scalp, as the book predicted."

"The emblem appeared?" Kobel asked in astonishment.

"Yes, exactly as you said it would when I pressed my blade

to her scalp." Malakai paused. "There's just something off, missing."

"What is it?" Kobel asked trying to calm his frustration.

"I can't be sure just yet," he said after a moment. "Call a meeting. It's time to start our preparations."

4

Remi sat in the waiting room with his elbows resting on his knees and his partially shaved head cradled in his hands. Nova paced a trail in front of him, while Journey leaned against the wall absently rubbing his bruised neck, gazing at nothing.

Remi watched as Nova dripped a trail of blood from a gash that ran through his right eyebrow, and then turned to walk through it. Each time he did so, he left a smear of bloody footprints. For some reason this, paired with the flickering of the bright overhead lights, was agitating Remi to no end. Finally he snapped.

"You're bleeding all over the floor," he yelled, stopping Nova in his tracks.

Nova looked at the floor and then touched his face, as if he hadn't noticed that he was bleeding at all. Then he turned his gaze to Remi. His eyes narrowed with such intense anger that Remi got to his feet just as Nova lunged at him.

Nova wound his fists into what was left of Remi's soiled shirt. "This is your fault! You had one job! Keep us invisible. How in the gods name did they know where we were?"

"Get off me!" Remi said shoving at Nova to no avail. "I didn't see you lifting a finger to save us with your *awesome* fire powers either."

"Do you really think I didn't try?" Nova growled.

"Do you think I didn't? I screwed up, okay? I don't know what happened, but trust me, I'm tearing myself up enough about it already without you laying into me. I know I'm a complete failure and I'm not worthy of her. Is that what you want me to say?

Nova glared at Remi, but backed off. "If I had my powers you wouldn't still be standing here!"

Journey took the opportunity to get between his brawling friends. "Listen to yourselves. None of us can use our powers. Obviously something strange is going on here."

"Exactly!" Remi spat, anger still pulsing through him.

Nova lunged for him again but Journey held him back.

"It's not his fault, mate," Journey said softly.

Nova's fury crumbled and he put his hands through what was left of his hair in frustration.

"The girls," he breathed in agony. "We couldn't protect them. I'll never forgive myself if – "

But Nova couldn't even finish his sentence. Journey pulled him into a fierce hold and just nodded, mirroring his friend's pain.

Nova squeezed his eyes shut trying to control his emotions. He couldn't let himself breakdown in front of the guys. Instead he pushed Journey away and punched a wall right as the door to their room opened. The startled man, dressed in a crisp white coat, looked at the ragged group of teenage boys and then nervously back at his clipboard. He cleared his throat and called out a name.

"Asher, please follow me."

The boys all stared at the man, but didn't move. The man sighed in obvious frustration.

"Which-one-of-you-is-named-Asher?" he asked slowly as if he thought they were hard of hearing.

The boys now looked at each other, but still didn't speak or move. The man looked at the clipboard again and glanced back up with a bit of a grin.

"Nova Asher?" he asked looking directly at Nova.

A shockwave of surprise lit up Nova's features and it was clear that this was the first time he was hearing confirmation of his last name. Finally he nodded.

"Come with me, please," the man in the white coat instructed, shaking his head in disbelief as he led Nova from the room.

~

"OUCH!"

I could hear Jemma protesting from the other room. Her shrill cries echoed from behind the door and were making me nervous. Sparrow squirmed closer.

"We'll be okay," I whispered to her, praying my words were true.

Sparrow and I silently waited for our turn with the medics in the newly renovated infirmary. It seemed like Jemma had been gone forever. Time dragged on as we listened to her whimpering. When we couldn't hear her, we heard the shouts and protests of the boys. They sounded muffled and far away, but there was no misinterpreting that they sounded unhappy. I heard Nova's familiar voice and my heart crumbled, but I stayed strong for Sparrow, who was falling to pieces in my arms. Finally, everything grew silent and the white coat woman returned to our room. This time she was here for me.

"Sommers, Geneva?"

"Here," I said stepping forward.

"Follow me," she said.

Sparrow made a whimpering sound and grabbed my hand.

"It's okay," I whispered to her again. "Where's my sister?" I asked still standing my ground and holding Sparrow's trembling hand.

The cold woman raised an eyebrow at me. "Who?"

"My sister, Jemma."

She continued to stare at me blankly.

"The girl you just took back with you. Where is she?"

"Follow me," was all she said.

I could tell I wasn't going to get anything from this woman, so I turned to Sparrow and gave her my best reassuring smile.

"Please, don't leave me," she whispered through her sobs.

"It's okay. I'll come find you," I whispered as I pulled my hand from hers, begging myself to believe my own words.

Once on the other side, I followed the woman down a narrow white hall and through another closed white door into an even smaller white room. There was a cold looking silver table and a wall lined with all kinds of strange looking tools inside the room. I had a feeling the team of eager white coats staring at me were planning to use them on me and I shuddered.

Now I saw why Jemma had been howling. I tried to keep my protests to a minimum for Sparrow's sake, knowing she could hear me.

The team of white coats stripped off my ragged clothing and bathed me, ignoring my struggles for modesty. Afterward, they put me on the hard metal table to examine me, peering into my eyes, checking my reflexes and trying to look into my mouth. Although they refused to answer any of my questions, they were much gentler than the Luxors had been, so I decided to conserve my energy and stop fighting them.

Somehow I survived all the poking and prodding. When the team of medics backed away from me I felt raw, but better somehow. They had bathed me and scrubbed my skin pink.

Despite my feelings of humiliation at being bathed by strangers, it actually felt good to be clean for a change. The white coats had treated all my scrapes and wounds with some sort of salve that was soothing and smelled pretty, like mint and flowers. It reminded me of the sweet fragrance from the red flower Jovi had put in my hair while we were in the forest. My heart panged when I thought of her, but it also steeled my reasons for being here.

When the white coats finally left me alone, I sat up on the table, letting my legs swing under me. I examined my trimmed nails and the foreign paint that covered them. I looked down at my wiggling toes, watching the light shimmer over the fresh coat of matching onyx polish that coated them. But another shimmer suddenly caught my eye.

There was a mirror on the nearby wall. I hopped off the table and padded barefoot to it and let out a tiny gasp! My hair was cut short; blonde waves rioting every which way. But the most shocking discovery was the large bald patch on the left side of my head, just above my ear. The white coats had spent a lot of time trying to repair the hack job the Luxors had welcomed me with and now I was left with a shiny bald spot that ran from my left temple to the nape of my neck! I ran my hands across the smooth skin. It was a bizarre feeling. I surveyed my new look. I couldn't believe that my mop of blonde curls was gone! I'd spent so much time despising my quirky locks and now that they were gone, I felt naked. It was like they had taken some of my identity with them. I saw a strange dark mark above my left ear and leaned in closer to the mirror to examine it.

It was another tattoo, the same LVX I had on my shoulder, but much smaller. Had it been there all my life? I was engrossed in examining this new tiny tattoo in the mirror. It seemed like there was a red mark just behind my tattoo. Was it another scrape from the Luxors who'd savagely hacked off my hair? I twisted and turned but I couldn't get the exact angle to see it clearly. I was so close that I rested my hands against the cool glass. The brightness of my eyes caught my attention. They'd never looked so blue. As I was gazing at the way my eyelids glittered I thought I noticed a familiar celestial shimmer in the upper corner of the mirror. "No mom, not here," I whispered to myself, closing my eyes tightly.

"What do you think?" asked a cheerful voice.

My eyes flew open and I jumped back when I saw a new form reflected in the mirror. My heart pounded as I spun around to face the person standing in my room. She must have entered when I had my eyes closed.

I let out a sigh of relief. For a moment I had feared, yet half-hoped, that it was my mother's voice I had heard. I collected myself and answered.

"Um, I don't know," I replied honestly to the young woman. "I feel naked," I said rubbing my arms with a shiver. The light smock that tied in the back did nothing to insulate me against the chill of the stark medical room.

"I brought something to help with that," she said walking toward me with an armful of white material. "But what about the rest of you?"

I turned back to the mirror warily to examine my reflection. No sign of my mother.

Of course not, Geneva. Jemma veiled your powers. Stop letting your imagination run away with you, I mentally scolded myself.

I refocused on my reflection and if I was looking past the shock of my new hairstyle; I guess I could say I'd never looked better. My skin glowed and my eyes seemed bluer and more sparkly than usual. My normally plain features looked like the painted perfection I'd seen on the students' faces when we'd arrived.

"What's on my face?" I asked, gently rubbing my fingers over my rosy cheeks.

"That's called rouge. Isn't it fun?" she said sounding delighted as she walked up behind me. "They're cosmetics. Here, you have your own set."

She handed me a tiny white bag. It was soft with braided grey cording to tie it closed. I stared at it in my hands, not sure what to do.

"It's a lot to get used to, I know, but it's all for the best, you'll see," the girl reassured me.

"What's that supposed to mean?" I asked turning my attention to look at the girl face to face.

"Oh, I didn't mean to imply you need it or anything," she added apologetically, scrunching her up-turned nose in embarrassment. "It's just another luxury Headmaster has brought from Lux for us to enjoy."

"And what about this?" I pointed to the tattoo on my scalp.

"Oh, that. You've had that all your life, or at least all your life that you've spent as an orphan. The Troian Academy gave it to you when you got the one on your shoulder. I guess it was a precaution so that no one would think of getting clever and trying to change their identities."

"Don't you mean the Troian Center?"

"No, it's called the Troian Academy now. You'll learn all about it during orientation."

I looked at her skeptically, but she only smiled.

"Anyway, I imagine Headmaster shaved your head to verify you are who you say you are."

"Seems a bit harsh," I said bitterly.

"Don't worry. He didn't single you out. He did it to all the orphans when he took over." She leaned in closer and whispered, "He does seem a little paranoid if you ask me."

"So you're not an orphan?" I asked noticing that she didn't have a tattoo on her arm.

"It's complicated," she said handing me the stack of clothes. "Here, try these on."

I'd never worn a garment that fit me so well. I examined the new Troian Academy uniform I was wearing, how the white tunic flowed effortlessly over my body, fluttering with a light movement when I swayed from side to side, falling right above my knee. It was sleeveless, with a high cut angle that started at my left shoulder and ran down to the right, creating a sharp geometric neckline.

"Perfect fit!" the girl exclaimed when I emerged from behind the dressing curtain.

I stared intently at her. At second glance I noticed she looked familiar, but I couldn't place her. I had initially thought she was much older than me, but now up close I realized we were nearer in age than I'd first thought. She might still have been older, but not by much. It was hard to tell because she was tall and lean and moved with such graceful poise. Her auburn hair was cut short, adding angles to her cherub-like features. I admired the way her unruly hair tussled, giving her a pixie-ish look. She smiled at me warmly and the feeling of familiarity grew even more. Suddenly the image of riding horses popped into my head.

"Mala?" I whispered.

The smile disappeared from the girl's face instantly and she suddenly looked younger, scared even. She rushed in close to me.

"You knew my sister?" she whispered desperately.

My hopes that I'd finally crossed paths with my favorite Grift evaporated.

"Mala is your sister?" I asked.

She nodded.

"I remember her from when she was a Grift here. She was always nice to me."

Tears welled in the girl's haunted blue eyes.

"You said *knew*?" I asked apprehensively, afraid of what the answer would be.

She swallowed hard and nodded. "Yes, my sister was arrested by the Luxors. She was caught stealing food for us and they threw her in prison. It was only because she couldn't find work after she was fired from the Troian Center and we were going hungry. My father was too sick to work. He'd been crippled during the Flood. Mala was only looking out for us," she added as she ruefully shook her head.

I sighed a breath of relief. Prison was better than death. But then again, some might argue that death was actually better than the Luxor prison. I'd heard horror stories about that place. But still, there was no coming back from death.

Unless you're the Ponte deorum, my subconscious reminded me. I shrugged that thought away and asked, "How did you end up here?"

"My father passed away last month and with Mala in prison, the law states I have to come here until I turn seventeen and I'm of age," she said bitterly.

"I'm sorry about your father," I said. "And I'm sorry you ended up here. Mala was my friend, so I'm pleased to meet her sister."

"I'm Sadira, but everyone calls me Sadie."

"Geneva." I extended my hand.

When our hands connected I felt a cold wave wash over me. It was like her touch sent a surge of icy water through my veins! Gooseflesh rushed up my arm like a current of electricity. Even without my powers, I knew she was one of us. And this connection sparked a hopeful thought: Sadie might be one of the Pillars!

The more I thought about it, the more I believed she had to be. This feeling... it was different, yet the same, as when I touched Nova. It was a deep-rooted connection, something that was predestined and unexplainable, but it was there nonetheless. With Nova, I had thought it was because I was hopelessly in love with him, but then I realized I had a similar feeling when I was around Jovi too. Now that I had another experience to go off of, I was sure I was right.

I hadn't ever wondered why I felt such a kinship with Jovi. I had attributed it to her magnetic personality, but in this moment I knew it was more than that. It was because she was a Pillar. I hadn't even known about the Pillars when I met Jovi, or Nova, but now that I was feeling this same connection to Sadie it clicked. It all made sense and I grinned with relief, finally feeling confident that we could complete our mission to find the Pillars, when minutes ago it had felt like a lost cause.

Just as I was wondering if she could feel it too, her liquid blue eyes swelled with fear. I pulled my hand away quickly, not wanting to alert suspicion. I didn't know who could be watching us in here. This new Troian Academy had me on edge."

"Sorry," I said. "My hands are always cold." I rubbed them together rapidly trying to think of a way to change the subject when I noticed the startled look on Sadie's face wasn't fading. "That's a cool bracelet," I said looking at her black shimmering cuff.

"Oh!" she said shaking herself back to reality and bursting into action again. "I almost forgot. You need your bracelet."

Sadie scurried to the table I had been lying on and pulled a small wooden box out from under it. She brought it to me and timidly nodded for me to open it.

I hesitantly obliged, pulled the thin gold latch up and opened the box. Inside was the same black metal cuff that Sadie wore.

"Put it on," she said.

"It's for me?"

"Yes. We all get one. It's Headmaster's gift to us. It's how much he believes in our promising future."

I was about to slide it onto my wrist when I heard her say Malakai's name.

"Why would he give us a gift? It seems kind of suspicious to me," I said hesitating.

"What's taking so long?" called a shrill voice.

We both turned to see a tiny woman in a white coat in the doorway.

"Sorry, ma'am. I was just securing Geneva's bracelet."

"Finish your task quickly and return her to the waiting room. The next one is almost ready for you." And with that she closed the door.

"Just put it on, Geneva, you heard her. I have to get you to the waiting room."

"I don't know if I want to wear this. Something doesn't seem right about it," I said, turning it over and over in my hand. It was much heavier than it looked and had a strange dull shimmer to it. It gave me an uneasy feeling of déjà vu, but before I could think on it further, Sadie snatched it from my hands and clasped it on my wrist.

"Sadie!" I shouted.

"It's just a piece of jewelry. Come on, you heard her. We have to go! Please?"

There was a look of fearful panic in her pleading blue eyes that compelled me to give up my protests and follow. I could tell I made her nervous after our handshake. And, if she truly was one of the Pillars, I needed to keep on her good side.

"Fine," I sighed.

Sadie thrust a small jar into my hand. "Here, put this on each night. It helps your hair grow back faster."

"What?"

"Just do it," she urged and dashed from the room.

5

I followed a different white coat woman from my exam room after Sadie left, eagerly asking her where my friends were and where she was taking me. She gave me the silent treatment until we walked through the door to another waiting room, where I caught the first glimpse of my friends. I breathed a sigh of relief when I looked passed her and saw all of them. All except Sparrow, that is.

"Ah, much better. You all look splendid!" the white coat woman said, greeting my friends.

I had to agree. Despite our strange haircuts, I'd never seen my friends look better. When I first caught sight of Nova after his makeover I let out an audible gasp.

He shot to his feet when he saw me, but the white coat woman sternly warned him to sit down.

I was glad she had stopped him, because in a moment of weakness I'd forgotten about Jemma's trick and I wanted nothing more than to run into his arms. I regained my composure and nodded to him, trying to wordlessly convey that I was all right.

But I couldn't take my eyes off him. Partly for sheer relief to see he was okay and also because I'd never seen him look like this. He had a habit of making me drool over his gorgeous features, but this was something all together different. I'd only known him as John #18 here at the Troian Center, or Nova, the fugitive, while we hid in the forest. We'd been in the forest so long that we'd all started to look a little unkempt. But now, he was Nova the Troian Academy student. He looked older and handsome in his new crisp white linen uniform. The starched mandarin collar of his uniform fit snuggly under his tan, chiseled jawbones. I gazed up to his perfect lips and watched them part slightly as he released a frustrated breath. They were in the perfect shape of a resting bow, with the corners slightly turned down at his discontent. I followed the sweeping lines of his face up to his blond crew cut. I mourned his golden waves that so often made me think of flames. But without his hair gently curling about his face, he had nothing to distract from his gorgeous features. His beauty was more raw and defined than ever.

I started to feel a bit light-headed and realized I'd been holding my breath. Being this close to Nova was impossible. I tried to look away from him but I couldn't. My eyes strayed to his furrowed brows. His right eyebrow had a tiny pink line through it, interrupting his perfection. I felt anger at who or what had caused him pain and injury, but I'd already cataloged the scar as yet another endearing part of Nova that I loved. I allowed my gaze to wander to his green eyes and was struck by the intensity with which they glowed. They were so brilliant that they seemed made of luminescent moonstones from some distant planet.

Nova's eyes locked with mine for an instant and I felt my cheeks flush brightly under the rouge the white coats had caked on me. I averted my eyes when I heard someone clear their throat. It was Remi. I found myself startled and gawking at his appearance too. His transformation may have been the most dramatic of all. He looked so grown up. If I hadn't heard Remi's familiar voice come out of the strange looking boy's mouth, I may not have even recognized him. Remi had shaggy, brown hair framing his round boyish face for as long as I could remember. He was constantly sweeping it away from his bashful, chocolate eyes. The boy I stared at now had a short buzz cut. His cropped hair was dark, like the color of his keen eyes and arched brows. I watched the angular lines of his face twitch into that smile I'd known all my life. I followed the curve of his face to the tiny tattoo on his scalp. XXVI, #26. Just as Sadie had said, it matched the one on his arm. Not knowing we'd had them all this time unnerved me.

What else didn't we know about ourselves, I wondered.

I pulled my eyes from Remi to survey the rest of my friends. Journey looked mostly the same. His tawny hair was shorter and he had a shaved spot above his left ear as well, revealing his tattoo; but other than that, he was just a cleaner version of his normal hulking self. His sharp amber eyes scanned the room uneasily. He was no doubt searching for Sparrow.

"She's okay," I mouthed silently to him.

He nodded, but still couldn't relax.

I looked away from his nervously bouncing leg and settled my gaze on Jemma. Somehow she still looked perfect. She had struggled hard against the Luxors, resulting in a few high scalp marks. Her shiny black hair was now shaved high above her left ear, with the rest of it swept to the right and cut into a fierce bob that fell chin length and angled shorter toward the back of her head. Her dark eyes sparkled, reflecting the shimmer of the cosmetics that had been expertly painted on her face, highlighting her beautiful features.

I shook my head in disbelief. Only my sister could get partially scalped and come out looking more beautiful than ever. I sighed, knowing though I was clean and made up too, I could never hold a candle to Jemma. It was impossible having a gorgeous sibling, but I reminded myself, looks weren't everything. Jemma was cruel and deceitful and no amount of beauty could conceal such darkness for long.

Journey's voice interrupted my thoughts.

"Where's Sparrow?"

He had apparently hit his limit for patience and approached the white coat woman.

"We are waiting on one more. You will wait *silently* and then you will be joining the rest of the student body for dinner," she replied without ever looking up from her paperwork.

My stomach grumbled at the word, but my brain protested. I was way too edgy to even think about eating. My eyes darted around the room taking it all in. This place was a bit less sterile looking than everywhere else in the medical wing. The walls were still white, but paintings of strangely dressed men hung on them. The white coat woman sat at a rich mahogany desk, in a wing backed upholstered chair. We were afforded comfortable leather chairs that sat on a pale grey woven rug that looked much too expensive to stand on, let alone get sick on.

We only had to endure a few more moments of uncomfortable silence before the door to our waiting room opened once more. All eyes darted to the slight figure that walked through. Poor Sparrow. She seemed to have gotten the worst of it. Either her Luxor had never learned his left from right or he was particularly cruel. Sparrow's head had been shaved on both sides. It was apparent that the white coats had done the best they could, but her fine, mousy brown hair - though still long - only ran down the center portion of her head. Her amber eyes, which had an uncanny resemblance to Journey's, were red and watering. Either the white coats had given up on the idea of cosmetics, or perhaps Sparrow had cried them all off. Tears streaked her cheeks and I stood to hug her.

I caught a glimpse at Journey over Sparrow's quivering shoulders. The concern on his face was so endearing. It warmed my heart to know they could always offer each other comfort. I felt a twinge of sadness as I passed Sparrow to Journey, who drew her so near that it almost seemed she dissolved into him. *Remi used to be that for me,* my heart whispered as I watched Journey's arms protectively encircle Sparrow, while he gently stroked her head. Now Remi stood rigidly against the wall. He hadn't said two words to me since we arrived and seemed to be avoiding my gaze. I fixed my eyes on him, standing next to Nova. Somehow I'd lost them both.

BUZZ BUZZ BUZZ.

An alarm pierced the air startling us.

"Time to go," the white coat woman said ushering us to the door.

When she opened it, the hallways were alive again. Groups of white clad students marched past us. Two familiar looking Luxors waited outside the infirmary door. I recognized one as the soldier that had bound and gagged me. I glared at him and he wordlessly motioned for us to line up and follow. He paid no attention to my scowl and I was forced to comply, lining up behind Journey, with Remi on my heels.

6

We followed the Luxors a short distance to the dining hall. My heart skipped a beat as I recognized the familiar double doors. The dining hall had always been a refuge for us at the Troian Center. It's where we laughed and become friends. It harbored us as we discussed theories and made our many plans. As I walked in past the doors, the fond memories instantly evaporated. Everything familiar was gone.

Our comforting little tables had been replaced with sleek long ones that appeared to be made of black marble. I could have cried, longing for those worn wooden tables where we'd etched our names and numbers. Our humble table in the corner had harbored us through so much. I felt I had taken it for granted as I stared into the abyss of strange students dressed in white.

It appeared we had arrived right in time for dinner. The nerves that had been suppressing my appetite could resist no longer. My stomach growled as the sweet aroma of food lured me forward, overpowering my wariness. The soldiers stopped beside the open double doors. They hadn't uttered a word since their assault. I looked to my friends to see if they had any idea what we were to do next but they all looked a bit shell-shocked and tentative.

"Look out," Remi said pulling me aside as a large Luxor rushed past, followed by a line of well-dressed students.

"I guess we're allowed to go get something to eat," I said motioning to the orderly line forming in the dining hall.

"Yeah, let's get some food," Nova said cautiously.

We hesitantly got in line with the other students. Even though we had been given identical uniforms and similar appearances, we didn't have the courtesy of being able to blend in. I could feel all eyes upon us and I knew the hushed whispers were no doubt aimed at our arrival.

"Next!"

The voice broke me out of my scattered thoughts, and when I looked to see where it had come from I saw a familiar face. She was wearing gloves and a bonnet and motioning to me because I was next in line. I rushed over to her, so happy and confused.

"Ms. Breia! What are you doing in the dining hall?"

"Hush, deary. I'm not allowed to fraternize with the students. Just point to the protein you want."

"Huh?"

This caught me off guard. Since when did we get a choice of what we wanted to eat at the Troian Center?

"But why are you in here? You're our nurse," I whispered as I surveyed the delicious looking meats. I pointed to the largest filet and she speared it and put it on a plate for me.

"Not anymore. I'm not good enough for the likes of them," she said bitterly as she jutted her chin to the sea of white behind me. "Keep your head down, deary." She turned away from me to serve Remi. "Next!"

I decided to heed her warning as I moved down the meal line. I chose my vegetable, fruit and starch from each labeled station. I could have taken forever staring at all the tantalizing options, but somehow I knew that would just land me another beating from the Luxors. My stomach growled louder and louder, and I knew I wanted to make sure I got a chance to eat this delicious meal. Before I knew it, the line ended abruptly and I was standing all alone in a swarm of foreign students.

"Let's keep going," Remi said softly as he put his hand on the small of my back.

"Where?"

"Just follow him," Remi said motioning to the boy walking a few yards ahead of me.

I gingerly placed my plate of food next to the boy I had followed to the long table in the center of the dining hall. I smiled weakly at him but he ignored me. I slung my legs over the bench and sat down. Remi sat beside me and moved in close, pushing me uncomfortably close to the boy on my left. My elbow grazed his and he glared at me before getting up and changing tables.

Still great at making friends, Geneva, I thought glumly.

"Well some things are still the same," I said looking sadly at Remi.

He smiled sympathetically at me. We were the only ones of our friends who were used to being outcasts. I watched as Nova, Sparrow, Journey and Jemma were given the cold shoulder as well and felt bad for them. I imagined they would have a tough time getting used to being treated like social pariahs.

As soon as Nova sat down he started talking.

"We have to get out of here, now. We weren't prepared for this."

"No, Nova. We have to find the Pillars and we're already here," I pleaded. "Besides – "

"Tippy! It's too dangerous. Malakai is here. We have to leave as soon as possible," Nova interrupted.

"I told you not to call me that," I fumed. "And you don't get to tell me what to do. Leave if you want, but I'm staying. I have a destiny to fulfill."

"Geneva," Journey said calmly, "we're here to help you, but I have to agree with Nova. We should regroup and come up with a new plan now that we know what we're dealing with."

"It was hard enough getting here. I think we should stay," Remi said coming to my aid.

I smiled gratefully at him as he put his calm hand over my clenched fist, squeezing it reassuringly.

"Of course you do," Nova said sarcastically.

"What does that mean?" Remi shot back.

"Knock it off," Journey warned them both, his eyes darting around the table to alert us to the fact that everyone in the dining hall was watching us.

Our raised voices had attracted unwanted attention.

"Great," I muttered. "Listen, we can't just waltz out of here at this very moment, so let's try to get through today and see what we learn."

Nova looked like he was ready to interject but I didn't let him.

"If you all feel like we should leave tomorrow we can discuss it, but I at least need one day to explore this place to see what we're up against. It'll be helpful information if we need to escape or break back in."

Nova shook his head but didn't meet my gaze. The strategist in him knew I was right.

"Can we please just eat?" Journey asked. "I'm starving and whatever we decide we'll need to eat first and then come up with a plan."

I sighed and turned back to my tray of food. I was ready to dig in just as someone else sat down in the empty spot next to me. I bumped his tray as he was setting it down, knocking his silverware to the floor.

"I'm so sorry," I cried not believing my luck.

"Not a problem," he answered politely.

I hadn't expected to be met with pleasantness. I turned to look at the dark haired boy sitting next to me and was greeted with a friendly smile, instantly offering my anxiety some relief. He had smooth olive skin and a kind, dimpled smile that lit up his face and made him look younger than he was. I was guessing he was probably about Nova's age, sixteen. I looked into his deep dark eyes; they were contradictory to the rest of him. They seemed sinister, like they were concealing secrets. I shook the nervous feeling away and took in the rest of him. He sat anxiously pushing his shoulder length hair behind his ears. He was tall, with a lanky athletic build that he hadn't grown into it yet.

"I'm Kai," he said extending his hand.

His name caught me off guard, knocking the wind out of me. I felt Remi grab my leg to steady its shaking under the table. He was saying something to me too, but I couldn't hear it over the pounding of my heart. I was staring at the boy named Kai and he just kept warmly grinning back at me, hand extended. His dark eyes, friendly and bright, seemed concerned.

"Did I say something wrong?" he asked.

"No, no. It's just that your name, Kai...that's my father's name," I whispered, finally shaking his hand.

"I know."

"You know?"

"Yes. But keep your voice down. We'll talk about this later. You need to eat your food. I'll be taking you and your friends to orientation after this."

Eat? How could I eat? My mind was reeling. Who was this boy named Kai? How did he know my father shared his name? What else did he know about me? Maybe we were related somehow? The *Book of Secrets* didn't say anything about me having any other siblings or relatives, but at this point nothing would surprise me. Although I was certain I didn't know him, something was familiar about him.

I pushed my food around my plate absentmindedly trying to pinpoint what was causing my feelings of recognition until Kai nudged me.

"You really need to eat something, Geneva."

I dropped my fork.

"How do you know my name?"

He just smiled at me, his white teeth shining, but I was so confused I could barely concentrate on his features.

"I asked you a question," I said desperately, unable to control my hands from shaking. I wasn't sure if I was mad or scared, but Kai took pity on me.

"I'm sorry, I wasn't trying to upset you. But everyone knows who you are. We've been expecting you."

"You have?"

"Yes. Father and I arrived here the day after Headmistress Greeley's demise. The rumor was that she chased a few orphans off into the forest for some unknown reason and then was attacked by vicious creatures. They suspect tarcats were the culprits and that's why Father had them banished."

I gulped and felt the color drain from my face.

"Is that so?" I asked weakly.

"Yep. Everyone here said Greeley had gone mad! My father did everything in his power to find you and bring you all back. He sent Luxors out looking for you. We'd just about given up hope. Some of the students were even taking bets on how long you'd survive out there."

"Pruxes," Journey muttered in disgust.

"Journey!" Sparrow scolded. "Don't use that foul word."

"Why? It's the truth. They're all a bunch of spoiled, pampered brats from Lux with perfect, privileged lives and no grasp of the real world. They were taking bets on whether we were dead or alive."

Kai looked terribly embarrassed. “I’m sorry, I didn’t mean it like that...”

“I’m sure,” Journey muttered sarcastically.

“Anyway, you were telling me about your father?” I asked, ignoring Journey’s vulgar comment.

“Yes, Headmaster Malakai. That’s how I got my name. My mother said it was the perfect name because it gave me part of my father’s namesake and part of the great Kai’s,” he said with obvious pride.

“The great Kai?” I whispered. “Did your mother know him?”

The boy laughed, almost spilling his drink.

“Oh, you’re serious?” he asked when he caught me still staring, waiting for him to continue. “No, I doubt she knew *the* Kai. You know he was just a legend, right? Besides, I never got the chance to ask her. She died when I was born. Everything I know about her, my father has told me.”

“Oh, I’m really sorry. My mother is dead too,” I said ruefully.

“I know.”

“What? How come you always say that? How do you know?”

“Well you’re in an orphanage, aren’t you?”

“Oh... good point,” I said blushing.

“Are you sure you’re okay? You ask a lot of strange questions,” Kai said with a playful grin.

“Yeah. Maybe I’m just hungry,” I said with a shrug.

I could see Remi trying to catch my eye, but I didn’t want to try to explain the conversation I was having with Kai to him. I needed more answers first. He was probably just being overprotective anyway.

I distractedly shoveled a spoonful of food into my mouth and my taste buds felt like they had been hit by lightning.

“Oh my gods!” I exclaimed.

“What?” Remi shouted, jumping to my aid.

"The food's great, huh?" Kai asked with a sly smile.

"It's incredible," I mumbled as I shoved another spoonful into my mouth.

And it was. Each bite was bursting with flavor. I'd never tasted anything so amazing before. The fish was flaky, buttery and melted in my mouth. The vegetables were crisp and fresh, and the fruit, oh the fruit was divine. I shoved a large chunk of pineapple into my mouth and moaned. It was so sweet it made my jawbone ache. It was juicy and sticky and I couldn't get enough. I felt like Journey as I sloppily piled food from my plate to my mouth, barely having time to chew or breathe between mouthfuls.

Remi shook his head and Kai grinned, trying to hide his amusement.

BUZZ BUZZ BUZZ.

That awful alarm blared through the dining hall, echoing wretchedly and splitting my ears. It was so loud I squinted my eyes, already loathing its torturous blasts. Especially since they signaled the end of my delectable feast. I'd never tasted such heavenly food and I was in mourning as I followed the slow, single file line to the trash receptacles to dispose of our dishes and exit the dining hall.

Kai motioned for us to follow him. We stood aside and watched orderly groups of students follow assorted Luxors out of the dining hall and down the hallway. I searched for familiar faces in the crowd as I wondered where they were all headed.

"They're going to study hall," Kai whispered, as if reading my mind. "You'll get to experience that tomorrow. All students attend study hall after dinner each day, you'll get the hang of the schedule in a few days."

"Why aren't we going?" I asked, starting to feel a bit nervous that we were being singled out. *Was this when Malakai was going to strike?*

"Orientation. Remember?" Kai said warmly.

"Oh," was all I could muster as I tried to smile back.

Journey stood next to me still licking his fingers. I grinned at him, knowing he must have enjoyed his meal immensely since he was such a food hog.

"Can you believe they were throwing away scraps?" he fumed incredulously.

Sparrow appeared at his side and silently handed him a napkin, simultaneously wiping a crumb from his chiseled chin. He grinned at her and she smiled for the first time since we arrived at the Troian Center.

"All right then," Kai said clearing his throat as the room cleared out. "My name is Kai and I'll be taking you to your orientation. You can consider me your guide at the Troian Academy. My father said to make you feel at home, so I'm at your service."

My friends all stared at him, looking a bit dumbfounded.

"Chatty group, aren't they?" he said to me with a smirk. "Well, don't all make your introductions at once. Better yet, let me try. I've already met Geneva, so... you must be Sparrow," he said looking at my slight friend who was standing in Journey's hulking shadow.

She nodded and he clapped his hands.

"Then that would make you Journey?"

Journey only stared back at him, unblinking.

"I'll take your silence as confirmation. So, moving on," he said cheerfully. "That means you would be Jemma," he said bowing in my sister's direction.

She grinned at him and nodded.

"And that leaves you two. Remi and Nova, I presume?" he said accurately labeling each of my friends.

"How did you do that?" Nova asked skeptically.

Kai smiled genuinely.

"You really underestimate the rumor mill around here,

don't you? How many other escaped orphans do you think there are on this island? Follow me."

He turned and marched down the hall ahead of us. I felt Nova rush past me and I instinctively jumped aside, remembering I couldn't let him touch me.

"How do you know our names? Our *real* names?" Nova said grabbing Kai by the collar and pushing him up against the wall.

"Nova! No!" I called. I wanted to run over and pull him off of Kai, but Jemma's stupid threats danced in my head.

Luckily, Journey was levelheaded enough to pull Nova off.

"Knock it off, Nova. Unless you want another beating from the Luxors, I think we need to cool it. Give the kid a chance to answer your questions, mate."

Nova glared at Journey and then at Kai, but he agreed to release him.

"Well?" he demanded.

Kai was collecting himself and smoothing the wrinkles in his white uniform, but he still seemed calm when he responded.

"I assure you, I'll answer any questions you have without having to be prompted by threats. First, please follow me to your orientation. We're expected and it's bad manners to show up late."

No one moved.

"I think it will help answer many of your questions," Kai urged.

I don't know why, but my initial instinct was to trust him. Even though his father was the suspicious Headmaster, Kai seemed nothing like him. He was so genuine and unassuming. I knew I'd have to keep my guard up, but still there was something familiar about Kai that put me at ease.

Nova looked to me, his eyes asking the unspoken question of if we should follow. I nodded.

"Kai, lead the way please," I said.

7

"Welcome students. Welcome! Right on time, you are! Now let us get started. My name is Professor Kobel. I am from the Luxor Academy and I am honored to be the one to orientate you to your new home, the Troian Academy."

"Troian Academy?" Journey asked, eyebrows raised.

"Yes, yes. Headmaster Malakai has updated the name to reflect the new status of this institution."

Institution? What a joke, I thought to myself. This place was more like a military prison. "I'm never calling it that," I muttered under my breath and Journey smirked in agreement.

"Ah, let me start with his history and bring you all up to speed," Kobel said, scurrying to the front of the classroom. He paused halfway there and turned back to us. "Oh and by the way, my boy, we raise our hands when we have questions. It's rude to speak out of turn."

I could tell from his tan, leathered skin that he was ancient. But he moved with such energy and excitement, despite an apparent limp, it was hard to guess his age. His slim frame seemed to be swimming in his white robes as his boney feet, clad in rope sandals, shuffled across the glistening floor.

Once he reached the front of the room, he stretched to grab a dangling gold ring attached to a rope. When he pulled it, an elaborate chart unrolled gracefully stopping at his feet. He grabbed his pointer and motioned for us to find a seat.

I followed Kai to a table and sat next to him. Sparrow and Remi joined us and the others sat at the table in front of us. I was barely in my seat before Professor Kobel burst into his lecture.

"Malakai Vanir is of noble pedigree and has been head official of the Luxor Militia for over twenty years. When he heard of the incident with Headmistress Greeley here at the Troian Center, he selflessly volunteered to take over the investigation. Once he discovered the unfortunate situation of how she had been running the Troian Center, using you poor orphans as slaves to increase her own personal power and wealth, he took immediate action to rectify it. Headmaster Malakai has committed himself, along with his expertise and personal resources, to turn the orphanage you used to call home, into the Troian Academy; an elite institution for studies in academia, militia, fine arts and athleticism. And he has kindly agreed to sponsor the tuition for those who cannot afford it, so each orphan can stay on as a student."

Kobel paused to clear his throat and survey us. Nova had a skeptical scowl on his handsome face and Kobel noticed it. He narrowed his eyes and swiftly hobbled up to Nova, getting uncomfortably close to his face.

"Young man, I can see you are doubtful, but you should know that you children owe your futures to Headmaster Malakai," he growled. "After the late Headmistress Greeley despicably used the funding for this orphanage for her own needs rather than those of the children, effectively running this institution into the ground, the city of Lux was ready to wash its hands of you. After hearing that the Troian Center was on the verge of being demolished, Malakai stepped in and saved you all."

"What would have happened to us?" Jemma asked with fear in her voice.

"Students will raise their hand if they have a question!" he bellowed, but then said, "Who knows? You most likely would have been sold into servitude." Then he seemed to return to his former happy professor demeanor as he spun on his heels and returned to the front of the room, rapping on the chart."

"Now back to orientation!" he said. "Headmaster Malakai's goal, besides educating you and helping you grow into responsible, well-mannered individuals, is to teach you the importance of family. That is why he has lifted the barbaric practice of tattooing orphans and the ban on your real names. He has spent countless hours combing the libraries of Lux for your lineage and we are happy to report that we have found a manuscript that is the key to all of your names and families. He has been working tirelessly to reunite the orphaned students with any surviving members of their families."

"Now that you've joined us, there is hope that the staff here can locate your families. For those orphans that are truly unfortunate and do not have any blood relatives, Headmaster has cultivated excellent relationships with respected families in Lux who have expressed a desire to adopt you. All students meet with the headmaster each week for counseling to discuss education tracks at the Academy and any adoption developments."

I could see Sparrow sitting a little taller in her seat after she heard this. It broke my heart to see her getting her hopes up. I didn't believe any of the glowing things that Professor Kobel was saying. It all seemed too good to be true, like a fairytale with a happy ending. The past year had taught me not to trust such fantasies. Not to mention that this was all just an elaborate cover story. Thanks to Hollis, we knew who Malakai really was. However, I was interested in this mysterious manuscript that listed all of our names. It could be the key to finding the Pillars.

Professor Kobel droned on and on about the new programs and rules of the Troian Academy. According to him, we now had better accommodations and food. New bright white uniforms replaced our old tattered ones. No longer was the school run by Grifts, and the local teachers we'd had before were deemed unfit to instruct us. Instead, the Luxors now policed the academy and new prestigious professors from Lux had been brought in to educate us. We even had choices on what lessons we wanted to study. Fine art and sculptures had been brought in from the Royal Museum in Lux to expose us to beauty and culture. There was some sort of athletic tournament that we would now have the honor to attend. I tried to listen to all the *exciting* new details that Professor Kobel rattled off, but warning bells were going off in my mind as it swam with questions. It all seemed like the Headmaster was trying too hard. Why would he bring this academy here? Why should so much be given to us? To orphans? There had to be something here that he was trying to get to or to cover up. My best chance to figure all of this out was Kai. Perhaps if I could get close enough to him, make him trust me, he would expose his father's secrets.

I looked over at him and he smiled warmly at me. I grinned back at him, all the while calculating what his father was up to. Right then and there I made it my vow to use whatever means necessary to find out.

~

AFTER AN EXHAUSTING two-hour lecture from Professor Kobel about the rules and regulations of the new Troian *Academy*, we had been excused to retire to our rooms. Kai passed out our new curriculum schedule and told us we would begin tomorrow. He was appointed to lead us to our quarters, where we were to get settled in for the rest of the night. I stretched my stiff muscles as I stood to follow him out of the classroom.

Everything seemed to be referred to with proper military authority now. Words like *academy, curriculum, retire* and *quarters* didn't roll off the tongue of most teenagers I knew. This vocabulary was going to take some getting used to. So were all the new lessons we had to study: Arithmetic, Astronomy, Ancestry, Athletics, Elective Arts, Foreign Language, Medicinal Horticulture and Military Studies.

I followed Kai silently into the hall, letting my mind snap to attention. Suddenly, I was wishing I'd paid better attention during orientation.

Kobel had rambled on about the heavy cuffs we wore and the reasons we had to be identified by our scalp tattoos, but I could scarcely focus. My mind was churning, trying to match Hollis's story of Malakai to this new shiny one that Kobel was feeding us.

"So what do you think?" Kai asked me once we were in the hall. He led us through the still corridors of the Troian Academy to our quarters.

"What do you mean?" I asked.

"Well, aren't you excited that you get to go to school here?" he asked excitedly.

I wanted to say, *Why? Because I'm nothing but a poor orphan that your conniving father has turned into a charity case?*

My cheeks flushed with anger and embarrassment. I didn't think Kai meant to make me feel humiliated, but he had. I took a deep breath to collect myself before answering. I needed to get close to Kai so I could work his father's secrets from him.

"Yes. I'm very excited, Kai. It's an honor, really. Please, thank your father for his kindness," I said painting on a cheesy smile.

Kai grinned broadly at me. His eyes shined with genuine joy.

"You can thank him personally, if you'd like. I'm having breakfast with him tomorrow. We always spend breakfast together and I know he wouldn't mind if you joined us."

"Oh... thank you for the offer, but I wouldn't want to intrude."

"No, really. It wouldn't be a big deal."

"Um, maybe another time. I'm still feeling a little overwhelmed."

"Sure, I understand," he said with a smile, but he looked hurt.

Smooth Geneva! I scolded myself.

I probably should have taken Kai up on his offer for breakfast with his father. What better opportunity to learn more about Malakai than spending time with him? But truthfully, he terrified me. The thought of being in a room with him made my veins run cold. But now I had probably offended Kai and blew my chances of ever getting another invitation.

Why was I so bad at flirting? Perhaps I should ask Jemma for some tips, I thought bitterly as I glanced behind me to where she was clinging to Nova.

We walked in silence for a while before Kai finally stopped us.

"This is it," he said pausing outside the door to our quarters with a grin. "Get some rest and enjoy."

I walked past his outstretched arm, gallantly gesturing for me to enter my new room. Once through the doorway, I paused and took a quick breath. The room was white like the infirmary had been, but warm and luxurious as well. There were thick wood beams bracing the white ceiling. At closer look, what I thought were dark grains in the cocoa colored wood were actually intricate carvings. They looked like swirling waves and clouds intertwined in a heavenly dance. My eyes followed the beautiful woodwork around the room in awe until distracted by dozens of tiny chandeliers hung from the rafters, casting shimmering prisms of light in every direction. Tall glittering windows trimmed in beautiful, sheer white curtains shimmered in the fading sunlight. Polished wardrobes and overstuffed chairs; bunk beds piled high with fluffy white blankets. It was the most beautiful bedroom I'd ever seen. There was no way it was meant for us!

I was busy taking in the rest of the opulent room, when I heard a scuffle behind me.

"I'm sorry, you can't go in there," Kai shouted.

I made my way back to the doorway where Nova and Journey looked like they wanted to smash Kai to pieces. Remi rubbed his visibly red wrist.

"I assumed you knew," Kai said apologetically looking at Remi's welting wrist. "This is the girls wing."

"Girls wing?" Journey seethed.

"Yes. Boys and girls have separate wings."

The startled look on all of our faces must have clued Kai in that this was something new to us.

"Did you all bunk together before?" he asked sounding shocked.

"I'm surprised that wasn't part of the orientation," Nova added sarcastically.

Sparrow and Jemma stood by, useless and mute. I pushed past them to the boys who were boiling to a standoff in the hall.

"Guys, cool it. Luxors, remember!"

They all sighed, and resigned their stances a bit.

"Remi, what happened to your wrist?" I asked staring at the red welt he was rubbing.

"This stupid bracelet," he grimaced. "It burned me!"

"Well that's because you tried to enter the girls bunkroom," Kai said matter-of-factly.

"What are these things?" Nova hissed. "I thought they were

a gift for our future or some rubbish. What kind of gift burns you when you step out of line?"

"Ah, the very kind that will serve to train you to become respectable young adults, I suspect."

We turned to see Malakai smiling behind us. His smile was sly and off-putting as he sauntered closer. No matter how soothing he tried to make his voice, I couldn't shake the horrible images of him Hollis had showed us.

"You can think of the bracelets as a gift with many purposes," he continued. "Not only are they aesthetically appealing and a symbol of wealth and status, but they will serve to remind you of your responsibilities and boundaries as students of the Troian Academy. Should you ever forget, they are set to gently help you recall such things."

Somehow, I doubted there was anything gentle about the way the bracelet had left the growing red welt on Remi's wrist. Malakai caught my eye and his grin grew even sharper when he noticed the red mark on my friend's arm. It was like he was enjoying the pain that his bracelet caused Remi. He was taking pleasure in our pain! Surprisingly, I wasn't that shocked. From what I'd heard of Malakai, I expected such wickedness. That kind of evil scared me to the core. At least with Greeley, she didn't hide her distaste for us. I always knew where I stood with her, but Headmaster Malakai was a whole different kind of enemy. He was the kind that hid from you in the formalities of manners and pleasantry, killing you with kindness, earning your trust so that you would never see him coming. But I felt it, deep in the pit of my stomach, like a poison spreading through my veins whenever he was near. He was not to be trusted.

8

I hadn't even had time to say goodbye to the boys. Malakai made sure of that. He had Kai usher them away with the brush of his hand and he pointed me to my room. I resentfully obeyed and heard the door slam closed behind me as I barely finished crossing the threshold.

"What are we going to do?" Jemma cried the minute the door shut.

"We're going to find the Pillars and get the heck out of here as fast as we can!" I said appreciating my sister's proactive question.

"No! I meant about our hair!" she squealed already in front of a full length mirror fretting over her new hairdo. "Sparrow, can't you make it grow back for us?"

I rolled my eyes. Of course my vain sister was more worried about her appearance than actually coming up with a useful solution.

"Jemma, no, that would be too suspicious. Besides, this ointment is supposed to help it grow back," I said holding up the jar Sadie had given me.

"Good idea. Put it on me," Jemma ordered.

"Jemma. We have bigger problems than your hair."

"Just because you don't care how you look doesn't mean the rest of us feel the same."

"I'll do it," Sparrow interjected when she saw me narrow my eyes at Jemma.

I resigned to help apply a thick coat of the cold ointment to Sparrow's head since she had done Jemma's and mine.

"Who cares about our hair?" I grumbled. "Did you not just see the headmaster reveling in Remi's pain? That man is evil and we need to stay as far away from him as we can until we figure out who the Pillars are and come up with a plan to get out of here."

"I don't know, I didn't think he seemed all bad," Jemma said admiring the dull sparkle of her new bracelet. She rubbed it on the hem of her new white tunic trying to get it to shimmer even more. "These uniforms are great too!" she said absently.

"Are you mental?" I hissed at her. "He's Malakai Vanir. The leader of the Ravinori. The very group *trying-to-kill-us*!" I quipped the last few words slow and snarky so she would understand the severity of it.

"Oh, because Hollis said so?" Jemma shot back. "It seems to me if Malakai wanted us dead he would have done so already. Not bothered making us pretty and giving us new clothes and jewelry," she said matching my tone while holding up her bracelet to let it sparkle in the last of the sunlight filtering in from the high windows.

She had a point. What was he waiting for? It seemed like he was just toying with us since he obviously knew who we were.

"He's up to something," I said. "We can't trust him."

Jemma just shrugged.

As usual, reasoning with my sister was useless. I rolled my eyes and turned to Sparrow.

"I don't buy it," I said to Sparrow.

"What?"

"All of it. It doesn't make sense. Why would Malakai be doing all of this? Pretending to care so much about making our lives better? He's sure laying it on pretty thick to cover up his real goals and his Ravinori connection."

"He's a humanitarian," Sparrow said reciting the orientation.

"Come on! You don't actually believe all that stuff Professor Kobel said, do you?"

"No," she sighed. "But it would be nice if it were true," she said looking deflated.

"Well it's not."

"How can you be so sure? Maybe Hollis was wrong about him. We're here. Don't you think we should explore the possibility?"

Sparrow gazed dreamily around the beautiful bunkroom we were now calling home. It was easy to see why she wanted to believe that Hollis was wrong and Malakai truly was just a wonderful humanitarian, swooping in to rescue us. I'm sure that was his plan and the reason for all this prosperity. I gently reached for Sparrow's hand.

"Sparrow, you know that's what he wants you to think. It's what he's counting on; that we'll like it here and get comfortable and not fight back. I would love nothing more than for this to be our future, but I know it's not. We can't ignore the *Book of Secrets* and I can't ignore my destiny."

"I know," she whispered.

"You know what I can't stop thinking about? I don't get how Malakai found everyone's names so easily. I wouldn't have gone through hell and back to get the *Book of Secrets* to find out my identity if I could have just gone to the library in Lux and asked someone to help me find my parents."

"So you don't think there's a book like Professor Kobel said?"

"I don't know, but if there is, we'd better find it. That could be the key we need to help us find the Pillars."

Sparrow nodded. "It does sound possible that they kept records of some sort in Lux. We've just never had access to them."

I fidgeted with the collar of my uniform. It felt too high, like it was choking me. I pushed the distraction from my mind. Something Sparrow said got me thinking. What if there were records or files about us somewhere? It almost seemed like there had to be in order for Malakai to know so much about us. Maybe if I could get Kai to help get me access to them I'd be able to find the Pillars. I turned to tell Sparrow my thoughts and realized she was no longer standing next to me. I looked around; Jemma was still glued to her reflection in the mirror, fretting over her hair.

Typical I fumed.

I stomped past her and found Sparrow a few feet away, sitting on a soft white blanket on the end of a low, metal framed bunk bed. Her name was scrawled in loopy penmanship on a small, framed chalkboard tied to the end of the bedframe with a pink satin ribbon.

"Sparrow Menders," I said reading the chalkboard.

She looked up at me sniffling.

"Sparrow. That's your last name," I said with excitement.

"I guess it is," she squeaked without enthusiasm.

"I thought you'd be excited about this." But then a thought occurred to me. "Unless... Did you already know your last name too?" I asked.

She shook her head.

"No, but now that I've seen it, it feels like I've known it all along. It's on my curriculum too," she sniffled handing me the sheet of paper.

I looked at it. Sure enough, it matched the name scrawled on her bedframe. I instantly wondered about the boys. What was Nova's last name? And Remi's and Journey's? Were they having this same conversation right now? I hated not being able to talk to them. I hadn't even thought to ask them about their last names. I heard mine so often in the *Book of Secrets* that I didn't think anything of it when I saw in on my curriculum. I glanced up at the bed above Sparrow's and sighed when I saw my name wasn't on the matching chalkboard hanging from the bunk above hers. *Ella Mayberry*, was scrawled upon it in the same loopy writing.

I searched the large room, my footsteps echoing as I wandered through the maze of bunk beds until I found my name. As I'd suspected, it was with my sister's, in proper alphabetically order of course. *Geneva Sommers*. That was the first time I'd ever seen it written out like that, in actual handwriting. I'd seen it in the *Book of Secrets*, but there it was scrawled on ancient parchment, written by someone long deceased. Somehow, seeing it now, knowing it had been written by someone here at the Troian Center made it more real. My emotions swelled as a single tear trickled down my cheek while I stared at my name.

"What's in a name?" I whispered to myself, recalling a quote from a poem we'd read in Miss Neilia's lessons once.

Those days seemed so long ago. I shook myself from my nostalgia and turned away from my bed. "At least I have the top bunk," I muttered to myself.

I walked back over to Sparrow and sat next to her on her bed. She leaned her head on my shoulder as tears streamed silently down her rouged cheeks. I hated seeing her cry.

"Sparrow, it's okay. We're going to figure this out. I think I met one of the Pillars today so that means we only have one more to find. Hopefully we won't even be here that long."

She sniffled and sat up to look at me. "You did?"

"Well I think I did. I need to talk to her again to be sure, but it's a start."

"Good," she nodded. Her teary amber eyes met mine, but it didn't seem like anything I said was putting her mind at ease.

"Are you worried about your hair?" I whispered trying to think like a girl for a moment.

She shook her head.

"Then what is it?" I asked.

"The boys... I... It feels weird to be separated from them," she whispered letting a tiny sob crack her voice.

I pulled her close and hugged her. She was right. It did feel strange not to be able to see the boys or communicate with them at all. I had a sneaking suspicion that Malakai was purposely separating us to weaken us. All it accomplished was fueling my hatred toward him. But I tried to push his agenda out of my mind and focus on Sparrow. She and Journey had been best friends forever. She thought of him as a brother. They came to the Troian Center together and it dawned on me that they had probably never spent a day apart since. Maybe this was hitting her harder than I could understand.

"I know it's hard, but the boys will be okay. They can take care of themselves," I said reassuringly. "Besides, I'm sure they have a beautiful room just like this. I mean have you ever seen something so lavish? Journey's probably stretched out on one of these comfy beds trying to come up with a plan right now."

Jemma let out a snide snicker. "The only thing Sparrow's sad about is that she can't be near *her Remi*," she sneered in a malicious tone.

"Shut up, Jemma!" Sparrow yelled, instantly getting to her feet.

I was shocked by both Jemma's taunt and Sparrow's reaction. She never bought into Jemma's unfounded gossip or teasing.

Could she really have a thing for Remi? I asked myself in astonishment.

She had been trying to tell me she liked someone when we were in the forest but we got interrupted.

"What's she talking about?" I asked Sparrow.

"Oh you really didn't know?" Jemma said sauntering toward me, her eyes bright and her perfect lips curving into a mischievous smirk.

She was so pretty with her flawlessly applied makeup that I wanted to punch her.

"This is too much!" she said laughing as she circled me and Sparrow, who was shaking. "You two have honestly got to be the most oblivious twits I've ever met. Both in love with the wrong boys and too blind to notice the ones who actually like you. You really are the perfect friends, aren't you? The blind leading the blind." She laughed.

"Jemma, I don't care if Sparrow likes Remi. I don't care who likes who, honestly. All I care about is finding the Pillars and getting out of here before Malakai locks us up or worse! And I'd really appreciate if you could focus on helping me accomplish that!" I yelled.

"Tst, tst, tst, somebody's got her britches in a bunch, huh?" Jemma said already back in front of the mirror.

"Geneva, I don't – "

I cut Sparrow off before she could start in on her feelings for Remi. He'd always been my best friend, but when he kissed me, it was obvious that he wanted more and everything got complicated. Truthfully, I didn't know how I felt about it. I just knew I didn't have time to process that right now.

"Sparrow, it's fine. I don't care and you don't need to explain anything to me. I just wish we could talk to the boys right now. It's so inconvenient that I can't telepath. We need to come up with a plan. Can you telepath to them?"

Sparrow shook her head. “I’ve been trying since we got here and I can’t. I get nothing,” she groaned.

“That’s strange. Maybe you were in shock. Try now,” I encouraged.

She closed her eyes tight and was silent for a moment.

“Nothing,” she said.

“Jemma, can you try?” I asked, swallowing my pride to ask her for help.

“Try what?” she replied absently from the large oval mirror.

I watched as she tilted it in its ornate stand to achieve her most flattering angle. I gave Sparrow a look of tired desperation and rolled my eyes, which actually got a tiny smirk from her. It was the first sign of my old friend since we had entered the new Troian Center. I sighed and walked over to Jemma, trying to calmly pry my shallow sister from her reflection.

“No!” she cried when I reached her side

My eyes focused on what hers had seen and I reacted quickly, spinning the mirror downward violently in one swift movement. The mirror was lighter than I’d anticipated and I’d pushed it with too much force. I watched in horror as the entire mirror and stand crashed to the floor in an explosion of glass. I reflexively put my body between the mirror and Jemma, trying to protect her from the cloud of raining glass. As the mirror splintered and smashed, I thrust my hand over Jemma’s mouth to stifle her scream.

“Jemma! You were supposed to stop this! You said it wouldn’t happen anymore! We shouldn’t be able to see her,” I hissed in her ear still clamping my hand over her open mouth.

Her eyes were searching the shards of the mirror wildly as she struggled against me.

Sparrow was by our side now too. “What’s going on?” she asked.

“I’m going to let you go and you’re going to stay quiet,” I commanded Jemma.

She nodded in agreement and complied when I removed my hand.

"What's wrong?" Sparrow asked looking more anxious by the second.

"I saw Nesia. Which means our timeline just got a lot shorter," I said to Sparrow, still staring at my traitorous sister.

9

"It's her, Master. I can feel it," Kobel said. "She's the one I saw in my visions when I was connecting to her mind."

"Yes, I believe it's her as well. But we must be absolutely certain," Malakai said. "We'll know soon enough when I test her cuff. In the meantime, I'd like you all to watch her this week. Catalog her behavior and whom she interacts with. The *Book of the Gods* says she will lead us to the Pillars. That is why we've brought all the children on the island to the Troian Academy. If the Pillars are here, the Eva will find them."

There was a resounding agreement from the group he addressed.

"I myself will be observing the six that came from the forest through my own methods, but I'm counting on your eyes and ears as well. This is what we've been preparing for. It won't be long now," Malakai said.

He looked at the faces of the Ravinori in the tightly packed room. The candlelight cast eerie shadows dancing along the rounded walls of the underground chamber. The figures in attendance were hooded, shadowing the looks of hungry anticipation that he knew lay upon their faces. They had gathered shortly after dark and traded their Luxor uniforms and professor robes for dark grey shawls as they met in their secret room in the Troian Academy. The mood in the room was electric.

“Do you suspect any of her accomplices to be Pillars?” one hooded woman asked.

“Yes, we do suspect at least one of them. I'll know more after I read their cuffs.”

“Why are we waiting, Master? I say we torture it out of them,” a gruff man grumbled.

“Mr. Flint, you're posing as a professor now. That's not how professors speak. And we've been over this, the *Book of Gods* tells us to let the Eva lead us to the Pillars. We must obey the book. Besides, our methods of torture tend to get out of hand. We don't want to accidentally kill one of them after waiting so long to find them, do we? I believe they will be an instrumental bargaining tool in locating the other Pillars. It's in our best interest to preserve them.”

“Let us not wait too long, Master,” came another voice. “That was Mistress Greeley's demise.”

“I will not make the same mistake twice,” Malakai thundered. “Greeley should never have been trusted to watch such valuable assets unsupervised. If you recall, I voiced this to you on several occasions, but you agreed I was needed in Lux. After all, I am but one man. I can only be in one place at a time; for now, that is. Our Liege may make other things possible.”

“So it can truly be done? We can bring him back now, Master?” another deep voice asked.

“Dare you disbelieve?” hissed the woman who'd spoke earlier.

“Now, now, Miss Kaul. I think Commander Gray is merely excited that the dawn of His rising is nearly upon us, aren't you Commander Gray? After all, a true Ravinori knows it's illegal to renounce faith in me, for that is the same as renouncing Ravin himself."

A low murmur rippled through the hooded crowd at the mention of Ravin.

"You all know what to do. This meeting is adjourned."

After the room cleared out, Malakai stalked over to Kobel.

"This had better work, Kobel, or they'll lynch me like they were prepared to do to Greeley."

"Yes, Master. It has to work. It was written in the *Book of Gods* so it will be. You've seen it with your own eyes. The Eva will lead us to the Pillars."

I LAY awake in my bed, snuggled beneath the white, down blanket. I was warm and comfortable, despite the nasty gash I'd gotten on my hand from a piece of the broken mirror, but sleep still wouldn't come. I flopped onto my back in frustration and stared up at the tiny chandelier above my bed. It cast dancing flickers of illumination each time a teardrop of glass caught the moonlight. They reminded me of my orbs and I suddenly ached for my powers. Perhaps giving them up had been more foolish than I'd thought. Although, I reminded myself that it didn't seem my friends could use any of their perfectly unveiled powers at the moment either. But the whole reason I'd done it was to conceal my identity as the *Ponte deorum* and it obviously hadn't work since Jemma and I had seen our mother in the mirror before I smashed it. My mind whirled with frustrating thoughts. Had the veiling not worked? Did Jemma purposely do it wrong? Was the *Ponte deorum* something that couldn't be veiled? Did Malakai already know I was the *Ponte deorum*? Was it all some sort of trick or test?

I shook myself from the endless circle of thoughts that had no answers and rolled onto my stomach, burying my face in my pillow. I wanted to scream. Nothing was going according to plan. Malakai was onto us, I was sure of it. Why else would he have Luxors policing the Troian Center? And we weren't doing a great job of infiltrating the new students to figure out if they were Pillars. I thought I'd had immediate success with Sadie, but of course, the rest of the girls in our room, including Sadie, had returned as I'd smashed the mirror. After watching wide-eyed while Sparrow and I desperately tried to clean up the shattered glass, they avoided us like the plague the rest of the night.

Great first impression, I thought.

Sparrow had helped me clean my cut, but the white coat woman who came in for bed check noticed my makeshift bandage and sent me swiftly to the infirmary. When I'd returned, it was lights out and everyone was already in bed.

Though I was exhausted, my mind was reeling. I was haunted with sleeplessness as I tossed and turned. I found myself thinking about the boys and wondering how the rest of their night had gone. I wondered where they were at this exact moment and what they were doing. Perhaps they were staring at the ceiling and thinking of us. An image of Nova faded against the backs of my eyelids as the darkness finally quieted my mind.

~

"No! Nova! Don't!" I screamed.

A Luxor was clutching Nova by the throat, his face contorted with pain, as a wall of flames raced up encircling them.

"Please don't," I cried.

Nova broke free of the Luxor's grasp and I screamed again as I recognized his face.

"Remi?" I gasped.

Both of them stood apart now, staring at me with muscles tensed and ready to attack each other again.

"Choose," said a voice.

It was unmistakably Malakai's.

"I can't! I won't!" I cried.

The wall of flames sprung up, engulfing them both.

"No!" I screamed again, this time from my bed.

I sat up and ripped the tangled blankets off, begging my mind to stop the madness.

"It was just a nightmare," I whispered to myself as I gulped in ragged breaths and shivered against the icy chill that clung to my sweat-drenched nightshirt. "It was just a nightmare."

Professor Kobel had stayed behind after everyone left the secret Ravinori meeting. He was busy pouring over charts and ancient manuscripts. A single candle burned on the table, lighting the room. The wax pooled dangerously, evidence that Kobel had stayed much longer than he'd meant to. The flame gave a tiny flicker and Kobel looked up.

"Can I help you?" he asked.

A woman in a white coat stood in front of him.

"There's been a development," she said handing him a clipboard.

Kobel took it, reading the pages until a sneer crept slowly across his face.

"And this happened this evening?" he asked.

"Yes. In her bunkroom."

"Thank you. This will please the headmaster very much," Kobel said with a smirk.

10

We finally regrouped in the dining hall for breakfast and I filled the boys in on what had happened in our room after they left. Despite our plush sleeping accommodations and delicious food, everyone was in a pretty foul mood.

"You said you took my powers away, Jemma. *All* my powers," I accosted her under my breath in the dining hall.

"I did. I swear I did," Jemma blubbered.

"Obviously not," I hissed holding up my bandaged hand that I cut when I smashed the mirror. "Is anything you told me true?"

I was implying to Nova being the talisman for my veiled powers and she knew it. She sat up straighter, her eyes desperately big and bloodshot.

"Yes, Geneva. I'm not lying to you. I veiled your powers. I did everything Eja told me to do. Everything I told you that night was true."

The nervousness and confusion in her voice was clear. I believed her. I let my shoulders slump and my hand fell back to the table, making me wince.

"That looks pretty bad," Remi said motioning to my bandaged hand.

"It's fine," I dismissed.

"It's still bleeding," Nova said, reaching across the table to where my hand rested.

"I said it's fine!" I barked more harshly than I'd meant, jerking my hand away.

Nova looked wounded.

"Shhh..." Sparrow warned.

I ignored her and turned back to Jemma.

"Jemma, if you did what you were supposed to, how do you explain how we saw our mother in that mirror last night?" I whispered.

Jemma just stared at me with a scared look on her face, tears still pooling in the corners of her eyes.

"Pull it together will you? You're starting to draw attention," Journey whispered to her. "We don't need these Pruxes giving us any trouble."

"Journey," Sparrow warned. "I've told you I don't like that word."

He grumbled but refrained from anymore comments. He was right about not wanting to draw extra attention though. We were outnumbered by students from Lux and we weren't doing a good job blending in. The bald patches of our hair had surprisingly grown back to a fine bit of peach fuzz over night, dulling the shine of the shaved parts. We looked like they did now. But even still, the other students seemed to want nothing to do with us. Our hectic arrival at the Troian Center had sparked rumors and ever since Kai had been ushering us around no one wanted to make eye contact with us. And now, after I'd smashed a mirror in front of the majority of the girls my age, everyone was convinced I was a violent psycho who bullied her sister.

A girl sitting next to Jemma gave her a pinched looking

scowl and inched her tray as far away from her as she could manage without practically sitting on her friend's lap.

"Geez, do they think we're contagious or something?" I muttered.

"Who cares," Nova scowled. "I'm more concerned that we're in over our heads here. We weren't prepared for this. I think we need to signal to Isby and get out of here while we can."

It was hard to believe that it had only been yesterday that we'd been standing on the hill overlooking the Troian Center, with our freedom and futures still in our possession. Now everything felt hopeless.

As if reading my mind Sparrow said, "We can't leave yet. Geneva's already found one of the Pillars."

"You did?" the boys asked in unison.

"Good, let's grab the Pillar and get out of here!" Nova said.

"Allegedly," I said waving away their looks of excitement. "I allegedly found a Pillar. Her name is Sadie and I met her in the infirmary yesterday. And we can't just kidnap her. Besides I'm not even one hundred percent sure she is one."

"What made you think she's a Pillar?" Nova asked.

I didn't know what to say. I wanted to say, 'she made me feel the way I feel when I touch you,' but it seemed too intimate to speak out loud in front of the others. I knew it would only bring up old feelings between us and probably confuse Nova even more about how I felt. I was confused myself. I couldn't turn off my undeniable attraction to him, yet I was behaving so cold and standoffish since Jemma decided to use him as a talisman for my veiled powers. I could feel the tension building between us, pushing us further apart.

"It was just a feeling," I shrugged.

"Well that gets us nowhere," Nova barked. "How are we supposed to confirm it?"

"I need a little more time with her. She's in our bunkroom. Maybe I can talk to her tonight?"

"Whoa, who says we're staying tonight?" Nova said. "We need to leave while we still can. The incident with the mirror is proof of that."

"No, I just need more time. I can't explain it, but I'm sure Sadie is one of us," I pleaded.

"Geneva, even if she is a Pillar that doesn't solve our problem. We still have one more to find," Journey chimed it. "I agree with Nova. It's too dangerous here."

I looked to Remi. He was the only one that was always on my side, but even he looked grim. "If we knew who the last Pillar was or how we go about finding them it would be different, but..." Remi trailed off unable to meet my pleading eyes.

"But we do know how to find them. You all heard Kobel yesterday. He said that Malakai has a book that has all of our names in it. I'm sure it will help us figure out who the last Pillar is. All we need to do is find it."

"Oh great! So we're searching for another book? That went so well last time," Nova commented, sarcastically referring to our epically disastrous plan to get the *Book of Secrets* that almost got us all killed.

"Hey, we did find it, didn't we? And besides, I think Kai is the key to getting access to this mysterious manuscript. We need to get close to him, get him to trust us so we can find out what he knows. His father is the headmaster; he has to be privy to his plan."

"Geneva, this is stupid. We're all in danger here. Don't you see that?" Nova said, all the bitterness and sarcasm absent from his voice now.

He stared at me with pained concern that stabbed at my heart and threatened my resolve. Maybe we should leave now. Maybe I could run from my destiny and disappear with Nova somewhere far away and safe. It was clear that we were outmatched here. No one would fault me for retreating, would they?

I swallowed hard, gathering my courage. As tempting as my daydreams were, I knew I couldn't give up. I was the only one who could save my island from the evil of the Ravinori. I was the chosen one. I didn't know why I had been chosen for this fate, but I had faith that there was a reason. I knew it was my duty to try my hardest to fulfill the destiny bestowed upon me. Running wasn't an option. I thought of the Beto's, my parents, Talon. I couldn't let everything they had fought for and sacrificed be for nothing. I had to stay and fight.

I softened my voice before replying.

"Look, I'm not oblivious. I know staying here is a risk, but I can't leave. I have to find the Pillars and stop the Ravinori in order to fulfill my destiny. The Pillars are here, I know it. If I leave now I'll just have to find another way to get back here. It was already hard enough the first time. I'm not asking any of you to stay, but I have to. I'm the only one who can end this. None of you will be safe until I do."

I was addressing all of my friends, but I was staring at Nova. He was why I had to stay here. He was why I had to fulfill my destiny. He was a Pillar and so was Jovi. I had to keep them safe. If I failed, that meant the Ravinori would win. They would use the Pillars to bring Ravin back and then we would all be doomed. But if I could somehow succeed, if I could stop the Ravinori, then I was sure I could fulfill my destiny as predicted in the *Book of Secrets* and we'd all be free. I could finally live the life I wanted, which of course was one in which Nova and I could finally be together without all of these secrets and lies strangling our hearts.

Nova's green eyes paled and he looked like he was glimpsing into a dismal future that I couldn't see as he shook his head slowly at me.

"You know I won't leave you here alone," he said softly.

The way Nova looked at me made everything else fade away. Even though we were in a room full of hundreds of students, the undeniable connection between us swallowed me whole. My chest tightened as his eyes pleaded with mine; sea green to clear blue. Our unspoken conversation must have been getting too personal because Journey finally interrupted by clearing his throat.

"So... we're staying then?"

"If Geneva is staying, so am I," Nova said, never tearing his eyes from mine.

My eyes watered as he reached a hand across the table. He wanted to make a pact, just like we had before in this very room when this whole crazy adventure had started. My heart splintered. I wanted to feel the warmth of his familiar rough hands on my own. My skin ached to remember the way each scar on his calloused hands felt as they caressed mine, but I couldn't. I had to shut him down in order to protect him. I pulled my own hands off the table and onto my lap.

"Just remember, I never asked you to stay," I said.

Emotions erupted like fireworks across his beautifully planed face; hurt, confusion, anger, betrayal. I couldn't bear to look at him. Instead, I stared at my hands that lay shaking in my lap.

"So what's the plan?" Sparrow asked trying to diffuse the situation after a long awkward silence.

"We continue looking for Pillars and try to get info from Kai as to where the book is that his father used to find our names," I said.

"Well *you* shouldn't have any trouble getting to know Kai," Nova said bitterly. "Here he is right now. Why don't you ask him?"

"Ask me what?" Kai said suddenly appearing behind me.

I jumped, wondering how long he'd been standing there.

"Hi, Kai," I stammered. "Nothing important. I was just wondering where you've been? I was hoping you'd show us around some more today," I said patting the bench next to me for him to sit, trying to change the subject. "Everything is so different around here, I'm having a hard time adjusting to all the changes."

Kai beamed and sat down next to me, forcing Remi to move over.

"I'd be happy to. I was with my father. Breakfast, remember?" he questioned. "Father was grilling me to make sure I did a good job of showing you all around and making sure you got settled in. I did a good job, right?"

"Fantastic," Nova added sarcastically.

I shot him a look.

"How was your night?" Kai asked me. "Did you sleep well?'

"Well, it was eventful," I replied holding up my bandaged hand.

"Oh no. What happened?" Kai gasped, immediately seizing my hand to exam it.

"Ouch!"

"Sorry," he replied letting it go.

"It's okay, just a little sore," I said gently, trying to take my own advice of drawing him in.

"What did you do?" he asked, gingerly examining my hand. This time he gently ran his fingers over mine.

"I'm so clumsy, I knocked over the mirror in our room and I guess I cut myself on a piece of the broken glass." I batted my eyelashes, giving a go at what I thought was flirting.

I didn't know if it was working on Kai, but it certainly pissed Nova off. His face grew so red that I was sure smoke was going to start coming out his ears and Remi squirmed uncomfortably in his seat. I consciously ignored their irritated glances and focused on Kai's dark features.

"Oh, that explains what they were talking about," Kai said absently.

My eyes widened.

"Who was talking about it?" Jemma asked suddenly joining the conversation.

"Oh just some people in my father's office. I overheard them say something about a mirror as I was leaving."

"What were they saying?" Jemma drilled. "What, *exactly*, were they saying?" She was practically leaning across the table, looking like she was possessed.

Kai looked shocked and confused.

"It's okay, Jemma," I said firing Journey a look. He was sitting next to her and pulled her back to her seat. I turned to Kai, touching his arm. "My big sister is just being overprotective. She hates when people talk about me or pick on me for being clumsy," I gushed.

I had Kai's attention again.

"Oh no one was making fun of you. They were just talking about how strange it was that the mirror in your room broke the day you arrived. It almost sounded like they were arguing over whether you could have broken it at all. I guess it must have been a special mirror or something," he shrugged.

"Oh no. Was it expensive? I'm really sorry. I'm so clumsy," I said doing my best to look embarrassed, but this was worse than I thought.

They were on to me. And something about the last sentence Kai said was unsettling. Perhaps the mirror had been a trap.

"Ouch," I whimpered when I brought my hand to my head. I guess I didn't have to try to fake it too hard. My hand was still sore and I was better at being clumsy then I thought.

"It's just a mirror," Kai said. "I'm sure it's replaceable. But you are not. Are you sure you're okay?" he asked, suddenly looking concerned.

"Yeah, my hand hurts a little still, but I'll be okay."

"Can I take you to the infirmary? They can give you something for the pain."

I paused for a moment and then thought this would be the perfect opportunity to be alone with Kai and ask him some more questions. And maybe Sadie would be back at the infirmary so I could talk to her again. It would also hopefully give my friends some time to talk without Kai around and come up with a plan for getting out of here once we did have all the Pillars.

Ugh, I wished I could telepath that to them.

After a desperate look at my friends, pleading for their understanding, I turned to Kai and grinned. "Yes, Kai. That would be great."

11

"What do you mean, Kobel? Why does this matter?" Malakai asked looking over the infirmary clipboard that Kobel had handed him.

"Master, when you told me to prepare this building like a fortress, I did. I took every measure, every precaution, so that when we encountered the Eva, we would be able to contain her until we could force her to work with us. We built the impenetrable Cayo fence, made of steel harvested from the ore of the sacred caves so that no magic could be used within its walls. We used the same cavernous ore when creating the cuffs the students wear, to absorb their magic so we can power the Soul Cells that keep this facility running. I charmed the entire premises so that we can track the movements of everyone here. These are not simple feats."

"Kobel, I'm losing patience, get to the point. Just tell me why I'm interested in this," Malakai shouted throwing the clipboard to the floor with a loud crash.

Kobel limped over to pick it up.

"I enchanted every mirror in this building to seek what we seek most. *Ponte deorum.*"

"Kobel, I've told you before to stop chasing this foolishness. We are focusing on the Pillars!"

"But Master, it worked! The mirror worked. We no longer need to find the Pillars if we have the *Ponte deorum*."

"How does a broken mirror prove that Geneva is the *Ponte deorum?*"

"Because only the *Ponte deorum* would be able to smash it. I used a very powerful enchantment. The mirrors aren't actually mirrors anymore. They're more like portals to the in-between, thinning the veil between our worlds. Only the *Ponte deorum* would command the strength to shatter such a portal."

"I'm going to need more proof then some broken glass - "

"I have a way to prove it, Master," Kobel interrupted, holding up a small glass vial filled with dark liquid.

"No. We are doing this my way, Kobel! Do you understand me?"

"So do you like it here?" I asked Kai as we walked down the hall toward the infirmary.

I'd convinced him to take me the long way so he could show me more of the Troian Academy on our way to the infirmary. After inspecting my hand and determining I didn't have a fatal injury, Kai was more than happy to oblige.

"Yes," he said, but he looked like he wanted to say more.

"What is it?"

"Well sometimes I miss home," he said bashfully. "I know Father says this is our home now, but I can't help being homesick sometimes."

"Tell me about it," I said.

"About my home?"

"Yes. I've only ever been to Lux for the New Year Galas and even then, I didn't get to see much of it."

"Lux is beautiful," Kai said with a warm smile. "You would love it there."

"Well that part I know," I said with a laugh. "Tell me about your house? What parts do you miss? Did you have your own room? Did you have any pets? Did you have a library? I love books," I said thinking of my goal.

"Oh! Well yes. I guess I miss my old room, mostly because I was used to it. Things here are just as comfortable though. I have my own room here too, you know?"

"You do?" I asked genuinely surprised.

"Yes. Father and I have our own private residence. He had it built when we arrived. He said he didn't want me staying with..." he trailed off suddenly.

"With orphans?" I guessed.

"Yes," he said as his cheeks flushed. "But I don't feel that way. Truthfully my home was rather lonely. I would be happy to stay in a bunkroom with the other boys."

From the longing in his tone, I believed him. He truly seemed like he just wanted to fit in.

"What else?" I asked. "Did you leave anything or anyone you miss behind? A pet, a friend, a girlfriend?" I inquired shyly.

Kai's cheeks burned again and he coughed uncomfortably.

"No, none of the above. I was never allowed to have pets, although I begged for one every year for my birthday. Father would never allow it. He was always too busy entertaining guests and working in his study."

"His study? Is that like a library?"

"Yes, I guess you could call it that. Father has more books in his private collection than the Troian Academy library has," he boasted proudly.

"Wow, I would love to see it someday," I swooned.

"Really?" he asked sounding surprised and a bit doubtful.

"Absolutely. I love books. I especially love writing. I used to have a journal and I wrote in it nearly every day, but I lost it when we were in the forest. I miss it a lot. It felt like a little piece of home, I guess, because I had so many memories in it."

This was mostly true. I did miss my journal terribly, but it wasn't lost. I had purposely left it with Hollis, not wanting it to fall into the wrong hands. My nostalgia must have shown on my face because Kai instantly perked up.

"I can get you a new journal. I've seen tons in my father's study. I'm sure he wouldn't mind if I borrowed one."

"I wouldn't want to make you go through the trouble. Lux is so far and – "

"No, I wouldn't have to go to Lux. Father has a small study here. It would be no trouble at all."

"He does?" I tried to keep the hopefulness in my voice from getting away from me.

"Of course. He brought some of his more important manuscripts with him so he wouldn't have to travel back and forth."

"Like the one he found our names in that Professor Kobel told us about?"

"Maybe," Kai said with a shrug.

"Can we go right now?"

"Oh, but what about your hand?"

"Oh yeah, my hand," I said glumly. "But I'm dying to find out more about my family."

"I'm sure my father will be happy to tell you everything he knows during your counseling session, but I should really get you to the infirmary now. We've gotten a bit off track."

"Where are we now?" I asked.

"This is the music wing."

"It's peaceful here," I said taking in the soft melodies that floated down the hall. "Do you play?"

"Yes. The piano. Do you?"

"No, I'm afraid I don't have any musical talent. I do enjoy listening though."

"Maybe I can play for you sometime," Kai said, smiling at me again.

He really did look so familiar. It was maddening that I couldn't put my finger on why.

"Kai, this might sound weird, but we haven't met before, have we?"

"No, I would remember a face like yours."

I flushed and we walked in silence back toward the infirmary.

"I bet you miss your friends and family in Lux," I said after a while.

"Well, my father is the only family I have, and I guess I don't really have any friends," he said sounding a bit embarrassed.

"I don't believe that for a minute," I said trying to cheer him up.

I barely knew Kai, but seeing him sad was painful. I studied his sullen eyes, rimmed by a forest of impossibly long, thick lashes. Something about the way he nervously blinked them reminded me of Niv and my soft spot for Kai grew even further.

"Thanks, but I guess no one wants to get too close to the headmaster's son."

"Why's that?"

"I'm not really sure why. They think I'll rat out their secrets I suppose. Everyone here seems to have a lot of secrets."

"But your father just recently became the headmaster, right? At orientation, didn't the professor say he was in the militia before coming to the Troian Center? I mean Academy."

Kai stopped walking. My heart dropped. Did I push him too far with all these questions?

"What is it?"

"I guess you're right. I can't use that as an excuse as to why I have no friends. People just don't like me," he said with a hint of honest realization in his voice.

Now he looked like an injured marmouse. I acted impulsively and did the only thing I could think to cheer him up. It's what I did to Niv when he looked sad and pathetic. I hugged him. He went rigid against me, snapping me back to reality, and suddenly it felt strange to be embracing him. Maybe I was violating some rule we had learned about in orientation. Was there no touching allowed at the Troian Academy? I hadn't paid attention too closely. My mind had been racing ahead with how impossible our task of rescuing the Pillars had become.

"Sorry," I mumbled letting him go.

"No, don't be. It just caught me off guard. No one's ever hugged me before."

"What? You can't be serious."

He gave an awkward shrug.

"My mother died right after I was born and my father's not an affectionate man. He says it makes people weak."

My hate for Malakai grew even further. How could he be so cold to his own son? I hadn't had a love filled childhood either, but at least I always had Remi. We were there to pick each other up, hold each other tight, and be a shoulder to cry on. I remembered many a night spent curled up in his lap crying myself to sleep when I was a child. He'd been the only one who could calm my night terrors when I was even younger. He used to lock his arms around my flailing limbs, letting me scream into his chest while he stroked my sweat drenched hair. I'd also been there for him when he awoke from nightmares and when he came back from his terrifying first trip to the Locker. He'd just wanted to sit quietly and hold my hand. We were a constant source of comfort for each other. I couldn't imagine surviving the Troian Center without Remi in my life. The thought sent a shiver through me.

"You never had anyone else in your life?" I asked with astonishment.

"Well we had servants, but Father never permitted me to speak to them about personal things."

My heart hardened against the headmaster, but it instantly reached out to Kai. This poor boy. I guess I needed to rethink everything. I had assumed that all the students who had come from Lux were a bunch of Pruxes. But it sounded like Kai was as starved for love and family as I was. As usual, nothing was what it seemed.

I reached out for Kai's hand with my good one and squeezed it tight. "Well you have a friend now."

His smile lit up his face as he squeezed back.

"WHAT THE HECK does Geneva think she's doing?" Nova growled from his seat in dining hall.

"Calm down, mate," Journey said. "She's pumping him for intel. She's gotta get close to him and gain his trust so he'll give her what she's looking for."

"Intel? What are you some sort of Beto super spy now?"

"You got all that from her batting her eyelashes and touching his arm?" Remi asked.

"Yeah, and if you two weren't so blindly in love with her, it's pretty plain to see. I swear that's her superpower, even with a bad haircut." Journey shook his head at Nova and Remi.

The boys stared at each other, but neither said anything to deny it. Nova scowled and Remi's cheeks burned red. Finally Sparrow broke the stalemate.

"Well, what exactly *is* she looking for?"

"She's trying to see if she can get him to slip up and say what his father is up to. Geneva's right. There's no way he's here acting as Headmaster of this rundown hunk of stone out of the kindness of his heart. I mean you met the guy, right? No one brings in soldiers to an orphanage and scalps heads like that..." Journey trailed off, remembering their brutal attack from earlier.

"Are you two telepathing or something?" Sparrow asked.

"No," Journey replied. "But I know it's what I'd be doing if I were her. She's smart. Give her some credit."

"About that," Remi said, "I haven't been able to telepath since we've been here. I haven't been able to use any of my powers actually."

"No kidding, invisible boy wonder!" Nova said.

"I already told you that wasn't my fault! I swear I kept us all covered. I don't know how they were able to see us. I would never endanger *an*y of my friends, Nova. Not even you," Remi said in an angry whisper.

"Are you accusing him of doing that on purpose?" Sparrow asked incredulously.

"If the shoe fits," Nova shrugged.

"Here we go again," Journey grumbled between mouthfuls as he picked at the scraps on Geneva's abandoned tray.

"Guys, stop it," Jemma interrupted before the conversation could go any further. "Your arguing is giving me a headache."

"There's obviously something here preventing us from using our powers if none of us are able to use them. I bet it has something to do with that fence around the Center. Maybe it's some sort of force field. I mean why would they build a fence? There's already a stone wall. Its overkill, don't you think?" Journey asked.

"Not this again," Nova groaned.

"What am I missing?" Sparrow asked.

"Journey hasn't stopped speculating about why our powers won't work since we got here," Remi explained.

"Something has to be causing it. I think it's the fence," Journey whispered.

"Will you please stop with your crazy theories?" Nova scoffed.

"Geneva can still use her powers," Jemma whispered.

"That's not true," Sparrow interjected.

"What do you mean?" Remi whispered. "I thought you veiled her powers to keep her safe, Jemma!"

"I thought so too," she said still sounding shell-shocked. "But you heard what she did. She saw our mother in the mirror, that's why she broke it. Maybe I'm not strong enough to veil the *Ponte* – "

"Shhhhh! Jemma, don't even say that word in here," Nova hissed, pounding the table angrily with his fist.

Jemma jumped while other students looked on, stifling their gasps.

"I don't know what that was with the mirror, but Geneva can't use her powers either. She's been trying to telepath to you since we got here," Sparrow said to Nova. "You heard what Kai said. Malakai knew about the mirror. Maybe it was some sort of trick."

"That *was* kind of strange that they were talking about Geneva breaking the mirror," Journey agreed.

"I know what I saw," Jemma said. "It wasn't a trick."

"This is impossible," Sparrow whined. "We can't telepath, we stay in separate wings, what are we going to do?"

"We'll figure it out," Nova said, a bit of his usual optimism returning. "Let's give Geneva a chance to talk to Kai and see if she can learn anything."

"Let me see your curriculum," Sparrow said. After briefly comparing them she put on a brave face and smiled. "We still have some lessons together and there's study hall on the schedule every night after dinner. We can talk then. In the meantime, we all need to be looking for the Pillars."

The others looked over their schedules too, nodding.

"I know it's going to be a lot harder now with all the new students and no powers. And not to mention our every move being monitored by Luxors, but we can't give up," Remi said.

No one argued, they just all looked at each other with trepidation.

12

Kai and I walked hand-in-hand making our way to the infirmary slowly. It felt increasingly awkward to be holding his hand, but once I offered it, he hadn't wanted to let go. I kept reminding myself I was doing whatever it took to get the information I needed, but I couldn't help feeling guilty. Kai was openly chatting with me, explaining the ancient stories intricately woven into the large tapestries we passed. He was back to his cheerful mood as he boasted proudly about the rich culture his father aimed to bring to the Troian Academy.

"You're proud of him, aren't you?"

"Very," Kai beamed. "I'm fortunate to be his son."

"I'm sure he feels the same for you," I added.

"He doesn't," Kai said sullenly. "But one day I know he will. I will make him proud."

I found it strange that Kai felt his own father wasn't proud of him and made a mental note to use that against him if I had to. I knew I would do anything to make my father proud, I thought wistfully, missing him as we walked in awkward silence for the next few paces.

"You miss your father, don't you?" Kai asked as if reading my thoughts.

I stopped walking and stared at him. It was unnerving the way Kai made me think of my father so often. It was more than the fact that they shared the same name.

My brain was itching for answers when Kai grinned, instantly disarming me. There was something so maddeningly familiar about him. Whatever it was that made me feel instantly comfortable around Kai, also made me feel guilty of my plans to use him.

"How did you know I was just thinking that?" I asked with more accusation in my voice than I had expected.

"I know that look of longing. It's how I get when I think about my mother," he replied giving me a sincere smile that tapped into my core.

He did get it; how bad it hurt not having parents and how the hurt could sneak up on you unexpectedly.

"Can I tell you something, Kai?"

He nodded.

"I miss my parents a lot, but when I'm around you, I think about my father more, and somehow that makes it hurt less. Does that make sense?"

"Absolutely. We have kindred hearts, Geneva. I am proud to share your father's namesake and that of the great Kai. I hope we can both find strength and peace in that."

I smiled, while cringing on the inside, wondering what Kai would say if I told him my father and the great Kai were one and the same.

We continued meandering down the hallway to the infirmary. We were in no rush, enjoying each other's company and conversation. But the whole time I was loathing my dishonest intentions. Why did Kai have to be so nice? Wasn't there some other kid I could exploit to gain access to the headmaster and his evil plans?

My face burned with shame every time Kai grinned at me or chivalrously ran ahead to open a door in my path. There was something so likable about him. He was honest and open, pouring forth facts about himself and his family and what life was like growing up in Lux. How was it possible that he had come from someone like Malakai?

I found myself shocked that he had no friends. How could his classmates not like him? Were they jealous of his dimpled smile, his flawless olive skin, his perfectly manicured hands? What was I missing? It wasn't his stunning white teeth or mysterious dark eyes that seemed to sparkle like the night sky every time a ray of light caught them. Try as I might, I kept coming up empty as I searched for his faults.

He caught me staring at him a little too long and gave me a strange look.

"What?" he asked.

"Nothing, sorry," I said mentally scolding my subpar sleuth skills.

Kai shrugged. It was refreshing to have someone take me for my word. I was so used to arguing about everything with Nova, it was strange to carry such an easy conversation for once.

Again I found myself shaking my head. What did all the other students see that I didn't? Perhaps Kai's charm and manners masked some murky secret behind his dark lashes and shiny shoulder length hair. I watched as he constantly tucked his black locks behind his ears as we walked. Maybe his father had taught him to be a master of deception. He would have had years to groom him for such a task. But somehow, I still had a feeling that whatever Malakai was up to - and I was sure he was up to something terrible - Kai wasn't privy to it. At least that's what I found myself wanting to believe.

It was increasingly difficult to keep my guard up around Kai, but I kept reminding myself that Malakai was his father.

"Are you feeling all right, Geneva?" he asked me.

"Yes, why?"

"Well you look kind of pale."

I laughed. "I always look like this, Kai. Remi teases me and says if it wasn't for my freckles I'd be translucent."

He leaned in close to me and touched my cheek, letting his thumb graze lightly over a cluster of freckles. He smiled, gazing at me.

"They suit you, Geneva. Don't let anyone tell you otherwise. Your face without freckles would be like the heavens without stars," he whispered.

I caught my breath and swallowed hard. *Oh boy. What do I say to that?* I had a feeling I was in over my head already. That was perhaps the most romantic thing anyone had every said to me. I was sure it was a line but I could tell he believed it, which made the comment even sweeter. I took a step back from him, feeling guilty and awkward.

"I'm sorry," he apologized dropping his hand. "I'm talking too much, aren't I? Sorry. Father says I do that. It's probably because I don't usually have anyone to talk to."

"No Kai, you're not talking too much," I reassured him. "And stop apologizing for who you are. I don't care what your father says, I think you're pretty great."

He smiled warmly back at me.

"I'm just taking it all in."

"It's a lot isn't it?" he asked. "My father can go overboard sometimes, but I know he means well. I guess we're alike in that way."

"In what way?" I asked suddenly shaken by this comment. I was holding my breath; secretly hoping that Kai was nothing like his father.

"We both try too hard."

I sighed with relief internally.

"And we can be misunderstood," he continued sparking my

suspicion again.

"Kai, I don't mean to be offensive, but I don't think anyone could ever misunderstand your father. He had an army attack us and shave our heads. He knows what he wants and he gets to the point."

"See! That's what I mean," Kai protested. "You probably all took him to be some brutal monster, but you have to look at it from his point of view. He's ordered the Luxors to protect the students here at all costs. When the six of you stormed the building, they were only acting on his orders of protection."

"Stormed?" I glared at him. He was talking like he was brainwashed. He must have sat through one too many orientations with Professor Kobel if he actually believed that. "And what about shaving our heads? I suppose that was a protective measure too? Did we have weapons hidden in our hair or something?" I retorted sarcastically, my temper growing.

"I know you don't want to hear this, but it was. It's a precaution against spreading disease."

"Seriously?" I asked him in disbelief.

"And other things..." he trailed off.

My blood was boiling and I wanted to shake him, but I bit my tongue. I had to keep my cool and keep Kai on my side. I didn't want to undo all the ground I'd just gained in my friendship with him. I'd probably already said too much.

"What other things?" I asked.

"They had to make sure you were really who you said you were."

"I don't follow, Kai."

"The tattoos on your heads. They had to make sure they matched the ones on your arms so they knew you weren't imposters."

"Imposters! Who would pretend to want to be an orphan?"

"I don't know, but I overheard my father and Kobel talking

about it. They said it was the only way to be sure of who you were."

Now we were getting somewhere.

Kai hung his head. "Forget it. This is what always happens. This is why I have no friends. He's my father, Geneva, and he's a good man. You don't know him like I do. No one does, and no one gives him a chance. And then no one wants to give me a chance."

I stood silently watching Kai for a moment. His eyes avoided mine and he looked uncomfortable as he shifted his weight from one foot to the other, scuffing the toe of his shoe on the floor while he fidgeted with his hair.

I took a deep breath and grabbed his hand. "I'll give you a chance. Both of you."

Kai suddenly pulled me into an embrace, almost knocking me off my feet.

"Thank you, Geneva! You won't regret it. You'll see. I'll prove it to you somehow," Kai said excitedly. "I'm not sure how, but I will!"

I couldn't help but laugh; Kai's exuberance was infectious.

"Okay, okay," I said steadying myself against his chest to regain my balance.

The alarm buzzed to signal the end of the period and Kai let me go as the halls filled with students. He ushered me to the side as we waited for the students to march past us, heading to their lessons. I tripped over my own feet while getting out of their way. Kai put his arm around me protectively. I grinned at him and assured him I was okay. I pulled away, but not before I caught the wounded glare that Nova shot in my direction when he filed by.

I only saw it for a moment before he steeled his eyes and squared his shoulders, but his hurt had been unmistakable and the pain quickly seared my heart. I wanted to call out to him, but he was already vanishing, into the stream of white-clad students flooding the hallway.

I cursed Jemma for veiling my powers. I wished I could telepath to Nova so badly. But I took a deep breath and reminded myself that he knew I was doing this for all of us. Still, even knowing all of that, it didn't help dull that nauseating feeling I had knowing that I had caused Nova pain.

"Well this is where I leave you, I'm afraid." Kai's voice interrupted my thoughts.

I blinked, looking up at him and refocusing. We were at the infirmary. I felt like I had barely gotten anything to go on from Kai. All these baby steps were testing my patience. I wished I could blurt out, 'I think your father is an evil man with ties to a secret society bent on capturing me, and using my powers to take over the island and I need your help to prove it and stop him!'

But since I knew that wasn't going to happen I just smiled sweetly.

"Kai, when will I see you again?" I asked.

"I'll be around," he said.

13

Once inside the infirmary, I had a moment to catch my breath. All this investigating and acting was wearing me out. I felt so tired suddenly. I guess it was because I was living a double life more than usual these days. Plus not having magic powers made everything more difficult. But for now, I was just a regular orphan, flirting with the headmaster's son and pretending not to be the savior of our island.

Next on the agenda; Sadie. I had a strong feeling my old friend's sister was one of the four Pillars. The water Pillar to be exact. I was starting to understand how my feelings related to each Pillar. Nova always made me feel full of warmth, which I had attributed to his ability to drive me crazy, making me either want to strangle him or kiss him. But then I met Jovi, whose zest for life always made me feel happy and full of energy. It made sense when I figured out she was the wind Pillar. Yesterday, when I'd met Sadie, she had a calming effect on me. And when I shook her hand, I was overwhelmed with a feeling of coldness, the exact opposite of what I felt for Nova, who was the fire Pillar. So that meant Sadie had to be water. The pieces were falling together. Nova controlled fire, Jovi the wind and if I was right about Sadie, she'd command the water.

I was praying Sadie was still in the infirmary so I could talk to her some more and see if my hunch was right. She hadn't been there last night when I went to get my hand bandaged, but perhaps I'd have better luck this time.

Before I could formulate a plan to find Sadie, I found myself locked in the sights of one of the white coats. She had walked through the door into the waiting room and looked surprised to see me. Her mousy hair was pulled back so tightly in a bun that when she narrowed her eyes at me, I was terrified the creases near the hallows of her temples would split. Somehow they didn't. Instead, she smoothed the wrinkles from the front of her white coat and marched over to me.

"Why are you back?" she barked.

She must have been one of the medical team that *welcomed* me. Or perhaps she was here when my hand was patched up last night. Honestly, I couldn't tell them apart. They all looked so much alike with their stern expressions and dark hair severely swept up in buns. One thing was for sure, they were nothing like our old nurse, Miss Breia. My heart sunk, thinking of her serving food to over privileged children, rather than healing those in need with her kind words and touch.

"I asked you a question," she said, snapping me back to attention.

I simply raised my bandaged hand, suddenly wishing I hadn't decided to come back to the infirmary to find Sadie. Maybe all I would accomplish was getting the both of us in trouble.

"Follow me," was all she said.

MALAKAI LOOKED UP, surprised by the knock at the door, as it swung open.

"Father," Kai said, striding past Kobel to Malakai's desk. "Father, I - "

"Kai, what have I told you about interrupting me?"

"I know. I'm sorry, Father, but this is important."

"What are you doing back here?"

"I thought you'd want to know that Geneva is injured. She cut her hand on a mirror last night. I walked her to the infirmary this morning."

"I know. It's very unfortunate. I'm glad you were there to help her, son. Did she say how it happened?"

"Yes, she said she's really clumsy and she accidentally knocked over the mirror in her room."

Malakai glared at Kobel, conveying his doubt in the old man's theories.

"You told me to keep an eye on her and report anything strange, so I figured you'd want to know. But you know what else is strange? I heard the Luxors talking about a broken mirror when I was leaving your office after breakfast this morning. Why would they be talking about it? Was it a special mirror or something?"

"It's nothing for you to worry about, son. Is there anything else?"

"Her friends were being strange about it. Especially her sister."

"How so?" asked Kobel.

"I don't know, really. They were acting kind of secretive and nervous when we were talking about it."

Malakai smiled slowly. "Thank you for coming to me. I'll be sure to talk to them about it during their counseling session. Remember what we talked about Kai. Keep doing as I asked you. Get to know them. It's very important to me that you make them feel welcome here."

"I will, Father."

"Now run along to your lessons. Professor Kobel and I have business to discuss."

"Yes, Sir."

"Master, I worry about the boy," Kobel said after Kai had left the room.

"Let me worry about my son, Kobel. He's not your concern."

"Yes, of course, Master. It's only... I worry for his safety being so close to the Eva. She's dangerous. I can sense it."

"Nonsense, Kobel. She's a child. A potentially powerful one, but we've taken the necessary precautions."

"That's what Greeley thought."

The movement was so swift that Kobel didn't have time to react. His hand went to his cheek as blood trickled down, staining the expensive Persian rug beneath him. With his eyes wide, he focused on the razor sharp dagger with the bone carved handle that was now lodged in the thick mahogany door of Malakai's office. His blood boiled, he couldn't believe Malakai had thrown the blade at him. Kobel had asked him time and time again not to toile with the important relic, but he bit his tongue.

"I apologize, Master. I only speak out of worry for you."

"It's not necessary. I know what I'm doing and Kai is a part of my plan."

I DIDN'T HAVE any luck finding Sadie at the infirmary. One of the robotic white coats had changed my bandage and wrote some notes on her clipboard before sending me on my way.

I was currently in arithmetic, sitting next to Kai and Sparrow. I groaned as Professor Flint assigned us more homework. Math was my least favorite subject, and the new professor wasn't doing anything to change my feelings. He loved the sound of his own voice and every time I looked at him, he seemed to be glaring at me. I struggled my way through complex equations on my abacus and leapt to my feet when the alarm finally blared, dismissing us.

Next I had medicinal horticulture. This was one of the few lessons that Kai wasn't in. He walked me to the door though, carrying my books.

"Kai, you don't have to carry my books for me. I'm perfectly capable."

"But your hand," he started.

"It's getting better," I said.

"Fine, I just like to do it, okay? It makes me feel important."

"Okay," I laughed.

"I'll see you after music theory," he said disappearing down the hall.

I was elated that Remi and Sadie were in medicinal horticulture with me. The subject peaked my interest. It was really just a fancy name for plants and poisons, which had been my favorite lesson at the Troian Center. The room had been spruced up since the new professor had taken it over from Miss Banna. I noticed that the exterior stone wall had been removed and opened up to a large, glassed in greenhouse, filled with dangerous looking plants. Some even had cages around them! I was dismayed to see Professor Kobel limp to the front of the room. Apparently he was our professor, and after spending orientation with him, I wasn't a fan.

Professor Kobel aptly introduced us to the plants we would be working with during our tour of the steamy garden. I noticed Wolfsbane, Belladonna, Mandrake, Wormwood and Foxglove, among the caged plants. There were signs with skulls and crossbones posted near each exhibit, warning not to touch, smell or eat any of the plants in the garden. Each sign labeled the plant with its proper Latin name, as well as its uses to remedy ailments. There were an alarming number of potentially lethal side effects listed for most of them.

I was kneeling next to the caged Belladonna plant when Remi sauntered over.

"Did you know that Rhubarb is poisonous?" he asked. "I'm pretty sure they served us Rhubarb candied dragonfly wings at the New Years feast."

"Only the leaves are poisonous," I said pointing to a section I'd underlined in my textbook. "But look at this little beauty." I nodded to the delicate purple flowers in front of me. "Atropa Belladonna. Uses – pain relief, muscle relaxer, anti-inflammatory, twilight sleep. Side effect – paralysis, convulsions, blurred vision, rash, slowed heart rate, shallow breathing, death."

"It will either kill you or cure you, I always say," Professor Kobel quipped from behind us. "Are you feeling all right, Miss Sommers?" he asked me.

"Yes, why?"

"I'd heard you cut your hand."

"Oh!" I said, slightly alarmed he knew about that. Perhaps he had been one of the people Kai had overheard talking to his father. "I'm fine," I said pulling it behind my back.

"Good to hear," Kobel smiled. "If you ever find yourself in need of any pain relief for it, let me know and I'd be happy to mix you up a tincture. After all, that's what this beautiful garden is for."

"Thanks," I said, moving slightly closer to Remi as I noticed a trickle of blood ooze from the cut on Professor Kobel's cheek.

"Sir, your face," Remi said pointing to Kobel's cheek.

"Ah, yes," he said, pressing a handkerchief to his face. "Thank you, Mr. Cleary. No matter how careful I am, some of these plants always find a way to fight back," Kobel said before quickly hobbling away.

"You thinking what I'm thinking?" Remi whispered.

"That we can't trust Kobel?"

Remi nodded.

"Then we're in agreement, *Mr. Cleary,*" I added with

a smirk.

Remi grinned.

"I like it, you know. The name suits you."

"Thanks," he beamed.

In the short time that we'd been here, I'd learned the last names of all of my friends. They were all spot on and resembled their personalities and special powers in a subtle way. I was looking forward to ancestry. It was one of the few lessons we all had together and I was anxious to learn what our names meant. I was also hopeful that I would learn the last names of more of my classmates, thus aiding our search for the Pillars. It wasn't going too well right now. Sadie was our only lead and I wasn't having any luck getting her alone long enough to talk to her. This was the first time we shared a lesson.

"Why don't you talk to her now?" Remi asked following my gaze as I watched Sadie from afar.

"There are too many people around. Besides, I think she's afraid of me, along with every other girl in this place," I muttered.

"Come on. I'll go with you."

"What difference does that make?"

"I'm approachable," he said with a confident smile.

I gave him a light shove as I rolled me eyes, but followed him.

"Sadie, right?" Remi asked.

She was knelt down near a strange looking plant and lifted her big blue eyes up at us, squinting against the sunlight. Her pretty features twisted with puzzlement, when she saw me.

"I was wondering since you work in the infirmary and all, if you might know if any of these plants were good for preventing scars?" Remi asked.

Sadie straightened up and frowned. "Why?"

"Well, Geneva is going to end up with a pretty gnarly one on her hand if she doesn't do something about it soon."

Sadie looked from Remi to me and then nodded.

"Yeah, I heard it's pretty bad," she said. "The textbook says to use aloe flesh and lemon root, but in my experience, that cream I gave you to help your hair grow back works the best."

"Thanks for the tip," I said smiling. "I really appreciate it and I'm sorry if we got off to a rocky start."

"Sure, anything for a friend of Mala's."

"Have you heard any news about her?" I asked.

"No and I don't suspect I will. The Luxor prison is a death sentence."

"Maybe I could help you get a message to her," I offered.

"How?"

"I'm friends with Kai. Maybe he could ask for a favor."

I saw a glimmer of hope in her eyes.

"I'll see what I can do. Catch up with you at study hall?"

"I have a shift at the infirmary tonight, but I'll be there tomorrow."

"Great. We'll talk then."

"Mr. Cleary you're brilliant!" I squealed when Sadie was out of earshot.

"Yeah, but now you better follow through with Kai. Do you truly think you have him wrapped around your little finger enough to pull a favor like that?"

"I don't have to wrap him around my finger. We're actually friends."

Now Remi rolled his eyes. "Don't tell me you trust his nice guy act. You've known him for a day, Geneva."

"He's actually not so bad. You guys should stop giving him such a hard time. Why don't you use some of your approachable charm on him? He knows you don't like him."

"Yeah, because I still remember he's the headmaster's son."

"I know who he is, Remi. But your parents don't determine everything about you."

BUZZ BUZZ BUZZ.

14

The rest of the day was uneventful. Lessons, meals, lessons. Kai walked me from room to room, filling my mind with idle chatter. Sometimes it was a welcomed distraction. Other times it drove me crazy, his words disrupting my mind from stringing together single thoughts.

After dinner, he followed me into the hallway. "Where are you going after this?" he asked.

"Study hall. You coming?"

"I don't have study hall."

"Why? Too smart for studying?" I joked.

His cheeks flushed. "No. Father has me tutored privately."

"Oh, bummer. I was hoping to ask you about something."

"Do you need help studying?"

"Well, probably. Honestly, I don't know how I'm going to keep up with all of these courses, but that's not what I was going to ask you."

"What is it?"

"Well I heard a rumor that a friend of mine is in prison in Lux."

"That's terrible. She must have done something awful.

Geneva, you should be careful not to make friends with the wrong people."

I swallowed my anger at Kai's stereotypical comment and forged forward for the greater good.

"Yes, well the problem is, I'm not even sure if the rumor is true. My friend would never do something to get herself thrown in prison. That's why I was hoping maybe you could help me find out if she's actually there."

"Well, I could ask my father I guess."

"No," I snapped. "I mean, I'd rather not cause any more trouble. Like you said, I don't want him to think I hang around with the wrong people. Maybe we could just look it up or something. There has to be a book that has records of those kinds of things, right?"

"I'm sure there is, but I wouldn't know where to look without asking my father."

"It's okay. Forget I asked. I shouldn't have imposed my worries on you," I said, turning away and doing my best to look sad and helpless. It must have worked, because Kai took the bait.

"Hey," he said stopping me so he could look into my eyes. "Don't apologize. You can always ask me for help. That's what friends are for, right? Let me look in my father's study tonight. Maybe I can find something."

"Thank you, Kai." I smiled and threw my arms around his neck, the way I'd seen Jemma throw herself at Nova.

"You're welcome," he beamed.

My heart flip-flopped. I felt so conflicted. I wasn't any good at having fake feelings for people and I could tell Kai liked me. The way he hugged me back, his constant smiles and attentiveness. It was how Nova used to treat me. I felt a stab of pain in my tangled heart as I thought of Nova. Maybe if I could pretend Kai was Nova, this would be easier. I knew it wasn't fair to Kai, but for all I knew, he was playing me too. Everything in me wanted to trust him, but the tiny voice in the back of my mind reminding me he was Malakai's son refused to be quieted.

"Maybe I can come with you to help you look in your father's study. Two minds are better than one," I offered.

"I don't know... Father is pretty strict about not letting anyone into our residence."

"Oh, I understand," I said, genuinely frustrated. *It was worth a try*, I thought to myself.

"I promise I'll look into it for you," Kai smiled. "Do you want me to walk you to study hall?"

"Sure," I said, letting him take my hand.

With only one hand to balance my tower of books, I lost my grip and dropped half of them on the floor. I bent to pick up the scattered paper, but Kai beat me to it.

"You know, you're just proving that you actually *do* need me to carry your books," he laughed looking up at me.

As I looked down at him, the wheels that had been turning since I met him clicked. All at once I knew him. His face, looking up at me like this, the way the afternoon light cast shadows, darkening his face ominously; he was the boy from the cave. The one from my vision or nightmare, whatever it was that my mother had shown me. The one where all of my friends were dead and a boy knelt over their bodies. Kai was the boy.

A chill swept through me and stole my breath. I gasped for air, my eyes wide with fear.

"Geneva? What's wrong?"

"You! You're him – you're the boy I dreamt about!"

My words weren't coming out right. Terror gripped my heart, but my mind fought it. Kai grinned at me and blushed a bit. I was thankful that he'd misunderstood my stammering. I didn't want to freak him out, but I was thoroughly rattled myself.

"I have to go," I said and turned on my heels and ran,

leaving Kai standing in the hall clutching my books and wondering what in the world was wrong with me.

"So you just left him there? With all your books?" Sparrow asked.

I'd retreated to our bunkroom and ran into her there. She instantly made me spill my guts by threatening to take me to the infirmary, saying I looked like I'd seen a ghost.

"Why haven't you told me about this before?" she asked softly. "Do the others know?"

I shook my head.

"Have you had other dreams like this?"

"Yes," I nodded. "I've been having strange nightmares ever since we decided to come back here to look for the Pillars," I added weakly, thinking of my fire filled dreams.

"Geneva. You can't keep secrets. We've been over this before."

"I don't even know what they are. They're probably just nightmares. You don't go around telling me what you dream about."

Sparrow flushed. "Yes, but I don't dream about us all being killed by another student. Plus this could have been more than a dream, Geneva. What if it was a vision?"

"I don't know that he's the one who killed you," I whispered.

"Right, he was just crouching over our dead bodies," Sparrow added skeptically.

I knew she was right, but I didn't want to deal with it. I didn't have the mental capacity for it right now. My brain still quivered with the memory of that image. I thought I had blocked it. I know I had tried to. Perhaps that's why it took me so long to make the connection between Kai and the boy in my vision. I was haunted by it and I knew beyond reason that it was more than a dream. It felt tangible, in the worst way. I couldn't explain it, but I knew it somehow already existed. It was a destiny I was rushing toward, like a waterfall, without anything to slow my inevitable drift.

SPARROW MANAGED to drag me to study hall where I sat numbly among my friends while she filled them in on my vision. As I'd anticipated, they were less than pleased to hear of the vision and even more upset that I'd kept it from them.

"I've already scolded her," Sparrow said taking mercy on me. "Now we need to figure out what it means."

"There's nothing to figure out. It will either happen or it won't. Talking it to death doesn't change anything," Nova said hastily. "We're here for the Pillars, not to interpret dreams."

"Well does anyone have any Pillar news?" Sparrow asked.

"Yes," Remi piped up. "Geneva and I actually spoke to Sadie today and made some headway."

"Oh yeah?" Journey asked, sounding optimistic.

"Well she's at least speaking to us now, but Geneva made her a lofty promise to help get a letter to her sister in the Luxor Prison."

"I thought I could ask Kai for a favor," I said quietly.

"Now was that before or after you remembered he's going to murder us?" Jemma chimed in.

I didn't have any fight left to come up with a clever retort to her teasing. "He said he'd help me. Kai's going to try to find out where she's being held. If he follows through we'll know we can trust him."

"Or that you're walking right into some trap he and his father are setting for you," Remi said.

"We're getting nowhere!" Sparrow sighed, sounding as hopeless as I felt.

"We have ancestry and athletics together this week. Let's research our classmates in ancestry and scope out escape routes in athletics. It's on the beach so they have to take us outside the fence to get there," Journey offered.

After we'd agreed to that plan, we went our separate ways, trying to work our way into the cliques of students in the library in search of the last Pillar. Jemma and Nova seemed to have no trouble fitting in. Apparently their good looks and charm overshadowed their initial outcast status. I watched Jemma laughing with a group of beautiful girls her age. They were trading lipsticks and gossip, while Nova mingled with a group of athletic looking boys, whose muscles flexed under their white uniforms like they didn't have a care in the world. But for me, some things never changed. Even with its new name, I still didn't fit in at the Troian Center.

After countless failed attempts to join a group, I retreated to a corner and pulled out the list we'd been compiling since morning. It consisted of orphans we knew from before Malakai took over and the new students we'd met so far. I'd even started a list of professors that seemed suspicious. In the short time we'd been at the Troian Academy, we'd made some headway, crossing off names of students we knew couldn't be Pillars and circling ones we needed to explore further. My mind was still spinning when the alarm finally blared signaling it was time to head back to our rooms for the night.

15

After another sleepless night, filled with the same dreams of fire engulfing my friends and Kai standing over their lifeless bodies, I decided to skip breakfast and go to the infirmary. In my restlessness, I must have torn open the cut on my hand and awoke to blood smeared all over my white bed linens. I stripped my bed and put on fresh sheets, before heading to the infirmary. I was disappointed in myself for protesting against stitches initially. If I hadn't been so terrified of needles, I'd be enjoying a delicious meal instead of another dreadful encounter with the white coats. I pushed open the door to the infirmary and plastered a fake smile on my face.

"Good morning."

The white coat woman didn't look that surprised to see me again.

"I thought you'd be back," she said. "You want those stitches after all?"

I nodded and fought the urge to run. I could already feel the clammy sweat breaking out on the back of my neck. I swallowed back the bile rising in my throat at the mere thought of a needle sewing together my flesh.

"Come with me."

"PROFESSOR, SHE'S BACK."

"Excellent," Professor Kobel replied, letting a smug smirk spread across his thin lips.

"Why are you still standing here?" he asked the white coat woman.

"I was wondering if it was safe to continue with our treatment plan. I've already given her three doses this week."

"Yes! Keep giving her the potion. I need to gain access to her mind."

"Yes, Professor."

WHEN I LEFT THE INFIRMARY, I was white as a ghost and my knees were shaking, but I had seven solid stitches and was assured that my hand would heal properly. At least the white coat woman had given me something to dull the pain a bit.

When I pushed my way out into the hall, I was surprised to see Kai waiting for me.

"Geneva! Are you all right? I came as soon as I heard."

"You heard I was in the infirmary already? Man, the rumor mill works fast here."

"Well I was worried about you after the way you ran off yesterday."

"Yeah, sorry about that."

"It's fine. Did you get your books? I left them outside your bunkroom."

"Yes, thank you, Kai. I'm sorry I flaked out yesterday. I haven't been feeling like myself lately."

"That's why I came straight here to find you when I heard you were in the infirmary again. I was in my father's office when he got the message."

"What, is he checking up on me or something?" I asked with nervous laughter.

"No, not at all. He was alerted by the Orbiture."

My blank stare prompted him to continue.

"It's how he's able to keep track of everything at the Troian Academy. The cuffs we all wear monitor our electrodermal activity and are linked to the Orbiture so he can see where each student is."

"That's really creepy," I said before I could stop myself.

"No, it's not. It's for your own protection."

"Protection from what?"

"Say you're hurt, like you are, it shows up on the Orbiture and someone can come help you in case you're too injured to help yourself. Or say you were to get lost in the Academy or something, it'll help you be located."

This was good. Kai was feeding me information about how these stupid bracelets worked. I took the opportunity to pump him for more.

"Well I guess that is a relief," I said changing my tune and trying to sound convincing. "So we can be tracked anywhere in the Troian Center, I mean Academy?"

"Yes. As long as you're wearing your cuff, the Orbiture can see you anywhere within the grounds."

"What if we leave the grounds?"

"Go beyond the fence?" he asked in shock. "Why would you want to do that?"

"Oh, I wouldn't. I was just curious. I mean what if someone kidnapped me or something?"

“Are you worried that might happen, Geneva?” he asked with genuine concern.

“Maybe,” I lied. “I met some dangerous people in the forest.”

“We won’t let anything happen to you. My father wants to protect you.”

“He said that?”

“Yes, he even asked me to spend extra time with you and your friends to show you around the Academy and make you feel welcome and safe.”

I continued to look at him skeptically.

“Come on. I want to show you something,” he said.

I hurried after Kai. Two Luxors halted us as we entered the courtyard, but upon recognizing Kai, let us pass under the archway, onto the stone floor baked by the bright midday sun. It felt amazing to have the sun on my skin once more. Even though the Troian Center was now opulent and bright, I still felt claustrophobic spending so much time indoors after having lived among the Betos in the forest for so long. I hadn’t realized it until I was outside, drinking in the sweet aromatic fresh air, like it was the first time I’d actually taken a breath since entering the stone structure.

Two more Luxors stood by the opening in the courtyard that led out to the manicured gardens. I hadn’t been back here since our brutal attack. I shuddered as I looked at the hibiscus blooms. They were the last things I’d seen before the heavy nets were cast over us and my whole world changed.

“Kai, where are we going?” I asked looking at their menacing weapons.

“I want to show you something.”

The Luxors never moved. They held their heavy lances still as we passed them, their gazes fixed forward, like we didn’t even exist.

"Kai," I whispered.

"Here we are," he said finally halting.

We were standing in the middle of a beautiful garden. There were stunning hibiscus bushes nestled among tall cypress trees, swaying in the gentle ocean breeze. Kai picked up a pebble from one of the gurgling fountains. He felt the weight of it in his hand for a moment and then took me by surprise by throwing it at the black iron fence that loomed up behind the trees. It sailed high and arced on a path meant to clear the fence, but as soon as it passed over it, a flash of red light exploded and the pebble disappeared.

"See. You have nothing to be afraid of. Nothing can get past the fence, in or out. You're safe," he said with a bright smile.

I swallowed hard and tried to choke back my panic. I returned a weak grin, but I felt like a cornered animal, suddenly realizing they'd wandered into a trap.

"WHAT ELSE DID HE SAY?" Remi asked as I filled my friends in on what happened with Kai and the fence while we were together for our study hall session in the library.

It had been a long and frustrating day. Even though I'd seen my friends at meals and in a few other lessons, it seemed that Kai was always there, eavesdropping. Now, finally free of him, we took advantage of our opportunity to converse candidly.

"So between the cuffs and the fence, we're basically trapped," Nova fumed.

"I knew it! I told you the fence was something," Journey said. "That has to be what's stopping our powers."

"Great. You were right. Happy now?" Nova growled. "Any ideas of how to get past the fence, genius?"

Journey shook his head.

"Shhh!" Sparrow hissed.

Nova's voice had echoed through the opulent room. Despite there being about two hundred students in the library, it was as quiet as a tomb. This was likely due to the fact that there were roughly a dozen Luxors stationed around the room. Something Professor Kobel said in orientation snapped back into my mind. 'The library is a place to exercise our minds, not our voices.'

The library was housed in an area of the Troian Center that I wasn't familiar with. I wasn't certain if it had always been there or whether it was something that Malakai had added. It was a gigantic room with impossibly high ceilings, chock full of shelves stacked floor to ceiling with books in neat rows jutting out from each wall. There were beautiful stained glass windows on the East wall, but most of the light came from the heavily beaded chandeliers. Their massive frames hung high from the rafters, reflecting showers of golden light throughout the room onto the plush upholstered chairs and ornately carved tables. There were tapestries and encased artifacts lining every inch of the walls that weren't covered in books. Long narrow tables sat between the rows of bookshelves, providing sheltered alcoves, promising to harbor our secrets. We were huddled in one such alcove. The room was actually cozy, and seemed immune to the Troian Academy's crisp military standards, yet it didn't resemble the old, humble atmosphere of the Troian Center either. It was more like a medieval castle might have been. The stark white uniforms of the students looked out of place in this grand room filled will rich history and texture.

I waited until a Luxor walked past our table before continuing our conversation in a hushed tone.

"Listen, stop arguing. The fence doesn't really matter unless we can find the Pillars, because we're not leaving until we do."

"She's right," Sparrow said. "Speaking of Pillars, have you been able to talk to Sadie again?"

"Not really," I mumbled. "She's supposed to be here now

actually." I looked around the quiet library, but I didn't spot her bright auburn hair anywhere.

"She was in my foreign language lesson today, but that professor only allows us to speak in Latin, so I just sat there with my mouth shut," I groaned. "I'll try again tomorrow."

"You don't have that lesson tomorrow," Sparrow said pointing to the curriculum schedule that lay atop my haphazard stack of books. "Look, we have a different schedule each day. They don't repeat until the following week. That's how we're able to study so many more subjects."

"Could you try not to sound so excited about all the extra studying we're going to have to do?" Jemma groaned.

"Oh. Okay, well as long as Kai isn't in all of my lessons again tomorrow, I'll try to talk to some more students and get a feel for them," I said ignoring Jemma.

"Kai was in all of your lessons today?" Remi asked.

"Yeah. All except foreign language." My friends stared at me with apprehensive expressions. "What? It's a good thing. The more time I spend with him, the more I can pump him for information. Look at all I found out today about the fence and the Orbiture."

"I think it's a little suspicious," Remi remarked.

"I hadn't thought about it I guess," I replied.

"You need to be careful, Geneva," Nova said. "I have a feeling Kai might be watching you as much as you're watching him."

"You said yourself that his father asked him to spend time with us," Remi added. "That's proof that he's spying on us."

"I'll handle Kai. I need you guys to start weeding out the rest of the students so we can find the last Pillar." I jerked my chin toward the large group of white clad students that littered the library. "We may need to revise our plan a bit though."

"Yeah, I guess we can all just focus on looking for the earth Pillar," Sparrow said.

"Yes. But, I think we need to consider the new students too."

"What? Those Pruxes?" Journey asked. "I thought the *Book of Secrets* eluded to the Pillars being orphans?"

"I thought so too, but Sadie wasn't here before, and Mala's her legal guardian, so she's not really an orphan." *And neither is* Jovi I thought to myself. "We have to consider everyone."

We spent a few more minutes reviewing what we knew about the Pillars. I shared my hunch about how I'd recognized each Pillar's power, hoping it might be helpful to my friends. Then we divided into pairs and started our mission; Jemma with Nova, Sparrow with Remi, and Journey with me.

"I'M sorry that she's being this way," Jemma said gently touching Nova's arm as they walked toward a group of unfamiliar students.

"What do you mean?" he asked.

"So rude and standoffish."

"So you noticed it too?"

Jemma nodded.

"Did she say..." He hesitated. "Do you know why?"

"I probably shouldn't tell you this because she told me in confidence, but she's still afraid of you."

Hurt rushed across Nova's face and his lips pressed into a thin line as he frowned.

"It's the Kull prophecy isn't it?"

Jemma nodded again.

"I knew it," he muttered. "I wish she would have told me herself. I mean I get it. She has every right to think the worst of me."

"Don't say that," Jemma said rubbing Nova's arm. "You're the best guy I know."

"No, I'm not, Jemma. Geneva's probably smart to stay away

from me," he resigned with a sigh, letting his shoulders slump. "You probably should too. I've always known there was something wrong with me. The Kull prophecy proves it."

"I'm not scared of you," Jemma said slipping her hand into Nova's.

~

"WELL THAT WENT WELL," Sparrow said beaming.

"Yeah, not too bad, I guess," Remi replied unconvincingly.

"You didn't expect to find a Pillar on our first try did you?"

"It's not that."

"Then what is it?"

"I've never been good at making new friends here. I was always an outsider."

"You did fine," Sparrow complimented.

"Yeah, only because you did most of the talking. I don't know how to talk to girls. I would never have been able to go up to a group of them on my own and introduce myself like we did just now."

"Oh, please. Give yourself some credit. You're best friend is a girl. This isn't any different."

"Geneva's not a girl," he snorted.

"I don't think she'd be thrilled to hear that."

"You know what I mean. I've known her my whole life... It's different."

"So you don't look at her as more than a friend?" Sparrow asked.

"I don't know? I mean she's – it's not – we're like – " Remi sighed deeply. "It's complicated."

"What about me?" Sparrow pressed. "I'm a girl and we talk all the time."

"That's different," Remi said.

"How?"

"I don't know? It just is. You're you. You're not some intimidating, giggly, beautiful creature that looks at me like a nobody."

Sparrow frowned and tried to hide the hurt she felt at Remi's comment.

"Remi, you're not a nobody, so stop thinking you are and everyone else will too. Also I *am* a girl, and so is Geneva. We can be intimidating and beautiful too! So stop taking us for granted," Sparrow huffed, stalking off leaving Remi open-mouthed and stunned.

"THAT WAS EASIER THAN I THOUGHT," Journey said.

"Yeah, I guess everyone wants the gossip from the famous escapee orphans," I replied.

"We are pretty gossip worthy," he laughed.

"Oh if they only knew the truth!"

"So, did you get any Pillar vibes?" Journey asked.

"Pillar vibes?"

"What? I don't know what you call it. You always say you just get a feeling. You know, like vibes."

"No. No one felt particularly earthy," I laughed.

I was trying to contain my laughter at Journey's spot on, yet humorous observations, when something choked the air from my lungs.

"What is it?" Journey asked.

He followed my eyes to where Nova and Jemma were, their hands intertwined, intimately. Journey turned me away from them and stared directly into my eyes with his big hands clamped firmly on my shoulders.

"Don't fall for Jemma's tricks. Don't give her the satisfaction. Let's just find these Pillars and get out of here. You'll have time to sort things out with Nova after all of this," Journey offered tenderly.

I nodded, but I felt my heart splintering. I wasn't so sure there would ever be a time for me and Nova. Jemma was making sure of that.

16

I sat at the breakfast table puffy eyed as I quietly ate another lavish meal. The food was as delectable as usual, but I couldn't focus on enjoying it much.

The night before had been another sleepless one, filled with horrible nightmares. Nova and Jemma haunted my mind and then Sparrow and Remi. Kai's face was a regular in my nightmares now too. The only constant was that they all ended with death and fire when I was asked to choose between which of my friends to save. It was an impossible choice and I didn't know what it all meant. I was more sure than ever that these nightmares were actually some sort of vision, but I couldn't figure out what I was supposed to be getting from them. Usually my visions were more like a premonition rather than some internal battle. I didn't want to be responsible for the fate of my friends, but my dreams kept forcing me to. Who was I to decide which life was more important? Is this what being the Eva would come to? I was frustrated by the fact that the visions didn't have anything to do with the Pillars, which made them feel useless. Each time I would awake, I would beg my mind to focus on finding the last Pillar, but it stubbornly reverted to more tortuous dreams about my friends being engulfed in flames because I'd once again made the wrong choice. The weight of my destiny was crushing me.

At one point, I awoke screaming and covered in sweat. Jemma had kicked my bunk from beneath a few times trying to quiet me in her less than sisterly way, until I finally gave up on sleep completely and got out of bed. I sat next to the crackling fireplace to try to drive the chill away. I found myself longing for my journal. Writing always soothed me and helped me work out my problems. It would have been wonderful to read my old entries, being comforted by memories of happier times, but I guess I should be grateful that I hadn't brought my journal with me. I wouldn't have been able to use it with my veiled powers and worse, it may have fallen into the hands of Malakai, who could probably read it since powers and enchantments didn't seem to work inside the walls of the new Troian Academy. Instead I had pulled open my medicinal horticulture book. I figured I might as well get a jump on the research paper that was due next week since it looked like we were going to be here a while. Failing lessons wasn't an option at the Troian Academy.

About twelve pages into my reading I came across a potion with peculiar side effects. It sparked an idea. It was dangerous, but it might work. I just needed to figure out how to get the ingredients I required. A trip to the infirmary should do the trick. I knew this was something I couldn't tell my friends. It was a risky idea and they would never allow me to do it.

"Earth to Eva!" Jemma said shaking me from my thoughts. "What's wrong with you. You're being weirder than ever and it looks like a bee stung your face!"

I'd momentarily forgotten I was in the dining hall, but as I tried to blink the fogginess from my mind I realized all of my friends were staring at me over their breakfast. "Huh?" I questioned.

"Your face is really puffy," Sparrow said. "Are you feeling all right?"

"Yeah, just couldn't sleep. So what lessons do we have together today?" I asked trying to change the subject.

"We all have ancestry and athletics today. We discussed this. Remember? Are you sure you're all right?" Sparrow questioned.

"I won't be in athletics today," Nova said.

"What? Why not?" I asked.

"Some of the guys asked if I wanted to try out for Cadets."

"They did?" Journey asked, sounding a little hurt at not getting an invitation.

"Yeah, I figured it'd be a good chance to get in with the Pruxes a bit more and search the ranks for Pillars. Want me to see if I can get you an invite?" Nova asked Journey.

"Nah, mate. Thanks, but I think one of us should stick with the girls to make sure they're safe."

"I can do that," Remi said resentfully.

"Good idea," Nova nodded, purposely ignoring Remi.

"Nova, that means you'll be in training to become a Luxor!" I said with concern. "They take that seriously. It's too dangerous."

"Oh and I suppose you're the only one around here allowed to take risks?" he challenged.

"We're all taking a risk just being here. I'm not doing anything idiotic, like throwing my name in the mix to be a Luxor."

"You can't be a Luxor. You're a girl," Journey scoffed.

I glared at him and Nova ignored his comment completely.

"Oh, so I suppose spending every waking hour with the headmaster's son isn't an added risk? Do you just like spending time with him, then? I'm surprised you're not with him right now."

"I don't know how many times I have to tell you that I'm spending time with him to try to get him to help me find that book with all our names in it and to gain information about Malakai!"

"Well you must truly think I'm an idiot if you think I believe that," Nova yelled. "Why don't you just admit that you have a problem with me? I'm a big boy, Geneva, I can handle it. You don't have to flaunt another guy around in front of me to keep me away from you."

I stared at him, at a complete loss for words. His face flushed scarlet, starting from the starched mandarin collar of his uniform to his beautiful cheekbones, and he was visibly shaking.

"What are you talking about?" I asked when I finally found my voice.

"I've seen the way he looks at you, Geneva. You're in way over your head this time."

"Thanks for the vote of confidence, Nova." I stood, grabbed my tray and stormed off.

~

"Nova! Why would you say that to her?" Sparrow fretted.

"Oh let her stomp off if she wants to be a baby about it," Jemma replied.

"I didn't mean to upset her," Nova said under his breath. He was slumped in his seat. All the fight had gone out of him the moment Geneva had left the dining hall. "I'm worried about her. She doesn't seem to be taking this seriously. She's just romping around with Kai and keeping things from us again."

"Funny way of showing it," Remi mumbled.

"Do you have something to say to me?" Nova growled, bristling.

"Stop!" Journey said pulling Nova back to his seat. "New rule. No more talking unless it's about a Pillar or how to get out of this place."

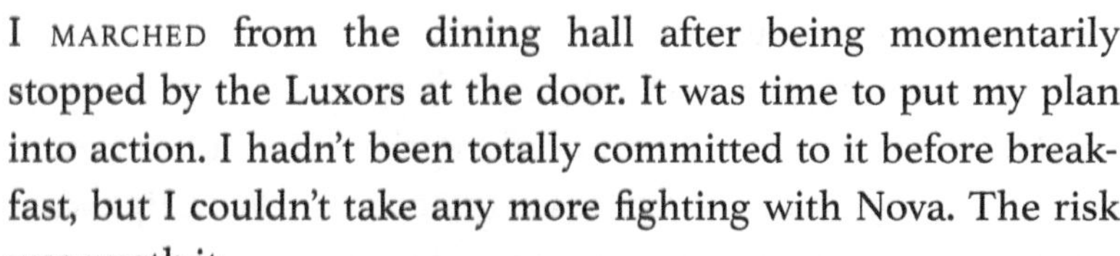

I MARCHED from the dining hall after being momentarily stopped by the Luxors at the door. It was time to put my plan into action. I hadn't been totally committed to it before breakfast, but I couldn't take any more fighting with Nova. The risk was worth it.

I held up my bandaged hand and the Luxors nodded to each other, silently agreeing one of them would lead me to the infirmary. I followed the silent soldier into the hall until I ran into Kai.

"Geneva. Good morning. I was hoping to catch you at breakfast. Where are you headed?"

I held up my injured hand to him as well.

"Again? I can take her the rest of the way," he said to the Luxor, who nodded and turned away without a word.

"Are you all right?"

"I don't know. Everyone's been asking me that and I really don't know," I said, my voice cracking.

I didn't intend to cry, but before I knew it, Kai was hugging me and I was shaking in his arms. I knew that the lack of sleep and sting of Nova's words were finally catching up to me. Not to mention the impossible task of finding and rescuing the Pillars. I was trying to put on a brave face for my friends, but truthfully, I was scared. I tried not to enjoy the comfort of Kai's warm arms, but he smelled like cinnamon and soap and I wanted to melt into him and disappear from all my problems.

"What's wrong?" Kai asked softly.

"I'm just having a hard time here," I stammered.

"Well, I have something that might cheer you up."

I pulled away from him and saw the tiny package he held.

"It's not much, but I thought you might like it," he said pushing the gold foiled bundle into my hands.

"What's this?" I asked.

"Open it." His dark eyes gleamed as he smiled.

I was halfway through peeling the wrapping off when he blurted out, "It's a journal!"

"Kai! Thank you. It's beautiful."

And it was. I ran my hands along the soft leather bound cover, feeling the smoothness under my fingertips and thumbing through the empty pages, letting the smell of rich leather and new paper waft over me. I loved the smell of leather and books.

"And I have something else for you too. Unless... do you need to go to the infirmary first?"

I hesitated for a moment before deciding that my plan could wait. I needed to see what Kai was up to.

"No, honestly I just needed to get some space from my friends."

"Okay. Come with me."

"Where are we going, Kai?"

"Do you trust me?"

That was a loaded question. But I did my best to convince him when I nodded.

"Then come on," he grinned.

17

I'd finally given up asking Kai where we were going. We were in an area of the Troian Academy that I'd never been to before. It was newly built, and separated from the rest of the Troian Center by a narrow stone tunnel. He motioned for me to keep quiet, so I did. I followed him through the heavy mahogany double doors that led to a miniature version of our library. The only difference was that instead of reds and golds, everything in this room was grey and blue, giving it a cold, uninviting feeling. The lights were off adding long, sinister shadows to the already eerie room. Books lined the walls on polished wooden shelves for two stories. There was a tall wheeled ladder running along a track that followed the curves of the walls. I noticed two desks on opposite ends of the room. We breezed past plush chairs and statues of important looking busts atop marble columns. I pulled against Kai's hand, wanting to explore. This room had to be where Malakai kept his important documents, like prison manifests, names of the students and maybe even the fabled *Book of Gods.*

"Kai, wait. What is this place?"

"This is my father's study," he said still pulling me forward. "Come on I have something you need to see."

"But – "

"We don't have a lot of time. I don't think my father would be happy if I brought you here."

The slight fear in his tone urged me forward. I followed him soundlessly through another doorway, down a short hallway and through one more door.

"This is my room," he beamed.

The hair on my neck prickled. *Why did he bring me to his room?* I suddenly felt uncomfortable being alone in a room with a boy I barely knew. His father was the leader of a secret society bent on destroying me. Even if Kai wasn't involved with the Ravinori's plot, being here with him, where no one else knew I was, seemed risky. The words of my friends echoed in my mind.

'He's a spy - I don't trust him - I've seen the way he looks at you.'

And he was looking at me now. He looked nervous and excited all at once, and I mirrored his feelings. Even if being here was risky, I had discovered Malakai's secret study. If Kai tried something, I felt confident enough in my self-defense that I'd be able to fight him off long enough to escape. My muscles tensed as I formulated my exit strategy and waited for him to make the next move.

"Why did you bring me here, Kai?" I asked nervously.

"I think I found what you're looking for," he said moving across the bright room to the tall wardrobe in the corner. He opened the carved door and pulled a large book out, carrying it over to his four-poster bed in the center of the room. He sat down on the white unmade sheets and patted them for me to join.

"I found this in the study yesterday. It's a list of prisoners. I think it may have information about your friend in it, but you never told me her name so I'm not sure."

"Kai, this is amazing! Thank you," I beamed hopping onto

the bed next to him, my reservations vanishing. I opened the large book and set it between our laps. My heart sank. There had to be thousands of pages. It would take forever to sift through the tiny writing on each page. "I don't know where to start."

"If you tell me her name I can tell you if she's in here."

"Kai, there has to be millions of names in here," I said, mournfully letting my fingers skim across the names of the unfortunate, sentenced to prison in Lux.

Kai reached over and took my hand, stopping its slow decent over the scrawling text.

"I need to tell you something," he said.

I looked at his eyes and shivered. They were such a deep black that I felt like they could look through me; like maybe he knew who I truly was. My breath caught in my throat.

"I have a secret, Geneva, and I've never told anyone. Not even my father. But I think I can use it to help you. But promise me you won't freak out first, okay?"

"Kai," I whispered. "You can tell me anything."

"What's your friend's name?"

I sat silently for a moment, not sure if I should divulge Mala's name to Kai.

"You can trust me, Geneva," he urged, placing his warm hand on mine and squeezing it sincerely.

"Mala Calder."

Kai pulled the book onto his lap and held his hands over it, letting his dark eyes close. I stared at his impossible long eyelashes as they cast dark shadows over his olive skin in the sunlight. I hadn't realized how beautiful he was before and I had a sudden urge to touch his smooth, black hair. It fell like a curtain over his cheek and I wanted to push it away from his face so I could see him better. Thankfully, the rustling of pages interrupted my wandering mind.

I looked down in astonishment. Kai held his hands well

above the book in his lap, with his eyes closed tight in concentration. My eyes widened as I watched the pages of the book rapidly flip unassisted under Kai's hovering hand. Suddenly the pages stopped and Kai opened his eyes. He stared at the open pages for a moment and then grinned.

"Here," he said pointing to a column on the right hand page.

I moved closer to see what he was pointing at and I shivered with excitement when I saw Mala's name leap from the page just above Kai's finger.

Mala Calder, cell 547: sentence - life

"Kai, that was amazing," I said squeezing his hand.

"So you don't think I'm a freak?" he asked with disbelief.

"No. I think you're incredible. How do you do it?"

"I don't know. I've always had a photographic memory and one day I was searching for something that I'd read before and when I was picturing it in my mind, the book I was thinking of just leapt off the shelf and opened to the page I was thinking of."

"How old were you when that happened?"

"I don't know? Maybe 8 or 9?"

"And your father doesn't know?"

"No."

"Why haven't you told him?"

"I know he would think I'm a freak. He doesn't have a tolerance for people that are different. He's already disappointed in my shortcomings and I figured that if he knew what I could do… that I was different… it would only make it worse."

We were both silent for a moment.

"I don't know. It's probably stupid, but I just have this feeling I shouldn't tell him. Please don't tell anyone else, Geneva."

"I won't, Kai. I promise."

"Thanks," he said with a nervous smirk.

"I truly won't tell anyone," I said trying to ease his worry. "But can I ask you something? Why did you decide to tell me?"

"I really want to help you," he said shyly. "And I don't know why, but I feel like I can trust you."

I was struggling with sympathy for Kai. I knew what it was like to be different, to feel isolated and confused. I wished I could tell him that he wasn't alone. That I was more like him than he knew, but I couldn't. I would expose my friends if I did. And what if this was all a trap? What if he thought I'd show him my powers if he shared his? I couldn't even if I wanted to since I'd veiled them, but for the millionth time I wished I hadn't. If I could absorb Kai's powers, I could probably find the Pillars and even the *Book of Gods* if it was here. But how was Kai able to use his powers? If what we suspected was true of the fence, Kai shouldn't be able to use magic within the walls of the Troian Center.

"Kai? Can you do this anywhere?"

"What do you mean?"

"Can you only do this in your room or can you do it in the library or lesson rooms too?"

"I would never try it anywhere else and risk someone seeing me."

I wrinkled my nose in thought.

"What is it?"

"Probably nothing. But – "

"Shhh – Did you hear that?" Kai asked.

I strained to listen, wishing for my hunter powers. He was right, I heard footsteps rapidly approaching.

In one swift move, Kai pulled his shirt off, pushed the book off his lap and under the sheets, pushing me back on top of them and pinning me down with his body. My eyes were wild with fear as his warm chest pressed against mine, our hearts pounding against each other.

"Kai!" I shrieked, but his hand was over my mouth now.

My chest heaved with panic. What was happening? Was Kai trying to take advantage of me? Had I fallen into some sort of trap? Was he turning me over to his father and the Ravinori? My mind was in a free fall of fear as I struggled against Kai, but he was deceptively strong. His body was corded with lean muscle coiled rigidly against mine. My efforts were useless, I couldn't budge him. I felt his hipbones digging into mine as tears welled in my eyes.

"Please don't do this," I attempted to say against his suffocating hand.

I could feel his heart pounding as his lips brushed against my ear, sending a terrifying shiver through my body.

"Please trust me, Geneva," he whispered as the door burst open.

Three fully armed Luxors surged through the doors, weapons leveled at us.

"Halt!" one screamed while another hauled Kai off of me.

I was about to thank them for coming to my rescue when I felt a catastrophic jolt of pain take over my body and I fell from the bed.

"Stop!" Kai screamed, flailing uselessly against the massive Luxor restraining him. "My father does not tolerate Luxor's in our private residence."

"Relax kid. Who do you think sent us?"

I could barely hear them arguing over the pain coursing through me. I was writhing on the floor gripping my wrist, trying to pry the cuff off by any means possible. It was the source of the pain and I was convinced I'd rather lose my hand then feel another second of this torture.

"I command you to stop! You're hurting her! My father will not be pleased," Kai shouted.

Two of the Luxors exchanged a nervous glance.

"He's right," the one holding Kai said.

And just like that the pain ceased.

"Deliver this message - Threat contained. Suspects have been apprehended. Awaiting your instructions," Kai's captor said.

One of the other two Luxors saluted and promptly left the room, while the empty handed Luxor turned his focus to me. He grabbed me by the nap of my neck and hoisted me to my feet before throwing me back onto the bed. Kai was shoved toward me as well and he wrapped his arms protectively around my shaking body.

"You two wait here."

18

We sat on the edge of the bed, waiting. My cheeks burned red as I stared down at my lap. Kai sat shirtless, next to me, doing the same. The Luxors stood guard at the door making sure we complied, arms crossed, silently judging us.

It had only been a moment that I had been trapped beneath Kai, but in my panicked mind, it seemed like forever. Now that we sat silently next to each other on his rumpled bed I was more confused than ever as to what was going on. I did know that Kai had tried to fight off the Luxors for me. It made me believe that whatever he had meant by throwing himself on top of me before they barged in had been for my protection

Before I could think too much on it, I heard more footsteps and Malakai strode into the room, black robe billowing theatrically about him. As soon as Kai saw him he quickly withdrew his arm from around my shoulders.

"What is the meaning – " he started, but when he saw us both sitting shamefully on the disheveled bed, his eyes darting to Kai's shirt strewn on the floor, he stopped and I finally caught onto Kai's quick thinking.

"Well, well, well," Malakai chuckled. "My boy, I can see you fancy this one, but rules are rules. And even you must follow them, son. This is an academic academy. Education comes first. We shall not let affections of the heart lead us astray. These kinds of affairs are not permitted on the premises."

"But we're not on the premises," Kai interrupted.

"Our private residence is off limits to students," Malakai said, the sharpness back in his tone. He stared at his son and sighed. "I will make an exception this time. But this will not happen again. Understood?"

We both nodded.

"Please see to it Miss Sommers finds her way to her next lesson," Malakai said to the Luxors. "I need a word with my son."

They nodded and approached the bed. I stood up and pushed passed them, lurching my arms from their attempts to grab hold of me.

"I know the way," I hissed.

I looked over my shoulder as Malakai shut the door and my heart shuddered for Kai.

"WHAT IN KULL'S name do you think you were doing bringing her to your room?" Malakai thundered.

"I – " Kai started.

"Never mind. I know what you were thinking, but you can't do this. Not here and especially not with her."

"But you told me to get to know her."

"Not like that, Kai." Malakai threw his son's shirt in his face.

Kai shrugged it on and stared at his father in confusion.

"Father, I'm sorry. I shouldn't have broken the rules and brought her here without your permission. But since I've been spending so much time with her, I think I've started to like her."

"Son, she's dangerous. She has a lot of secrets that you don't know about. I shouldn't have asked you to get close to her. Kobel was right, it was a mistake to involve you."

"What are you talking about? Involve me in what? What secrets?"

"Kai, you're not ready to know yet."

"So it's okay for you to have secrets, but Geneva can't have any?"

His movements were so fast that it took a moment for Kai to comprehend where the pain had come from. His face stung where Malakai had swiftly struck him.

"Back talk is not tolerated!" Malakai bellowed.

Kai put a shocked hand to his face where his father had backhanded him. The humiliation he felt was much worse than the pain.

"Kai, remember what we spoke about? Soon you will have a kingdom at your feet. All I've done, all I've built, you will inherit. On your seventeenth birthday, the world will be yours. Then you will be ready to know these things, our guarded secrets."

"Maybe I don't want all of that, Father. Maybe I just want to be a normal 16 year old boy and hang out with a girl that I like."

"She's not a normal girl, Kai! That's what I'm trying to tell you. She's manipulating you."

"No she's not!"

"Kai, you don't know her. There's something she wants and she'll do anything to get it. She's already been using you; lying to you so she can get what she needs."

"She wouldn't do that to me," he said looking crestfallen.

"Think about it, son. Has she asked you for things?"

Kai's eyes softened ever so slightly with recognition and Malakai stepped closer to him, grabbing his shoulders.

"Have you given her anything, Kai?"

Kai swallowed hard as he shook his head, preparing to lie to his father.

"No, Father. I'm not stupid."

"Good," Malakai said, relaxing his grip on his son. "From now on, you will stay away from her."

"But, Father – "

"This is not a request, Kai. Geneva Sommers is off limits," he bellowed before storming out of his son's room, slamming the door on his way out.

I WAITED for Kai outside the ancestry lesson room. When he finally showed up, I rushed over to him. His lip was already turning red.

"Are you okay?" I asked gently reaching up to touch his swollen mouth. "Did he hit you?"

"I'm fine," he said moodily brushing my hand away. "What about you?" He lightly touched my arms as he looked at them with worry. There were already the beginnings of bruises forming on my pale arms from where the Luxors had grabbed me on their not so gentle escort from Kai's room.

"Yes, I'm fine," I smiled, biting my lip a bit to hide my embarrassment.

"I'm so sorry. I knew it was a risk bringing you there, but I wanted to help you find your friend."

"Thank you Kai. For taking a risk to help me and for trying to protect me from the Luxors," I said. "Quick thinking too. That bit with the bed was brilliant."

"Yeah," he said with a crooked grin, not meeting my eyes as his cheeks flushed.

It was nice to see that he was as embarrassed as I was at being caught in a promiscuous situation. It made me like him even more. It was far better to let Malakai think we'd been hormonal teenagers rather than letting him know what we were really up to. I was grateful to Kai for his willingness to take such risks for me.

"Too bad it can't happen again," he added sullenly.

"What do you mean? What happened after I left?" I asked glancing at his lip again. "If he's hurting you – "

Kai laughed. "What? Tell someone? Like who? The headmaster?"

"Kai – "

"Geneva, I can take care of myself. I'm almost seventeen and then I'll be a legal adult and won't have to answer to him. But right now we have a bigger problem. My father forbid me from seeing you again."

"What? How can he do that? We have almost every lesson together."

"I'm sure that will change by tomorrow."

"I don't understand," I said. "Wasn't it his idea to have you show me around?"

"Yeah, well he changed his mind."

"Why?"

Kai shook his head and shrugged. His expression was stormy and he wouldn't meet my eyes.

"Kai, what did he say?"

"He said you're using me and lying about who you really are."

I tensed and my eyes widened.

"I told him he was wrong, but from the look on your face and the fact that you're not denying it, maybe I'm the one who's wrong," Kai said before stalking away from me.

Crud! That didn't take long. I guess I thought my acting skills were good enough to buy me more time with Kai. But then again, I hadn't expected Malakai to rat me out. I had to figure out a way to patch this up and fast. I was finally starting to make some headway with Kai.

"Wait," I said running after him. I barely caught him before he entered the lesson room. "Kai, please let me explain. I really do like spending time with you, but there *is* something I need to tell you."

"What is it?"

"Not here. It's not safe."

"You can trust me, Geneva," he said, his genuine warmth returning to his dark features.

"I know that now," I said. "Can you trust me for a little while longer? I promise, we'll talk the first opportunity we have to be alone."

Kai laced his fingers with mine, making my whole body feel warm. He pulled my hand up to his mouth and kissed it. Perhaps I was better at acting than I thought, because I was even making myself start to believe that there was something between Kai and me.

"Of course," he said.

"Come on," I said pulling Kai with me. "We're late for lessons. I don't want to get you in any more trouble."

19

We showed up late to ancestry and I squeezed in next to Remi and Sparrow, while Kai exchanged words with our professor.

"I'll explain later," I whispered to Sparrow when she raised her eyebrows in concern.

Professor Greene, a portly little man, welcomed us without too much unpleasantness about our late arrival. He gave a brief recap of what we'd missed at Kai's request, and then picked up where he'd left off: page 36, *The History of Surnames*. My mind pricked to attention. This was perfect. Maybe this would reveal the last Pillar, or at least help us eliminate more students.

After Professor Greene had finished his readings, he called each student in alphabetical order to the large, black chalkboard in the front of the room, asking them to write their full names. Nova was first. I eagerly read each name as it was written on the board, hoping for some sign of the last Pillar. I copied the names down in the back of the journal Kai had given me, scribbling question marks next to the ones I wanted to explore and putting lines through ones I was sure weren't possibilities. It was finally my turn at the board. I grasped the brittle chalk and wrote my name. I felt a rush of gooseflesh as I completed it. Professor Greene was right, names were powerful things. Seeing mine among the others on the board felt strange. I felt like I was staring at a list of prisoners, and perhaps I was. The list on the blackboard wasn't much different than the one Kai and me had been leafing through earlier. I wondered if any of the other students here felt like they were trapped at the Troian Center. After all, they had been dragged from Lux, away from their homes and loved ones to go to this Academy, as Malakai called it. They too, where just pawns in his master plan. Back at my seat, I stared at the list of names on the board, wondering who among them I could convince to join my side.

Once all the names were listed on the board, I drew my attention to the names of my friends.

Nova Asher
Remi Cleary
Journey Mason
Sparrow Menders
Geneva Sommers
Jemma Sommers

I stared at the last names of my friends on the chalkboard. We'd discussed them over breakfast on our first morning here. They were equally shocked to see their last names for the first time on their curriculum and then scrawled on their bedframes. Even Nova, who'd been using his first name the longest, seemed excited to have confirmation of his surname.

"It seemed familiar to me the moment I saw it," he'd said, but then his green eyes had grown stormy and now I saw why.

In the silence of the lesson room, with nothing to distract me from the names scrawled on the blackboard, I finally saw what he had. His last name was Asher, like ashes, like his power or, as he surely thought, like his prophecy of Kull, who had been condemned to Limbo for all eternity for his deceitful ways.

It was odd that his last name resembled his power, and so did Remi's, Journey's and Sparrow's for that matter. But what about Jemma and me? Sommers? What did that mean? Savior maybe, in some other language? Or maybe it meant doomed, I thought grimly.

My pondering was interrupted by Professor Greene's voice.

"For example, Asher is of Middle English descent and although most people take it for it's literal translation of fire, it actually means blessed."

My heart skipped a beat and I tried to catch Nova's eye at this revelation, but he was too far away, sitting on the opposite side of the room with Jemma and two other boys I didn't know.

"Your assignment for the rest of this lesson is to work in groups of four and decipher each others genealogical origin along with at least four meanings for your name and one misconstrued meaning."

I was relieved to see that even without our powers to telepath, my friends and I were still on the same page. We split up so that none of us were working together. We could meet more students that way. I hadn't been able to shake Kai, but I did meet two other girls at our table. Ruby McCray and Fallon Crane. The girls were nice enough but seemed uninterested in talking to me about anything other than our assignment once they realized I didn't have any juicy gossip for them, like if I had a boyfriend or any other cool tattoos. Ruby had asked me who I was taking to the ball and when I replied, "What ball?" she looked appalled and lost interest completely. I was sure neither of them were Pillars at least. I hoped working through each lesson like this, we'd be able to eliminate suspects quickly. My friends didn't have the ability to *feel* the Pillar vibe, as Journey called it, but I had faith that they were sharp enough to identify gossipy twits from potential Pillars.

"Look," Kai said. "I found mine. Vanir is Dutch. It means most high, valor, bravery and honor!"

"Well that's a lot to live up to," Fallon sneered. "You know I've heard every good definition is trying to cover up at least two bad ones. With adjectives like that, your family must be trying to cover up something pretty awful."

"Yeah, in German Vanir means bird of death, oppressor and bringer of war," Ruby added.

Kai looked dejected.

"Just because Crane means awkward bird in every language, doesn't mean you should take it out on Kai," I said defending him.

Fallon glared at me, but turned back to her textbook.

"Thanks," Kai whispered. "But they're right, you know. There are a lot of negative associations with my name. I know what people say about my family."

"Like what?"

"Like my father is evil and practices black magic. That he killed my mother and other cruel things. It's all talk. But I'd be lying if I said it didn't get to me."

I swallowed hard, remembering the rumors Hollis had shared with us. If tales of Malakai had reached the forest, I could only imagine what Kai must have had to endure inside the walls of Lux and now the Troian Academy.

"Don't worry about it, Kai. People can be cruel. They fear things they don't understand. I got picked on a lot too when this was the Troian Center. All you can do is hold your head up and learn the truth for yourself."

"How am I supposed to find the truth about all my terrible family rumors?

"Have you ever tried asking your father?"

"Yes," he flinched. "That didn't really work out."

I could see Kai didn't want to talk about it so I changed the subject.

"So what ball were they talking about?" I asked him, gesturing to the girls at our table.

"The Genesis Tournament ball," he replied.

When I shook my head and returned a confused stare he smiled and launched into a detailed explanation about Genesis Tournament.

"It's a yearly event that takes place in Lux, where the most elite of the Luxors compete in athletic competitions for honor and prowess. It's also how they advance in ranks more quickly. Before the tournament, there's always an elegant ball, where the citizens of Lux come dressed in their finest to meet the competitors, so they can size them up and decide who to bet on the following day. There's music and dancing and all sorts of merriment," Kai boasted. "Since Father has been head of the Luxor militia for so long, I've been able to attend many balls. And now that he is the Headmaster of the Troian Academy, he wants to bring his own version of the Genesis Tournament and ball here."

I tried to envision what this beautiful ball must have looked like in Lux. Soldiers dressed in uniform, citizens in expensive suits and extravagant gowns, all swirling to the rhythm of sophisticated music.

"So when is the ball?" I asked.

"At the end of the semester."

I sighed, that was still six weeks away according to my curriculum. It would have been nice to see such an elegant event, but I knew my destiny didn't allow for such luxuries. I had to get the Pillars and get out of the Troian Academy as soon as possible. It was probably just as well that I wouldn't be here for the ball. I don't think my heart could handle watching Nova dance with someone else. My mind flashed back to the night of my Eva ceremony, the one and only time I'd ever danced with Nova. I was enjoying my daydream, when I realized Kai was staring at me.

"What?"

"Who are you planning on going with?" he asked.

"To the dance? I haven't really thought about it," I said.

"Well, you shouldn't have any trouble finding a date."

I shook my head uncomfortably, wishing I hadn't brought the subject up. The last thing I wanted was for Kai to ask me to be his date for the dance. I'd have to say yes to keep up pretenses, but the thought of standing him up pained me. But I couldn't very well tell him that I didn't plan on being here by then.

"I assumed you would be going with him," he continued, nodding toward Nova's table. "I thought you two were... you know... together?"

My heart lurched. *Yeah, me too* it screamed.

"Nova? No," I said averting my eyes. "We're not together."

We're not anything anymore, I thought with a heavy heart.

"I'm not really into dances and that kind of stuff," I added hoping to prevent Kai from pursuing the subject any further.

"Oh... You're not?" he asked sounding slightly disappointed.

"I think they're kind of lame," I said.

"Oh, yeah. Me too," he said not meeting my eyes.

Luckily for me, Professor Greene walked past our table, halting all conversations and I busied myself by burying my head in my ancestry book.

20

"You what?" Sparrow squeaked as we made our way through the winding pathways in the garden.

We were crunching along the pebble path in the hedge maze on our way to the Athlesium and I was quickly trying to fill my friends in on why I'd been late to ancestry. Journey trailed behind looking for possible escape routes, while Jemma, Sparrow, Remi and me kept up with the rest of our lesson. Nova had left ancestry to go to his Cadet training without a word to me.

"Keep your voice down," I hissed. "I think this proves we should trust Kai."

"I don't know," Remi said. "It could have been all part of Malakai's master plan."

I knew I couldn't tell them why I truly trusted Kai, that he was one of us and had amazing powers that could help us find anything we were looking for. I promised Kai that I wouldn't tell anyone. It would just have to be one more secret I had to tuck away for now, leaving me to convince my friends to trust him based on nothing more than my instinct.

"I thought of that too, but Kai didn't have to help me. He

risked a lot by doing it, but he did it anyway. Malakai wasn't happy to find me in his room."

"How did you get out of there?" Sparrow asked.

"Kai came up with a quick excuse," I said, my cheeks blushing.

"I bet he did," Jemma smirked. "Listen little sister, if you want to go around trusting every boy who smiles at you, go ahead, but don't expect me to do the same."

"Keep your friends close and your enemies closer," I jeered at her. "Isn't that what you always say?"

"So what do you expect Kai to do for us then? Ask his father for the key out of this prison and see if he minds if you take a few suspected Pillars with you?" she shot back.

"No Jemma, but I do think he can help us find what we're looking for in Malakai's study. There has to be information about the Pillars in there."

"I'm glad you were able to get news of Mala. It should help Sadie trust us," Sparrow said. "I don't know what to think of Kai yet, but next time you go off spying let us in on your plan so we don't worry, okay?"

"I agree with Sparrow. Going off with Kai without telling us wasn't a smart idea," Remi said.

"Why? Nova gets to come up with his own plans all the time. He's off playing Cadets with a bunch of Pruxes right now while we're being subjected to barbaric forms of exercise in the sweltering sun!"

"Easy, Geneva. Remi just meant you should tell us your plans. We're on your side, remember?" Sparrow said.

I was about to give a smart retort when we finally emerged from the maze of hedges, but the path was starting to angle steeply. We kept following it down. Down until it grew dark. We were in an underground tunnel. The damp walls were lined with torches every few yards and smelled strongly of sulfur. Halfway through the tunnel, we passed through a heavy iron gate. It looked like it was made of the same metal as the fence surrounding the Troian Center, but it was rusted, oxidized from the salt air that hung thickly in the humid tunnel.

"Well so much for an escape route," Journey mumbled from behind me.

"I guess you were right," I said. "There isn't an opening in the fence."

We continued through the dank tunnel until it suddenly spilled out onto the beach. I was hit with a warm blast of sea breeze and smiled, instantly reminded of the days spent with Nova, sneaking to the courtyard to steal looks at the sea and feel the salty breeze on our skin. My heart panged again, defying me of my reasons for staying away from him.

"What is this place?" Sparrow asked.

"It looks like the Coliseum!" Journey said coming up behind us.

"I have a bad feeling about this," Remi said.

The dark hulking structure loomed before us. It looked like a giant dome that had mysteriously rose from the sea, and decided to rest on the white sand beaches. It's colossal form, adorned with ornate carvings, looked so foreign on the soft flowing sand. It had massive columned archways marking the entrances all the way around the gigantic circular structure. The sides nearest the sea were being battered by a barrage of waves as the tide rolled in.

We walked under an archway and into the arena. I instantly felt a chill as the enormous shadow of the structure engulfed us. There was a giant hole in the center of the ceiling, letting the sunlight spill in. I looked up, shading my eyes to take in the immense feat of architecture. There was a second level of seating arranged above us. My mind reeled. This surely was meant for spectators. Despite the thick humidity, a cold damp chill crept up my spine. There was something sinister about this place.

"Nothing good can happen in here," Sparrow whispered by my side.

I agreed with her, but tried not to show my fear.

"How could a place like this have been built in the time we were gone?" Remi asked.

"I was wondering that same thing," I replied. "Malakai sure had a lot of unusual additions added to the Troian Center while we were gone. It seems a little excessive for a school."

"I have a feeling we're not meant to learn here," Jemma said.

For once I agreed with my sister.

"Welcome to the Athlesium!" bellowed a voice behind me.

I jumped as a Luxor strode past. This was the first time I'd heard one address us in anything other than an order.

"I am Commander Gray. You are now in my house. My house, my rules! There are some new recruits here today. For their sake, I will repeat the rules of the Athlesium one time and one time only. The rest of you, fall in line."

We watched as all the students in our lesson silently marched into formation. They stood in perfectly straight lines, alternating, girl, boy.

"This is the Athlesium. This is where you will be trained in six different athletic trials. You should try your best to excel because you are required to compete in at least one event at the Genesis Tournament at the end of the semester. You will learn grappling, fencing, climbing, archery, flails and quarter-staffs. I will decide which trial you will compete in. I will decide whom you spar with. I am not someone you want on your bad side. You will address my soldiers and I as 'Sir.' You will answer our questions with 'Sir, yes, Sir.' Do we understand each other?"

"Sir, yes, Sir!" rang out in unison, echoing off the domed fortress.

I swallowed hard, trying to push the foreboding feeling of doom back down into the pit of my stomach. I didn't like anything about the Athlesium. I felt like I was an animal marching to slaughter.

"Today we will be studying quarterstaffs. Get suited up."

Quarterstaffs, I learned, were flaming club-like weapons that were wielded at each other while holding a shield and trying not to get bludgeoned to death. Prior to training, I'd been hustled into the dressing room with the rest of my classmates, where I traded my white uniform for a pair of rough brown shorts with a drawstring that I could barely pull tight enough to hang on my boney hips. Then I'd selected a lightweight grey tunic with the Troian Academy logo emblazoned on the left breast; a black crest, outlined in gold, with the crimson letters TA intertwined in the center. I grabbed a soft red sash and wrapped it around my waist twice before securing it in a knot below my navel. Commander Gray was kind enough to supply us with leather helmets and pauldrons to protect our shoulders and upper arms, but it was still a barbaric sport.

I did my best to stay on my feet, but that was no simple task. I was easily one of the shortest girls and was still nursing an injured hand. The heavy shield and quarterstaff were hard enough to hold without the weight of the leather armor and someone bearing down on top of me.

When I wasn't fighting, I was guzzling water and watching the boys battle. Journey excelled at quarterstaffs. I had little doubt that Commander Gray would place him in this trial for the Genesis Tournament. I winced as I watched Remi get clubbed hard. He was holding his own, but he was nowhere near Journey's caliber. I found myself relieved that Nova wasn't here. I was sure he'd be good at quarterstaffs. I'd yet to find anything Nova wasn't good at, well besides communicating with me, perhaps, but I still didn't want to watch him be attacked by a bunch of Pruxes. It was hard enough to watch Remi and Journey.

A whistle blew and it was my turn in the ring again. Jemma

stepped into the circle with me this time and I grinned behind my shield. Maybe this wasn't such a bad sport after all. It felt healthy to take my aggression out on my sister. With each swing of my club I vented my frustrations.

This is for using Nova as a talisman. My club slammed into Jemma's shield, making her stumble backward.

This is for all the years you were cruel to me. I swung hard, connecting club-to-club, sending bits of flames dancing to the ground as the impact sent a bone-jarring tremor through my arm.

This is for being a terrible sister. I dodged her advance and attacked her shield with a solid blow.

And this is for –

I didn't get to finish the last thought. Instead I felt my jaw slam into the backside of my shield and my head snapped, hard. I saw stars and fell flat on my back. When I opened my eyes, I was looking up at the oculus. I stared at the bright sunbeam bursting into the Athlesium when Jemma came to peer down at me.

"You okay?" she asked

"I'm fine," I sputtered trying to shake my mind clear.

"Hold your shield higher, Sommers," Commander Gray yelled.

I tasted the bitter metallic flavor of blood in my mouth and spit it out on the sand.

"Sir, yes, Sir," I yelled.

"Go again," he bellowed.

My jaw throbbed and I was shaking but I managed to get into position. On the whistle I lunged at Jemma, but she was faster. She spun and came around at me with a hard blow to the side. I wasn't expecting it and couldn't get my shield around fast enough. My arm took the full brunt of the club, knocking me off my feet again. I thanked heaven for the leather armor or my arm would have been broken and probably on fire. It was throbbing with a searing pain as it was, but I managed to get back to my feet and deflect Jemma's advances to make it through the rest of our match. When I heard the alarm blare in the distance signaling the end of our lesson I was elated. I sunk to my knees dripping with sweat as we stripped off our gear.

"Ouch!" I cried as I tried to pull off my pauldron.

There was a large splinter stuck through the leather, piercing my arm. I struggled in vain to get the armor off but each time I moved to pull it over my head it pushed the spike further into my skin. I was having no luck and the pain was excruciating. Another girl in the group took pity on me. I remembered her from ancestry; she'd been in my group. Her name was Ruby McCray.

"Stand still," she said. "I'll try to pull the splinter out."

"Ouch!" I screamed again, but I was relieved to see she'd pulled it out.

"Thanks, Ruby," I said smiling weakly at the girl.

Sparrow and Remi had run over to see what was wrong and so had Commander Gray.

"Sommers, what happened here?" he asked.

"I had a splinter, Sir. Ruby pulled it out."

As I uttered the words, Ruby collapsed with the bloody shard clutched in her hand. Commander Gray blew his whistle startling me.

"Call for Professor Kobel and get them to the infirmary right away!" Gray ordered.

Before I knew what was happening I was on a stretcher, bouncing up the beach toward the Troian Center. I watched the cloudless blue sky swirling above me. Sun flares shot prisms of rainbows exploding before my eyes. I remember feeling cold, even though I knew the sun was caressing me.

Blackness.

~

"Gray, how could you let this happen?" Malakai bellowed.

"Master, you know the risks. These trials are dangerous. We shouldn't have the Eva competing. I've already pulled the fire Pillar out at your request. He'll be safe under my watch at Cadets, but we still don't know who the others are. We are risking too much by subjecting them to these trials. What if they're killed before they're discovered? We've already had one casualty," Gray pleaded.

"How dare you speak to me in that tone!" Malakai said, fuming behind his desk.

"Gentlemen, we have the situation under control," Kobel said trying to diffuse the situation. "Commander, you were wise to call me. We have stabilized the Eva. Don't worry about the other girl. She was expendable. We must continue to execute our plan. We can't start treating the Eva and her friends differently or they will suspect us."

"We got lucky this time. I'm not comfortable with continuing this way," Gray said.

"Commander Gray, may I remind you that you serve at my pleasure," Malakai added.

"Don't think that will stop me from bringing this up at the next Ravinori meeting," Gray answered with a cold stare.

"As you wish, Commander. Just remember everyone can be replaced," Malakai purred. "Dismissed."

With that, Commander Gray turned sharply and left Malakai's office. Kobel and Malakai sat in momentary silence.

"Perhaps he has a point, Master. It was a close call. I tested the antidote on the McCray girl first and she wasn't strong enough for it. We were fortunate the Eva is so strong," Kobel said. "I was able to recalculate the dose, but it was still taxing on her body."

"Of course she's strong enough. She's the Eva, isn't she?" Malakai barked. "I'm not changing my plans. The danger of the trials is my intension. It will expedite her urgency to find the Pillars, which is what we want."

"Yes, but – "

The doors to Malakai's office flew open and Kai burst in, followed by an apologetic Luxor.

"I'm sorry, Sir. He ducked passed me," the embarrassed Luxor mumbled.

"It's fine," Malakai said, waving him away. "Kai, we've talked about this."

"But Father, something's happened to Geneva!"

"I know son, that's what we were discussing before you rudely interrupted."

"Is she going to be all right?"

"Kai, sit down. We need to talk about Geneva. You need to be careful around her."

21

I later learned that the oil used on the quarterstaff clubs to keep the flame from going out comes from the Monkshood plant and is extremely poisonous if absorbed through the skin. It slows the heart and will result in death if not treated immediately. Lucky for me, Professor Kobel had an antidote. Unlucky for Ruby, he'd only had enough to save one of us.

I'd been in and out of consciousness in waves. When I found out that Ruby was dead I was hysterical. I'd barely known her, but she'd tried to help me and paid the ultimate price. I felt cursed. Everyone who came near me was in danger. Talon and now this poor girl, Ruby, had died because of me. Why had Kobel decided to use the antidote on me? It didn't make sense? Why was my life worth more than hers?

I hated everything about this new Troian Center. One minute they were showering me with luxury, the next I was being put in dangerous situations, like dueling in the Athlesium. It was like some confusing test that I couldn't comprehend. I was convinced that Malakai and the Ravinori knew who I was and wanted to use me to bring Ravin back, but what were they waiting for? Why were they toying with me? Kobel was involved somehow. His decision to save me proved that he needed me for something.

When I finally awoke, I found Kobel sitting by my bedside. After he examined me, he wrote a few quick notes on my chart and came back to sit with me.

"You were quite lucky, my dear. Perhaps quarterstaffs is not in your future," he said with a sincere smile as he patted my hand.

I flinched. My whole body hurt and even his light touch was painful.

"Ah yes, one of the side effects from the antidote, I'm afraid. You'll have some bruising, but you'll recover. I'm having you moved to your room where you'll be more comfortable. A few days of bed rest should set you straight. And apply this to the wound for pain." He placed a tiny vial into the palm of my hand.

"Ruby," I mumbled groggily.

"We've been over this. I'm sorry about your friend. Unfortunately, there are times when we can't save everyone. Sometimes we have to choose."

His words haunted me. It was just like what Malakai said to me in my nightmares. I watched him slowly hobble from my room, while I clutched the tiny vial in my shaking hand. When he was gone, I squeezed two droplets into the oozing gash on my arm and sunk back into my pillow, letting the darkness come.

"Stop! You can't go in there! Stop!"

There was a terrible commotion going on in the hall outside my room. It woke me from the most restful sleep I'd had since coming back to the Troian Center. I struggled to sit up in my bed. When I cleared my vision, I thought maybe I was still dreaming as I watched Nova burst into my room.

"Mr. Asher! You are not allowed in the girls bunkroom!"

Nova scanned the room and locked eyes with me. His jaw was set, but his eyes were tender with worry. He ran over to me, ignoring the other girls who shrieked and scurried out of his way.

"Geneva, thank the gods. Are you okay?" he asked breathlessly when he got to my bedside.

His face was level with my shoulders and I could feel his breath on my bare skin. It instantly sobered me. I couldn't let him touch me! I recoiled from him and pulled my knees to my chest. He had been raising his hands to touch me. I'd seen that look in his eyes before, when we were in the forest after Khan saved us. He was going to scoop me up and hold me close and it was what I wanted most in the world, but I couldn't let him.

"Don't touch me!" I yelled, halting his motion.

He stopped short. Shock and pain contorted his face. He was plainly shocked by my outburst.

"Geneva?"

"You shouldn't be here, Nova," I said through tears.

He put his hands on his head in baffled frustration. I saw a giant red welt crawling from under his cuff, up his forearm and suddenly realized what he must be going through. He wasn't allowed to be in the girls bunkroom, his cuff restricted it. The pain must have been blinding, but he'd fought through it to come see me. I felt sick; I knew I was causing him more pain than that cuff ever could.

Our eyes were locked on each other's, trying to read the others unspoken misery. Before either of us could say another word, two Luxors burst into the room and tore Nova away from me, breaking the spell.

22

The next few days were uneventful. I was more than happy to stay in bed as ordered. The antidote may have saved my life but it didn't spare me any pain. Kobel had understated the bruising. My entire arm and chest were covered in deep purple patches that stretched up my neck. Moving was excruciating. The only relief I had came from the vial Professor Kobel had given me for the pain. The down side was that it made me sleepy. I found myself lost in my thoughts, in and out of consciousness. I had vivid dreams about the Ravinori and finding the Pillars. I clung to them, hoping somehow I'd find an answer in the jumbled visions.

"Geneva?" a voice called out to me.

"Geneva?" it called again, pulling me from another mind-searing vision.

I struggled to sit up and rubbed my palms against my throbbing temples. When I opened my eyes, Sparrow and Jemma stared back at me.

"You look terrible," Jemma said in her usual callousness.

"Thanks," I grumbled.

"Come on," Sparrow urged offering me her hand. "We have

to go to counseling today. Professor Greene sent us to help get you ready. Let's get you cleaned up."

Jemma was right. I did look terrible. I sat in a chair in front of the new mirror that replaced the one I shattered, staring at my sallow reflection. Sparrow had helped me wash my hair since my arms were too sore to hold above my head. She steadily combed it, trying to tame the wet curls. I frowned at my hair. It had grown back with the help of Sadie's lotion. The length of my curls measured the time we had been at the Troian Center. Too long. Much longer that I had anticipated. And now we were getting ready for our counseling session with Malakai. The thought of being in a room alone with him made my skin crawl. I was terrified of what he might say or do to me. I hadn't seen him since he'd found me in Kai's room and he didn't look too happy. Kai! I had promised to explain everything to him and then ended up in the infirmary. It had been days since I'd seen him. I hoped Malakai hadn't turned him against me in our time apart.

"There," Sparrow said, smiling at me and the masterpiece she'd created with my hair. "You ready?

I set my jaw and squared my shoulders. I supposed now was as good a time as any to face my destiny. It was evident that things were getting worse and quickly. It was time to face Malakai and find out what he was up to.

"Ready," I said.

Before we went to our counseling session Sparrow made me stop at the infirmary. She was concerned that I was still bleeding through my bandage from the quarterstaff wound and no matter how gentle she was, every time she tried to change it, I winced.

"Do you want me to wait here for you?"

"No, that's okay. You go. I don't want you to be late. I'll meet you there. Good luck."

"You too," Sparrow said, squeezing my hand.

I watched her and Jemma hurry down the hall before I turned to walk through the infirmary door. Even pushing the door open required more exertion than I had the energy for. By the time I made it up to the desk, my forehead was glistening with sweat again. There was no one at the desk, so I slumped in the comfortable chair next to it to catch my breath.

A white coat woman walked through the door and was momentarily startled, but recovered when she recognized me.

"What is it this time?" she asked harshly.

"My arm," I grimaced, pointing to the blood soaked bandage.

The woman sighed. "Follow me."

I sat waiting in the cold, white exam room to have my arm treated and re-bandaged again. By now, I knew the drill. I would wait in the exam room. A white coat would pull off the old, blood-soaked bandage, poke and prod at it, scribble some notes on a clipboard and then send someone in to apply a new bandage.

I held my breath and looked away as the exam was done. The cut was painful and looking at it made me feel light-headed, not to mention nauseated. Finally, it was note-taking time and I mustered up some courage to enact the plan I'd thought of while reading my medicinal horticulture book a few nights back. I knew it was dangerous and a bit desperate, but these were desperate times.

"Excuse me?" I started. "I'm almost out of the vial that Professor Kobel gave me for the pain. It keeps me up at night," I lied. "I was wondering if you had anything you could give me to help me sleep? I'm afraid my studies are suffering."

The white coat only stared at me over the rim of her wire-framed glasses. After a moment, she looked back down and scribbled more notes on the clipboard before leaving the room without another word.

Well it was worth a try, I thought to myself.

Moments later the door swung open and Sadie walked in.

"Sadie, hi," I said. "I'm so glad to see you."

"Hello, Geneva. Back again?"

"Yeah," I shrugged. "It's not getting better."

She washed her hands at the small sink basin and then applied a pair of thin stretching gloves.

"I'm glad you're here. I have some news for you," I said.

"You do?"

"Yes, I think – "

"Why don't you let me complete your exam first and then we'll talk," she said interrupting me.

She pulled the curtain around the table I was on with one quick motion.

"It's not always safe to talk here," she whispered to me.

I nodded.

"You've really done a number on yourself," she said loudly, examining my wound gently. "Hmm..."

"What?"

"It's puzzling that it hasn't started healing. Did it always look this bad?"

I looked down at the gash on my arm and gasped.

"It looks worse!" I cried

"How much worse?"

Beads of sweat started forming on my brow as I looked at the puckered flesh of my arm. It was bright red and swollen. My skin was orange with heat from the infection and the pink fleshy muscle underneath was severed and gleaming. The last image I saw was a tiny purple vein pulsing.

"I'm going to be sick" I said rushing off the exam table.

I hit the floor and crumpled weak-kneed to the cold ground, vomiting at Sadie's feet.

Blackness.

~

When I woke, I was back on the exam table, my throbbing arm, neatly bandaged, lay strapped across my chest.

"Don't move too quickly," came a familiar voice.

"What happened?"

"You got sick," Sadie said helping me sit up. "It happens all the time. Some people are a bit squeamish."

"Sorry," I said, my cheeks burning with embarrassment.

"Don't mention it."

Sadie was eyeing me skeptically.

"What is it?"

"I am a bit concerned about your chart."

"What do you mean?"

"Here," she said thrusting it into my lap as she nervously looked over her shoulder. "They're charting your injury and they keep recording that it is getting worse. It's clearly infected, but they aren't doing anything about it."

"And that's not normal?" I asked.

"No. There are a number of potions we can give you to stave off infection, but they're giving you something I've never heard of before. That's not even the most worrisome part. They keep charting that you are getting closer to this prognosis, but I don't know what it means. Do you?"

My heart about leapt out of my chest when I saw the words she pointed at blazing from the medical chart.

Ponte deorum.

I fought the dizzy spell that sent my mind whirling.

"Sadie, I have to tell you something, but you have to promise not to tell anyone else."

"Okay."

"I'm serious, Sadie. I need you to swear on Mala."

Her big blue eyes met mine and she nodded.

"I swear on Mala."

"Take off your gloves and give me your hand."

"Geneva, you can't be serious."

"I am. You know I am. I can feel it and I know you can too."

"Yes, but it's... it can't be possible. It's not that I don't believe you, but I don't think I'm who you're looking for."

"Sadie, you are. I've already located and confirmed two of the Pillars and I know you're the third. It feels the same when I touch you. It's like an electric charge, but then it's followed by a feeling of coldness, like water. I even looked up your last name. Calder means strong water. You're the water Pillar. You can't deny you've felt it."

"Yes, I felt something strange when you touched me, but that doesn't mean I can do... " She looked over her shoulder and then whispered, "Magic."

"Think about it. Have you ever done something you couldn't explain? I know it sounds crazy but – "

I saw a flicker of recognition rush across her features.

"You have! What was it?"

"It was probably nothing."

"Just tell me about it," I pleaded.

"Not here, okay?"

"Will you tell me later?"

"Yes, but if what you say is true, this place might not be safe."

"So you believe me?"

"I'm not sure what I believe, but you're right, something strange is going on here. Especially with your wound." Sadie glanced back at the chart in her hand.

"Can you do me one more favor?" I asked. "I need some Verilium potion."

"Verilium? But that's an anesthetic. It'll knock you out."

"I know, but I was reading about it. It's made with Henbane and Belladonna and if used in small doses it's said to allow you to open your mind to visions. I've been having these nightmares and they always end in flames. I feel like it means something, like maybe it's a clue. I think if I could stay in these dreams long enough it might help me find the last Pillar."

"Yeah, if it doesn't kill you first."

"Sadie, if I don't find a way out of here Malakai is going to kill me anyway."

Saying the words out loud made them so real that I started to tremble.

"Okay, I'll see what I can do. But for now you need to go back to lessons. I'll catch up with you later."

"Wait. In case something happens to me, you need to know about Mala."

I handed Sadie a tiny piece of crumbled paper that I pulled from my pocket. She unfolded it and her eyes welled with tears.

"Thank you," she whispered.

"If we get out of here, I'll help you get to her, Sadie. I promise."

23

I sat next to Jemma in the hallway outside of Malakai's office. Sparrow was currently inside, having her first counseling session with the headmaster. Everyone said it was nothing to worry about, that Malakai only talked about your studies and family, but that did little to ease the frenzy of butterflies in my stomach. I couldn't stop thinking about what Sadie had shown me in the infirmary. If Malakai knew I was the *Ponte deorum*, it was game over. He would probably sacrifice me to the Ravinori right now. I was mentally kicking myself. I should have told Sadie to warn my friends that someone suspected me of being the *Ponte deorum.* If I didn't come back from this counseling session they would worry. I should've told her to get my friends and run the first chance they got. Perhaps if I had been waiting with anyone other than my sister I would've been less terrified. We weren't speaking much since she nearly killed me in the Athlesium.

I looked over at her, skeptical if I should confide in her. Her black hair fell over the side of her face to the edge of her perfect jawbone. She was examining her nails painted black and gold. I could tell she liked it here. The plush accommodations, the fancy clothes; they all suited her. She had found her way back into a clique of popular girls and she seemed to have Nova wrapped around her finger. I didn't know if I could trust her to tell my friends I suspected that Malakai was on to us. She could very well ignore my warning and choose to stay in this comfortable world she was building for herself. I thought of my mother, urging me to work with my sister and give her a chance. I felt like I had tried and I regretted every time I'd trusted Jemma. But I didn't seem to have any other option at the moment.

"I need to tell you something," I finally said breaking the awkward silence.

"THAT DOESN'T MAKE ANY SENSE," Jemma said.

Once I had started talking, everything spilled out. I told her that I'd confided in Sadie and told her that I thought she was the water Pillar and how I'd discovered on my chart in the infirmary that Malakai knew I was the *Ponte deorum*.

"Jemma, of course it does. We knew Malakai was part of the Ravinori and that they are seeking the Pillars to bring Ravin back. But if they could find the *Ponte deorum* instead, they wouldn't care about the Pillars."

"Eva, we've been over this. If Malakai truly was the big bad leader of the Ravinori, why would he be pretending to be the headmaster of a school? Why would he be so nice to us and give us all these amazing things? If he knew who you were he would just kill you now or whatever he's supposed to do to bring Ravin back. He wouldn't have wasted that antidote on you to save your life and let that poor Rooni girl die."

"Ruby! Her name was Ruby," I corrected my aloof sister.

"Whatever," she said coldly.

"Jemma, I don't know what his plan is yet, but I know he's

waiting for something. I'm telling you all of this because this will be the first time I've been alone with Malakai. If he really is who I think he is, he might... I'm just saying I might not see you all again and I didn't want to miss the opportunity to tell you what I think is going on."

Jemma stared at me with her piercing dark eyes. I wished I could read them. It was hard to know what she was thinking. Was she worried for me? Was she hoping what I said was true, that I would be out of the picture so she could have Nova all to herself?

"Look, you don't have to believe me," I said after I grew impatient of her silence. "But please warn the others. If I don't come back after counseling with Malakai, you all need to get out of here. Find a way to get your cuffs off so Malakai can't track you and take Sadie with you. We need to get as many Pillars out of here and away from the Ravinori as possible."

"If the Ravinori have you, won't we all be safe?" Jemma asked, confirming her distaste for me.

"I think the Pillars will still be in danger because they are a source of power and the Ravinori are power hungry."

She scowled at me. I could tell she wasn't convinced. I felt a tiny tear in my heart, realizing my own sister hoped I'd just give myself over to the Ravinori so I'd get out of the way of her happily ever after. I guess somewhere deep down, I'd still held out hope that she would act like a sister and be on my side.

I took a deep breath and used the only ammunition I had. The only thing I was sure Jemma cared about.

"Jemma, Nova is a Pillar. He won't be safe here, especially if he thinks Malakai did something to me. You saw how even the cuff couldn't stop him from coming into our room after you impaled me with the quarterstaff. Imagine what he'll do if he thinks – "

My voice cracked. I couldn't say the words out loud. They

terrified me, just thinking them. *Imagine what he'll do if he thinks I'm dead.*

"Don't let him be a hero, Jemma. He'll get himself killed."

"Fine," was all she said, but from the pinched expression on her face I could tell she knew I was right and that she wouldn't let Nova die for me.

That was my final comforting thought as the door to Malakai's office swung open. I saw Sparrow's slim silhouette in the light spilling forth from the massive doorframe.

"Geneva Sommers," a deep voice bellowed.

I stood shakily and shuffled toward the door. Sparrow and I passed each other, but she didn't even look at me. She looked like an empty shell, moving silently in a trance. I didn't have a chance to say anything to her. She was passed me in a moment and I stood alone in the doorway, at the threshold of my destiny.

24

"Ah... Welcome, Miss Sommers." Malakai's voice purred.

"Malakai," I said curtly from the chair in front of his desk.

"I've been looking forward to our counseling session." He'd motioned for me to sit.

"I'd prefer to stand," I said. But Malakai spun toward me so quickly that I fell backward into the seat. I tried to recover my composure while he grinned at me like a cat does its' prey, knowing he had me rattled with nowhere to run.

My feet didn't even touch the ground while I was perched in the massive carved chair, which made it hard to feel strong. The chair looked more like a throne, yet it was miniature in comparison to his. The tall back of his ornately carved chair wound up and around, curling like flames until they melted into two towering spindles that framed either side of Malakai's head like a crown of spikes.

I shivered involuntarily, waiting for him to make the next move.

"You know, I prefer that you call me Headmaster," he said through a sneer.

"Why? I know who you really are. You're the leader of the Ravinori. Don't you think it's time we stop pretending?"

He grinned so wide that he couldn't contain his laughter. It rang sharply though the room and reached the hollow pit of my stomach. His laugh was worse than any scolding could ever be.

"Miss Sommers, you have a very wild imagination indeed. I hope you're putting it to good use in your studies. How are they going, by the way?"

I didn't know what to say. It seemed he was going to keep playing his game of cat and mouse. "They're fine. But I don't think they're going to do me much good."

"No?" he purred. "You don't think a proper education will compliment your future?"

"I don't think you want me to have much of a future," I said trying to keep my voice steady.

"Miss Sommers. I know you have been through a lot. You had to endure time at this establishment under Headmistress Greeley and I apologize for how she may have mistreated you. But I assure you that I am here to help you," Malakai said. "If you are willing to work with me, we can achieve great things together," he added softly, his eyes keenly surveying me for understanding.

Finally, he was alluding to the real reason he'd called me here. He may not be willing to come out and say what he wanted, but I was.

"I want you to know that as long as I have a breath left in my body, I will never work with you. I know who you are and what you hope to accomplish, but you won't be able to. I won't help you, no matter how long you keep me locked up in this place."

His smile disappeared and I saw a flash of anger dance across his face before he narrowed his eyes and leaned forward, so close that I could feel his breath. It was a struggle to keep my eyes open and not recoil, but I couldn't let him know I was afraid.

"It's a shame you feel that way, Miss Sommers. I think you will find that you will work with me in the end, whether it is against your will or with it. I have a way of getting what I want. I urge you to reconsider your stance. If you don't, you will have a lonely road ahead of you," he said with a sinister smirk.

"What do you mean?" I asked before I could stop myself.

"Let me show you."

Before I knew what was happening, two Luxors grabbed me from behind and secured me to the chair by my arms while a third one removed my cuff.

"Excessive force seems to be your style," I spat while I uselessly struggled against them.

"Merely a precaution, Miss Sommers. You must have had some life to make you so distrustful of others. You'll come to see that everything I do is to protect you."

"How is strapping me to a chair for my protection?"

Malakai grinned as he methodically moved his hands in a strange pattern above a large stone tablet on his desk. It began to glow when he placed my cuff upon it.

"Some of the images you are about to see tend to be a bit... graphic. They may cause adverse reactions. I wouldn't want you to harm yourself."

His gaze met mine and I saw true evil behind his black eyes. It made my insides shiver to see his barely contained smile twitch across his sharp face.

"Remember, you mustn't look away or we'll be forced to start over. Watch them all to grasp the true meaning."

"Watch all of what?" I asked.

"Only you know what you'll see," he answered coyly. "Shall we begin?"

The question had been rhetorical. A searing pain bit into

my mind and my entire body convulsed for a split second before I went rigid against my restraints. I was sure someone had cracked my skull like an egg; letting all my secrets, desires and fears ooze out in a strange glowing orb for the world to see. I watched in horror as the orb hovered above the stone tablet and filled with a grey fog that formed into blurry images that prickled my memory. Malakai frowned and waved his hands through the cloud chanting undecipherable words. When the mist cleared, the orb displayed a glowing round map. A globe of sorts. It spun, rapidly shifting to new scenes.

At first I saw the Troian Center, not how it was now, but before Malakai had taken over. But then the scene spun and expanded to all of Hullabee Island, turning until it was focused on the forest, and then the Betos. I watched in horror as the spinning orb showed Jovi and Vida outside their tent in the forest. The orb swirled their images into a churning smoke that reappeared as Jaka and Mali, their faces stern as they silently discussed something. They evaporated into the smoke that whirled out of focus again, tilting my world with it. I felt sick as the misty orb replayed the last year of my life; the escape from the Troian Center, my battle with Greeley, my friends and me in the forest, the mercenary attacks. Then it knocked the wind out of me by showing Jovi and Nova standing among a circle of flames. It looked just like my nightmares! *'Choose,'* his voice thundered in my ears.

It wasn't a choice at all. I already knew I would never allow him to harm any of my friends. Sensing my resistance, the orb changed once more and Remi, Sparrow, Journey and Jemma joined Nova and Jovi in the wall of flames suspended before me. I squeezed my hands into fists so hard that my nails bit into my skin until they drew blood. My mind lurched and I felt my consciousness slipping. I fought the nausea that pounded my bulging mind as the fiery images of my friends scarred my retinas and I let go.

Blackness.

WHEN I LEFT Malakai's office I was shaking. A cold sweat crawled down my neck and arms, and I shivered when I walked into the chilly hallway. I scarcely heard Jemma saying my name, my mind reeling too much to even find my voice to respond. Instead I kept moving. Placing one foot in front of the other. I didn't know where I was going, but it seemed to be the only thing my body could do at the moment. If I stopped moving, if I sat down, I was sure I would never have the strength to get up again.

MY MIND WAS HAUNTED STILL by the visions Malakai had shown me in his Orbiture. He knew everything. He had figured out that Jovi and Nova were Pillars even though I had tried so hard to conceal it and keep them safe. Malakai was just toying with me. In that instance I finally figured out what he wanted with me. He wanted me to find the last two Pillars for him. He was showing me that he'd been watching me and he already knew I'd found Nova and Jovi. He'd shown me the rest of my friends as a threat. Proving he knew who I cared about and that he would use them against me to get what he wanted. That was my choice. He wanted me to *'Choose,'* to find the Pillars willingly. If not, I knew he would harm my friends in order to get me to do his bidding.

I wandered aimlessly down the empty hallway, Malakai's voice still echoed in my head.

'One way or the other, you will help me. You can work with me and you will be rewarded, or you can try to fight me. But I promise you, if you resist, all those you care about will suffer. And it will all be for nothing. Because in the end, you will help me, willing or not. The only question remains, how many will you let suffer before you bend to my will? Three have already died by your fault. I can see to it that there are many more.'

I looked down at my bloody palms and felt dizzy. How had I been so stupid? There was no way for me to beat Malakai. I was no match for him. He had an entire army of Ravinori behind him. Plus he was prepared, he'd been preparing for this his entire life. I'd only just learned of this world of magic and mystery. I was still trying to figure out my role in it all and how I was ever going to fulfill my destiny. The one thing that was clear, was that if I didn't surrender and help Malakai, he would kill everyone I cared about. I couldn't let that happen. If he was going to win in the end, it would be better to tell him I was the *Ponte deorum* and let him use me to get what he wanted. Perhaps then I could barter to save the lives of my friends and the Pillars. It was my fault they were a part of this anyway.

That realization overwhelmed me and I started to shake uncontrollably. I had to steady myself against the wall to keep from collapsing. I watched as my hands trailed bloody prints down the stone wall as I started to sink to my knees. I felt hands encircle my waist and heard a familiar voice. When I looked up, I was met with dark worried eyes. Kai's.

"Geneva? What's wrong?"

"Everything," I sobbed into his arms, letting him scoop me up.

He effortlessly carried me folded in his arms. I had only glimpsed his wiry strength when I was pinned beneath him in his room, but now I could feel the definition of each muscle as I clung to him and curled into his chest. I was comforted by his warmth, suddenly realizing how cold I felt. I watched the walls swirl by through my tears. I didn't know where he as taking me. It could be back to his father's office to turn me over for all I knew, but for once, I didn't care. I didn't have any fight left. What did it matter? My fate was sealed anyway. Malakai would win. I was no match for him. All that was left to do now was to beg him to take me and spare my friends.

We took multiple turns and weaved through hallways and doors before Kai stopped and set me down on the ground. He kept his strong arms around me protectively while I tried to stop shaking. We were in a small dark room that I'd never been in before. All around me, I heard the soft tinkering of pianos.

"Where are we?" I asked.

"It's a practice room in the music wing," Kai said. "It's where I come when I need ... some space," he said shyly.

"Oh," was all I could muster.

I felt drunk with weariness and I wanted nothing more than to stay right where I was, wrapped in Kai's warm arms, drinking in his comforting scent of cinnamon and soap.

"Geneva, please tell me what's wrong?"

"I can't," I whispered.

I sank to the floor. Kai was right beside me, anxiously holding me in his gaze. I began sobbing uncontrollably. I shuddered and gulped for air, hiding my dreadful expressions with my hands. I felt Kai gently pull them away and then he gasped.

"Geneva! You're bleeding! What happened? Are you hurt? Do you need to go to the infirmary?"

"No! Please, I just want to stay here."

I held out my hands showing him it was my battered palms that were bleeding. I'd accidentally ripped open my stitches, causing a stream of blood to trickle to drip onto the floor.

Kai pulled a handkerchief from his pocket and moved closer to me. I could feel his breath on my face as he gently dabbed at my cheeks, wiping away the blood and tears. I tried not to stare directly into his beautiful midnight eyes. Instead, I awkwardly stared at my mangled hands. He pulled them into his lap and applied pressure to my palms with the handkerchief to stop the bleeding.

I let him quietly hold my hands while I tried to catch my

breath and stop the tears from flowing. After a few minutes, Kai closed my right hand, around the handkerchief while he continued to hold my left. He stared at me, reaching his hand up to my face and tilting my chin so I was looking at him. His face was close to mine. Something in my chest felt hot and tight being this close to him.

"It's okay," he whispered soothingly, while wiping tears away from my face.

His thumb brushed across my temple and he gently tucked a stray, damp curl behind my ear. I shuddered at the intimacy of his touch. Only Nova had ever touched me like that.

"You're going to be okay," he whispered again, this time putting both hands on either side of my face.

I stared at his sharp exotic features. He was beautiful, but he looked like his father and it made me tremble. Kai didn't let go. Instead he stroked my face trying to comfort me. I felt so tiny and breakable in his strong hands. He continued to wipe away the slowing stream of tears from my face while whispering comforting words and closing the gap between our bodies. He was so close I could feel his breath mingle with my own. His forehead was nearly touching mine. I was spellbound, staring at my pale reflection in his endless obsidian eyes. When his thumb brushed slowly over the corner of my mouth, my lips parted and I let out a tiny gasp.

"Did I hurt you?" Kai asked pulling back and breaking the spell I'd been under.

"No, I… I'm not hurt, I just… Kai, I'm so sorry. I can't talk to you about this."

"Of course you can. You can tell me anything, Geneva. I care about you. I've told you my deepest, darkest secrets and you promised me you were going to tell me what I needed to know about you."

"I know, Kai. Thank you for being so kind to me," I said staring into his pleading eyes. "I don't deserve it."

"Why do you say that?"

"I'm sorry. It's just... you're probably the only person who wouldn't understand."

"It's because I'm different, isn't it?" he said letting his eyes drop to the floor.

"No! No, Kai. We are more alike then you could ever know, but I can't involve you in my problems."

"Why not? I want to help you, Geneva. I care about you."

"I know, Kai, and that's why I shouldn't spend any more time with you. Everyone I care about ends up getting hurt. Ruby is dead because of me."

"No. I don't accept that. Ruby wasn't your fault. I don't care what my father says, I know you and I know you would never purposely hurt anyone."

"He said I hurt Ruby on purpose?" I asked in shock. "I never even sparred with her."

"Father said you took a cheap shot at her when she came over to help you with your armor."

My huge eyes brimmed with tears. Was it not enough that she was dead because the Ravinori needed me alive? Malakai had to poison everyone against me by making up some vicious rumor as well?

"It's okay, Geneva. You were scared and probably only trying to protect yourself, right? No one would blame you if you thought she was trying to harm you."

"I never touched her, Kai! She was trying to help me with the splinter in my arm and she must have pricked herself with the Monkshood oil. I never took a shot at her. Your father is lying to you!"

"Geneva, why would he – "

"Because your father is the problem!" I blurted out cutting him off. "He's the reason I'm so upset, he's the reason I'm in danger! And he's the reason I shouldn't be telling you any of this!"

"My father?" Kai asked, stunned.

"Yes! So you see why I can't talk to you about this?"

"But what happened? What did he say? Maybe I can talk to him."

"No, you can't! Promise me you won't. If he thinks you're involved with me in any way, you'll be in danger too. He was right to tell you to stay away from me."

"Geneva. None of this makes any sense."

"I know and I wish I could explain it to you."

"Then try. I'm willing to listen. I promise I'll keep an open mind. You did it for me when I showed you what I can do."

"Kai..."

"Please, Geneva. Don't shut me out. You're my only friend here." He reached for my hand. "I've missed you so much these past few days. I was desperate to see you, but my father forbid it..." He trailed off, starting to notice the trend with his father.

There was such honesty in his eyes that I felt my resolve crumbling. I hadn't been able to talk to any of my friends lately. Malakai made sure that I barely had any unsupervised time with them. And even when I did, I was so caught up in all the secrets and lies I'd been keeping that I was starting to revert to my old ways of shutting everyone out. Keeping everything bottled up was taking so much energy and I just didn't have any left. I gripped Kai's hand and looked into his dark eyes that reminded me so much of how the night sky looked in the forest. I felt a sudden ache for it. Perhaps I would be joining my friends and family among the stars soon. I squeezed my eyes shut, fighting the tears and held onto the warmth I felt in Kai's hands. It was like he was the only thing keeping me connected to this world. The rest of me felt like it had given up, like it was already gone.

"Oh what does it matter?" I sighed. "Your father already knows who I am. It can't hurt to tell you now."

"What do you mean, he knows who you are?"

"He's right, Kai. I've been lying to you. You know what you can do? Your magic power?"

Kai nodded slowly.

"I have powers too. Lots of them. Dangerous powers, and that's why I'm not safe. Your father knows about them and he wants to take them from me. You were right not to tell him what you can do, Kai. He wants to take my powers and he's going to use them to do something terrible. If he finds out about you, he'll use you too."

"Geneva, he's my father. I know he can be extreme, but he would never truly hurt me."

"Kai, you're father isn't who you think he is. Have you ever heard of the Ravinori?"

"The elite secret society of Ravin worshipers? Yes, who hasn't, Geneva? But that's just a myth. Another crazy rumor that people spread around here about me and my family. I've already told you that I've heard much worse. I just didn't think you'd join in."

"It's not a rumor, Kai. All of the legends and fairytales you've heard are real."

Kai stared at me.

"I know it sounds crazy, but I believe your father is their leader and he's going to use my powers to further his cause."

"And do you have any proof?"

I racked my brain. Of course, I sounded crazy. I didn't have any hard evidence against Malakai. It was my word against his father's. Trying to tell Kai had been a mistake. It was useless. I shook my head in frustration.

"Geneva, I can't take what you're saying seriously. I really like you, but what you're saying sounds crazy. We're talking about my father. The man who raised me my entire life. I'm going to need a little something to go on if you expect me to believe you."

"I believed you when you showed me what you could do. I didn't question you or run away or tell anyone about it."

"I know," Kai said taking a deep breath. He ran his hands through his dark hair in frustration. "Okay, prove it," he said. "I want to believe you. Prove anything you told me is real. Show me one of your powers or something."

"I can't."

Kai shook his head and started to get up until I grabbed his hand and pulled him back down.

"Wait. Please, Kai. I know this sounds insane, but I promise you I've never been more truthful than I'm being right now. I can't use my powers here and I think it's because of the fence around this place. It's some sort of magic-preventing force field."

"Then why can I still do what I can?" he asked.

"Try to do it right now!" I said excitedly, wanting to test my theory.

"Geneva..."

"Just try it, please."

Sighing, he grabbed a music book off a nearby stand and said, "Pick a page number."

I stared at the book and smiled.

"65."

He closed his eyes and held his hands above the book in his lap. Nothing happened. He peeked them open and then tried again. Still nothing.

"I knew it," I whispered.

"I don't get it?" Kai said.

"I have a theory. The fence is a force field and no one can do magic inside its walls. But when I was with you in your room, we weren't in the Troian Center. We were in a new wing that your father had built for your residence. If he *is* the leader of the Ravinori, he'd need somewhere that he could still practice magic. The fence mustn't affect your residence. That's how he's been keeping tabs on me and how he's able to use the Orbiture. That thing is definitely some kind of dark magic."

Kai looked perplexed. He scratched his head in frustration.

"Geneva, there has to be some other explanation. I mean this sounds nuts. You know that, right? If my father was the leader of the Ravinori, don't you think I would know?"

"You're telling me you've never seen your father do anything suspicious? He's never said anything to you that sounded off? You never overheard anything that made you ask questions?"

"I mean... "

A wave of understanding crashed down on Kai as I saw his expression change from confusion to recognition. He sat in rigid stillness and closed his almond-shaped eyes. Thick, black lashes cast shadows onto the delicate skin just above his cheeks. When he opened his eyes, they glistened with tears.

"I can't believe how stupid I am," he whispered. "For years he's been telling me that he's grooming me to take over everything he's built. That I'll have the world at my feet. That once I turn seventeen all of my questions will be answered, and that I will understand everything he's done for me. This whole time I thought he was talking about the stupid Luxor militia and now the Troian Academy. I had no idea that it was something... something like this."

Kai was trembling, and I reached a hand up to wipe the tears streaking his warm cheeks. It broke him out of his thoughts and he quickly swiped at his wet face before fumbling in his pockets looking for something. I offered him the blood-stained handkerchief I still held onto and he smirked. He wiped his face with it. A flash of gold woven into the corner of the handkerchief caught my eye and I froze. The gold thread practically made the letters glow.

"Kai, what is this?" I asked apprehensively touching the monogram.

"It's my family crest."

My mind spiraled, racing away with more thoughts than I could gather. All the pieces of the puzzle I had been reaching for, trying to make my mind stretch around so they would fit together, all fell perfectly into place when I gazed at the emblem emblazoned on the white handkerchief in Kai's hand. I laughed. I'd been holding the proof of Malakai's involvement with the Ravinori for the past ten minutes and didn't even know it.

"Geneva, what is it? What's wrong?" Kai asked, spooked by my expression.

"Kai, I've seen this symbol before. It's not what you think it is," I said hesitantly.

"Of course it is," he said. "It's my family crest. My father even wears the ring."

"Kai, this is going to sound crazy, but this is exactly the proof I've been looking for. Can I keep this?"

"Sure, but what proof? You're freaking me out."

"I'm sorry, Kai. I know none of this makes any sense to you now, but I promise I'll explain it all later."

"Geneva... – " he started.

"Do you trust me?"

"Yes," he replied.

"Good. I'm going to need your help."

"Okay..." he said warily.

"My friends and I are in trouble and if anything happens to me I need you to help get them out of the Troian Academy, okay?"

"What's going to happen to you? What kind of trouble?"

"Kai, I swear I'll explain everything as soon as I can. But I need you to promise you'll help my friends if I have to go away for a while. Nova, Sparrow, Remi, Journey, Jemma and Sadie. If something goes wrong, they can't stay here. You have to help them escape."

"Escape? What are you talking about? What's going to go wrong?"

"Kai," I pleaded staring into his dark searching eyes. "They're like us and they mean everything to me."

"Okay. I promise I'll help them," he said. "But I don't understand. What kind of trouble are you in? Maybe I can help you."

"You already have, Kai. I know none of this makes much sense yet, but it's hard to explain."

"Can't you try?"

I took a deep breath. I didn't know how much more I could risk telling him, but the longing in his eyes pulled at my heart, prodding me to trust him.

"Have you ever had dreams that came true?"

I saw a flicker of recognition. "You mean like a premonition?"

"Yes," I nodded. "I have them a lot. And I've been having bad ones since I came back here."

"Is that why you left the first time?" Kai asked.

"Sort of. My friends and I were in danger and I think it's going to happen again. And this symbol," I said holding up the handkerchief, "I've seen it before. It belongs to a set of twin books. I have one and I believe someone extremely dangerous has the other."

"My father? That's why you don't trust him," Kai said.

I nodded.

"I've seen it other places, too." My mind snapped back to random images I recalled; the tattered leather cover of the *Book of Secrets*, all the times I'd seen it referenced on the pages of legends that Eja and I had scoured over in the forest, some of the *Stregga Carta* documents that Jaka had shared with us.

I wished I had Kai's photographic memory so I could remember exactly what I'd read in the passages with that symbol. But if I was right, this proved Malakai was the head of the Raviniori. It may say MV to Kai, meaning Malakai Vanir, but when I saw it upside down it spelled NW, as in New World, or *Novae terrae* in Latin. The Ravinori's mantra for total world domination. It represented the fire and brimstone the Ravinori would release upon the earth if they succeeded in bringing Ravin back.

"Have you ever seen this symbol anywhere else?" I asked Kai.

"Of course! It's all over everything I own. It's my family crest."

"Look at it like this." I flipped it upside down for him, but he shook his head. "Are you sure?"

"Geneva, of course I'm sure. I showed you what I can do. I would know if I'd seen it anywhere else."

BUZZ BUZZ BUZZ.

The alarm signaling lesson change rang though our quiet room making me jump.

"Kai, I have to go. Promise you won't mention this to anyone else. Especially your father. I'll tell you more as soon as I can. I still have a lot to figure out."

I got to my feet and was about to open the door of the practice room when he caught my hand.

"You can trust me, Geneva. I don't know what's going on, but I'm here for you, okay?" His brows furrowed with worry.

"Okay," I said squeezing his hand.

"Be careful," he said before letting me go.

"You too."

25

"She isn't the *Ponte deorum*, Kobel. You've seen the Orbiture results yourself. I'm not even convinced she's the Eva! Her cuff revealed nothing! Her orb was completely grey. I forced all of those visions upon her from what we already know, but still she gave me nothing. She has no powers!"

"Master, that's impossible. She's hiding them somehow. The *Book of Gods* does not lie. She's the one that will lead the attack against us. She will try to defeat the Ravinori. We watched her through my visions. She bares the correct tattoos and the secret mark. And she's found two of the Pillars already. We know the Asher boy is the fire Pillar. I say we use him as leverage to get her to cooperate and tell us where she's hiding the others. She's in love with him. She will reveal her true self to save him."

"The *Book of Gods* also said she will lead us to the Pillars. We don't need to interfere, Kobel. Besides, I've already threatened her. She will be back to surrender herself to save her friends. I could see it in her eyes."

"Are you sure, Master? What if she runs? If we lose her, we have nothing."

"Let her try. She won't get far wearing that cuff. I can track her every move. Look." Malakai tapped the stone tablet on his desk. The Orbiture flickered to life, displaying a map in the glowing ball.

"She's cowering in the music wing, sobbing her eyes out. She's in shock. Tomorrow she'll be in denial and then she will accept her fate and turn herself over to me."

"Yes, Master. That is a wise plan. But the others are anxious. They will not be pleased to hear these results. We were hoping to start the preparations for the Pillar ceremony at our next meeting."

"Correct me if I am wrong, Kobel, but I am the one in charge of the Ravinori! And from what I know, we can't bring Ravin back with only the fire Pillar and the blood of the Eva. And since you have failed to locate any of the other Pillars we will have to continue to wait until the Eva helps us locate them," Malakai bellowed.

Kobel cowered but didn't respond.

"Besides, I always have a back up plan. I learned a lot about the other Sommer's girl today. She may be easier to manipulate than her sister. She has a weak mind, easily swayed. She's jealous of the Eva. With the right coaxing I think she will come willingly to us. I have given her a test. We will soon see if she is destined for greatness along side us."

"But Master, Jemma is not the Eva," Kobel said.

"At the moment, it appears that she has more power than her sister. They share the same blood. If we have the four Pillars and the blood of Zophia's descendant we should have everything you need to do the ritual and bring Ravin back. Is that not what you told me?" Malakai thundered, turning on the old professor.

"Yes, you are correct, Master. Your plan is wise. I only wish to serve you, so I must think of every possibility so that you will have success."

"Then what am I missing?"

"Nothing, Master. I'm merely suggesting we act soon. The longer we let the Eva stay here, the more time she will have to act against us."

Malakai laughed. "Don't be a fool. She is completely outmatched. And we have Kai. My son has served us well. He has gotten close to her and she trusts him. He's with her now gathering information for us. He doesn't know that I can hear his thoughts. I know everything she confides in him."

"Well played, Master."

"I've isolated her at every turn. Soon she will be completely alone. I've made arrangements for her friends to be sold. I have a buyer for the slim one already. She will make a great servant once I have absorbed her powers."

"What of the others?" Kobel asked.

"I haven't decided yet. The boys might make good soldiers in my army. Wouldn't it be fitting to have the Eva watch her own friends destroy everything she was supposed to protect?" He smirked shrewdly.

"You are very wise indeed, Master."

I SAT at our normal table in the library, anxiously waiting for my friends to meet me for study hall. I had so much to tell them. The past few days had been a whirlwind. I'd learned so much and I'd felt my mission to rescue the Pillars go from bleak to probable and back again multiple times over. Now I teetered somewhere in the middle. I'd finally talked to Sadie and was sure she was the water Pillar. Giving her information about her sister seemed to make her trust me. I could tell I had sparked a memory when I mentioned being able to do things she couldn't explain, and she'd wanted to tell me something, but had been wary of who might be listening. I just needed a little more time with her and I was sure I could convince her to come with us when we fled the Troian Center.

I also knew Malakai was onto me now and he knew that Nova and Jovi were Pillars. But he didn't seem to know about Sadie yet or that I had finally found the proof I needed from his son to pin him as the leader of the Ravinori. All I needed to do now was get it to Jaka. I was sure the Betos could launch an attack against him with the right evidence. And that could be the distraction we needed to escape. We had three of the four Pillars and I had a suspicion that I now knew the name of the fourth one. The monogram that Kai believed to be his family crest, when flipped upside down actually meant *Novae terrae* and it was the Ravinori mantra, meaning new world. There was no way that Novae, meaning new, as in *'born anew from the ashes,'* was coincidentally also a version of Nova's name. I was counting on Terrae being the name of the fourth Pillar. It meant world in the Ravinori mantra, but world could also mean earth, as in the earth Pillar.

My heart was beating out of my chest with this realization. I scanned the room for my friends. Where were they? As I looked around, I studied the faces of the other students. I'd met most of them in the time we'd been here. None of them went by the name Terrae. Maybe Kai could get his hands on a list of names of everyone here at the Troian Academy to help us find anyone named Terrae. After our conversation in the music wing I was convinced I could trust him to help me.

Finally I saw Jemma stroll into the library. She made a beeline for my table, instead of stopping to talk to the girls she normally hung out with. I looked passed her but still didn't see Sparrow or any of my other friends.

"Can I talk to you for a minute?" she asked when she sat down.

"Um, okay," I said, shocked by her sudden interest to talk to me.

"I wanted to apologize for how I've been acting. I've been a terrible sister."

'You just realized this now,' was what I wanted to say, but I bit my lip and said, "Okay," instead.

"Malakai is a monster. You were right about him."

"Counseling didn't go well for you either?" I asked.

"No. He kept asking me all these weird questions, like where do my loyalties lie, and what did I know about our parents. It made me think, you really are all I have left. We're each other's only family and it's time I start doing a better job of acting like it."

I was stunned. I'd never expected a conversation with Malakai would have woken Jemma up. Nothing I ever said got through to her. But I guess fear was a good motivator.

"Here," Jemma said sliding next to me and reaching out her hand.

I watched her blood, red nails curl toward me. Sinful; that's what she called the color the other night when I'd watched her paint them in our bunkroom, while laughing carefree with the other girls. My own nails were bare, chewed down to the quick with nerves. I let Jemma open my palm and put something cool and metal into my hand. It was a tiny skeleton key on a thin gold chain.

It was actually quite beautiful for a key. The hilt had been shaped into an intricate pattern; a diamond, with four smaller diamonds on each corner. I didn't recognize it and was confused as to what it meant or why Jemma was giving it to me.

"WHAT IS IT?" I asked looking up from the necklace to her expectant eyes.

"It was mom's. I've had it for a long time and I want you to have it now." She beamed.

I hadn't seen her grin like that in a long time. Not since we were in the forest getting ready for my Eva ceremony. She looked so beautiful when she smiled. I was rarely graced with it.

I knew I should say thank you, but "Why?" was all I could muster.

"Well, talking about family so much today got me thinking. Do you know what today is?" she asked cheerfully.

I shook my head.

"Sorry, of course you don't. It's June 14th. It's your birthday, Geneva."

I couldn't believe my ears. "My birthday?" I said breathlessly.

"Yes," she said, beaming.

"How do you know that?"

"I pulled some strings. It's the least I could do," she replied leaning over to give me a hug.

It felt awkward to have her hug me. I sat stiffly against her embrace, letting my mind absorb what she'd just told me. I never imagined I would ever know my real birthday. I always celebrated it on January 1st, with all the other orphans. Birthdays weren't a part of my world at the Troian Center. I didn't know how to react. I was filled with a bittersweet feeling, thinking of all the birthdays I never got to celebrate with my family.

Jemma let go and took the necklace from my cupped palm with her painted fingers and fastened it around my neck.

"There," she said. "Keep it close to your heart; someday it will bring you home."

"What?" I whispered, still in shock to learn today was my birthday and have my sister show me so much kindness.

"It's what mom said when she gave it to me."

"But this is yours, Jemma. Mom gave it to you."

"Well, I have a lot of making up to do. Let's start with this, okay? I want it to be yours."

"Where has it been all this time" I asked. "I've never seen you wear it."

"I never risked wearing it before. You know we weren't allowed to have extravagant things like that when this was the Troian Center. I hid it here a long time ago and I was racking my brain for something I could give you for your birthday that would have great meaning and it just popped into my head."

"Where was it hidden, Jemma? Nothing about this place is the same," I said suspiciously. "And how do you remember what she said when she gave it to you?"

"LET'S just say things have been coming back to me since I veiled your powers," she said with a coy smirk. Suddenly Jemma stood and waved her hands. "Hey, babe," she called scurrying to the other side of the table as Nova moved in eyeing me apprehensively.

I shuddered back to reality. She was calling him *babe* now? My heart sank. He used to call me that.

"Hey," he said sitting down across from me. "What's going on?" he asked no doubt noticing the shock on my face from finding out today was my birthday and that my sister now called the boy I love *babe.*

Nova always said he could read my face like an open book. I wonder what he was reading now.

"Today's Eva's birthday!" Jemma said clapping her hands together in excitement. "Isn't that great?"

Nova stared at me hard, his green eyes soaking in my

confliction. I could see my pale reflection in them and I felt myself blush. His hands were folded on the table in front of him, only inches from my own. I hadn't been this close to him since Jemma veiled my powers. I could feel the heat his body gave off from across the table. Now that Malakai knew who I was and that Nova was a Pillar, did I have to keep my powers veiled? I flinched when he drummed his fingers against the wooden table. He almost looked angry, with his jaw set and his mouth in a firm line, not speaking, just staring at me like he was trying to tell me something that I couldn't understand. My heart felt like it was trying to claw its way out of my chest toward him, ready to betray all my efforts to keep my true feelings from him.

"Is that true?" he finally asked.

"I... I guess," I stammered trying to find my voice under his steady gaze.

"Happy birthday, then," he said still staring.

"We should celebrate," Jemma said breaking our trance.

She practically sat on top of him, forcing him to slide down the bench, farther away from me.

"What could we possibly be celebrating?" came Journey's deep voice. "You all must have had a much better *counseling* session than I did."

He and Remi finally showed up, and sat on either side of me. But still no Sparrow.

"Today is Geneva's birthday," Jemma said proudly.

"We'll have to celebrate later. I have a lot to tell you guys," I said and launched into my discoveries.

26

"So we have a fighting chance!" Journey said with enthusiasm when I finished.

"Don't get ahead of yourself," Nova said. "We've searched this whole place and haven't come across anyone named Terrae."

"I think Kai can help us with that."

"I don't like that you're involving him in this," Nova replied.

"He's helped me so far and he gave us what we need to pin Malakai," I argued.

"Yeah, by accident. I don't trust him," Nova said.

"Come off it, mate," Journey said rolling his eyes.

"Well, I do," I said firmly. "So you're just going to have to trust me."

Our stare down ended quickly when Nova shook his head and put his hands up in concession.

"Fine, I can take care of getting a message to the Beto's," he said.

"How?" I asked.

"You're just going to have to trust me," he replied sarcastically mimicking my voice.

I took a deep breath. “Fine. So what else did we learn from counseling?” I asked. “All of you made the Orbiture glow blue?”

They nodded.

“And you said yours didn’t?” Remi asked.

“No,” I said with a shudder. “It must be because my powers are veiled.”

I had already told them about my experience. It had been much different then theirs. Their cuffs had created blue orbs and Malakai told them what fields of study he recommended for them. Using the glowing orb to show them prestigious careers they might have. He assigned Nova, Journey and Remi to Cadet training, telling them they’d all make great Luxors. Then he asked them questions about their families and said he was sorry that he had been unable to locate any remaining relatives to place them with, but that he would continue to explore adoptive family options.

“What if he finds a family that wants to adopt us before we can get the last Pillar and find a way out of here?” Remi asked.

“He’s not sending me anywhere?” Journey said.

“Let’s not add more things to worry about,” Nova said. “We’ll cross that bridge if it comes to it.”

“Yeah and if the blue glow indicates we have powers, then Malakai’s probably going to want to keep us around since the Ravinori think collecting Truiet powers will help them bring Ravin back,” Journey added.

“If that’s true, we could start talking to the other students and find out who else got a blue reading. That would mean they’re Truiets too and we could potentially get them on our side,” I said.

“Yeah, but we can’t prove it without being able to use our powers. They’ll think we’re crazy and possibly report us to Malakai,” Remi said.

“Well, we should at least try to find out. We have to try to save as many Truiets as we can,” I argued.

Everyone nodded. We stood at the sound of the alarm and filed out of the library. As I strode through the door, Nova suddenly turned and blocked my path. I jumped to a halt, catching my breath at how close I'd come to colliding with him. He jerked his chin to the side, motioning to a row of bookcases and headed in that direction. I looked over my shoulder before following him there.

My heart was pounding. I was alone with Nova for the first time in months. Jemma wasn't around to stop me from telling him the truth. The words itched in my throat, *You're the talisman!*

"I need the handkerchief," he said when we were alone.

"Oh." I was relieved and disappointed all at once. "Here," I said pulling it from my pocket. I held it out gingerly, only touching the material at the very corner, careful I wouldn't brush his skin when I handed it to him.

He grabbed it, his eyes never leaving mine.

"Make sure you warn Jovi when you send the message," I said tensely, remembering the fiery image of Jovi and Nova the Orbiture had burnt into my mind.

"I will," he said staring at me.

"Okay," I replied.

Nova continued to hold my gaze. I hadn't realized it, but I must have been gradually backing away from him because I felt my back slide up against the bookcase behind me.

"Is there anything else?" I asked, breathlessly as he moved a step closer.

"You tell me," he asked.

I couldn't stand there another moment without breaking down and telling him everything. His deep green eyes bore into me like he was trying to solve a complex puzzle. His face, still as beautiful as ever, looked gaunt with tension and I knew I was the cause of much of it. I had to leave now. My defenses were crumbling today. I'd already spilled my guts to Kai and now I felt the truth bubbling up inside me, threatening to spill over into a waterfall of confessions.

"If that's all," I said turning to leave.

I took two steps before I felt my heart plummet. I don't know which sensation felt stronger, the feeling of Nova's flesh on mine or the fear that my powers were about to come rushing back to me and completely blow what was left of our cover.

"Nova! Don't!" I cried, but it was too late.

He had laced his strong fingers around my boney wrist and pulled me back into the protective cove of bookcases. I yanked my arm from him and fell to the ground, balling myself up in anticipation.

"I didn't want to believe it, but Jemma was right. You're actually afraid of me, aren't you?" he said, his voice shaking.

I opened my eyes one at a time and saw that everything was exactly as it was a moment ago. Everything except Nova's face. He knelt across from me looking wounded.

"Geneva, you have to know I would never hurt you," he groaned. "You have to know that."

I was stunned. Why hadn't my powers come back to me? I closed my eyes again trying to call on my hunter skills, but nothing happened. Jemma told me that Nova was the talisman and that I couldn't touch him without releasing my powers. Was it because we were within the fence of the Troian Academy? I was still contemplating why nothing happened, when Nova moved closer to me.

I flinched away from him reflexively.

"You're truly afraid of me?" he asked, pain cracking his voice.

"You're the one who should be afraid of me, Nova. I can hurt you, but I don't want to. Please, you have to stay away from me. I don't want to hurt you."

"Tippy, just tell me what's going on?" he begged.

My caged heart slammed against my ribs, cracking what

was left of the walls I had built up around it, walls meant to conceal my feelings for Nova in order to keep him safe.

"Nova, I – "

"Geneva?" called another voice.

Nova and I both turned our heads in surprise. We had been so wrapped up in ourselves that we hadn't noticed someone else come into the room. We both scrambled to our feet.

"Are you all right?" Kai asked.

"Yes, Kai. I'm fine," I said giving him a weak smile.

He moved closer to me, until he was between Nova and me. He looked nervously at Nova and then back at me. Side by side like this, I noticed that they were almost negative images of each other. Kai's black hair was long, while Nova's blond locks had been cropped short, but both boys had the same tall, wiry build. Nova, all golden and lightness. Kai, all shadows and dark. The boys stared at each other. The tension in the room was palpable.

"Is he bothering you?" Kai asked without taking his eyes off of Nova.

Nova's mouth moved from a thin line to an angry scowl. I could tell from the way his muscles coiled under his skin he was restraining himself from lunging at Kai. Truthfully, I was grateful for his interruption. Not that I was afraid of Nova, but rather of my own resolve. I could feel it crumbling and I knew if I had to withstand Nova's pained gaze much longer I would cave and tell him everything.

"No. We were just talking," I said staring past Kai to Nova. "Would you mind waiting for me in the hall while we finish?" I asked Kai.

He shot me a questioning glance, still unsure if he should leave me alone with Nova.

"Don't bother," Nova grumbled. "We don't have anything left to discuss."

Nova pushed past Kai, and I watched him march away from us, his shoulders rigid and square.

"Nova!" I called after him, not knowing what else I could say.

His step faltered but he didn't stop.

"Kai, I'll be right back," I said reassuringly, before running after Nova.

I caught up with him outside the library doors. I almost ran into him actually. I was expecting him to be halfway down the hall with his long strides, but he had stopped right outside the doors to lean against the wall. His forearms pressed high on the wall with his head leaning against them. He was breathing hard, like he was trying to catch his breath. Seeing him like this startled me.

"Nova?" I whispered.

He stiffened when he heard my voice and turned around abruptly. He looked so wounded that I thought he might cry and I felt my chest splintering apart under the barrage from my heart.

"What?" he asked, all the fight and anger gone from his voice now. His jaw was slack and his eyes were a stormy shade of green.

"Nova. I know this doesn't make any sense, but please trust me… I need you to stay away from me."

"If that's what you really want," he said quietly.

'It's not what I want! But because of my horrible sister it's what I need to do. I want to tell you everything! I want to leave this place and spend the rest of my days with you in the forest away from all of these problems. I love you, Nova!'

But I couldn't say any of those things. So instead I took a deep breath and lied with as much conviction as I could muster.

"That's what I want, Nova," I said.

He said nothing. He hadn't nodded or frowned, he'd just

held my gaze for a moment before turning silently away from me. After I watched him disappear down the hallway I leaned against the wall, where he had been. It still felt warm somehow, as if heated by the ghost of him. I clung to that feeling as I slid down the wall, wishing it were his body warming mine, rather than the memory of him. I buried my head between my knees, sucking in ragged breaths as I sobbed uncontrollably.

Why was this my life? Why did I have to lie to the people I loved in order to protect them? Was hurting Nova to protect him truly any better than telling him the truth and letting him have the opportunity to make up his own mind? Malakai already seemed to know Nova was a Pillar and if he found out he was the talisman for all my powers, I knew I would be putting him in even more danger. But if Malakai knew I was in love with him, he'd surely use that against me too. Either way Nova was doomed. I couldn't live with myself if something happened to him because of me. No, I couldn't be selfish. It was better to let him believe I didn't have feelings for him, rather than telling him how I truly felt so he'd risk his life doing something foolish to save me from my destiny. I prayed that I'd somehow be able to defeat Malakai and the Ravinori. Only then could I try to rebuild my relationship with Nova. I shuddered, knowing I still had a long road ahead of me. I could feel what Nova and I had slipping away as the lies piled up between us. My only hope was we would be strong enough to rebuild our love from the ashes left behind.

I shivered as a line Eja had read to me about the Ravinori from the *Book of Secrets* popped into my mind; '*They will scorch the earth with flame, burning out all that was good, only to start anew.*' I couldn't let that happen to us.

I don't know how long I sat there, but after a while Kai came out into the hall to look for me. He didn't say anything. He didn't touch me, he just sat near me as I tried to collect myself.

After a while I looked over at him and tried to smile.

"Are you all right?" he asked.

"No," I said, surprised by my own honestly.

Kai had a way of putting me at ease and making me want to open up to him. Maybe it was because he was so unassuming, or maybe Malakai had taught him to be that way. I wasn't sure, but I was too tired to guard my words with him anymore.

"But I will be," I added.

"I know I've asked you this before and I promise I won't ask again, but is there something going on between you and Nova?" Kai asked. "If there is, you can tell me. I don't want to get in the middle of it and make things harder for you, Geneva."

"There's nothing between us, Kai," I said sadly. "Not anymore."

He reached for my hands clasped around my knees.

"Okay. If you ever need to talk, you know I'm here for you, right?"

"Thanks, Kai."

"Come on," he said pulling me to my feet. "I need to show you something."

I followed Kai to the tiny practice room at the end of the music wing. It was dark and too still without the students filling the wing with music. I tried to shake the eerie feeling that crept up my spine as we strolled through the shadows. Kai started talking as soon as he shut the door.

"So. I went back to my father's study after we talked and I found that symbol."

"Your family crest?" I asked with surprise.

"Yes. I was trying to find proof that you were wrong," he said bashfully. "But I'm afraid I found something else."

"What do you mean?"

"I found a book in my father's private study that had this symbol on the cover." He slipped a small pale blue book from his leather shoulder bag.

It looked silver in the moonlight that filtered in from the

windows. I watched as he opened the cover, revealing a hand drawn copy of the symbol I had seen stitched into his handkerchief. The same symbol that adorned the cover of the *Book of Secrets.* The same symbol that was said to be on the cover of it's opposite. I shivered as gooseflesh flooded my skin. Had Kai found what I thought he had?

"You found a book with this symbol on it?" I asked in disbelief.

"I thought it must have been a book with my family's history in it..." He paused as if deciding how to continue. "But it wasn't. It was something... about you."

I shuddered as I gazed at the symbol drawn on the page of the open journal.

"I DIDN'T DARE to take the book out of his office. He'd know it was missing, but I copied down some of the passages I thought were important." He pushed the book toward me.

My eyes flitted across the pages, tracing the graceful letters with intrigue. They were drawn with such elegant penmanship that I doubted Kai could have written them. I'd seen him take notes in lessons before. He wrote like a boy with small blockish handwriting. This was large, looping and slanted, like the writing in the *Book of Secrets*.

"Kai, you wrote this?" I asked, my mind churning with doubt.

"I copied it from memory," he said sheepishly. "I see things exactly how they are. Photographic memory, remember?"

"Oh, yeah," I said pressing on, reading the words that I knew held my secrets.

Kai had found the legendary *Book of Gods*.

I flipped through the pages in disbelief. My tattoo was on one of them. Not just LVX, but the crescent shape I'd created with Lux's laurel leaves and the Beto's tribal bands. How could this symbol been in the *Book of Gods*? I had created it and I'd never seen it before the moment I painted it onto Eja's arm.

THE NEXT PAGE was filed with more looping words. '*The prophecy has begun; the bringer of light will blind those to the fear and doubt you have seeded in this land. A single nation will be united when your darkness is driven out by her light.*'

Another page had details about my Eva ceremony. '*The four Pillars, with which our very existence was founded, grow deeper still. Today they have been awakened, called to connect with their creator, offering power and obedience. Thee who controls the sacred four controls all.'*

There was even an excerpt that seemed to predict that I would return to the Troian Center to fight those who want to bring Ravin back. *'The light shall seek out the dark. It shall be drawn to it with sacred force, piercing the shadows until all are free from its shackles. Though he has fallen, he is not forgotten, he will rise again and he will not forget who served his side in his absence. Seek the bringer of light, for after light comes the darkness. The battle shall be great, only the truth shall prevail. Which is purest, the lightness or the darkness?'*

I was trembling when I put the book down. Malakai had known my every move. He knew I would come to him even before I had known it. Nothing I'd done or could have done would have protected me or my friends. Somehow, the *Book of Gods* could predict my destiny.

"Geneva? What does this mean?" Kai asked.

I looked at him as if seeing him clearly for the first time. His dark eyes reflected the moonlight back to me. I saw my own reflection floating in them and I realized that's how I felt; as if floating uncontrollably in orbit, unable to maintain my direction. Kai's expression begged for answers. He was kept in the dark by Malakai as much as I was. I knew how that hunger for truth felt. Now was my chance to tell him the truth. His eyes were open and he teetered on the brink of understanding. If I could get him to believe me, maybe he would help me stop his father.

I took a deep breath, deciding how much to tell Kai. It was risky. The only solace I had was that it seemed the ending to my story had yet to be written. The *Book of Gods* said the battle would be great, but not who would win it. Maybe with Kai on my side, we would have a slight advantage. It had never been clearer to me that I was alone; one girl, facing an army of Ravinori, bent on bringing back their leader, who would bring darkness to Hullabee Island. I needed all the help I could get.

"Kai, I'm going to tell you the truth. It's going to sound crazy, but you deserve to know. I'm tired of all the secrets and lies. It doesn't seem like they're doing any good, no matter how much I mean them to."

I FELT HOLLOW when I left the music wing. Telling Kai the truth about who I really was had left me feeling exhausted, yet lighter. I told him about the Legend of Lux and the Immortal War and my role as the Eva in all of it. I told him about Greeley and why we had to flee the Troian Center. I told him how we had been attacked in the forest and why we had come back. He didn't seem to question any of it until I got to what Hollis told us about his father being the leader of the Ravinori.

"I know you're telling me what you believe to be true, but he's my father," Kai said with torn loyalty.

I don't know what I expected. I don't know if I would have been able to believe it had the roles been reversed. I didn't have any real memories of my father. I only knew what I'd been told from a legend. But if I did, would I be able to disown what I believed about him so easily?

Kai had excused himself, saying it was getting late and I would get in trouble if I missed bed check. I begged him not to tell his father or anyone else about what I'd shared with him. He'd looked uncomfortable, but agreed. I had even been so bold as to ask him for a favor. I knew if anyone could help find a needle in a haystack, it was Kai. I asked him to use his gift to search his father's records for anyone at the Troian Academy by the name of Terrae. He hadn't made any promises, but said he would see what he could do.

As he turned to walk away, he paused and looked back at me. "Thank you for telling me," he said.

"You're welcome, Kai. I know it's a lot and I know you'll have more questions. I hope you'll come to me with them. I promise I'll do my best to answer."

"That's all I could ask," he replied with a sad smile.

I tried to shake the image of Kai's deflated face from my mind as I hurried down the dark hallways of the Troian Academy. I breathed a sigh of relief when I made it back to my room unnoticed.

By the time I arrived in the bunkroom, everyone was deep in their nightly rituals. All the girls were milling about, applying face cream, combing their hair and gossiping about who liked who. I pushed passed them just wanting to be alone, but then I saw Sparrow sitting on her bed already in her nightshirt. My mind snapped to attention. I had been on my way to find her after study hall before Nova, and then Kai, had distracted me.

"Hey," I said changing direction and moving toward her. "Why weren't you in study hall?" I asked as I approached.

When she looked up at me, her big amber eyes were watery. She'd been crying.

"Sparrow? What's wrong?"

"Everything," she sobbed.

27

"He can't do that!" I cried.

Sparrow had just finished telling me about her counseling meeting with Malakai. Her session seemed to have gone like the rest of our friends' had. Her cuff made the Orbiture glow blue, he questioned her about her family and academic interests, and said he was sad to report that he found she had no remaining family members. But then, he told her that he found an adoptive family for her and she would soon be sent to live with them.

"I won't let it happen!"

"I don't think I have a choice," she said. "He told me that my new family wants me to come live with them in Lux."

"When?"

"Soon," she said through a hiccup.

"Sparrow, how soon?"

"Two weeks," she whispered.

I threw my arms around her and let her shake against my chest.

"I won't let that happen, Sparrow. We'll figure something out. I promise."

"I know," Sparrow whispered. "It's just hard to accept, you know? I guess I always held out hope that somehow, my family was still alive. Still out there somewhere, missing me."

I squeezed her tighter, knowing that was the false hope we all clung to.

"I don't want to leave you, Geneva. You're my family now," she said breaking down into sobs again.

She continued to cry and shudder, while I panicked internally. I couldn't let Malakai send Sparrow away. I didn't know how to stop him yet, but I prayed I'd figure out a way to get us all out of here safely before I had to worry about that. I couldn't help thinking that sending Sparrow away was somehow a strike at me. A vision of her had been in the Orbiture when Malakai threatened to make me work with him. Perhaps this was his first move, proving to me that he was serious.

I sat quietly thinking on the bed with Sparrow until lights out. I had to scramble to get changed and into my bunk by bed check. Finally, the lights went out and all was still. I lay in my plush white blankets, staring up at the ceiling, cursing Malakai. I was fighting back tears of my own when I felt my bedframe lurch, suddenly. I sat upright and came face to face with a girl climbing onto my bunk. I had to stifle a scream when I recognized it was Sadie.

"What are you doing?" I whispered.

"I believe you. And I want to help you," she said. "But we need to talk."

"Okay." I sat up and swung my legs over the bed.

"Not here," she said holding her hand up to stop me from getting out of bed. "Too many people listening. Study hall tomorrow." Then she thrust something small and cool into the palm of my hand. "Here's what you asked for. Use it carefully."

And then she was gone, leaving me to roll the tiny vial of Verilium around in my palm. So much had happened tonight. It seemed with every step forward, I took two steps back. I stared at the bottle. The brown glass hid the green tinted liquid inside of it. Was this really a good idea? It seemed like a desperate move, but I couldn't let Malakai hurt my friends. I had to protect them by any means necessary. I uncapped the vial and squeezed the black rubber top, suctioning the liquid into the slender glass tube attached to it. I let it hover over my tongue for a fraction of a second, before letting two drops splash onto my tongue. It was bitter. I didn't think it was supposed to be bitter. I swallowed it anyway, quickly securing the cap back on and hiding it under my pillow.

I closed my eyes and waited for sleep to come, praying that I would find the answers I was searching for hidden somewhere in the darkest corners of my mind. My timeline was growing shorter. With Malakai using my friends, I needed answers more desperately than ever.

~

"MASTER, I AM TRULY SORRY," Kobel groveled. "Please forgive me. I didn't think anyone else would be able to find the *Book of Gods.*"

"Yes, it is most unfortunate that the Eva knows the book is here," Malakai replied calmly. "And this will most certainly be looked at as your error. You are in charge of the book's safe keeping, are you not?"

"Yes, Master. I am, but your son is getting too close. I think it may be time to send him back to Lux. For his own safety."

"Now how would that help us? I'm able to read Kai's thoughts and now that he is so close to the Eva, he's a source of valuable information. He's given us confirmation that she has the *Book of Secrets*. Who knows what else she will confide in him."

"But, Master – "

"Kobel, let me worry about my son and you the *Book of Gods.*"

"Yes, Master. I've moved it to a secure location. He will not find it again."

"Good," Malakai replied. "It does pose a question though. How is it possible that Kai was even able to use the book? I was under the impression it required a special *touch?*"

"It does, Master. I've been telling you for some time now that there is something special about your boy. Have you ever tested him?"

"Nonsense, Kobel! He is my son! I would know if he was gifted."

"Sometimes it is hardest to see what is right in front of us, Master."

"If Kai were to have powers it would mean that he had Truiet blood in his veins and then all we have done to prepare him will have been for nothing! Ravin needs a host when we bring him back. We cannot put his soul into my son's body if his blood had been defiled by those filthy Beto savages! The Ravinori law prohibits it."

"Shouldn't we find out, Master? Before it is too late? We still have time if we cannot use Kai. We have to wait until his seventeenth birthday. That gives us time to search for an alternate host. We should have a back up."

"You will not share your suspicions of my son and we will not need a back up! It's already been decided. Kai will host Ravin's soul and inherit the earth. This is not a role that we can give to just anyone. We can control my son. He can be manipulated to do our bidding. Look at what he's already done. He's working for us without even knowing it."

"I fear you were right to worry for him, Master. These are dangerous circumstances we are dealing with. What if something should happen to him?"

"Nothing had better happen to my son, Kobel or it will be you're head!"

KOBEL SHOOK his head in disgust as he recounted his conversation with Malakai. The Ravinori leader was a stubborn fool. He was being careless with the Eva and letting his son meddle too much in things he didn't understand. And despite everything Kobel had told him, he still didn't believe that the Eva was the *Ponte deorum.*

Kobel was glad that he had been clever enough to set his own plans in motion. He sat in his lab reviewing the clipboard that one of his trusted medics had given him. It brought him the news he had hoped for. It would only be a matter of time now. He just prayed his calculations were accurate, because even the slightest mistake would be fatal. He couldn't afford to be wrong when it came to the Eva.

28

I felt something poking me, pulling me from the dream world I floated in. I heard my name, but I didn't want to answer. I was warm and happy, laying in a meadow with Nova. Sparrow was there, too. She wore a beautiful dress and she sat with a kind eyed older woman who was brushing her hair. Three Luxors stood guard in the distance. Something was familiar about them. I begged my mind to focus on their faces and when they came into view, I recognized two of them; Remi and Journey. But who was the third boy? He was tall and muscular with dark skin. He had curly brown hair and hazel eyes that scanned the horizon. Suddenly he turned and looked at me. He opened his mouth to say something, but no words came out. I saw horses coming. A black one led the charge, with a dark haired boy on its back. It was Kai! The longer I looked at him, the more I realized something was wrong. He wasn't leading the charge, he was being chased. He too was trying to tell me something. I looked past him and saw two more dark haired figures on horseback. One was a girl with raven hair; the other was a towering man in a billowing black cape. They both wore angry expressions. My mind balked while Jemma and

Malakai rode toward me, mouths opened, screaming something I couldn't hear. I looked back at my friends and all of them said the same word in unison. This time I heard it loud and clear.

LIAR.

But who was the liar? Which one of them had betrayed me? Who was lying to me? Or was it me? Were they calling me the liar? I didn't know who to trust, but I felt the dream world slipping away in a dizzying spin.

"Help me get her up," Sparrow was saying when I opened my eyes.

"What's wrong with her?" Jemma asked when I stumbled out of bed.

I collapsed onto her bed below mine and tried rubbing the grogginess out of my eyes. My head pounded and my throat was so dry I could barely talk. It must have been the side effects of the Verilium. I had only taken two drops, they should have worn off by now. Had I miscalculated the dose? My mind was racing, trying to make sense over the pounding in my ears.

I opened my mouth to say something and a croaking sound came out.

"Stay with her, Jemma. I'll get her some water," Sparrow said.

Jemma sighed and sat on the bed with me. I flinched away from her when she pushed my damp hair away from my face. Her nails were a different color now, iridescent green, reminding me of some dangerous insect.

"Do you like it? It's called Envy. I could paint yours for you sometime, if you'd like."

My mind snapped back to the vision.

"You're a liar," I said hoarsely.

"What are you talking about?" she said staring at me.

"You know exactly what I'm talking about!" I spat. "But you know what? I don't care what you say anymore. I'm not going to stay away from Nova. I'm not going to let you lie to him and twist the truth and force him to be with you. I love him and you're not going to take something else away from me."

Jemma grabbed my arm right bellow the wound she'd given me and twisted. I winced in agony, but swallowed the scream in my throat.

"You'll do no such thing!" she hissed. "You can't go near him or – "

"Give it a rest, Jemma. I already touched him and nothing happened."

Shock and anger raced across her face.

"That's right," I said. "My powers didn't come back, which means it's safe for me to be near Nova. So either you lied and he's not the talisman or if he is you don't know how to make him give my powers back."

Her dark eyes squinted and her hand twitched for a moment, like she wanted to slap me, but she regained her composure.

"You're right, okay? I don't know how you'll get them back. I've never done this before. Maybe it's the fence or maybe I screwed up. But don't tell Nova yet. It won't do either of us any good. He'll just be mad at us both. And even if he finds out the truth, he won't want to give your powers back to you."

I looked at her, half-shocked she was admitting I was right and half-skeptical of what she was up to.

"Think about it," she said. "If he gave you your powers back, Malakai would be able to identify you. The only thing keeping you safe is that he thinks you have no powers. Nova would never risk giving them back if it would endanger you. Don't burden him with that. Give me a chance to fix it."

"How?"

"I don't know yet. But give me some time to figure it out."

Her round eyes pleaded and I let my shoulders slump in defeat, because I knew she was right. Nova would only be mad at me for lying to him this whole time and would never agree to put me in danger by giving my powers back while Malakai was monitoring us.

"Fine," I said bitterly.

"Eva, I'm sorry. I know you like him. I shouldn't have tried to get in your way. I won't do it anymore. I meant what I said. I want to start being a better sister. I care about Nova too and I don't want to see him get hurt. Don't tell him about the talisman. It'll only make him hate us both for putting him in that position."

I recognized the genuine concern on her face. She truly did care about Nova.

"I won't tell him. But you have to stop lying to him. He thinks I'm afraid of him because I believe he's like Kull and it's killing him. You have to let me talk to him. I can be his friend without telling him about the talisman."

"Okay," she nodded meekly as Sparrow came over with a glass of water.

"Come on. We're going to be late for breakfast."

IT HAD BEEN a struggle to make it to the dining hall. The effects of the Verilium were still weighing on me. I kept getting dizzy spells. I had no appetite at breakfast. I pushed my food around my plate while I tried to tell everyone the newest developments with Kai last night. I left out the fact that I'd taken Verilium and the strange visions I'd had since I still wasn't sure what they meant.

"Wow, bold move trusting him," Journey said through a mouthful of toast and eggs.

"I can't believe you!" Nova growled. "You had no right to tell Kai!"

"I was doing what I thought was right," I said putting my

hands to my throbbing temples. "I don't have all the answers, but I think he'll help us, Nova. If we can get him to show us where the *Book of Gods* is we will have everything we need. In the meantime I asked him to search for anyone here at the Troian Academy named Terrae. If we can find the last Pillar, we can get out of here."

"Are you okay?" Remi asked.

"I'm fine," I said through gritted teeth, but I wasn't. My vision was tunneling and I kept seeing dark spots dancing before me. I could feel beads of sweat rolling down my neck and my stomach was cramping.

"You really don't look too good," Sparrow said. "Your arm is bleeding through your bandage again. Maybe I should take you to the infirmary."

"No, I'm fine and we still need to figure out how to stop your adoption."

"What's she taking about," Journey said, letting his fork drop.

The clanging of Journey's fork off his tray was the last thing I heard. The room went white and I felt myself falling, drifting into the abyss of my mind again.

Blackness.

29

I awoke on a cold exam table. But something was strange, it was moving. I could see the lights above me flashing by, fading to darkness in the sections between them. When I tried to sit up I felt a stabbing pain in my arm. I looked down at my bandage in bewilderment. My eyes widened when I saw the once white dressing was now stained crimson. The center was such a deep color of red that it almost looked black. It was wet and spongy and gave me a bad taste in my mouth, which I commanded myself to swallow. Now was not the time to get queasy.

You'd think I'd seen enough blood in the last year to make me immune to my squeamishness, yet, the mere thought of it still made me light-headed.

I focused on the woman in the white coat who pushed me down the narrow white hallway. I opened my mouth to ask her where I was, but no sound came out. We passed through a set of double doors. It was dimly lit here, unlike the previous parts of the infirmary I'd visited. The grey shadows made it feel like the walls were closing in on me and the throbbing behind my ears didn't help any. It was adding to the blurry tunnel vision I was experiencing.

The woman in the white coated stopped.

"You wait right here," she said sternly before leaving me alone in the wavering hallway.

Odd, why would she leave me in the hall? I thought she was taking me to another exam room or perhaps a surgery room from the looks of my arm. How had it gotten so bad so fast? I sat up on the gurney and turned to look behind me, only to realize I was lost in the labyrinth of long white walls and doors. Nothing looked familiar.

A cloud of confusion confounded my mind, while hushed voices reached my ears. I swung my legs over the side of the gurney and slowly steadied myself to my feet. I approached the door the woman had gone through. To my surprise the door wasn't white like everything else in the infirmary seemed to be. It was a dull, lusterless black and seemed like some kind of magnetic dark abyss. My mind bowed when I looked directly into its sinister complexion, like it was going to suck my soul right out of me. But still I was drawn toward it, pushing myself closer until I could almost make out the muffled voices coming from within.

"You brought her here?"

"Yes, Sir. I didn't know what else to do with her."

"You shouldn't have! This type of risk is unacceptable."

"But, Sir, it's working. You must see her arm. It's what you were hoping for, Professor Kobel."

"Are you certain?"

"Yes, Sir."

"Ah, Malakai will be very pleased indeed."

Professor Kobel? Malakai? I backed away from the door and the disturbing conversation. A bubble of bile leapt into my throat, burning the back of my mouth. What was wrong with me? And what was Kobel hoping for? Why were he and

Malakai interested in my injured arm? I looked down to examine it again and gasped in horror.

"Help," was all I managed to get out before I lost the battle with my mind and slipped into unconsciousness again.

Blackness.

THE RUMORS WERE RUNNING wild by the time study hall rolled around. Remi, Sparrow, Journey, Jemma and Nova huddled around a heavy wooden table in the library trying to pick up bits and pieces of the hearsay for any clues about Geneva.

"I heard that her bandage was completely saturated and there was a trail of blood down the hallway."

"I heard that she was covered with blood because she lost her arm completely!"

"She's been spending a lot of time with the headmaster's creepy son. I bet he did something to her!"

"Serves her right for what she did to Ruby."

"This is ridiculous!" Remi said, fed up with the outrageous rumors that surged through the library like a storm.

"Shut up," Nova growled. "I'm trying to listen."

"I'm really starting to worry about Geneva," Sparrow whispered. "And where the heck is Kai? We need to get to the bottom of what happened."

Kai had been the last person they'd seen with Geneva. He'd shown up in the dining hall as the Luxors were carrying Geneva to the infirmary after she passed out. Nova, Sparrow and Remi had tried to follow Geneva's limp body as it was carted from the dining hall, but the Luxors stationed at the door stopped them. When Kai spotted them among the chaos of students he ran over and shoved a piece of paper into Sparrow's hand and said, "I'll find you in study hall," before racing out the door after Geneva. That was the last they had seen of them both.

"Oh we're going to get to the bottom of it, all right," Journey grumbled cracking his knuckles angrily.

Nova sat stoically, listening to the idle chatter as the other students speculated what might have happened to Geneva. He looked like a kettle about to whistle: collected on the surface, but boiling beneath.

"Tell me what they said again?" Remi asked the Sparrow.

"A woman from the infirmary came into our room and asked where Geneva's things were. I pointed to her bed and asked what was wrong and she just said that there had been an accident and then she took everything. Her bedding, her shoulder bag, her clothes, everything," Sparrow replied.

"That's it? No other explanations? You didn't ask where she was?" Remi pushed.

"I tried to find out more but they ignored me and rushed out of our room."

"What about the note that Kai gave you?"

"All it says is Private First Class, Clay," Sparrow said reading the paper she had folded in her lap.

"I don't get who or what that is?" Jemma said joining the conversation.

"Shhh...." Nova hissed, straining to hear the gossip happening a few tables away. "I'm trying to listen. I think they have some actual information," he said jutting his chin to the right. His friends turned their attention to a group a girls chatting a few tables away.

"You're being dramatic. Sadie said she just slipped on some blood and that's why it was smeared all over her uniform," a bossy brunette was saying to the blathering blonde who sat cross-armed next to her.

In a flash Nova was upon the table of gossiping girls, causing them to gasp.

"Who told you that?" Nova accosted the brunette who had been talking.

He was so close he could see the girl's frightened eyes dilating.

"My bunkmate," she whispered with wide eyes.

"Her name, what's your bunkmate's name?"

"Sadie," breathed the girl, falling into a dreamy trance.

"WHAT DOES he think he's doing?" Jemma hissed.

Remi rolled his eyes. "He's using his charm. And probably drawing too much attention to himself, as usual." Remi stood up with a sigh and started toward Nova, but Sparrow pulled him back.

"I know you don't like him very much, Remi, but we're all on the same team, and like it or not he always has Geneva's best interests at heart. I know you don't like his methods, but look, he knows what he's doing."

Remi was startled by Sparrow's forceful tone and hold on his arm, but he followed her gaze to where Nova was crouched at the tableful of girls. The one he was questioning pointed over to the bookshelves, where a slight girl, with an auburn pixie haircut gracefully leafed through rows of books. It was Sadie.

In a few quick strides Nova was at the bookshelves extending his hand, while the table of girls he had left giggled and swooned.

Remi watched as Nova unapologetically interrupted Sadie and introduced himself.

"I'm Nova," Remi said, adding his own sarcastic commentary for amusement. "Aren't I so handsome and charming? Look into my dreamy eyes."

"Stop it," Sparrow warned, lightly elbowing Remi in the ribs. "I'm trying to hear what they're *actually* saying."

Remi noticed Sadie didn't seem mesmerized by Nova's startling good looks, like every other girl he talked to, and that made him like her even more. Perhaps it was because Sadie was very beautiful herself. She had pale skin and bright blue eyes that sparkled across the room. She reminded Remi of a porcelain doll. He watched her subtle graceful movements, admiring how each of her motions seemed more fluid than they should be somehow.

Remi was still staring at Sadie when Sparrow sighed in resignation. "If you're going to stand here and stare like that, we might as well just go over and talk to her."

"I'm not staring," Remi said, following Sparrow, who was already making her way over to Nova and Sadie.

"Whatever," Sparrow grumbled.

SADIE LOOKED on suspiciously as a couple approached her and Nova.

"So this is Sadie?" the girl asked Nova when they reached them.

He nodded, looking perplexed.

"Great, I'm Sparrow and this is Remi. We need your help, so let's get on with it."

Both Nova and Remi looked at Sparrow, startled by her directness.

"To the point." Sadie grinned. "I like it. I've met Remi already, but it's nice to officially meet you. Geneva's told me so much about you all."

"We don't really have time for pleasantries, I'm afraid. Something has happened to Geneva and I think you may be the only one able to help us get to the bottom of it."

"I was getting to that when you strolled up," Nova said with frustration.

"Yes, he said you were worried about Geneva and coincidentally I've been looking for her myself."

"You have?" Remi asked.

"Yes, we were having a discussion we didn't get to finish and there's something I need to talk to her about."

"We know all about that," Sparrow said.

"You do?" Sadie asked, her delicate eyebrows raised. She looked nervously at the group, uncertain if she could trust them. Geneva had told her that they were her friends and that they were *special,* like she was. But she wasn't sure how they would react if they found out she'd given their friend a poisonous potion that may have sent her to the infirmary.

"I knew it wasn't a good idea," Sadie muttered.

"What wasn't a good idea?" Nova pressed.

"I told her to be careful and she promised she knew what she was doing," Sadie sighed chewing her bottom lip.

"Sadie, what are you talking about?" Sparrow asked gently.

"The Verilium Geneva asked me to get her from the infirmary. She said she wanted to use it to enhance her visions. She thought it would give her answers, but I'm not sure to what. I thought that's what you were talking about," she said apprehensively.

"What's Verilium?" Remi asked.

"Honestly! Do none of you follow along with our lesson work? We just learned about it in medicinal horticulture. That explains why Geneva has been pouring over her book day and night. I knew she was up to something," Sparrow said.

"Anyway..." Nova drawled. "For those of us who don't spend our free time memorizing texts books, would you care to explain what the heck Verilium is?"

"It's an anesthetic, and a hallucinogen," Sadie said. "But it can be lethal in the wrong dosage."

Nova's eye widened and the color drained from his face. He looked like he might pass out.

"Sit down," Sadie said pulling him to the nearby table.

"Listen, I know you're worried about your friend. I'm so sorry. I shouldn't have given her the Verilium. I knew it was risky, but she swore she knew what she was doing. Please don't report me," Sadie pleaded.

"We're not going to report you. We're in this together. Geneva said you're one of us and we protect each other. But we're going to need your help to find out what happened to her," Sparrow said.

"Okay," Sadie swallowed. "I'm so sorry. I'll do whatever I can to help."

"When was the last time you saw Geneva?" Nova asked.

"Last night, when I gave her the Verilium after lights out."

"Your bunkmate said you were talking about her," he pressed.

"Who? Nina? I was trying to stop her incessant gossiping. I was only repeating what I'd heard the other medics saying. I wasn't there when Geneva got checked in this morning."

"So she's still there?" Sparrow asked.

"That's the weird part. When I heard the medics talking about her I panicked, thinking I'd poisoned her. I checked every room to see if she was okay, but I couldn't find her."

"What were the medics saying?" Sparrow asked.

"I heard some of the other medics say she lost a lot of blood. The orderlies were still mopping the hallways when I got back there for my shift."

"What about your bunkmate saying you were covered in her blood?"

"That's just Nina being a gossip. I come back covered in blood and gross stuff all the time," Sadie dismissed.

"Sadie, how come you have to work in the infirmary?" Remi asked.

She averted her eyes momentarily and her cheeks flushed with shame.

"Oh, um, I'm sorry. I didn't mean to pry. You don't have to explain," Remi stammered, instantly feeling bad that he had obviously embarrassed Sadie.

"No, it's okay. I just don't get asked much about myself I guess, but I want to tell you. You're friends of Geneva's and she was a friend to my sister," Sadie said. "I work at the infirmary to pay my room and board here. I'm not from Lux like the other students, but I'm not an orphan either. My sister, Mala, is my guardian. She used to work here, but she's unable to pay for me right now, so the headmaster agreed to let me attend as long as I work to help pay my way."

"You look so much like her," Remi said absently.

"Did you know my sister too?"

"Yes. She used to let us ride the horses after we finished our chores in the stables. That was Geneva's favorite summer," Remi smiled wistfully.

"Listen, Geneva's been really nice to me. I want to help you however I can, but I have to be honest. Some of the things she's told me sound a little crazy and I don't want to get wrapped up in any sort of trouble. I try to keep my head down so I can stay here, ya know?"

"I understand, Sadie. We don't want to get you in any trouble. But can we ask you for one small favor? Can you find out if she's still in the infirmary?" Sparrow asked.

"And can you get us in to see her?" Nova added.

"I can check the log book tonight to try to figure out where she is and what her prognosis is," Sadie said hesitantly. "But I'm sorry, there's no way I can get you in to see her. I'm just an aid to the medics. I restock supplies and file charts, that sort of thing."

"But – " Nova started to argue, but Sparrow cut him off.

"Thank you, Sadie. We really appreciate your help. Can you come find me as soon as you know anything?"

"Sure," Sadie said looking concerned.

"What the heck was that?" Nova argued, pulling his arm from Sparrow's hold when they were almost back to Jemma and Journey at the table. They were out of earshot of Sadie now, who was still watching them cautiously.

"You're about as subtle as a tarcat, Nova. You were being too aggressive. Can't you see you were freaking her out? She's a Pillar. We need her to trust us and work with us. She agreed to help us so let's leave it at that and see what she finds out."

"I just have a bad feeling that Geneva is in trouble," interjected Remi, sounding like he was finally buying into the wild gossip. "Nova was only trying to find out a way to help her."

"So am I!" Sparrow snapped.

"What happened?" Journey asked as they sat back down.

"What's he doing here?" Nova shouted at Kai, who had since joined the table with Journey and Jemma.

"Our friend Kai here came by to ask if Geneva's all right. It seems he hasn't seen her either," Journey said dramatically raising his eyebrows.

"You don't know where she is?" Nova demanded.

"No, it's like Journey said, I'm concerned for her as well. I haven't seen her since I left her at the infirmary this morning."

Nova closed the gap between him and Kai in two brisk strides and grabbed him by his shirt.

"If I find out you had anything to do with this and I mean anything," Nova whispered into his ear, "I'll kill you myself. I don't care who your father is."

"I think you better leave, Kai," Journey said stepping between them. "We'll let you know if we hear from her and you do the same."

Kai smoothed his rumpled uniform trying to regain his composure and nodded to Journey before leaving the library.

"Well that went well," Journey said. "You should probably go easy on him, mate, being that he knows our secrets and all.

Anyway, can anyone elaborate on what happened over there while we were babysitting Kai?"

"We spoke to Sadie and asked her to help us find out if Geneva is still in the infirmary," replied Remi.

"That's it?" Journey asked eyebrows raised. "You were over there for a while."

"Well, that's all Sparrow would let me ask her before she dragged us away," Nova retorted.

"You were being too pushy about wanting to get into the infirmary to see Geneva," Sparrow replied. "She did say that Geneva took something called Verilium to help her with her visions and that may be what made her so sick."

"What did Kai say? Did you ask him about the note?" Remi asked.

"Yeah. He said Geneva asked him to look for anyone named Terrae. He found someone named Terran Clay, and said it was the only name that came close."

"Terran Clay? Oh my gods! Do you know what that means? Kai found the last Pillar!" Sparrow practically shrieked. "Does he know who he is?" she asked, her eyes excitedly darting around the room.

"You won't find him here," Journey said. "Private First Class, Terran Clay is a Luxor."

"What?" Sparrow and Remi said in unison.

"That can't be right," Nova argued. "The Pillars are all supposed to be orphans."

"Well, we're all in Cadet training. If we graduated, we'd be Luxors," Remi pointed out.

"What if Kai's lying?" Nova asked.

"We don't have any other leads," Sparrow argued. "And besides, Geneva trusts him."

"Well, I don't."

"Nova, come on! We may actually know who all the Pillars are! This is good news," Sparrow said.

“Yeah, great news,” Nova said. “This keeps getting easier. Now all we have to do is convince a thick-headed Luxor that he’s part of a magic legend, grab that little Sadie chick, find Geneva, and then bust our way out of here. Should be a cake walk.”

“How do we even know we can trust Sadie?” Jemma asked. “What if she’s not someone we should be asking for help?”

“Geneva thinks we should trust her,” Remi said. “And I agree with her. I knew her sister. Mala’s a good person.”

“Of course, you do!” Jemma spat.

“I can feel it, she’s one of us,” Nova said, ignoring Jemma’s interjections.

“How can you feel it? We don’t even have any powers in here,” Sparrow argued.

“I can’t explain it, but when I shook her hand I felt it,” Nova said. “You wouldn’t understand,” he muttered.

“That’s what Geneva said,” Sparrow sighed, throwing up her hands in frustration.

“Enough arguing about my needy sister!” Jemma whined. “Let’s just drop it. Besides, for all we know Geneva could be back in our bunkroom already.”

30

"What have you done, Kobel?" Malakai bellowed. "You have directly disobeyed my orders! I told you before this is too risky. We need her alive!"

"Master, you must come see for yourself. It is too late to undo the spell, but I know you will feel differently once you see how well it is working."

Malakai paced back and forth, barely containing his anger. The contents of his desk lay littered about the floor from his sudden burst of rage when he realized what Kobel had done. The old fool had taken matters into his own hands to prove his insane theory that the Eva was the fabled *Ponte deorum;* the Bridge of the Gods. Could it be true? Could the Bridge of the Gods be here in this very building? According to Kobel it was true. He had dosed her with a potion that would activate a spell to access her powers and suspend her life cycle. Once the spell was complete, she would be frozen and at their complete mercy; ready to be used as a single weapon to bring Ravin back when the time was right.

If Kobel was correct, the Ravinori would be ecstatic.

Malakai allowed a small sneer to spread across his lips, knowing he would be celebrated as the most successful ruler of all time if he could bring this to fruition. But if he was wrong, they would both hang for potentially endangering the Eva. She was imperative to the ceremony that would bring Ravin back.

"How did you even get her to take the potion?" Malakai asked.

"Simple, really. The Sanguin de Salvator is a coupled spell; it required two separate steps. First, the subject must take a small sample of Black Cohosh, which is completely harmless on its own in the correct dosage. I slipped it into her pain medication after I gave her the antidote for the Monkshood oil that she sustained during her quarterstaff injury. My idea was to have this plan in place as a last resort. But – "

"But you decided to go ahead and act on it anyway," Malakai grumbled.

"Well, yes. But look how well it turned out."

"Finish telling me how this all works, Kobel."

"Yes. The second step is delivering the Kenna potion, which is quite complicated to make. It activates the Sanguin de Salvator spell, rendering the subject in a dreamlike state. I wasn't sure how I was going to execute that, but when my staff alerted me that a particular aid that the Eva has gotten close to was asking about how to make Verilium, I knew that was the perfect delivery method. It was too good to pass up. I used a trusted friend to deliver it and the Eva administered it to herself," Kobel boasted proudly. "It was the perfect plan. With both drugs in her system, it was only a matter of time before she fell under its spell."

"Which aid?"

"Miss Calder. She and the Eva have grown close and I suspect that she may be a Pillar."

"Do you have proof of that?"

"No, but we don't need the Pillars now."

"Kobel, I employ you for your expertise in these dark arts. I do not share your experience in such potions and spells. I don't understand how the effects of these drugs prove you've found the *Ponte deorum.* To me, it merely sounds like you've given poison to someone extremely important to our cause."

"That's why you need to come see her for yourself. Then you'll understand."

"How?"

"The Sanguin de Salvator spell is a blood curse. If applied to the *Ponte deorum* it will form this symbol over their heart permanently activating their powers."

KOBEL LIMPED over offering a page for Malakai to look at. His eyes widened as he focused on the intertwining shape that Kobel pointed to in the *Book of Gods.*

"It's the mark she had hidden on her scalp. The one we were looking for when you suggested we shave their heads."

Kobel smiled. "Yes, the very mark that identified her as the Eva when your knife was applied."

"I still don't understand the power the knife holds," Malakai said.

"It's an ancient relic. It has many powers yet to be revealed. I've told you before - "

"Yes, yes. It's priceless and important," Malakai said impatiently. "Enough of all this talking. Bring me to see the Eva," he demanded.

I KEPT GOING in and out of consciousness. It felt like my mind was clouded with a thick veil of fog. I could hear muffled voices and the sounds of shoes squeaking. Shadowy figures loomed above me. I could feel them touching me, but it was as if I was asleep, unable to interact with them or truly comprehend what was happening.

A dark shadow parted the sea of white and the noise stopped. It came closer to me and the scent of sharp cologne cut the air. *Malakai! Malakai*, my mind shouted, recoiling instinctively. I wanted to get up and run away from him but my body wouldn't respond.

Something tickled my cheek. It must've been his hair and I cringed inside but still I couldn't move. I was panicking but my body wouldn't respond. It was as if it had detached from my mind and drifted into a peaceful sleep. It reminded me of when I'd first seen my mother in the forest; like I was floating above myself watching my life unfold rather than living it. I tried hard to focus on the voices I heard.

"Good work Kobel. I'm sorry I doubted you, old friend."

"I live to serve you, Master."

"So what do we do next?" Malakai asked the withered old professor.

"We wait. Her reaction to the potion proves that she's the *Ponte deorum*. Once the symbol is complete it will have dissolved whatever magic is veiling her powers and she will be ready to test."

"Keep me apprised," Malakai said. "And Kobel, no more unnecessary risks. This one seems to have worked in our favor, but I am the one in charge here. Understood?"

"Yes, Master."

"Call a meeting. It's time the Ravinori celebrate the first step in our victory!"

A sinister smile spread across Malakai's shadowy lips as he tilted his head back in thunderous laughter. Kobel, bowed and Malakai stalked away, trailed by the sound of his billowing black robe. The dark shadows were blotted out by white ones again and hands groped me. I was moving, floating. But, was I? I couldn't follow the blurring visions and I succumbed to them again, seeking comfort in the soft quiet darkness that my mind was craving.

Blackness.

SADIE WAS SITTING on the end of Sparrow's bed, filling her and Jemma in on what she'd seen during her latest shift at the infirmary. It had already been two days since they'd last seen Geneva and everyone except Jemma was on edge.

"Okay, so this is weird. I went to the infirmary just now and Geneva is nowhere to be found, but the strange part is she's still listed on the patient log," Sadie quickly whispered.

"So, they forgot to check her out," Jemma shrugged, unconcerned.

"Could that happen?" Sparrow asked Sadie.

"No way. They're particularly strict about the paperwork there. They log everything and everyone we bring in and out of that place."

"Great, now what do we do?" Sparrow whined, dreading what the boys would do when she told them the latest news.

Two days of failed attempts to contact the last Pillar had

only added to their restlessness. That, coupled with Geneva's unknown whereabouts was tearing their group apart. Remi and Nova were practically at each other's throats and Journey was frantic about Sparrow's impending adoption, which left him short on patience when breaking up their fights. And it didn't help any that Kai stubbornly ignored suggestions to give everyone space. Nova had already been hauled away twice by the Luxors for attacking Kai. The first time was because Kai tried sitting with them in the dining hall and Nova punched him in the jaw. The next day, Kai caught up with them in the hall outside of the library and Nova put him in a headlock, but Kai didn't back down. He swept Nova's feet out from under him and pinned him to the ground. "I care about her too!" He'd screeched through Nova's chokehold. That had resulted in both of them being sent to the Locker to cool off.

"There's nothing to do," Jemma said as she continued to apply glossy coats of polish to her gleaming nails. "She's the freaking Eva for heaven's sake. I'm sure she can take care of herself. Maybe she finally gave up on this crazy plan and ditched us."

"Jemma!" Sparrow hissed in an angry whisper as she looked around the busy bunkroom.

Girls were milling about in little cliques; studying, gossiping and primping for bed. None of them were paying any attention to Sparrow, Jemma and Sadie. It seemed all the drama surrounding Geneva's disappearance had reinstated their outcast status. For the most part it served them well, because no one gave them a second look, which was helpful while they were scheming. Jemma, however, was not adjusting well to being a social pariah again since she had worked so hard to get back in the graces of the popular girls. She had been on her way to regaining her status among the girls who ruled the halls of the Troian Academy before Geneva's disappearance.

"What is she talking about?" Sadie asked. "What's an Eva?"

"Nothing," Sparrow said trying to change the subject. "You need to go back and look again, okay?"

"No, not until you tell me what's really going on here. Geneva trusted me. She already told me she thinks I'm a Pillar and I know you guys are involved somehow. Stop being so mysterious and tell me the truth already! I'm the one risking everything. It's not easy to sneak around the infirmary, you know? They have that place on lockdown. I can't just wander from room to room without reason. I have to come up with all these explanations to restock and clean things. I'm running out of excuses and I don't want anyone to suspect I'm up to something. That will put us all at risk. I need you to tell me what's going on for real so I know what I'm up against here."

Sparrow bit her lip, struggling with whether or not to trust the blue-eyed girl. So far Sadie had proven trustworthy. Still, she wasn't completely convinced Sadie was a Truiet, let alone one of the Pillars. She knew Geneva believed it, and now so did Nova, but neither had been able to give any solid proof other than a gut feeling. It seemed too risky to expose all their secrets to Sadie so soon.

But then again, time was running out. Soon she would be shipped off to her new adoptive family. Then who would be here to look for Geneva and make sure the boys didn't kill each other?

Sparrow wrestled with herself while staring at Sadie's unwavering blue eyes. She hadn't heard any new speculations about Geneva and none of the Luxors or professors seemed any wiser to their quest to find her. The rumor mill surrounding Geneva had died down. The running consensus seemed to be that Geneva had to have surgery on her injured arm and was recovering in the infirmary. Sadie herself had been essential in spreading that line of gossip. Of course, Sparrow knew that was a lie, but she appreciated the helpful cover.

Right as Sparrow started to speak, Jemma cut her off. "Oh will you stop dragging this out already? Give it up, Sparrow." Jemma rolled her eyes. "Sadie, it's a long story, you better get comfortable."

31

"Wow," was all Sadie could muster when Jemma finished telling her the unbelievable tale of her and Geneva's legend and filling her in on all the crazy adventures they'd been on since discovering their powers; stealing the *Book of Secrets,* escaping the Troian Center and surviving in the rainforest with the Betos. And now, the mission to return and recover the four Pillars before the Ravinori did.

"So you think I'm part of this?" Sadie whispered sounding spooked.

The three girls were huddled on Sparrow's bottom bunk whispering well after lights out. Luckily, Sparrow's top bunk-mate, Ella, was a heavy sleeper. The soothing rhythm of her snores helped drown out their whispers.

"I'm sorry, you guys, this is a lot to comprehend," Sadie said.

"I told you she wouldn't believe us," Sparrow scolded Jemma.

"I didn't say I didn't believe you. A lot of it makes more sense than you know, but I still have a lot of questions."

"Sadie, I'm sure you do. I still have a million questions myself, but now you can see why we are so desperate to find

Geneva. She could be in danger if the Ravinori are looking for her too. They could have found her already! We need you to go back and keep looking. Isn't there anywhere else she could be? Think," Sparrow pleaded.

"I swear I've checked everywhere. Exam rooms, recovery rooms, stock rooms. She's not there."

"Shhh!" Jemma hissed.

The bunk above them creaked and shifted. They held their breath until Ella's snores filled the room again.

"But she has to be," Sparrow whispered when she thought it was safe to speak again. She was losing hope and couldn't keep the longing out of her voice as she swiped at her teary eyes.

"Okay, okay. You're right. I'll go back and look for her again. Don't cry, Sparrow. I'm going to do everything I can to find Geneva."

I WAS AWAKE AGAIN. Or was I? I felt like I was in a bed, but it was made of white fluffy clouds. A bright light illuminated my vision, yet I knew my eyes were closed.

I heard a voice. "Darling, you need to fight. You can fight this."

"Mom?"

"I'm right here, my darling."

I couldn't see her. I saw nothing but white light. I could hear her clearly though.

"Mom, what's happening to me? Am I dead?"

"No, darling. You've been drugged. Malakai has that old professor working for him and –"

"Professor Kobel?" I interrupted.

"Yes, but he's not actually a professor. He's a sorcerer that Malakai has recruited into the Ravinori. He had Kobel set up all sorts of traps for you here."

My mind was spinning.

"Traps?"

"Yes, darling. You saw me in the mirror when you first arrived. Do you remember?"

So I hadn't been crazy when I smashed the mirror. It truly was our mother that Jemma and I had seen. "Yes, I remember."

"That's how I can get you out of here."

"But I shouldn't have been able to see you with my powers veiled. Jemma lied to me. She didn't do it right."

"No, darling. You and your sister share an exceptionally unique bond. Do you know why I named her Jemma? It comes from the word Jemina, meaning twin. Jemma has twin souls; that's why she was the only one strong enough to share your powers and the only one capable of veiling them. But it makes Jemma particularly susceptible to darkness. She can be easily influenced because her soul is divided between light and dark. That's why it's so important for you to work together. You need to fill her with your light so that she can aid you. And you are doing a great job, darling. Seeing me in the mirror was proof of that. Jemma is the only one who can save you now."

"What do you mean?"

"Kobel put a hex on all the mirrors in the Troian Center linking them together and turning them into portals to the other side. By doing so, he's given you access to us."

"Us?"

"Yes, darling. All of us on the other side. That's how he plans to make you bring Ravin back. Kobel is poisoning you to dissolve the talisman and reverse the veil, so that soon, all your powers will return and he'll be able to use you for the ritual to bring Ravin back."

I shivered. Dissolve the talisman?

"But Nova's the talisman! What will happen to him?"

My mother was silent and I knew she was keeping an answer from me that I didn't want to hear. I swallowed my fear.

"How do I stop him?" I asked.

"When you injured your arm, Kobel gave you a risky antidote. He tried it on your friend Ruby first, but she wasn't strong enough."

"He told me there wasn't enough to save her."

"He lied to you, darling. He's been lying to you this whole time. I'm so sorry I can't protect you. But listen to me. This is important. Kobel has suspected you were the *Ponte deorum* for a long time. The mirror raised his suspicions and when you responded so well to the antidote that he gave you, he was convinced. But he couldn't convince Malakai of it. Kobel dosed the medicine he gave you with a poison. It was for the pain after you injured your arm. It is harmless on its own, but Kobel was desperate to prove you were the *Ponte deorum,* so he had Sadie unknowingly deliver another poison activating an evil spell. It's an ancient blood ritual, *Sanguin de Salvator*. It means blood of the savior. For the blood of the one true savior will burn away all impurities leaving only the truth. It's meant to dissolve the veil hiding your powers so he can reveal you to Malakai for who you truly are. It takes time. It's slowly drawing a symbol over your heart. Once it's complete, it will be there forever and there will be no denying your identity."

"What do I do?"

"Only a blood relative can save you now."

"Jemma," I whispered.

"Yes, you need to call to her. Get her to come to you. Her blood will kill the poison coursing through your veins and then they will think they've been mistaken."

"But I can't telepath to her. I don't have any powers."

"You don't need powers to communicate with your sister, Geneva. Blood is the strongest bond there is. Just call out to her. She will hear you."

"But, Mom – "

"Someone's coming. Hold on, my darling. You must fight this. I love you."

~

"FATHER, please. It's been days! What's going on? Is she in some sort of trouble?"

"She's none of your concern, Kai."

"None of my concern? I care about her. I can't pretend I don't. She's my friend. Why won't you just tell me where she is?"

"Kai, we've been over this. I've told you before that she's fine. You can stop worrying about her. Please don't bring this subject up again. It's becoming insufferable."

"But if you told me where she was I wouldn't worry," Kai pleaded.

Malakai didn't answer. He continued looking over the paperwork on his desk.

"Unless you don't now where she is," Kai taunted.

"Of course, I know where she is! The Orbiture tells me all. Your friend is safe, I assure you."

"But where is she?"

"ENOUGH!" Malakai shouted. "We are done with this subject, do you understand me? Go to your lessons, Kai."

"Yes, Sir," Kai said quietly exiting the room.

Kai had seen his father angry before and knew better than to press him. But he was sure he was up to something. If there was nothing unusual going on, his father would have told him where Geneva was. Only people with something to hide tell lies.

Once outside his father's office, Kai decided if he was going to find Geneva, he needed to put his plan into action. He headed in search of Nova to tell him he had a deal.

32

"Any news?" Nova asked.

"No. I tried again just now but I got nothing. He knows where she is and he keeps saying she's safe, but I don't believe him," Kai replied.

Both boys stood in the bathroom. Nova waited by the door to watch for anyone heading in their direction, Kai stood in front of the sinks with the water running to muffle their voices. He had searched the stalls and given the all clear before they started talking.

"I even tried to trick him. He confirmed the Orbiture knew where she was, but I don't know how to use it. If that's true, it at least means she's still here in the Troian Academy."

"So, are you still willing to do what we talked about?" Nova asked.

"Yes."

"You're sure?"

"Are you sure you'll be able to talk to Clay?" Kai asked.

"Don't worry about me."

"I'm in," Kai replied.

"Fine. But I have two conditions," Nova said. "It has to look real and Geneva can never find out. Agreed?"

"Agreed."

SADIE ARRIVED BACK at the infirmary for her next shift with a new determination to find Geneva. She checked in with the medics and started her rounds, reading patient charts, restocking rooms, cleaning the medical instruments and cataloging the elixirs.

Speaking with Jemma and Sparrow last night had opened her eyes to things she hadn't thought about in years. One memory in particular kept dancing around Sadie's mind. It was from when she was a child, living in poverty with her sister and injured father. The Flood had devastated her home outside the rural village of Aviles. Their farm had lost most of its livestock and crops, and what little was left was dying because the well had dried up.

SADIE REMEMBERED it all so vividly.

Mala had come to talk to her.

"Sadie! Sadie, where are you?" Mala called out to her.

"Over here!" Sadie giggled, peeking out from behind a singed tree trunk.

"Sadie, come over here. I need to talk to you."

"Come catch me, Mala!" she said, laughing and running through the rows of dried crops.

"Sadie! This is no time for games," Mala said sternly, but then she ran after her little sister, making Sadie squeal with delight.

Sadie was no match for her long-legged sister. She scrambled and dodged her, laughing all the while, before Mala finally stopped goofing around and caught her as she ducked behind the well. They'd both been breathless and smiling. Sadie remembered her sister's smile, and how it slowly faded away.

"Sadie, I need to talk to you," Mala said. "Father isn't well, we need to go into town to get him some help."

"Can I come too?"

"Yes, Sadie. We're all going, but that's what I came to talk to you about. We're going there permanently."

"But what about the farm?"

"Sadie, the farm is dying. Look. Look at this well. We have no water. We can't live without water and neither can the farm."

"But I don't want to leave! And what about all our animals?"

"I'm going to sell them so we have some money to find a new place to live."

"NO! Mala, no! I want to stay here!"

"Sadie, it's not open for discussion. I'm sorry, but this is what we have to do. We won't survive if we stay here. We leave in the morning, so come back to the house and pack up your things."

"I'm not going!" Sadie wailed, throwing herself to the ground in a fit.

She remembered watching Mala walk away from her through her tear-blurred vision thinking this was so unfair! She didn't want to leave the only home she'd ever known. Sadie had stubbornly clung to the old dried up well and leaned her head on the dusty stones and cried. She felt her tears dampening the sun warmed walls of the well and wished that she could cry enough to fill it. Then maybe she wouldn't have to leave. She'd cried and cried, slumped over the well until the sun hung low in the sky, like a bright orange hourglass, ticking down the time she had left in her home.

Sadie finally rose, resigned to head back to the house and pack up her room. She took one last look around the barren farm and was about to turn away when a glimmer caught her eye. Something inside the well was shimmering. She peered down into it and shrieked with glee! It was water! Where there had been nothing but dust, there was now, a deep, dark pool of water!

She ran back to the house screaming for her sister.

"Mala, Mala! Come quick! There's water! There's water!"

Mala resisted the entire way as Sadie tugged her out toward the well. But when they were close enough to see it she went rigid and pulled to a stop. The water was bubbling over the top of the well, flowing out over the walls and through any little crevice it could find. It trickled down a meandering path toward them. Mala backed away from the water as if it were dangerous.

"Sadie, what did you do?" she whispered.

"Nothing. I was crying on the well and when I got up it was full of water! It's what I wished for! I thought if we had water we could stay!"

Mala looked frightened, but she pulled Sadie close into an embrace as she muttered something under her breath.

"Come on," Mala said. "Let's grab some buckets and collect the water. And Sadie," she said looking sternly into her eyes. "You will never speak of this to anyone."

SADIE JUMPED when she felt something wet splash her feet. She had been so engrossed in her memories that she had dropped one of the vials she was polishing. Its brown liquid contents slowly oozed from the shattered glass.

"Shoot!" she exclaimed, quickly moving to wipe it up. When she got near it, the putrid smell almost knocked her over. It stung her nose and her nostrils flared trying to push away the sulfuric smell. Sadie grabbed a rag and tried once again to get close enough to wipe it up, but her eyes started watering and she felt light-headed.

"What was that?" a woman in a white coat called, poking her head into the stock room.

"Um, I dropped this vial. I'm sorry. I'm going to clean it up."

The woman took one look at the brown liquid seeping across the floor and her eyes widened.

"Grab us both masks right now!" she shouted at Sadie.

Once their faces were sheltered from the fumes she looked at Sadie, narrowing her eyes.

"You stupid girl! What have you done? This is a powerful paralysis potion."

"I'm so sorry. I'm going to clean it up right away and I'll get you another vial."

She laughed petulantly, "You think Kenna potion just grows on trees? That was our last vial!"

"Ma'am, I'm so sorry. Please, let me clean it up," Sadie quivered.

"Malakai is going to be extremely displeased!" she said nervously. "Never mind, I'll take care of this. You go get cleaned up and get yourself a new uniform," the white coat woman said glaring at Sadie and her stained clothes.

"Yes, ma'am. I'll go straight to my room and get another uniform."

"There's not time for that! I'm short handed as it is tonight. Just go grab another uniform from the storeroom here," she said distractedly looking at the mess on the floor.

"Ma'am?" Sadie said looking confused.

"It's down the hall. Go!"

Sadie scrambled from the room and headed down the hallway in the direction the woman had pointed. She had never seen a storeroom here in the infirmary, but she was too scared to ask the angry white coat woman for more details.

She came to a set of double doors marked restricted and hesitantly pushed through them and into the unknown. Sadie was now in unfamiliar territory. The hallway pitched downward and the air was cooler. She had a feeling she was headed underground.

She passed by half a dozen doors before she found one that was labeled "storeroom facilities." She peeked her head inside the large cold room. There were rows of lockers, bathrooms, sinks, changing stalls, linen carts and rows of hooks with all sorts of things hanging from them; clothes, bags, even weapons. Whose things were these? When she got closer she realize they were Luxor weapon belts, teachers' satchels and lab coats. What a strange assortment to find inside the infirmary. Perhaps this hallway led to the staff's quarters? Either way, the room gave Sadie the creeps. She quickly got cleaned up and changed into a freshly pressed white uniform that she found in one of the closets, depositing her soiled one into a large linen cart. The room smelt of harsh cleaning solutions and she wanted to get out of there before the fumes made her sick.

As she poked her head back into the hallway, she noticed it was deserted. "Now or never," she said to herself as she decided to head further into the unknown in search of Geneva.

She cautiously poked her head into room after room, each time moving further away from the direction she had come. The light in the hall was much dimmer here and none of the doors were marked. She had found rooms with cots and wardrobes set up in them, probably for the staff on call, furthering her theory that she was nearing the staff quarters. But who would want to live down here? In this cold creepy crypt with no windows?

No thanks, Sadie thought to herself.

She found a few rooms that looked like laboratories of some kind, with glass vials in all different shapes and sizes, brewing liquids in various states of development. The odor was putrid so she moved on. She was about to push her way into another room when she heard voices on the other side of the door. She leaned up close to it so she could listen.

"It's as I suspected, Master," said a man's voice. "The pattern is nearly complete."

"So you're certain it confirms she is the *Ponte deorum* then?" another male voice purred. "How long until the veil is dissolved?"

"The Sanguin de Salvator is an ancient blood ritual. It takes time. But once the symbol has formed completely over her heart it will become permanent, disabling the veil blocking her powers and giving us access to the *Ponte deorum*. I'd give it another day or two, Master."

"Very well indeed! Has everyone been assembled?"

"Yes, Master. They are eagerly awaiting your arrival. I've told them we have much to celebrate."

Sadie ducked into the room across the hall just in time. She leaned against the cool wall holding her breath as she heard the echoing footsteps of the men fading away. She took a deep breath and opened the door a crack so she could peek out.

She caught sight of two backs as they disappeared around a corner. They were men. One figure was short and bald, dressed in a stark white robe and the other was tall, dressed in dark billowing robes. His long dark hair swayed neatly down his back.

33

"Help me!" I wordlessly screamed.

My mind was so hazy and a dull buzzing in my ears made it impossible to think. I still couldn't open my eyes and I saw nothing but the blank canvas that was the back of my eyelids. But I knew Malakai and Kobel had been in my room. They were talking about my wound and how they thought I was the *Ponte deorum*. I didn't have much time left. They said the veil would be dissolved in two days and then they would know who I was for sure. What did that mean for Nova? Was two days enough time for me to get out of here and make sure he was okay? My only comforting thought was that I knew they wanted me alive. For now at least.

I found myself longing for more of the drug they'd been giving me because I could feel my arm now. It was throbbing in excruciating pain. My stomach ached with hunger and my throat was scorched with thirst.

"They're doing a terrible job of keeping my alive," I thought to myself.

Someone else was in the room now. Someone new.

"Hello? Help me," I mentally shouted again.

"Geneva?"

"Can you hear me?" My heart was thundering with excitement. "Please get me out of here! Take me to my sister Jemma!"

"Geneva? Can you hear me? I need you to wake up. It's Sadie."

"I can hear you!" I shouted in my mind.

"Geneva, I don't know if you can hear me but all your friends are looking for you. They're going to be so happy I found you. I'm going to go get help, but I'll be back okay? I promise," Sadie said.

"No! Don't leave me!" I shouted, but it was too late. She'd already gone.

All my shouting was useless. No one could hear me. I was somehow trapped in my unresponsive body and my less than loving sister's blood was the only thing that could save me.

"How am I supposed to get Jemma to hear me if I can't even get someone in the same room to hear me?" I cried, letting my mind slip back into the grey hopeless oblivion.

"I FOUND HER!" Sadie whispered barely able to contain herself.

Sadie had everyone's attention as they gathered around a table in the library for study hall.

"When?" Nova asked in desperation.

"Where?" Remi added.

"You were right, Sparrow! She's in the infirmary. They have her in a restricted area that I've never been to before and they're drugging her with something called Kenna potion. Malakai and Professor Kobel were there. They know! They know who she is!" Sadie rambled, finally stopping to take a breath.

"What do you mean they know?" Nova asked through gritted teeth.

"They know she's one of us," she said to Nova locking eyes with him.

"One of us?" he asked suspiciously.

"Yes," she said looking at Jemma now.

"What did you tell her?" Nova raged standing from his chair and glaring at Jemma.

"Sit down!" Journey said, yanking Nova back to his seat. "Let Sadie finish."

"Sadie, start over, tell me what happened. How did you find her?" Remi asked.

"I was working my regular shift and I broke a vial of something called Kenna potion. I didn't know what it was but the smell was horrible and it almost made me pass out. One of the medics came in and flipped out. She made me put a mask on and was freaking out saying the headmaster was going to be mad because it was the last bottle. It's used for paralysis. Then she ordered me to go change my uniform because it had spilt on me and she sent me to the storeroom in the restricted area. I didn't even know there was a restricted area!"

"How'd you find Geneva?" Remi prodded.

"After I got changed I decided to look around to see if maybe she was in one of the rooms in the restricted section. None of them were labeled so I had to keep peeking in each one. I got to a room and before I could go in I heard voices. It was the headmaster and Professor Kobel. They were talking about Geneva, saying that some pattern was forming on her chest, confirming their suspicion that she was the *Ponte deorum* and that in two more days the veil would be dissolved and they could test her, whatever that means. They were heading to some sort of meeting to celebrate."

"And you know what this all means?" Journey questioned.

"Well most of it, yeah. Jemma filled me in on everything so that I would continue to help you guys."

"She what?" hissed Nova.

"Sparrow was there too!" Jemma said.

"She wouldn't agree to help us unless we told her the truth," Sparrow added apologetically.

"Calm down," Jemma droned. "It worked. She found Eva, didn't she?"

Nova looked like he would have strangled Jemma with his bare hands if no one else were watching.

"Guys, you can trust me," Sadie said. "I'm on your side."

"I guess we don't have a choice now, do we?" Nova grumbled.

"We don't have time to argue about this. We have to help get Geneva out of there and we're running out of time," Sadie pleaded.

"How?" Sparrow asked.

"After Malakai and Kobel left, I snuck into her room to make sure it was really Geneva they were talking about. It was, and I read her chart. That's how I know they're giving her Kenna potion. I think it's keeping her sedated because I couldn't get her to wake up. Her arm is still bandaged, but the charts say that the wound isn't healing; in fact, it's getting worse and her bandage has to be changed regularly because she keeps bleeding through it. And she had this weird rash on her chest. It looked like some sort of foreign letter or symbol."

"What are we supposed to do?" Jemma asked. "Sneak in and steal her?"

"No, we need to figure out a way to heal her and stop whatever pattern he's talking about from forming so Malakai thinks he's wrong about Geneva," Sadie said.

"How are we going to do that?" Journey asked. "Besides he's not wrong."

"When did you find her?" Nova asked for the second time.

"Late last night during my shift."

"And you're just telling us now?" Nova erupted.

"It's not like I can easily get ahold of you. I have lessons too, you know? I was trying not to raise suspicion. Besides, this is the only place I know to find you all together," Sadie said defensively.

"It's okay, Sadie. We appreciate all the risk you've been taking to help us," Sparrow said shooting Nova a warning look.

"I know time is of the essence. I told you as soon as I could."

"Not soon enough," Nova mumbled to himself.

"Feeling guilty about something?" Remi taunted Nova.

"Don't push me, Remi," Nova warned.

Journey moved between them and directed a question at the group. "What do we do to help Geneva? How are we going to get her out of there?"

"We need to get a message to Hollis. He'll know what to do," Sparrow said.

"How are we supposed to do that?" Jemma asked.

"Clay," Nova said.

Everyone turned to look at him.

"I found him. I think he's the fourth Pillar."

Nova was flooded with a barrage of questions from the group.

"What! When? Where? How? You're telling us now?"

"I had a rough go at Cadets today and got sent to the Locker. It's not a big deal!" Nova interjected when everyone started talking again. "That's where I met him."

"Kai might explain it a little differently," Remi said under his breath.

Journey gave him a cautionary shove. "Leave it, mate."

"How did you find him?" Sparrow asked, ignoring the boys' antics.

"Kai helped me find him."

"Kai?" Sparrow questioned.

Nova shrugged. "Turns out he's not totally useless. Anyway, Clay's one of us and he's agreed to help. If we need to get messages in and out, he's our guy."

"You trust him?" Journey asked.

"Yes. If he wasn't on our side, I'd still be in the Locker," Nova said confidently.

"Hollis can make her a potion. He told me about the one he made to heal Jovi. I bet he can make one for Geneva," Sparrow said sounding hopeful. "We just have to get a message to Isby and then Hollis can get us a cure."

"Who's Hollis and Isby?" Sadie asked looking lost.

"I'll fill you in as we go. But first I need you to help me write a message," Nova said. "Oh and someone might want to go visit Kai in the infirmary."

"What?" the girls asked.

"It was an accident," Nova said.

34

With Sadie's help, Nova drafted a letter to Hollis explaining Geneva's predicament. He described how they needed a cure to heal her wound as fast as possible and they were running out to time. He mentioned how Sadie had overheard that Geneva was hexed in some way to prevent her wounds from healing and that she was being drugged with something called Kenna. They also mentioned the part about some sort of pattern forming on her chest. Once complete it would dissolve the talisman veiling Geneva's powers and reveal her true identity. Sadie did her best to draw the rash-like symbol she'd seen on Geneva's chest. Nova seemed startled when he saw it.

"You're sure this is the symbol you saw?"

"Yes. I'm positive," Sadie replied. "Why? Have you seen it before?"

"Never mind..." Nova dismissed. "Look it over one more time. Is there anything else?" he asked Sadie.

"No, that's all correct," she said. "Do you think your friend Hollis can really get you the cure in time?"

"He's our only hope," Nova said.

"How are you going to get him this message?"

"That's where Isby comes in."

"And who's Isby?"

"He's a bird who lives inside Hollis, who's a rover tortoise."

"Um, okay then. I'm sure that's a long story and I know I don't really have time to ask, so just tell me how we're supposed to get this to Isby."

"Clay helped me get a good friend into the Troian Center today. Niv will take care of getting this to Isby for us," he said with a wink.

"And Niv is?"

The alarm sounded, signaling the end of their study session.

"Come with me, I'll introduce you," Nova said with a mischievous twinkle in his eye.

After everyone had cleared out of the library, Nova and Sadie peered out from the bookcase where they had been hiding.

"Come, on. Coast is clear," Nova said.

"Where are we going?" Sadie whispered.

"To get this letter to Niv. Just follow me and be quiet."

They crept down the main hall past the infirmary and the dining hall. Everyone was back in their rooms getting ready for bed.

"Nova, what about bed check?" Sadie said, hesitating. "They're going to lock this place down if we're not there."

"We'll be back in time. Come on," Nova said pulling Sadie behind him as he ducked in through a door.

"Nova! This is the boys' bathroom! Are you mental? I can't be in here!"

"Too late," he said letting go of her hand and disappearing into a stall.

He came out with a marmouse perched on his shoulder.

"Niv, meet Sadie. Sadie, this is Niv."

"Niv is a marmouse?"

"Yes, but not just any marmouse, are you buddy? He's Geneva's marmouse and well, he understands humans, don't you Niv?"

Niv nodded his head and stuck out his tiny paw, waiting for Sadie to take it. Nova nodded to her in encouragement and she took his paw and shook it delicately.

"Hi, Niv, it's a pleasure to meet you," she said unable to contain her smile when the little marmouse chattered a greeting to her. "How did you get him into the Troian Center?"

"Well, Geneva told him to stay put because it was too dangerous for him here, so naturally he disobeyed her and followed us. He has a mind of his own and figured out a way to sneak in. I found him here in the bathroom the first day we arrived. I've been sneaking him food ever since. It's the safest place for him. The Luxors and faculty have their own facilities and there aren't tarcats here anymore, so there's not too much threat to him. But I had to send him on an errand once already and I was starting to get worried because he hadn't come back yet. I told Clay about him and he knew exactly who I was talking about. Said he found him a few days ago stuck in a pipe. He was causing quite a ruckus. You're lucky it was one of the good guys that found you, buddy," Nova said scratching Niv's belly. "Getting stuck in pipes! Somebody's been feeding you too much!"

Nova turned his attention back to Sadie.

"Clay has offered to take care of Niv. That's how I know he's one of us. He can talk to animals too. It's a power called animyth. Both Geneva and I can do it, too, and if I'm correct, so can you."

Sadie stared into Nova's glowing green eyes and looked back at the marmouse perched on his shoulder. Niv winked at her and her lips parted into a smile. She nodded to Nova, whose grin lit up his handsome face.

"I knew it! It must be a trait that all Pillars have. That proves it. We've found all four Pillars. Now all we have to do is rescue Geneva and get out of this place."

"So Niv, the marmouse, is going to give our message to Isby, the bird, who's going to give it to Hollis, the rover tortoise?" she asked skeptically.

"Well, when you say it like *that* it sounds crazy!" Nova laughed. "But, yes." He turned to Niv and asked him a series of questions. "So you haven't heard back from Jaka? Do you know if he got the package?"

Niv shook his head.

"It's okay. I'm sure he'll get back to us soon," Nova said sounding distracted.

He told Niv exactly what he needed to do and that Geneva's life depended on it. The tiny marmouse made sad cooing noises, but he snatched the rolled up note and leapt off Nova's shoulder and disappeared into the stall he'd come out of.

"And that's that," Nova said brushing his hands back and forth. "Come on, let's get back before bed checks."

"Who's Jaka?" Sadie asked as they left the bathroom

"He's the leader of the Betos. I sent him a message a few days ago. It's strange that I haven't heard back from him yet."

"This is going to work, right?" Sadie asked with concern.

"It has too."

"Nova?" Sadie questioned quietly as they snuck back toward their rooms.

"Hmm?"

"Thanks for trusting me."

"Didn't have much choice," he said with a wink.

"No, you did actually. You could have told me to get lost, but you didn't."

"I'm just trying to help Geneva."

"I can tell how much you care about her. It must be why she dreams about you."

"What do you mean?" Nova said, stopping abruptly in the dark hall.

"I've heard her call your name out just about every night she's been here," Sadie said sheepishly.

"She does?"

Sadie watched the mix of strange emotion pass over Nova's face. It was a painful happiness, tinted with boyish confusion.

"Maybe I shouldn't have said anything. I'm sorry, I thought you two were... ya know... dating?"

"It's okay," Nova said shaking himself from Sadie's shocking words as he turned to continue down the hall. "I used to think that too," he mumbled mostly to himself.

"He what?" Sparrow gasped.

"He gave the message to Niv," Sadie said. "Was that bad?"

"No. I mean yes. I mean no! It was good. Niv can get the message to Isby, that's a great plan, but how did Niv even get here? He was supposed to stay with Hollis. Geneva is going to kill him when she finds out he snuck into the Troian Academy."

"Well, she might not be around to kill him if he doesn't get that message to Hollis," Jemma said dryly from her bunk. "She should be glad that crazy rodent followed her here."

"I can't believe Nova would keep that from us," Sparrow said.

"Why? You think he tells you all his secrets?" Jemma taunted.

"Well, you didn't know either so I guess you're not the one he's sharing secrets with these days!" Sparrow retorted.

"Girls, stop it. You all seriously need to stop with the secrets! This is way too much to keep track of. And anyway, our work isn't done here. Geneva's not out of the woods yet. Even if Hollis can make that cure and get it back to us in time, how are we going to deliver it to her? I can't just march into her room and give it to her? We have to figure out a way back into the restricted area of the infirmary."

"Do you have any thoughts?" Sparrow asked.

"Not yet, but if we put our heads together I'm sure we can come up with something."

"Bed check!" called a Luxor from the doorway as a cranky old white coat woman came into our room sending all the girls into a tizzy.

Chatter ceased and all the girls dashed to their beds as the old woman paced back and forth with her clipboard checking off names as she went.

"Lights out!" she called when she finished.

She slammed the door on her way out as the room slipped into darkness.

35

"Geneva! Geneva! I need you to try harder."

"No, Mom. I just want to sleep. Please, let me sleep," I begged my mother wearily.

"You can sleep after you contact your sister."

"I can't do it, Mom. She doesn't hear me or she does and she's ignoring me. She's not going to come."

"Geneva, you can't give up. You have to believe in yourself. Everyone else believes in you. Think of Nova and Remi and Sparrow and Journey. They all believe in you. They need you to lead them. And what about Niv? He won't be safe without you. And the Pillars? You swore you'd protect them."

Suddenly, I felt a blinding pain and my mind bowed. The fog lifted momentarily and I could see clearly.

"Mom, what just happened? I could see for a second."

"You could?" she asked sounding concerned.

"Yes!"

She was silent, but then the pain hit me full force and suddenly I could see again. Even through the pain, I felt stronger and although my eyes were still closed I could see clearly. I was looking at myself lying on a cot inside the infirmary. But then it was gone again.

"Mom, something's happening," I said excitedly.

"I'm touching you, darling. You know what happens each time I do that. It brings you closer to me, closer to the other side. Each time it steals a little piece of your soul and makes it harder for you to find your way back."

"But Mom, it's working. I was able to see myself laying in this bed."

"You're seeing as I do, through the portals in the mirrors."

"Can you see through any mirror?"

"Yes."

"Can you find Jemma? She's always looking in a mirror."

"Geneva," my mother warned with a stern tone. "Do you know why that is?"

Because she's terribly vain, I thought to myself, but I couldn't say that to my mother.

"She's searching for me. Her twin souls make her susceptible to darkness, remember? Jemma can see through the thin veils between worlds easier than most. She's always been able to see things in her reflection, but unlike you she sees dark shadows. You were the one to introduce her to the light. She's been searching for it ever since."

This shocked me. Did I have my sister all wrong? Was there really more to her than lipstick and wickedness?

"I didn't know," I mumbled.

"She's been talking to me in the mirrors since you arrived. I don't think she can see me, but I know she hears me."

"She didn't tell me," I said feeling hurt.

"Yes. We talk mostly about you and how she wants to be a better sister."

"Oh," I whispered in shock, thinking back to the birthday gift Jemma had given me. Maybe she'd really meant what she said. "If you can tell me where Jemma is right now maybe I can finally talk to her through the mirror."

My mother hesitated to answer. Just as I was about to call to her, she was back.

"I found her. She's in bed in the girls bunkroom. But Geneva, this isn't safe."

"Mom, please do it one more time and don't let go until I tell you to."

My mother sighed, but suddenly the fog lifted again and I could see through the searing pain that surged through me. I was looking at myself again. I looked so pale and fragile lying on the cot. I felt my mother's energy prodding me and I got back to the task at hand. I thought of my sister. I pictured her and our room and then I was there, staring at the rows of bunk beds and slumbering girls in the pale blue moonlight that bathed the quiet room. I could even see Jemma's bed from here. I called to her.

"Jemma! Jemma!"

Nothing happened. I closed my eyes and concentrated. I pictured my sister, her perfect face, her dark lashes fluttering as she peacefully slept, her pouty heart-shaped lips parted in slumber. I reached out to her mind, and to my surprise she was already thinking of me. Visions of me bleeding swirled around in her sleeping mind.

It startled me. Was she worrying about me or was this what she was hoping would happen to me? I didn't like being inside her mind so I tried one more time to wake her.

"JEMMA!"

This time it worked. She sat bolt upright in bed. She was looking around with a startled expression on her pretty face.

"Over here, Jemma, the mirror."

She slid out of bed, her cropped black hair disheveled as she padded barefoot to the mirror.

"Mom?" she whispered.

"No, it's me. Geneva," I said. "I might look like Mom, I'm not sure. I'm channeling her and she knows how to cure me. I need your blood, Jemma. It's the only way. I need you to come now, Jemma. I don't know how much longer I have. Malakai and Kobel are coming for me."

"My blood?"

"I need your help, Jemma! Please?"

She looked frightened, but she nodded.

That's all I got to see before my mother let go.

"SILENCE!" Malakai called, his voice echoing through the packed room.

He had just announced the news that he confirmed the suspected Eva was also the *Ponte deorum.* The Ravinori members were in an uproar, filling their secret meeting room with rushed voices.

"Professor Kobel tells me that the magic blocking her powers will be dissolved once the blood curse is complete. We not only have stolen the Eva from the foolish Betos, but we have secured the *Ponte deorum*. When she awakes, we will force her to call the Pillars and we will control the world!"

The room erupted into applause. Malakai basked in the glory. He would be hailed as the one who brought Ravin back and gave Him control of the universe.

The meeting was short. Kobel dispelled any doubts and in the end, Malakai was left with parting handshakes and congratulations. His future had been secured. Now all he had to do was wait for his son to turn seventeen and all the pieces would be in place.

He was collecting the last of his things, when there was a

knock on the dense metal door. Kobel answered it and spoke to a medic. When he returned his face was grim.

"What is it, Kobel?" Malakai asked.

"I'm afraid it's your son, Master. There's been an incident."

36

"Why are you still sitting here?" Sparrow asked lividly.

They were all sitting in the dining hall, discussing the events of Jemma's night while quietly eating their breakfast.

"I couldn't very well go wandering around the halls at night. Besides, I figured I needed to tell you guys first. What if the whole thing was a trap or something?" Jemma argued.

"I think you need to get to the infirmary as fast as you can, Jemma," Journey said.

"Sadie, can you help her get in there?" Remi asked.

"Yes, I think the best thing to do is fake that you're sick. I can take you there and say I'll help get you checked in. Then we can sneak down to Geneva's room."

"So you all think this is a good idea?" Jemma asked. "That I should really go give her my blood? I don't even know how I'm supposed to do that. I think we should wait for Nova. I want to hear what he has to say."

"Where is Nova anyway?" Sparrow asked.

"He said he had to go to the John's room," Journey said.

"It's not called that anymore," Sparrow corrected.

He shrugged his shoulders. "Old habits."

"I bet he went to find Niv," Sadie said.

"I did," Nova said cheerfully joining the conversation as he swung his long legs over the bench and slipped in next to Jemma. She grinned and cozied up to him, but he ignored her as he unrolled a tiny scroll after taking note that no one else was watching them.

"Niv brought it back this morning," he said.

"What's it say?" Remi asked anxiously.

"Don't know, I haven't read it yet. That's what I'm trying to do right now if you'd stop interrupting."

Remi glared at Nova but said nothing.

Dearest N,

I'm quite positive from your description that our dear friend is suffering from Sanguin de Salvator. It loosely translates to the blood of the savior. It's an ancient blood curse that I regretfully cannot cure. The only cure for this is blood for blood, I'm afraid. And not just any blood, as I know you would give up your life for our friend in a heartbeat, but it must be the blood of a direct relative. Luckily she has one nearby I trust? I'm thinking of a certain sister, but I'm not going to name any names in case our transcripts are intercepted, but I trust you know whom I mean.

It's a simple task. Drip the blood directly from one to the other. Let it fall onto her wound to heal it fastest.

Also, your first message has been received. J agrees. Our suspicions are confirmed. We can have what you need ready in two weeks time. We will assemble where I last saw you and await your order. You know how to signal us.

May the gods be with you all.

Please keep me apprised of the results.

H.

. . .

Everyone's eyes settled on Jemma once Nova finished reading the note from Hollis.

"Well, he's being cryptic," Jemma said.

"Jemma, he's not being cryptic, he's being cautious. But there's no denying what he was saying. You have to be the one to do this," Remi chimed in.

"But I hate blood. Isn't there any other way?" Jemma whined.

"No, Jemma. Hollis said it plain as day. It has to be you," Nova said pouring on the charm. "You can do this, Jemma. I believe in you. You can be the hero I know you were born to be. This could be the moment your whole life has been leading up to."

"You really think so?" Jemma said, turning to complete goo and hanging on Nova's every word.

"I know so. I'm going to be so proud of you, Jemma," Nova continued.

"How proud?" she toyed coyly.

"So proud, Jemma. I'll owe you big time. We all will."

"You'll owe me?" she asked.

"Yes. I'll do anything you want, Jemma. I promise," Nova pleaded.

"Anything?" she asked, her dark eyes narrowing.

"Yes! Jemma, anything!" Nova exhaled loosing patience.

Jemma leaned over to whisper something in his ear. Nova frowned but nodded.

"Okay! When do we go?" she said turning abruptly to Sadie. "Time's a wasting!"

They quickly discussed the rest of Hollis's message. Nova explained that it meant Jaka had received the handkerchief with the NW symbol on it and from what Kai had described, agreed that it indeed confirmed Malakai was in possession of the *Book of Gods* and, therefore, the leader of the Ravinori. Jaka would rally his men and fight to get Geneva and the Pillars out of the Troian Center if it came to that. The Betos would gather at the edge of the forest and await his signal, a flaming branch, carried by Isby.

After realizing how little time they had, they decided not to waste a moment more. Jemma feigned a stomachache brilliantly. She was wailing and doubling over in pain as Sadie dragged her from their breakfast table.

They had no trouble getting past the Luxors at the door once Jemma gagged herself and vomited all over the floor, narrowly missing their polished boots. They leapt out of her way and one of them even held the door for her.

The racket continued on down the hall.

"She's laying it on a little thick, don't you think?" Remi worried.

"Jemma doesn't do anything halfway," Nova smirked.

"I'm just glad she agreed to do it," Sparrow said.

"Yeah me too, but I knew I could convince her," Nova boasted.

"You're as bad as she is," Sparrow erupted. "You two deserve each other! Always manipulating people with your looks to get what you want! It's not right! And you went a little overboard with Kai too, don't you think? Someone should be going to check on him while they're in the infirmary."

"Sparrow!" Journey said in shock, reaching out to grab her hand.

She pulled it away, wiping at the tears rimming her amber eyes.

"I'm sorry," she apologized immediately. "I'm just so worried about Geneva," she sobbed. "But I shouldn't be taking it out on you," she said to Nova.

"It's okay," Nova said solemnly.

"No, it's really not," Remi added. "She has a point. I wish

we could all stop with the manipulation and secrecy and be friends again. And Nova, stop speaking for us. If you want to promise your life away to Jemma, fine by me, but don't lump us in with you. I don't want to owe that vindictive girl anything."

"Well, I guess we know which one of us is willing to go the extra mile for Geneva, don't we?" Nova spat back. "I was just doing whatever it would take to get Jemma to save Geneva's life. Sorry if I had to inconvenience you in any way, King Remi."

"I'll tell you what's inconvenient, Nova. Your – "

"Stop it! Both of you!" Sparrow yelled, drowning out whatever Remi was saying to Nova.

"Remi's right. When did we all stop being friends? I need you guys to be friends. I don't have much longer here with you all and I don't want to waste it fighting. Malakai will be sending me to meet my adoptive family soon."

Journey's eyes clouded to a deep amber and he moved protectively to Sparrow's side.

"They'll have to take you over my dead body," he said, his broad chest heaving.

Everyone was silent for a moment, taking in the gravity of their situation.

Geneva was being held captive by a poisonous blood curse, Sparrow was about to be adopted by strangers and the rest of them were at Malakai's mercy until the Beto warriors showed up, which wasn't for another two weeks time. They looked tensely at each other. Who knew if they would all still be here by then?

The alarm blared right at that moment, breaking their somber spell and taking the boys stalemate with it.

Nova and Remi almost collided on the way out the door and started shoving each other. Nova stepped aside and gave a dramatic bow, sweeping the floor until Remi marched past him.

"This is going nowhere," Journey mumbled as he elbowed

Nova to knock it off and followed Remi and the rest of the students out of the dining hall.

~

"I'LL KILL that insolent boy, I don't care who he thinks he is!" Malakai barked.

"Father, I'm fine. It wasn't Nova's fault," Kai said, wincing as the medics propped up his pillows.

Malakai had demanded that Kai be moved from the infirmary to his room as soon as he found out what happened to his son. Despite Kai's protests, he didn't want his son to be subjected to recover in such a modest place. That only depressed Kai further. The whole reason he'd come up with his plan was so he could have a reason to be in the infirmary and search for Geneva. He should have known his father would have never allowed it.

"Tell me again, what happened?" Malakai demanded.

"Nothing happened. We were sparring and I was outmatched," Kai replied.

"Then why did Commander Gray match you two together?"

"He didn't! I chose Nova."

"Why?"

"We were arguing."

"Ah, let me guess. Over a girl?"

Kai hung his head.

"I've told you that Geneva is no good. And she does nothing but prove my point. Stay away from her, Kai. I don't need you mixed up with her crowd. Look where it gets you. If you continue to disobey me, you'll force my hand and I will send you back to Lux."

37

Jemma carried on her act inside the infirmary. She was moaning and clutching her stomach. "It hurts! It hurts!" she wailed.

"What's wrong with this girl?" demanded the woman in the white coat as Sadie stumbled into the check in room with Jemma.

"I don't know, we were eating breakfast and she started feeling ill. She threw up on the way here. I think she may have eaten something bad," Sadie said.

"I think I'm allergic to something I ate," Jemma cried. "My throat feels so tight!"

"You have to help her!" Sadie screamed.

The white coat woman sprang into action. "Wait here," she said as she ran for the door leading to the exam rooms.

She was back in an instant with a rolling cot and three other white coats. They lifted Jemma onto the cot and whisked her away through the door and down the hall out of sight.

Sadie ran to catch up, but when she reached the door, a man in a white coat was pulling a curtain around Jemma's cot, blocking her view.

Sadie went to stand inside the door, when another white coat poked her head out of the curtain.

"You! Susie? You work here, don't you?"

"It's Sadie. Yes, I work here."

"Go grab me a patient gown and some extra gauze," she commanded before darting back behind the curtain.

Sadie stood frozen in place, watching the other medics scramble around the room, grabbing instruments and tubing.

"Charcoal!" called the medic in charge.

"What are they doing to her?" Sadie asked when the woman poked her head back out.

"They're pumping her stomach in case she ingested something she shouldn't have."

"Is she going to be all right?" Sadie worried, second-guessing their harebrained scheme.

"I don't know. There's nothing you can do for your friend right now. If you want to help her, go fetch those supplies!"

Sadie turned on her heels and ran down the hall to the supply room. She grabbed the gown and gauze and stopped for a moment to catch her breath and collect her thoughts.

"This was such a bad idea. How are we supposed to help rescue Geneva now?" Sadie said to herself. "All I've managed to do is get both sisters confined to the infirmary! Think, Sadie, think!" she scolded herself.

The only good thing was that Jemma and Geneva were now in the same place. All Sadie needed to do was to wait for the chaos to clear. Perhaps if she got the chance she could wheel Jemma down to Geneva's room?

Sadie took a deep breath and poked her head back into the hall. She looked right, then left. No one. She looked right again, pausing momentarily before taking off in that direction, heading straight for the double doors that led down to the restricted area.

~

"GENEVA, YOU HAVE TO KEEP TRYING."

"Mom, she's not coming."

"She's your sister, Geneva. Don't give up hope. You two need to trust in each other. If you could only work together there would be nothing you couldn't conquer."

"I wouldn't be so sure about that, Mom."

"What's keeping you apart?"

My heart panged as I thought instantly of Nova. My mind's image of his angelic face glowed before my closed eyelids. I sighed deeply, knowing I'd never be with the boy I loved. I'd probably never even get to see him again or say goodbye. A dry, painful lump ached in my throat.

"All of this is over a boy?" my mother asked.

"Oh, Mom," I sobbed, "I've been such a fool! I love him and he'll never know it."

"Darling, I know this is so hard on you and I'm sorry for your suffering. But you are better than this. You are the Eva, the chosen one. You must focus your energy on more important things. There will be time to follow your heart after you fulfill your destiny."

"But you told me to stay away from him!"

"I assume we're speaking about Nova?"

"Yes, you warned me to stay away from him the night that Jemma veiled my powers. It was the last thing you said to me."

"Darling, that's because I saw where Jemma planned to veil your powers. I know by now she has told you that she used Nova as the talisman."

"And you wonder why we don't get along? Can't you see she did that just to hurt me?"

"Or maybe it was for your protection?"

"Mom! No, she wants Nova for herself and she used that as the perfect excuse to keep me away from him."

"Maybe so, Geneva, but I choose to see the good in my children, because I know what incredible things you are both capable of. It is true, you both possess different qualities of light and dark, but that is why you must work together, to balance the lightness and darkness equally. While you two are feuding, nature is unbalanced and you will never be able to fulfill your destiny. Do you remember the passage in the *Book of Secrets*? '*to achieve harmony, the sun and the moon must work together, despite their inclination to chase after the stars –*' "

"'*The sun must give up the stars.*' Yes, I remember it, Mother."

At saying those words, I felt my barely mended heart ripping open again, knowing that Nova was the star I had to give up. For surely I was the sun, the child with the bright eyes, white hair and pale skin, and my perfect sister Jemma, who was dark like the night with her silken raven hair and her eyes like the night sky. She was the moon and she belonged with the stars, with Nova. She knew it and it seemed my mother knew it. I was the one who was holding on to something that could never be. It was time to let go.

I was melting into an abyss of self-loathing and pity, when I heard someone enter my room.

"Geneva? It's me. It's Sadie. Jemma and I are here to rescue you."

"Sadie!" I called to her. My eyes remained closed, my body still and unresponsive despite my mind screaming out to her.

"I told you, your sister would come for you," my mother whispered.

"We figured out the cure. It's Jemma's blood. She's here in the infirmary. I just need to figure out a way to sneak her back here and then we'll get you out. I promise we'll get you out, Geneva. Just hold on. I'll be back as soon as I can."

~

SADIE RAN from Geneva's room when she saw the coast was clear. She sprinted the whole way back to Jemma, trying to keep her footfall light so no one would hear her.

She stopped outside of Jemma's room to collect herself and slow her breathing. She heard the medics inside talking and took the opportunity to eavesdrop.

"She should be fine. I didn't find anything strange in the contents of her stomach, but keep her here overnight for observation to be sure," the medic said.

"Yes, Sir. Anything else?"

"Oh yes, I almost forgot."

There was a heavy thud, like metal on metal, which caused Sadie to jump.

"I removed this. Send it to Professor Kobel. If he discovers anything, have him report to the headmaster directly."

"Yes, Sir."

Sadie jumped for a second time when someone tapped her on the shoulder.

"What are you doing standing out here?"

It was the white coat woman from earlier.

"I... I... um..."

We've been waiting for you!" she grumbled. "Bring the supplies into the medics, Susie!"

Sadie breathed a sigh of relief and followed the rude woman into the room. She placed the gown and gauze on the table next to Jemma's bed. She wasn't sure if Jemma was passed out or sleeping, but she looked peaceful.

Sadie looked around the room. She was the only one in there. She was about to lean over to whisper into Jemma's ear when something on the bedside tray caught her eye. Its dull sparkle gleamed ominously.

Sadie instinctively looked to Jemma's wrist and sure enough her cuff wasn't there. That must have been the heavy thud she heard earlier. But why did the medic remove her bracelet for a stomachache? And why did he want it to go to the professor?

Before Sadie could make another move, a woman in a white coat returned and snatched the metal tray with the bracelet on it.

"I almost forgot this!" she said looking at Sadie. "Well, make yourself useful, young lady. This room needs to be cleaned."

38

"Mom you were right! It worked!" Geneva said with a renewed excitement in her voice. "Jemma is coming to get me! She and Sadie figured it out! I knew Sadie was one of us. She's a Pillar, isn't she?"

"I believe she is," my mother responded. "Once I figured out Kobel's mistake with the portals, I've been doing my best to help you from the other side. I've been monitoring all the students and reading their thoughts."

"You can do that?" I asked instantly feeling guilty about burdening my mother with my hateful thoughts of my sister. Not to mention all the personal thoughts I've been having about Nova, and more recently Remi. Ever since Sparrow told me she liked him, I'd been thinking of him differently for some reason. And then there was Kai. He was so kind and beautiful and gentle. He made me feel a guilty happiness every time I was close to him. I felt terrible for using him. He'd trusted me and proved to be a loyal friend. I knew he truly cared about me and the only thing I'd done for him, was get him into trouble with his father.

"I can't read minds or bend thoughts like Nova. It's more of reading emotions and feelings," my mother said interrupting my distracted thoughts.

"Oh." I breathed a sigh of relief. "Kind of like I could before Jemma veiled my powers?"

"Yes, exactly."

"Is there anyone else, Mom? Supposing Sadie is a Pillar, we're still searching for one more."

"There is ... " she hesitated.

"Who?"

"His name is Terran."

"I knew it! Just like *Novae terrae*! What makes you think he's a Pillar?"

"There's something about his thoughts that speak to me, louder and stronger than the rest. He seems grounded emotionally, yet also suspicious of how he feels different since he's come to the Troian Center. He's always felt different than his peers but there's something about being here that has him on edge."

"Since coming here? So, he's not an orphan," I said excitedly.

I had been right! The Pillars weren't necessarily orphans. That confirmed my suspicions about Jovi and Sadie and made me even more positive that I was now only hunting for the final Pillar. I guess I was getting ahead of myself. I still had to make it out of here alive first.

"Mom, can you show me what he looks like?"

"Darling, it's too risky."

"Mom, this may be our last chance before Jemma comes back for me. I have to find him. He's the last one. Once I find all the Pillars we can leave the Troian Center. We can go back to the forest, where the Beto's can help protect us while we restore balance to the island and finally fulfill my destiny!"

"Geneva, each time I let you look through my eyes I pull you closer to the other side."

"Mom, I know. I can handle it. You said it yourself. I was chosen to do this. I can handle it."

She was silent.

"One more time," I begged.

Then the room went white and I felt a rush of pain that sent my blood pumping through my veins. Something was pulling me away from my mother. I could hear her faintly whispering my name in my ear.

"Darling, I love you."

"Mom!" I shouted. "Mom, no! What's happening? I need more answers!"

But I was losing her. The bright glow of her presence was fading.

"Mom!" I shouted in desperation.

I didn't know what was happening but it was painful and I knew it was pulling me away from her before she could give me the answer I needed. I needed to find the last Pillar, but I also had so many more questions for her.

I felt like I was free falling into an endless atmosphere. My heart was in my throat and visions I couldn't explain flashed through my mind like forgotten memories.

Nova and Remi floated before me. Both of them looked so sad and confused. I tried to reach out to them, to hold onto them and somehow slow my fall, but they turned their backs on me and were suddenly blotted out by a tornado of dark shadows that reformed as my sister, her black hair whipping in the wind and lashing across her face. She looked so sinister that I felt a chill run through me.

My vision of Jemma dissolved into a vapor of black smoke. When it cleared I saw Sparrow, she was smiling at me and then she was falling. She kept falling, over and over. Her face changed from a smile to shock and panic. Journey was there reaching out to her but he couldn't get to her. His face was tortured and twisted as he called out to her. I tried to squeeze my eyes shut to make this nightmare stop, but they were already closed. Nothing could stop the slide show of horrors.

Then Sadie's blue eyes blinked before me, looming large and still, like the tranquil ocean on a calm day. She brought me a sense of peace and relief. She closed her eyes and when she opened them again I saw Jovi in their reflection. She was frolicking in the forest, chasing after Quin and giggling. My heart ached as I watched her disappear beyond the ferns. I strained my mind to follow her and as I looked closer, the ferns parted and I saw Kai.

He was standing with his back to me, in front of an entrance to a cave. He looked back over his shoulder and locked eyes with me. His face was smeared with blood and there were dark circles under his eyes. He didn't look like the warm, sincere boy I knew. He started running and I begged my mind to follow, but he blurred away.

The next vision took a while to materialize. I could tell I was inside the cave now because it was exceedingly dark and cold. The images took a moment to come into focus. The dull sparkle from the walls reflected off the eerie still water of the cave casting dancing shadows. I recognized this place. It was the cavern lake I fell into with Remi; Cayo Cave.

I saw Kai again. My mind raced toward him. He stood in front of something, a dark mound. I closed the distance between us and now I was standing next to him. He reached for my hand, looking at the shape in front of him. I followed his eyes and saw a boy kneeling in front of him, his face down, bowed away from us so I couldn't see who he was.

I looked beyond the kneeling figure and saw that the mound behind him wasn't a mound at all. They were bodies. Dead bodies! I'd been dragged back into my nightmare. But this time it felt so real. Too real. My stomach lurched and bile burned in my throat. I saw myself stagger forward and collapse onto the pile of bodies. I was looking from one tortured face to the next. – Eja, Jovi, Sparrow, Remi.... I clutched up the bodies of my fallen friends and screamed.

I actually heard myself scream!

So did everyone in my vision. The eyes of my dead friends flew open and stared angrily back at me.

I screamed even louder, desperate to stop the horror.

Kai stared at me, his feral black eyes unblinking. There was no white left; his midnight eyes had been taken over by the nightmare and exploded his pupils into a horrifying sight. I tried to get away, but I tripped over the boy who had been kneeling in front of Kai. He looked directly at me. His unfamiliar face was the last thing that flashed before me. The negative of his image danced on the backs of my eyelids as my mind finally let go of whatever dark dream it held me in.

~

"GENEVA? Shhh... Please. It's okay. It's just us. It's Sadie and Jemma."

"Make her stop screaming," Jemma hissed.

"I'm trying. Maybe you're hurting her," Sadie worried.

"Eva, shut up or you're going to get us all caught," Jemma crooned in a feeble attempt at kindness.

Sadie rolled her eyes and pushed Jemma out of the way, slowly stroking Geneva's arm.

"Just hold her still while I drip my blood into her wound. I don't plan on wasting any more than I have to," Jemma complained.

"I will," Sadie said. "Are you ready?"

"Yes, just make it quick. And pretty. I don't want a nasty scar."

"Okay. Give me your hand," Sadie said, skillfully wielding a scalpel over Jemma's palm. "Take a deep breath and count to five."

"One. Two. Three – Ouch!" Jemma cried. "You said five!"

"I know. It works every time," Sadie smirked. "Now, hurry. You're wasting blood."

"Ugh, it's disgusting," Jemma whined when Sadie pulled back the bloodstained bandage from Geneva's arm. The first drop of Jemma's blood that dripped into the wound made a hissing sound. With three more the wound began to glow and close up.

"Geneva. Open your eyes. It's us," she soothed. "It's Sadie and Jemma. We've come to get you out of here. You have to be quiet."

I HEARD familiar voices surrounding me and I felt the painful ache of my limbs moving, but I was afraid to open my eyes. I couldn't take another horrible nightmare.

I involuntarily sputtered a cough from my parched throat as I tried to tell whoever was moving me to stop. I took a rattling breath, mindfully filling my lungs for the first time that I could remember in a while. It felt strange and unnatural at first.

My eyelids opened and I saw the worried faces of my sister and Sadie hovering over me.

"Je – " I tried, but my voice seized and cracked into a coughing fit.

Sadie handed me a cup of water from my bedside.

I nodded my gratitude as I grasped it with shaky hands and swallowed in large, greedy gulps.

"Are you all right?" Sadie asked when I handed the empty cup back to her.

"I think so," I whispered.

The last thing I remembered was the face of the strange kneeling boy that I didn't know. It made me shiver involuntarily.

"Are you sure?" she asked skeptically. "You look cold."

"Of course, she's cold," Jemma scolded. "She was nearly dead and it's frigid in here. We don't have time for all these questions. Let's just get her dressed and get out of here!"

Sadie expertly disconnected me from the numerous bags of strange looking fluids I was hooked up to, while I struggled to get my stiff limbs to cooperate as Jemma tugged my uniform on and attempted to get me out of bed.

"What happened to me?" I whispered as they unsteadily propped me onto my feet.

"You were being poisoned by Professor Kobel," Sadie said. "He was giving you something to prove you were the *Ponte deorum* and prevent your wound from healing."

I looked instinctively to my arm. My triceps had a bright pink welt on it shaped like a jagged triangle. I held it up to exam it and a rapid flash of memories slammed into my head, unsteadying me.

"Whoa," Sadie said struggling to help me keep my balance.

But I couldn't help her, I was lost in my memories; Luxors carrying me, Kai calling after me, the worried medic, the long dim hallway, my throbbing dizzy head, the black door, so much blood, Malakai! My mother, the mirror, the visions, the Pillars, reaching out to my sister...

"You saved me?" I said suddenly looking at Jemma.

Her own hand was freshly bandaged. She must have cut it to give me her blood.

She shrugged. "I guess I could have done a better job. Sorry about your arm," she said wrinkling her nose at the sight of my scar. "It's kind of hideous. The rash on your chest mostly cleared up though."

I blinked dumbfounded at her for a moment before throwing my arms around her neck and hugging her.

"Thank you, Jemma. Thank you for coming."

"Okay, okay," she said awkwardly patting my back. "Let's get out of here first and then you can thank me."

Sadie peeked into the hallway to make sure the coast was clear, while Jemma held me up. There was no one in sight, so she waved for us to join her. We scurried down the hallway as quietly as we could despite my wobbly legs.

"Pick up your feet," Jemma hissed.

"I'm trying," I grumbled, but I felt like I was just learning to walk and Jemma wanted me to run.

"It's from the Kenna potion. It's a strong paralysis, but it should start to wear off soon," Sadie said. "In here," she whispered, pulling us behind her.

We followed her into a door marked, Storeroom and Utilities.

"What are we doing in here?" Jemma scolded Sadie. "We're supposed to be getting out of the infirmary, not cleaning it."

"You don't really think things through, do you?" Sadie retorted. "Did you think the three of us were just going to stroll out of here, Jemma?" Sadie retorted.

My sister was uncharacteristically speechless for a moment, but then she put her hands on her hips and said, "I suppose you have a better plan?"

"I hope so," Sadie said.

"Well, what is it?" Jemma demanded.

Sadie grinned and pointed to something in the corner that I couldn't see since I had collapsed to the floor the moment Jemma let go of me. She was standing in front of me, blocking my view of whatever Sadie was pointing at.

"Oh you've got to be kidding me!" Jemma cried incredulously.

39

Every few feet, a rhythmic bumping jarred my aching body as the wheels struck a crack in the floor. I listened to Jemma's quiet breathing and Sadie's steady footsteps as we whizzed down the hallway. I had already lost track of where I thought we were.

It was impossible to see anything through the thick linen sides of the laundry cart that Sadie had crammed us into. Jemma and I were wedged hip to hip and piled high with soiled sheets and dirty uniforms as we rolled down the hall, guided by Sadie's shaking hands.

"There has got to be a better way than this," Jemma complained next to me. "What *is* that smell?"

"Shhh," I reprimanded her. "Laundry doesn't talk back."

"Both of you shush... or we're going to get caught!" came Sadie's voice.

"Ugh, did it have to be *dirty* laundry?" Jemma whined.

"Well, it's more believable this way," I offered.

"Seriously! Be quiet you two! There's someone up ahead."

I felt Jemma tense next to me as I held my breath and waited for someone to stop us.

"You! Sally, where have you been?"

"It's Sadie, ma'am. I was gathering fresh linens for the rooms and I noticed there wasn't enough, so I thought I would get these washed," Sadie responded.

Her voice was higher than usual and I could sense nervousness in her tone. The woman didn't respond, but I heard her footsteps getting closer. The hair on my arms stood at attention. She surely was onto us and I expected the sheets to be peeled away revealing us as stowaways at any moment.

"There are no bed linens?" I heard the woman ask Sadie in a suspicious whisper.

I couldn't hear if Sadie responded, but the woman did.

"Wait right here," she said and I heard her hurried footsteps fade away from us.

"What's happening?" Jemma whispered.

"I don't know," Sadie whispered back in a panic. "What should I do?"

"Is she still out there?" I asked.

"No."

"Then go!" Jemma urged, panic now lacing her voice.

I felt our cart start to move again. We lurched forward, gaining speed.

"Wait! WAIT!" I heard the woman yelling behind us.

I could hear her footsteps following us. It sounded like she was gaining on us! I reached blindly for Jemma's hand among the sheets and when I found it I squeezed, hoping to convey my apology for dragging her into my mess once again. To my surprise, she squeezed back.

"Stop! Stop!" the woman was yelling behind us. "Agatha! Stop them."

Suddenly we came to a halt.

"What's going on here?" a new voice accosted Sadie.

"I... um... I...."

"Well?" she questioned Sadie.

"I was taking the laundry out."

"It's not laundry day," she responded.

Then the woman who was chasing us finally caught up and joined the conversation.

"Agatha, it's okay. I was just sending Susie here out with the linens. Can you believe we're out already?"

"Out of linens?" Agatha asked sounding confused.

"Yes, and you know how Headmaster feels about keeping things clean," whispered the other woman.

"Susie, I was calling you," she continued. "I wanted to give you the rest of the linens from the exam rooms."

"It's Sadie... but I don't think I have room," Sadie stuttered.

"Nonsense, come with me."

I felt our cart start to move again.

"Leave the cart and follow me," the woman commanded.

I didn't know what was happening. I heard Sadie hesitate for a moment, before her footsteps reluctantly followed the other woman's. Jemma and I sat in complete silence for what felt like forever, both of us too scared to speak. I held my sister's hand and concentrated on breathing quietly. I had no idea if the Agatha woman was still standing nearby.

Suddenly I heard shouting and a flurry of footsteps moving down the hall in the direction we had just come from.

"She's gone!"

"Where is she?"

"I don't understand."

"Who?"

"The Sommer's girl!"

"Jemma?" I heard Sadie's voice among the panic medics.

Jemma's body went rigid next to mine.

"Yes! Have you seen her?" questioned a medic.

"Yes, I saw her in the hall when I was collecting laundry a few minutes ago," Sadie responded innocently.

"Go! What are you waiting for?" one of the medics barked and the flurry of footsteps scattered away.

I heard a lone pair of feet heading in our direction and then our cart was in motion again.

"It's me, guys, I'm getting us out of here," Sadie whispered.

"Now what?" I asked from inside a stall in the Jane's room where we were hiding out.

While everyone searched for Jemma, Sadie had rapidly wheeled us out of the infirmary. It seemed we were an afterthought among the chaos of a missing patient. Sadie guided us safely into the girls bathroom, helped us out of the dirty laundry cart and ordered us to stay put while she ditched it so she wouldn't look suspicious.

I stretched my aching limbs stiffly and watched as Jemma fussed over her filthy clothes.

Jemma and I were waiting to change into new uniforms that Sadie promised to return with since our joyride in the dirty laundry cart had left ours looking less than desirable.

"Now we wait for Sadie," she whispered. "Where is she anyway?" she asked impatiently from her perch on the toilet seat.

I continued to stare at Jemma. She seemed different to me now that I had seen her through my mother's eyes. Was there actually more to her? Maybe all the time she spent looking in the mirror was more than vanity. Maybe she was searching for something more; something I had only begun to see.

"Why do you keep staring at me like that?" she asked with her usual venom.

"Why did you do it? Why did you decide to save me?"

"Uh, because I'm your sister, and the only one that could save you," she said looking at me like I was daft.

"But I could tell when I first spoke to you through the mirror, you didn't want to. You hesitated."

"You try being told you have to be part of a blood sacrifice."

I continued to stare at her, wanting to tell her that I *did* know what that was like. I was tied to an unthinkable destiny that would require the ultimate sacrifice in order to save her and my friends. I would have to give my blood and possibly my life if we didn't find a way out of the Troian Center soon. But I didn't try to explain that to her. I knew it would be useless with Jemma in the state she was in. She was wallowing in self-pity and fretting over her appearance.

I watched as she picked at the stains on her uniform with her perfectly manicured nails. They were a deep metallic purple today. I looked down at my own hands for a moment. They were pale and still shaking. My nails looked nothing like Jemma's. They took the brunt of my worry and were chewed down to the beds. I sighed; it was another subtle difference between us. We had so many, and when added together they always made me doubt that we could actually be related. But her blood had saved me, proving that she truly was my sister despite all of our differences. After what my mother said, I was determined to chip away Jemma's abrasive layers and connect with her.

"What made you change your mind?" I asked.

She met my gaze. Her large dark eyes looked soft and child-like for a moment. They were searching mine, deciding whether to tell me the truth or not.

"Nova," she said.

She had decided on truth.

"It always comes back to him, doesn't it?" I asked.

She steeled her eyes at me, but said nothing.

Before being trapped by the Sanguin de Salvator, I had been furious with Jemma for lying to me about having to stay away from Nova in order to keep my powers veiled. After he grabbed my arm in the library and nothing happened, I was determined to tell him the truth since it didn't seem like Jemma knew how I'd get my powers back. But now, it seemed useless. After the visions I'd had during my time in the infirmary, it seemed my only option was to give in to Malakai. He knew everything anyway. He was only toying with me. If I surrendered myself, maybe I could set my own terms and save my friends. I at least owed Jemma my thanks for giving me that opportunity. If she hadn't saved me, Nova may have been in mortal danger as well. I was uncertain what would have happened to him if the blood curse had been successful in dissolving the veil on my powers. Now I could at least tell Nova the truth before I died. He deserved that and so much more.

"For what it's worth," I said, "thank you."

"It's not like I had a choice."

"I'm trying to say thank you, Jemma."

"Well I don't need you to. I don't want to owe you anything, okay?"

"Fine," I muttered as Jemma hopped down off the toilet and pushed her way out of the stall. "We were supposed to wait in here," I called after her.

"Yes, you were!" rang Sadie's voice. "Geez, you're so impatient, Jemma. I was going as fast as I could." Sadie sounded out of breath.

I cracked the door open and she handed me a crisply folded uniform.

"Thanks, Sadie," I said while pulling the filthy uniform over my head.

My hands brushed against my unruly waves of short curls as I tugged the soft white fabric past my head. I righted my uniform, smoothing it gently and then gingerly reached my stiff arms above my head to try to tame my disorderly blonde locks.

"What's taking you so long?" Sadie called to me.

"I'm coming," I said, swinging the stall door open.

Jemma already stood in front of the mirror, examining how she looked in the clean uniform. Sadie rested against the wall waiting for us.

"You okay?" she asked when I ambled over to the mirror next to my sister.

"Yes," I answered distractedly.

"I thought you might be starving so I brought you something," Sadie said handing me an apple.

"Thanks," I replied absently. I was staring into the mirror, but not at my reflection. I was trying to look beyond it, knowing that my mother was probably somewhere on the other side watching us. It made my heart sad to be so close to her, yet so far apart. I put my hand to the glass and smiled ruefully. "*Thank you*," I mouthed silently to my reflection, hoping my mother could see me.

"Are you sure?" Sadie asked, not sounding convinced.

She was next to me now and when she touched my arm it brought me back to reality. I gave my reflection a quick once over and immediately regretted it. My eyes looked shallow and there were grey circles under them, as if I hadn't slept in days. And if possible I looked thinner; my cheeks were sunken in and my collarbone protruded more than usual. I still had bruises on my arms from quarterstaffs and as Jemma had pointed out, a pretty gnarly scar left among them. I traced my finger over it gingerly, wishing our uniforms had sleeves.

"I'll be all right. Thank you for everything, Sadie. I really appreciate you helping me."

"Don't mention it," she said kindly.

"How long was I out?" I questioned as I bit into the apple. The sweetness of it made my jaw ache. It must have been a while since I'd had real food.

"I don't know, a few days?" Jemma answered.

"You were in the infirmary for over a week, Geneva," Sadie said quietly.

"What? A week?" My mind raced. "What about Sparrow?"

"She's still here," Sadie said, reading my worry about Sparrow's impending adoption.

"Thank the gods," I whispered, letting my hands rest on the sink as I steadied myself.

I was shaking again. I splashed some water on my face to try to clear my mind and chase away my anxiousness. It didn't seem to help much. I rubbed my eyes until I saw stars and patted my cheeks roughly to put some color into them. I moved closer to the mirror to see if I'd made any improvement. I shook my head as I examined my hollow looking eyes. Nothing was going to help them, except maybe some sleep and that was a luxury I couldn't afford right now.

"What the - ?" I exclaimed jumping back from the mirror.

"What?" both Jemma and Sadie yelled at once.

"Did you guys see that?"

"See what?" Sadie asked nervously.

"Was it Mom?" Jemma questioned desperately searching the mirror.

"No, not in the mirror," I said already heading back toward the open door of the stall behind me.

I had seen a brown fuzzy blur skitter behind me when I was looking in the mirror and I'd know that scurry anywhere.

"I swear I saw him...." I trailed off disappearing into the stall.

"What's she doing?" Sadie asked Jemma.

"Beats me," Jemma shrugged. "Maybe I screwed up the blood cure or something and fried her brain?"

"Niv? Niv are you in here?" I called. "Niv, I promise I'm not mad at you, buddy. If you're hiding in here, please come out. I could really use a hug from my friend," I pleaded.

I heard a familiar squeak and my heart leapt!

"Niv!" I exclaimed scooping up the brown shaggy shadow that came waddling out from behind the toilet basin. I hugged him and let him lick my face and tickle me with his long whiskers. I came sauntering out of the stall, holding my squirming marmouse, smiling ear to ear.

"Sadie, I'd like you to meet Niv," I said laughing as he scurried up my arm to perch on my shoulder. He was sitting on his hindquarter examining my prickly hair. "I guess he doesn't like my haircut either," I laughed.

"We've met, but how did he get in here?" Sadie asked.

"You have?" I asked startled.

"Niv, did you bring us any news," she asked ignoring me.

He shook his head at her. I shivered, realizing they understood each other. Sadie was an animyth too!

"We should tell Nova he's back," Jemma said.

"Nova?" I asked.

"Yes, he's been using Niv to send messages back and forth to Hollis and Eja."

"What? You knew Niv was here?" I questioned, as a feeling of distrust and hurt washed over me. "Since when?"

"There's a lot we need to fill you in on," Sadie said as the alarm blared. "But we can't stay here much longer. They'll be looking for you. Luckily you both don't have cuffs on, so that might buy us some time. Can you walk?"

I nodded.

"Good, follow me."

40

Sadie quickly filled me in about the note Nova brought to breakfast and how they hadn't wasted a moment putting it into action. The only problem was they hadn't thought past rescuing me, so we were winging it now. We decided our best plan of action was to blend in, joining our class for whatever lesson was next. We agreed that letting the other students and teachers see us made us less likely to be abducted back to the infirmary. Jemma said she'd catch up with us, claiming she had to return to our bunkroom first to reapply her lipstick. Sadie persuaded me to leave Niv in the bathroom, convincing me it'd been the safest place for him to hide lately and then dragged me reluctantly into the busy hall. We timed it perfectly and slipped seamlessly into the single file line and marched alongside the rest of our class. I caught a few sideways glances from the other students, but no one said anything. I guess everyone knew better than to cross the Luxors that led us down the halls.

We kept marching, and my heart sank when we headed out into the courtyard. This wasn't good.

"Sadie?" I whispered, uneasiness heavy in my voice.

"It'll be okay," she said under her breath.

The bright sunlight blinded me. I had to shield my eyes. They hadn't seen sunlight in, in... well I guess more than a week, according to Sadie.

We were already outside the gates of the courtyard, and we rounded the curves of the hedge maze heading down the path that sloped toward the beach. The feeling of dread in my chest amplified. This could only mean one thing; we were heading to the Athlesium.

My heart was pounding and I shivered at the sheer memory of the violent arena. Of course, I had been rescued from the infirmary just in time for the most brutal class at the Troian Academy.

Just my luck, I thought.

I was getting winded from the brisk pace of the Luxor's march. It would be a miracle if I didn't get sent back to the infirmary from the hike to the Athlesium, let alone whatever barbaric sport we would be practicing today. Sadie grabbed my hand, offering her support as she towed me behind her. I was relieved for the momentary pause supplied by the Luxors who stopped to open the gate halfway through the tunnel. I closed my eyes relishing the faint ripple of the sea breeze in my hair. Then I felt a pair of hands lightly touch my arm. I tensed for a moment before I heard Sparrow's voice behind me.

"Thank the gods," she said.

I squeezed her hands as I watched tears stream down her face. I tried to smile, but I barely had the energy to stand.

"Are you okay?"

I nodded even though it was a lie. I felt like I was going to pass out at any moment. But Sparrow looked so worried, I couldn't add to her burden.

"You just need to get through this lesson and then we'll get word to Nova to signal for help."

"Help?" I asked.

"He's been speaking to Jaka. He's sending reinforcements to the edge of the forest ready to break us out of here at his signal. We were just waiting to find you," she said beaming.

I felt a tiny prickle of hope blossom somewhere deep inside me. It gave the pit in my stomach a moment of ease.

Just make it through today, I told myself. *Help them escape and then you can turn yourself in, Geneva.*

I smiled and squeezed Sparrow's hand. "I can do that," I said as Sadie gently nudged me to keep moving.

I followed my friends to the dressing room where we changed into our Athlesium uniforms. Jemma caught up with us there. She was out of breath, but looked radiant with her painted lips and shimmering eyes. I avoided my own reflection while I got ready, keeping my head down through the gossip surrounding me. The ugly scar on my arm was a point of interest to the leering girls in the dressing room.

"What's their problem?" I whispered to Sparrow.

"We had to make something up to stop the rumor mill, so we said you had surgery on your quarterstaff injury," she replied.

"Oh," I said glancing at the jagged pink flesh that marred my arm.

There was no hiding it, so I resigned myself to putting up with the whispers.

Commander Gray blew his whistle and I followed the orderly line from the dressing room to where the other girls were lined up around the edge of the sandy ring inside the sphere shaped structure. I watched while the boys lined up across from us. I scanned the crowd and noticed Remi, Nova and Journey were absent from the group. In fact, the group looked smaller than the last time I'd been in the Athlesium. My stomach dropped thinking perhaps I wasn't the only one to end up on the losing end of the violence that had happened here.

Sparrow noticed the panic on my face and moved close enough so I could hear her whisper.

"Don't worry. The boys are at Cadets," she said. "They only have to come to the Athlesium every other week now."

I breathed a sigh of relief.

"And everyone else?" I whispered, referring to the fact that there had been twice as many students the last time I'd been here.

"Adopted," Sadie said.

I looked to Sparrow, but she averted her eyes. I didn't have time to say anything else before one of the Luxors addressed us. Commander Gray's booming voice rang through the air.

"As you know, Headmaster Malakai wants each of you to find a trial that you can excel in for the Genesis Tournament. He regards self-defense and athleticism highly. Today we will be learning a new skill ..."

He paced back and forth, droning on about the rules of some athletic endeavor, but I couldn't pay attention. I was too busy trying to see past him to search the crowd of students. I scanned the row of boys across from me, studying their faces, moving methodically down the row, instinctively hoping that the boy from my vision would be among them. My brain ached as I tried to determine who was missing while I searched the faces of the boys in the Athlesium for the last Pillar. But Terran wasn't there.

"That would be too easy," I sighed to myself.

I watched the Luxors stride down the rows passing out helmets and equipment. I kept my head down and did my best not to groan under the weight of the heavy gear. I couldn't draw attention to myself and risk them turning me over to Malakai just yet. I needed to see Nova and convince him to signal for the Betos to get Niv and my friends safely out of here first.

I was at least pleased to find that whatever we were doing today required the helmets to be outfitted with mesh facemasks. That would make hiding my identity easier. I pulled on the white jacket with its thick chest guard and buckled it in place. Next I slipped on chainmail gloves. They were lighter than I expected and cool to the touch, making my skin quiver with a chill that ran the length of my arms.

The last piece of equipment was a long, thin saber. I picked up the curved silver hilt and felt it hum in my grip. I gulped back my fear and stood ready with the rest of my class. I glanced at Sadie and she gave me a look of encouragement as she pulled her mesh facemask down.

The Luxors ordered us to advance to the center of the arena where we lined up before them.

I stumbled in the soft sand, still feeling a bit unsteady on my feet. My unused muscles ached and were sluggish to respond. I was still fighting to catch my breath and a cold sweat ran down my back despite the heat of the humid salt air. I hurried to catch up to the others and heard a few malicious snickers from the students who saw my clumsy move. I shook it off, only focusing on surviving.

Just get through this. Just get through this, I repeated to myself.

THERE WAS a knock on the heavy mahogany doors to Malakai's office and he glared at Professor Kobel.

"I thought I told you we were not to be interrupted! Planning the Genesis Tournament is a tedious affair."

"I conveyed your instructions, Master. It must be an emergency."

Kobel went to the door and whispered hurriedly with a Luxor who handed him a note. The professor's creased face paled and he shut the door.

"Master, we have a situation." Kobel paused before continuing. Steadying himself for Malakai's wrath. "We've lost her."

Malakai looked up from the stack of plans on his desk. "Excuse me?"

"The Eva, Master. She's no longer in the infirmary. Both she and her sister are unaccounted for."

"They're not lost," he growled rising to his feet. "The Orbiture will give us their location."

Malakai was already whirling the stone tablet to life. The bright orb swirled with yellow light as Malakai waved his hands above it, tilting the images rapidly as he scanned the Troian Academy.

"I'm afraid you won't find them with the Orbiture," Kobel said as he placed two cuffs onto Malakai's desk with a soft thud. "The medics had these removed."

Malakai looked up in shock.

"What? Under whose orders?"

"Mine, Master."

"You old fool! This means you not only lost her, but were wrong about her too. She's not the *Ponte deorum* or she would still be frozen by your curse!"

"That can't be," Kobel said in utter confusion. "You saw the pattern forming yourself! There must be another explanation."

Malakai had closed the gap between himself and the elderly professor. He leaned in closely and spoke into his ear. "You were wrong. You've made me look like a fool in front of the entire Ravinori. You've failed me, Kobel. I told you what would happen if you failed me again."

Kobel began to shake as Malakai unsheathed his dagger.

"Please, Master. I am not wrong. She is deceiving us somehow. Please..."

A thundering knock at the door interrupted the men. After a moment it creaked open and a startled looking Luxor stared at Malakai and Kobel.

"This message was just delivered for you, Headmaster. I

would never normally intrude, but it's from one of your informants and they said it was urgent."

Malakai took the note and slammed the door in the wide-eyed Luxor's face. A slow smile spread across his face as he read the note.

"It seems I owe you an apology, Kobel."

Malakai sheathed his knife and passed the note to Kobel.

"Come, Kobel. I'm through waiting."

COMMANDER GRAY WAS BARKING ORDERS.

"Face your opponent. You will bow to them and then run through the basic moves I demonstrated."

Oh crud.

I hadn't been paying attention at all during his demonstration. My ears pricked up listening to the instructions the Luxors were shouting at us now. I lifted the thin metal saber. It was much heavier than it looked. I tried to mimic the maneuvers of the students around me without much success. I was definitely not at my best, so sword fighting seemed like it was going to be a pretty disastrous task for me.

"Bow," barked Gray.

I followed the boy in front of me, bending forward with both hands, the sword behind my back.

"Paces!" he called.

Everyone turned their backs and took a few paces away from each other.

"En garde!"

There was a swift sound, like whipping wind, as everyone changed direction, crouched and welded their sabers. As usual, I was a few steps behind. I could see my opponent shaking his head in disappointment as I stumbled through the next few foreign commands.

"Lunge. Parry. Riposte. Parry-riposte."

The Luxor kept shouting commands and everyone else kept up with the demanding dance that he was choreographing. Everyone except me. I was sweating and struggling to catch my breath. My opponent had stopped trying once he knocked the saber out of my hand for the second time. I apologized repeatedly, but he said nothing, silently shaking his head.

I finally breathed a sigh of relief when Commander Gray shouted, "Disengage!"

I let my arms drop to my sides and I pulled my mask up, drinking deep breaths of air into my burning lungs. Sadie and Sparrow gave me nervous looks when Gray marched down our row. He hesitated as he passed in front of Jemma and I. I held my breath and neither of us made eye contact with him. He paused momentarily and raised an eyebrow at me, but said nothing. He continued down the line and called out another command.

"Rotate and repeat!"

"Bow, Paces, En garde! Lunge, Parry, Riposte... repeat!"

The dizzy dance continued until I was starting to see spots swimming in my blurry vision. We'd rotated partners so many times I lost track of where everyone was, until I heard a familiar voice next to me.

"Geneva, are you okay?" Sadie whispered

"No! I can't do this anymore. I think I'm going to pass out or throw up or both."

"You have to hang in there or they'll send you back to the infirmary."

I knew she was right and I felt like I was going to burst into tears. There was no way I was going back there after what we'd just been through to escape. I took a deep breath and nodded to her.

"I'll be all right," I said as I steeled myself for attack.

"Go easy on her," she hissed to my opponent who looked

bewildered. His eyes had widened nervously when he'd heard me say I might throw up. I recognized him. I'd seen Nova talking to him in the library. His name was Luca.

He nodded at me and said, "Just stay on your feet."

"En garde!"

41

Somehow I made it through two more dizzying rounds. When the whistle blew, signaling the end of the final round, I sighed with relief. I had made it! I was dripping with sweat and seconds from vomiting, but I made it through the grueling lesson in the Athlesium. Sparrow was at my side and I gratefully let her put her shoulder under mine to hold me up. I lifted my mask and grinned at her as I panted to catch my breath.

The sudden sound of clapping in the distance stopped my feeling of relief. I turned around to see where it had come from and my stomach plummeted. I staggered backward. Sparrow was the only reason I stayed on my feet at all, her toned arms steadying me.

A dark line had appeared on the edge of the arena. Cadets, in crisp navy blue uniforms stood motionless in the sea breeze that drifted through the stone archways of the Athlesium.

I found Remi, Nova and Journey in the crowd and couldn't tell whether they looked frightened or relieved to see me. Remi was the only one who returned my confused stare with a meek smile. Journey and Nova remained stoic, their jaws set tightly, hiding any emotion they might be feeling, as they stood rigidly at attention with the elite group of boys.

My eyes moved instinctively back to Nova, studying his beautiful face. My knees went weak the moment I'd picked him out of the crowd of Cadets. At times, my need to see him again had been all that kept me going in the infirmary. I was desperate to make sure he wouldn't be harmed by whatever plan Malakai had to dissolve the veil on my powers. Nova looked paler and thinner than I'd ever seen him, but he was still alive and that was all I could ask for at the moment. He had tired bags under his eyes that matched my own and his pinched brow showed signs of worry. I knew instantly that I was the cause of his distress and I wanted to run to him and wipe it away with the tears that were welling in my eyes.

I followed Nova's piercing green eyes as they glanced nervously between me and the Luxors. He was trying to tell me something, but I didn't know what. If only I could talk to him or telepath. Not having powers was making everything impossible. I stood on my tiptoes to get a better view and Nova shot me a look of pain. I'd seen it before, in the forest when we'd battled the Ravinori. He was telling me to stop, stay put. I was in danger.

My eyes were drawn to a movement behind him. A tall figure with a dark billowing cape moved toward us and my body was instantly flooded with fear.

Malakai.

"Don't stop on my account," Malakai crooned. "I'm merely a spectator."

"We were actually just finishing, Sir," Commander Gray said as he greeted our headmaster. "Some of them are showing promise."

"Oh dear, I'm too late? I was so hoping my Cadets would get a chance to see a few rounds of fencing. I do love the sport so. It reminds me of my days at the academy in Lux," Malakai said ruefully.

"I suppose they could stand one more round," Gray said eager to please the headmaster.

"I have an idea," he said cunningly. "As luck would have it, the Cadets had a fencing drill this week. Why don't we have them spar with your students? That is, if you think their up for the task?" Malakai asked with a sinister grin.

I couldn't be certain, but I could have sworn he glanced at me when he asked that question. There's no way he could have recognized me with my helmet and gear on, could he? I could tell this sparring stunt wasn't something that Malakai had just thought of. He was orchestrating something.

"Of course, Headmaster," Gray replied.

"Splendid! Come, son. Let's watch how it's done!"

And that's when I first saw him. Kai had been in the wake of his father's shadow, trailing shamefully behind him. His arm was awkwardly strapped to his chest and he had a look of agony painted across his handsome face as he glanced in my direction. His dark eyes flashed me an apology before he lowered them to obediently follow Malakai.

"What happened to Kai?" I asked still staring after him.

"I'm surprised he's back on his feet," Jemma snickered.

"What's that supposed to mean?" I asked.

"He sort of got into it with Nova," Sadie whispered.

My temper flared. I could feel my cheeks flushing with anger at Nova's jealousy. "What happened?"

"Apparently they learned grappling last week. It's a form of defensive wrestling; pretty brutal stuff. Anyway, Kai had the misfortune of drawing Nova as his competitor," Sadie replied.

"Oh no," I groaned. "Do I even want to ask?"

"Oh, he'll be fine," Jemma shrugged. "They were just mismatched. Nova pinned him instantly," she said with a bit too much pride in her voice.

"He doesn't look fine," I said leering at the uncomfortable angle of his arm.

From the looks of it, Kai had suffered much more than a bruised ego at Nova's hands. Wrestling Kai was probably the perfect opportunity for Nova to get his hands on him. I remembered the way Nova had glared at Kai when we were in the library. He probably tried to take Kai's head off in a wrestling match.

"Nova broke his collarbone," Jemma said without any remorse. "We won't be seeing Kai in the ring at the Athlesium for a while."

"He broke his bones?"

Why did Nova always have to overreact? First with Remi and now with Kai. Poor Kai had done nothing but try to be a friend to me, but Nova couldn't see past his jealousy to realize that Kai was trying to help us. I was furious. This fighting among us had to stop.

I glared across the area, shooting daggers with my eyes. Nova stared right back at me, like he knew what I had just found out and he wasn't sorry. A strange protectiveness for Kai stormed inside of me and I was shaking mad. How could Nova be so selfish? Weren't we all supposed to be on the same team, with the same goal? How would we ever get Kai to help us if Nova was trying to kill him every chance he got? And why? All because he was jealous? He truly didn't understand me at all.

Kai was probably our best chance at finding Terran and now we had one less lesson with him or maybe worse. Maybe his father would pull him out of the Troian Academy altogether and send him back to Lux where he'd be safer. Part of me almost wished he would. Poor Kai, he didn't deserve any of this. He'd been nothing but kind to us and I'd done everything I could to lure him into my messed up life. He definitely thought I liked him, and I obviously wasn't very good at forming fake friendships, because the minute I heard that he was injured my heart fluttered with worry. Any feelings I'd forced myself to have for Kai felt surprisingly real.

A whistle blew, disrupting my thoughts. I numbly shuffled back into the ring after my friends in disbelief.

What was Malakai doing here? Did he know I'd be here? What was he up to?

I made sure my facemask was secure and fell into line with the rest of my class. We all waited in electric silence, while the Cadets filed in across from us after they'd donned their fencing gear. I breathed a sigh of relief when I drew Journey as an opponent. My arm was already shaking from the strain of holding the saber. I didn't have much faith that I'd last through another round of drills. At least Journey would do his best to help me. We took our positions and I was now close enough to chance talking to him.

"What's Malakai doing here?" I whispered to Journey. "Do you think he knows I escaped the infirmary?"

"I don't know. Just stay calm. Keep your mask down and stay on your feet and maybe he won't know it's you."

"Okay. Okay, I can do this," I said, giving myself a pep talk.

"Geneva, breathe," Journey reminded me.

"Bow," barked Commander Gray.

"Just a moment. Sorry to interrupt," called Malakai.

My veins went cold. Did he pick me out already? Was I about to get hauled away before I even had a chance to warn my friends about him and my visions?

"Do you not start your drills with synchronized rotations?" he asked innocently.

"Yes. Thank you, Sir," Gray said. "ROTATE!"

I followed the waltz-like steps, spinning past opponents in the sand. I did my best to stay on my feet and fight the dizzying paranoia I felt being trapped in the Athlesium with Malakai. When the dance came to a halt, I found myself face to face with Nova. My anger had evaporated, replaced by a trembling fear. I could barely make out Nova's piercing green eyes behind his mesh facemask. They were wide, but calm. I could tell he was trying to convey to me that everything was going to be all right. But how could it? I couldn't let Nova touch me, especially here in front of the headmaster. I knew he'd touched me before without unveiling my powers, but maybe that was because we were within the magical fenced in walls of the Troian Academy. Now I lacked their protection and I had no idea what would happen if and when my powers came unveiled. But I had a feeling it wouldn't be an inconspicuous event.

Malakai was already suspicious of me. Jemma saving me from the blood curse might have bought me some time and I needed every second of it. But I couldn't afford to confirm Malakai's beliefs. I hadn't expected him to figure out I wasn't in the infirmary so quickly. I'd hoped without my cuff to track me, I'd have had more time. Somehow, Malakai seemed to know everything that went on in the Troian Academy and I was sure showing up here to watch our fencing lesson was no accident. I now suspected that he had already located me and purposely had us rotate so I would be forced to fence Nova. I knew I was bordering on the edge of paranoia, but I guess that's to be expected after being in a poison induced coma.

"Geneva, you're shaking," Nova whispered. "I'm not going to let him get to you," he said reaching his hand out to steady me.

I lurched away from his outstretched hand, barely dodging it. I could see the hurt expression on his face and it killed me that I couldn't tell him the truth. But now was not the time. I couldn't risk unveiling my powers here in front of Malakai. I had to do the only thing I knew would keep Nova away from me. Push his temper.

"Don't touch me, Nova! I can't believe you would hurt Kai like that. I don't want to talk to you ever again, do you understand me?" I hissed at him in a rushed whisper.

He said nothing but he took a step back.

"I mean it, Nova. Stay away from me."

He nodded, but still said nothing.

"Bow, Paces, En garde!"

And it began, a flurry of dizzying commands. I did my best to keep up with them and Nova did his best to be terrible at fencing. He avoided me, backed off on all my advances and even dropped his saber at one point.

"Disengage," the Luxor finally called and I heaved to a panting halt.

I was dripping sweat and shaking. I could barely catch my breath but I had survived.

"Bravo! Bravo students. You're right, they certainly are picking it up quite nicely. See Kai, it doesn't look that hard, does it? You should aim to be more like your classmates. Perhaps you can join them for a round? After all, you only need one arm to fence."

Kai looked mortified. His eyes were wide and his mouth opened, but I didn't hear anything come out. How could his father be so cruel? Kai's arm was thickly bandaged and it was tied in a sling around his neck. He had been wincing in pain as he trailed his father through the Athlesium. There was no way he could fence.

"He's got to be joking, right?" I whispered to Nova.

He still said nothing to me.

"Why doesn't he just say no?"

I wanted to call out to Kai and tell him to say no to his father. He didn't need to impress him or earn his respect this way. It was too cruel.

"Well, what do you say, boy? Do you want to give it a go?"

Slowly, painfully, Kai nodded.

"Splendid! One more round!" Malakai bellowed to the Luxors.

Kai feebly made his way into the center of the arena, with

his father trailing him. The Luxors jogged over with sabers and equipment and helped get Kai ready.

"Ah, isn't this fun?" Malakai exclaimed, clapping his hands together. "Now, let's find you a worthy opponent,"

He spun around and his eyes settled immediately on me. I caught my breath and swallowed hard.

"You," he said pointing at me. "You'll do. Come here,"

I was frozen in place and before I could command my shaking legs to move, I felt someone stride past me. His long legs carried him gracefully around me and he was in front of Kai before I could even react.

Had Malakai been pointing to Nova or was he coming to my rescue again? I wanted to scream, but I couldn't. I was paralyzed with fear.

"You'll go easy on him this time," I heard Commander Gray say to Nova.

"No! He'll fight my son as he'd fight anyone. War doesn't afford privileges, it treats all men equal," Malakai hissed angrily, momentarily losing his composure as he stepped between Nova and Kai.

"Let's make things interesting, shall we? Remove the sheaths. I find fighting with a real weapon always inspires greatness, don't you agree?" he asked with a maniacal grin.

Not wanting to argue with the headmaster, Gray carefully removed the metal sheath from the boys' sabers. The metal hummed when it was uncovered and glinted back the sunlight filtering in through the Athlesium's oculus.

The Luxors motioned for us to take a step back. Journey physically dragged me because I was frozen in fear. He handed me over to Remi, who wrapped his arms around me. I wanted to melt into his familiar embrace, but I was trembling with fear. This couldn't be happening. Malakai couldn't truly be asking his son to fight Nova with a real weapon!

Surely he would stop them before the Luxors called for En garde, right?

But he didn't. The boys bowed to each other, each marched several paces and then turned to face each other. I held my breath, praying I would hear Malakai speak next and stop this foolishness, but I didn't hear that. Instead I heard, "En garde!"

Then I closed my eyes as a flurry of commands and clashing metal filled the air.

"This can't be happening! They're going to get hurt or worse," I blubbered.

Remi turned me away from the ring and I buried my face into his shoulder.

"Don't watch," he whispered into my hair.

He protectively covered my ears, trying his best to block out the sinister sounds of sabers slashing though the air.

"Parry! Parry means step backward," Nova whispered as he advanced on Kai.

Kai's eyes were wild with fear and confusion.

"Just listen to me and we'll both make it through this," Nova said.

Kai stared at Nova as he stumbled around in the sand, wincing in pain and trying to keep his saber raised.

"Kai, blink twice if you understand me. I promise, I'm trying to help you, but you've got to work with me here."

Finally, Kai gave some semblance of recognition and blinked twice in response.

Nova winked back at him and whispered, "Follow my lead."

Nova expertly waltzed through the series of maneuvers, quietly directing Kai so he could anticipate what moves would be coming next. Before too long, Kai was getting the hang of it.

~

"GENEVA, open you're eyes. It's all right, look," Remi coaxed.

My eyes popped open and to my amazement, he was right. Kai and Nova danced about, cautiously tapping blades as they gracefully rotated around the ring.

"Oh! They're doing it! How are they doing it?"

"Nova's helping him."

"He is?" I squeaked, my heart instantly melting and washing away the remaining anger that I'd been harboring toward him.

"Yeah, watch his lips; he's whispering his next move to Kai so he knows what to anticipate."

As soon as he pointed it out, it was blatantly obvious.

"Malakai's not going to be happy if he figures that out," I said as I looked across the ring to the headmaster.

And I was right. His face was twisted in frustration as he watched the two boys fence.

"No! No, no, no! Stop! I wanted to see a true duel!"

"Arret," called Commander Gray, giving them the sign to stop.

Both boys halted and raised their masks as Malakai strode toward them. Malakai grabbed the sword from his son's hands and whispered something angrily in his ear.

"And you," Malakai said turning on Nova. "Do you think I didn't notice that you were leading him? Feeding him your every move?"

Nova stood his ground. "I don't enjoy picking on a cripple. It's not a fair fight."

"Life's not fair, Mr. Asher. A win is a win. You should never be lenient to a foe. You never know when that will come back to be your undoing. Besides, where was this compassion for the weak earlier, hmm? You didn't seem to have an issue with breaking my son's collarbone then? I had higher hopes for you. Perhaps you're not the warrior I'd hoped you were."

Nova stared at him, but didn't answer.

"No matter," Malakai said, regaining his composure and turning to face us. "If they will not fight properly, I guess I'll have to show you how it's done myself."

Malakai pushed the boys aside but kept hold of Kai's sword. He stood alone, like a tall menacing shadow in the center of the Athlesium. The sunlight shining in from the oculus in the ceiling shone directly on him, ominously highlighting the sinister angles of his face. He slowly raised his free-hand chest high and uncoiled one of his long, boney fingers.

A collective inhalation resounded among my classmates as they watched our headmaster beckon me to the center of the ring with him.

42

"You'll spar with me won't you, Miss Sommers?"

I couldn't find my voice to respond, but I nodded and took a shaky step forward.

"Come, let's show them how this is done," Malakai encouraged.

Before I could take another step, Remi grabbed my hand, pulling me back.

"Don't," he said, his voice laced with concern.

"Remi, I know what I'm doing. Trust me," I pleaded as I squeezed his hand.

Journey grabbed a hold of him.

"Let her go, mate. She doesn't have a choice."

He was right. I didn't have a choice. Malakai had known I was here all along. I hadn't been acting paranoid. It was no accident that he pitted Nova and Kai against each other. He was trying to hurt me through those I cared about to prove that he was in control. And he *was* in control. I was a fool, completely out of my depth when it came to Malakai. He somehow knew everything. He had been expecting us all along and we played right into his hand. But what could I do now? I had nothing, no powers. I was just an ordinary girl. I was still weak from whatever poison Professor Kobel had laced my blood with.

I felt like I was marching to my death as I somehow convinced my leaden legs to carry me to the center of the Athlesium. I narrowed my eyes at Malakai. This man had already stolen a week of my life. I wasn't about to let him take anything else from me.

An evil smirk spread across his wicked face and he licked his lips in a sickening fashion as I approached. Before I could face him directly, Nova and Kai were back in the ring, both of them rushing to my aid and arguing to take my spot.

"If you want a worthy opponent, I'll fight you," Nova said. "Challenge me."

"Ah, the noble boy. Coming to the rescue of your love? Don't you know you're wasting your affection on her?"

My heart stuttered. How did Malakai know about my feelings for Nova? I'd been so careful.

"He's not my love," I said finally finding my voice.

"See, she doesn't even deny it. You can do better, Mr. Asher."

"I can fight my own battles, Nova," I said sternly.

"Father, please," Kai pleaded between us.

"Kai, is this not the girl you've been telling me about? You've had such praise for her. Is she not as great as you've said?"

"No, she is, but..." Kai's cheeks burned red with embarrassment. "I just don't want to see anyone get hurt."

"Ah, well both of your honorable intentions have been noted, but I strive to teach equality here. Unless, you're all aware of something that I am not. Is there some other reason that this girl isn't up to sparring with me?"

There was a long silent pause.

"Then it's settled. She'll prove a worthy opponent."

"Nothing would please me more than to spar with you, Malakai," I countered, refusing to let him shake me.

"Splendid!" he responded, motioning to the Luxors.

They sprang forward with sabers and gear. He arrogantly waved away the helmet and protective equipment. He simply motioned for them to pull Nova and Kai from the ring. I was securing my helmet when Malakai cleared his throat.

"For a proper duel, opponents must be equally outfitted. You won't be needing your helmet," Malakai said, and then he whispered for only me to hear, "I want to look into your eyes when I bring you to your knees."

I pulled off my helmet and gloves and looked toward my friends. I tried to convey with my eyes that it was okay, but it was a feeble attempt. Deep down I couldn't even convince myself that I'd be okay. But I felt that I was at least protecting my friends from the headmaster's cruelty. It was me he wanted. And I'd already decided that I was going to turn myself over to Malakai in order to spare them. Now was as good a time as any to start bargaining.

Also, I was fairly certain he wouldn't murder me in front of so many students and half a dozen Luxors, but even that wasn't comforting. Maybe his plan was only to injure me severely so I had to go back to the infirmary, where I'd be at his mercy again. I knew I was no match for Malakai. He had size and skill on me and who knows what other tricks he had up his sleeve, but I was past the point of caring. If I couldn't beat him, I'd at least try my damnedest to maim him, or make him show his true intentions to everyone in the Athlesium. Then maybe I'd gain a few more supporters.

I had no idea what Malakai was trying to prove but if he wanted a fight, he was going to get one.

We took our positions and waited for the commands to be called out.

My breathing came fast and shallow. Adrenaline spiked pushing the pain and weakness from my mind as I raised my saber. The unsheathed blade hummed and glistened before me and I morbidly imagined plunging it into Malakai's heart. The vision brought the taste of bile from my queasy stomach and gooseflesh tingled up my arms, despite the heavy humid air in the Athlesium.

"I'm the Eva, I can do this," I silently pep talked myself as we paced away from each other.

"Allez," called the troubled looking Luxor that Commander Gray had charged with our duel.

Then finally, after a painfully long hesitation, he said, "En garde!"

Malakai advanced on me quickly. This wasn't like our training. He wasn't waiting for choreographed commands. His saber whizzed past my shoulder as I narrowly dodged his lunge. I went into defense mode and put as much ground between us as I could. It seemed my speed and being a relatively small target was to my advantage.

My confidence was building. Even when Malakai closed the gap, I was able to stave off his attacks. I may have pushed it too far when I grinned after hopping over one of his leg swipes.

He yelled as he spun around and lashed out at me unexpectedly. I didn't even feel the sting of the blade, but the gasp from the crowd and the thick red liquid that blurred the vision in my left eye let me know I'd been hit! I was so shocked that I stumbled backward and fell out of the ring, stopping the duel.

"Now, this is how a real fencing duel should be!" Malakai bellowed, circling the confines of the ring in celebration. "Can you feel the electricity?" he called to the crowd of stunned students and Luxors.

I was seething mad; seeing red, both figuratively and literally. I was under the impression that he would be going for the target zone of my fencing jacket as we had been instructed to do in our lesson. But he didn't, he went for my head and drew blood! He was aiming to kill me!

I sprang to my feet and charged Malakai. His back was to

me as he addressed the crowd, but I didn't care. He wasn't going to play fair, so why should I? I jumped and swung my sword wildly. I watched in slow motion as he turned, his eyes wide with astonishment. He saw the lifeless pile of black locks lying unceremoniously upon the sand and his hand went instinctively to the back of his neck. He slowly pulled his hand away and examined the red liquid smeared across it.

I sneered at him, feeling a small dose of triumph as I saw his utter disbelief that his long black mane had been severed from his head.

"I figured you might enjoy the same haircut as me and my friends," I smirked.

"I didn't realize you would play without honor," he growled.

"Me?" I said incredulously while I wiped at the blood dripping down my face.

Malakai grinned, igniting a fire in my bones that stoked my hatred for him.

"A win's a win, right?" I sneered quoting him.

He lunged at me and we locked into a fierce battle. When he got close, I could see the fury in his eyes and smell the blood streaming down the back of his neck.

"I know who you are, Malakai. I know what you and the Ravinori want me for," I said as we tangled.

He laughed wildly and struck me hard on the arm, but my jacket protected me from the brutal sting of his razor sharp blade.

"Don't fool yourself, girl. You know nothing about us. But I know exactly who you are and what you think you can do. Actually it's becoming more apparent every day that I know more about who you are then you do yourself."

"So you knew I'd escape your little blood curse then?" I taunted.

He growled and lashed at me again, slicing a ribbon into the front of my fencing jacket. I needed to cool it. I was pushing him too far. But I could see my opportunity. I needed to try to sway him to let my friends go.

"You're right. I know I'm in over my head. So, I've thought about your offer," I panted as I blocked his swings.

"And?"

"I'm prepared to work with you, but I have conditions."

His eyebrows rose and he gave me a condescending grin. I continued anyway.

"I will work with you willingly. I'll do anything you want, on this condition," I panted through gritted teeth while I fought off his advance. "You have to let my friends go. You can only have me. I'm all you need."

Malakai laughed as he tangled our blades and pulled me in close. The feel of his breath on my neck made my skin crawl.

"The first rule of negotiation, my dear, is leverage. And you have none."

He kicked me away and lunged at me once more while I was off balance. His saber struck out at my fighting hand, knocking my weapon free.

"Then what are you waiting for?" I shouted, defenseless and scared.

He paused for the briefest moment to smile at me, and somehow that was the scariest moment of our duel. In that moment I knew he was only toying with me, that he could have killed me right then and there if he wanted. But he didn't. He wouldn't. He needed me. And I had nothing I could bargain with.

"You tell me, *Ponte deorum*," he whispered.

And then he dropped his sword and bowed.

43

"What in the gods name was that?" Nova accosted me during our hike back to the Troian Center?

I put my head down and kept marching. Malakai had laughed and thanked me graciously for a spirited duel and then left the Athlesium with Kai following painfully behind him. But not before commanding the Luxors to put cuffs back on Jemma and I.

"Are you trying to get yourself killed? Or perhaps you have a death wish I don't know about? Geneva, answer me!" he badgered.

Apparently watching me duel with Malakai had been enough to erase the hurtful words I'd said to him earlier. I sighed, not having the energy to argue with him right now.

"Nova, he's not going to kill me, all right?" I grumbled trying to keep some distance between us.

"Have you seen the gash on your forehead? You're going to have to do a little better than that to convince me."

"He can't kill me. He needs me."

"What does that mean, exactly?" he persisted.

"He knows," I spat. "He knows everything, okay! He knows

I'm the *Ponte deorum.* My only hope is that I'm worth enough to him that I can bargain for your lives."

"No. No, that's not the deal. You are not sacrificing yourself for us," Nova whispered urgently.

I met the burning green flames in his eyes with sorrow and had to look away to fight the sting of tears welling in my own.

"Please, Geneva. Just talk to me," Nova begged.

He was bending to be closer to my height. He was too close. I was out of breath and losing energy now that the adrenaline was wearing off.

"This isn't the time or place to explain it all to you," I muttered.

"The way things are going I'm afraid this might be the only time," he argued, reaching out for my hand to stop me from walking away from him.

"STOP!" I screamed at him. "How many different ways do I have to ask you not to touch me?"

"Until you make me understand why," he shouted back.

I hadn't expected him to yell at me with such resentment. We'd always bickered, but now he was really laying into me. His face was red and I could see a vein pulsing furiously in his neck. We'd stopped moving and so had most of our classmates, who were now gathered around, staring at us.

Nova, why can't you just leave this alone? I wished.

"Keep moving!" called a Luxor from the back of the line.

"Please, Nova. Not here, okay?"

"Then where?" he pleaded, his features finally softening back to the kind-faced boy I loved.

My heart lurched. I didn't know the answer to that question. He deserved the truth from me, about my feelings for him, why I had been keeping my distance, how Jemma was using him, all of it. But I didn't know if I could bring myself to confess it all to him. I didn't know if I'd even have the time to do so. So I did what I'd been doing since we came to this dreadful place; I lied to the boy I loved.

"Study hall, tonight. I promise."

"What's going on here?" called a Luxor. He'd caught up to us and wasn't happy we were disobeying his orders. "I said, keep moving!" he bellowed, giving me a swift shove in the back that knocked me to my knees.

I could tell he hadn't meant to push me to the ground, but I was so exhausted from fencing that staying on my feet was enough of a challenge. Nova moved protectively between us.

"Leave her alone," Nova warned.

"Unless you feel like being in a world of hurt, you better fall back in line, maggot," the Luxor scolded Nova. He stepped to the side and shifted his focus to me. "On your feet, 65!" called the irritated Luxor, reaching his hand down to help me up.

I hated how most of the Luxors continued to use our tattooed numbers as our names.

"My name is Geneva," I said. "And I don't need your help."

To my surprise Jemma stood suddenly by my side. She pulled me to my feet while Nova continued to argue with the group of Luxors now milling around us.

"I'll get back in line when you stop picking on girls," I heard Nova shout.

The Luxor leered and laughed in Nova's face.

"What are you sweet on this one? Come on, Cadet, you can do better. A big strapping lad like you? You don't want that one," the Luxor said pointing at me. "There's no meat on her bones. Look at her; knobby knees, no chest, and that hair. Besides, I can tell she's nothing but trouble. She's not worth it."

The Luxors joked and laughed at my expense as Nova shook with rage. I knew he wanted to protect me, but he knew it would only make things worse if he continued to face off with them. He took a deep breath and stepped aside, letting his head drop in defeat. I was proud of him for refraining from retaliating.

Jemma steadied me and pulled me away from them and back toward the haphazard line of students gawking at us. Sparrow ran to my side and slipped my other arm over her shoulder.

"Oh, now these two, they're worth fighting for, wouldn't you say?" the Luxors ribbed each other, referring to Jemma and Sparrow.

I heard a low whistle, followed by the Luxors laughing and cat-calling.

"Come on," Jemma said ignoring them and pulling me away from their snide remarks.

The next thing I knew I heard yelling behind us and all the Luxors were amuck. I turned around in time to see Journey pummeling one of the Luxors, blood staining his flying fists, just before two more Luxors leapt onto his back and tackled him to the ground.

"I DON'T CARE if you have to chain him to his bed! My son doesn't leave his room until I say so," Malakai screamed, slamming the door in the face of a frightened Luxor he ordered to escort Kai to his room.

Malakai paced back and forth furiously in his destroyed office. The massive desk was overturned and the room was in shambles from his outpouring of rage after his fencing session. A white coat trembled in the corner while Professor Kobel tried his best to calm the headmaster down enough for her to attempt stitches on the back of his neck.

"How dare she," Malakai repeated again. His black hair was damp from sweat and swung freely about his rage contorted face. With his hair cropped to shoulder length, he looked more like Kai than ever. "I'll have her head, Kobel! Do you hear me?"

"Yes, Master."

"I want you to get me inside her head. I will rip the remaining Pillars from her mind if she refuses to give them to me."

"I'm trying my best, Master, but the blood curse didn't have time to dissolve the veil completely."

"Try harder!"

44

"Well, I hope you're happy now," Sparrow scoffed at Journey through the bars of the Locker.

"Sparrow, you can't be mad at him. He was trying to protect you," Remi argued.

"Did you ever think I don't need protecting?" she retorted.

"I was defending your honor," Journey said sheepishly.

"My honor is not yours to defend," she yelled back, stinging Journey.

"Sparrow, honestly, Journey was doing you a favor," Remi said coming to his friend's aid. "They were saying some nasty things about you. I wouldn't want anyone talking about my girl that way."

"Really, Remi? I'm not his girl. I'm not anyone's girl. And I guess we know where you stand now, don't we? You don't care enough about any of us to defend us. Guess we're not good enough to be *your* girl," Sparrow snapped, hands on her hips and color splotching her cheeks.

"You just got finished reaming Journey out for defending you and now I'm in trouble for not defending you?"

"You don't get it," she yelled putting her hands to her face to cover her tears as she moved away from us.

Remi's mouth was open and he stared at Journey and Nova, speechless. Nova just shrugged.

"Sometimes you can't win, mate," Journey said to Remi under his breath.

"Girls," Remi muttered and shook his head.

"Cut her some slack. Sparrow's under a lot of stress," I whispered to my friends, motioning over my shoulder to where she was standing. "The adoption," I mimed.

Everyone nodded solemnly and seemed willing to forgive her outburst.

"What did the Luxors say anyway?" Sadie asked.

"I'm not going to repeat it, but it wasn't very nice," Journey said.

I didn't know what Journey had overheard the Luxors saying but whatever it was, I'm sure it wasn't flattering. It had angered him enough to attack one of them, which erupted into pandemonium. Sadie, Sparrow and I had rushed in to try to calm Journey down, but all it resulted in was getting us all sent to the Locker for our part in the mêlée. Everyone except for Jemma. Somehow she had disappeared during the commotion.

Remi, Nova, Journey, Sparrow, Sadie and I huddled together, quietly talking through the bars of the newly remodeled Locker. It was no longer cloaked in complete darkness. Rugs and tapestries had been added at the landing of the stairs leading to the Locker. And torchlight burned brightly, filling the air with the thick perfumed scent of burning oil that made my eyes water. I found myself wondering how safe the design was since there wasn't much ventilation down here.

There were also multiple cells dividing up the Locker now. Presently, the girls were in one cell, with the boys in the one right next to it. There was a Luxor stationed at the bottom of the staircase to make sure we didn't try anything. Although I'm not sure what we could do. We were deep underground, surrounded by dank stone walls and thick steel bars with no magic powers to aid us. I stared at the metal that caged us in the Locker and my mind hiccupped with sudden recognition. The bars of the Locker, they looked exactly like the material that made up the cuffs we wore and also of the mysterious fence that now surrounded the Troian Academy. That couldn't be a coincidence. They all had to be linked somehow. But how? The answer was swimming just outside my mind when Nova interrupted me.

"I don't know, getting stuck down here might be the best thing that could have happened to us."

"What are you talking about?" Sadie asked.

"Now Geneva can't avoid telling us what's going on," he said.

I sighed deeply. There was no way I was getting out of it this time. Who knew how long we'd be stuck down here, and maybe Nova was right. This was the perfect opportunity to tell my friends what I'd learned while in the infirmary. Plus, Jemma wasn't here, so if I decided to be completely honest with Nova, she couldn't stop me. And he was on the other side of a steel cage, so perhaps this would be the safest way to tell him that my sister was using him and I'd been lying to him about it.

"Yeah, what happened, Geneva? We were so worried about you?" Remi said.

"Some of it's fuzzy, but Malakai was having me drugged. He did some sort of blood curse on me that was supposed to prove I'm the *Ponte deorum* by forming an ancient symbol over my heart."

"Sanguin de Salvator. We know that part," Journey said.

"You do?" I asked.

"Yes, Sadie figured it out and we sent a message to Hollis to see if he knew how we could fight the poison," Nova said.

"How did you send him a message?" I asked suddenly remembering to be mad at him for keeping Niv from me.

"It's not important - " Nova started.

"Give it up. She knows," Sadie interrupted.

I glared at him. "How long were you going to keep him from me, Nova?"

"Me? What about you? How long are you going to keep hiding things from us? We're all a part of this, Geneva, or have you forgotten?"

"How could I ever forget that, Nova?" I said incredulously. "All I've been trying to do is protect you!"

"Well you sure have a fine way of showing it," he said.

"What's that supposed to mean?"

"It means you need to start acting like we're a team and tell us what in the gods' name is going on here so we have a fighting chance of surviving."

"Okay. Enough, mate," Journey said laying his hand on Nova's tense shoulder.

"Geneva, why don't you tell us what you learned while you were in the infirmary?" Sadie offered trying to diffuse the tension.

"Fine." I huffed. "I was having a lot of visions and I was able to talk to my mother."

"Isn't that dangerous?" Remi asked.

"Yes, but I couldn't help it. I think the poison was making it almost impossible not to access the other side. Perhaps that's how it works on the *Ponte deorum*. But my mother was helping me. She helped me contact Jemma and tell her that she had to save me with her blood. Sadie and Jemma got to me just in time. The symbol was almost complete, which would have dissolved the veil on my powers."

Nova put his hand to his chest absently and looked like he tasted something bitter. I watched as he shook his head. He was grumbling something under his breath.

"What is it?" I asked.

"Nothing. Go on," he said.

"My mother also told me that Professor Kobel is working with Malakai. He's actually a powerful sorcerer. He's the one who came up with the blood curse and he also enchanted all the mirrors in the Troian Academy. He turned them into portals to the other side. That's why I saw my mother when we first got here. It was a trap to prove I'm the *Ponte deorum*. Malakai didn't believe Kobel though, so he went out on his own to prove he was right by poisoning me and enacting this blood curse."

"So are your powers still veiled?" Remi asked.

"Yes, as far as I know. But it doesn't matter. Malakai knows everything now."

"What do you mean?" Sparrow asked, rejoining the group.

"He knows I'm the *Ponte deorum*. He's been speaking to me in my dreams since I got here and he was doing it again while I was in the infirmary. He kept telling me to choose."

"Choose what?" Remi asked.

"The easy way or the hard way? Who lives or who dies?" I said. "Malakai knows who I am. Despite our best efforts, he knows I'm the *Ponte deorum* and he knows about two of the Pillars."

"Which two?" Sadie asked.

"Not you," I said.

I glanced at Nova and our eyes locked for a moment.

"How did he find out?" Sadie questioned.

"Well none of us told him," Remi said.

I watched Nova shake his head, his expression turning hostile.

"Don't even say it, Nova! It wasn't Kai!" I said. "I never even told him about you being a Pillar. I'm not that stupid. Don't you know I would never do anything to put you at risk? Any of you." Tears were brimming in my eyes now as I wiped them away in frustration. "And by the way, thanks for being a complete jerk and breaking his collarbone. Kai was willing to help us, but I'm sure you completely ruined that!"

"I wasn't going to blame Kai," Nova said calmly when I'd finished my hysterical rant. "I see why you trust the guy now."

"Oh... You do?" I asked baffled.

"Yeah. He came through for us," Remi said grinning.

"What do you mean?" I asked.

"Thanks to Kai, we found the last Pillar. His name's Terran Clay," Nova said.

"What?" I asked in astonishment.

"We've already met him," Journey said with a smirk. "And he's on board."

This was too good to be true. If they knew who Terran was and had already convinced him that we weren't crazy then the last thing we needed to do was escape.

"My mother gave me his name too. She was helping me search for anything else to go on when I was rescued. How did you find him?"

"We've been busy while you were gone," Remi grinned.

"I can't believe it. You actually found him?" I asked, letting a hint of excitement catch hold of me.

"They're completely serious," said a voice from behind me.

I turned to see where it came from and my eyes nearly bugged out of my head.

Staring back at me was the face I'd seen in my visions, the last Pillar. He fit the memory I had of him perfectly; the same light brown eyes, chocolate skin, rugged looks and crooked smile, but the thing that had surprised me was that he was wearing a Luxor's uniform.

"It's about time we met," he grinned as he extended his hand through the bars. "I'm Terran Clay."

45

Terran had switched places with the Luxor who'd been on guard at the bottom of the stairs. He was eagerly filling us in on what he'd just heard.

"You guys stirred up some major trouble," Terran said.

"What do you mean?" I asked.

"Well, I don't know what you did to Malakai, but whatever it was it pissed him off. He's moved the Genesis Tournament up to this Saturday."

"What?" all of my friends exclaimed at once.

"Sparrow, isn't that the day you're supposed to be adopted?"

She smiled weakly. "Well, the good news is, maybe I won't have to compete in the tournament."

"Um, what am I missing?" I asked.

"We have a theory about the Genesis Tournament," Journey said.

"It's more than a theory," Terran jumped in. "Malakai is using it as a front to kill you."

"What?" I squeaked.

"If you don't do what he wants by then, he'll have you killed in the tournament. It's the easiest way to explain your death. An athletic trial gone wrong. No one will even question it."

"He can't kill me. He needs me for ... something," I said, not knowing how much information I should trust Terran with.

"Yeah, yeah you're the Eva and the *Ponte deorum,*" Terran said. "I know all that. But there's a few different theories floating around out there. One of them is that Malakai only needs your blood to complete the ceremony to resurrect Ravin. Another is that he already has some of it, so you're not really as valuable as you think."

My mouth was dry. Would he actually kill me? I had been under the impression that Malakai needed me alive. No wonder my bargaining chip to save my friends hadn't worked.

"But that was if he planned to use the Pillars," Remi interrupted. "If he knows she's the *Ponte deorum,* he doesn't need the Pillars. Just Geneva."

Terran nodded.

"Right, but what are the chances that Malakai's not interested in the power that the Pillars harness *and* the *Ponte deorum*? We're all at risk here. I've overheard Malakai and Kobel talking. They want everyone to think you're dead, Geneva. They can't bring Ravin back until the host is prepared. That's still a few months off from what I've heard. So while they're waiting for the timing to be right they don't want the Betos or anyone thinking you're still alive and waiting to be rescued. The plan is to hide you away and eventually use your powers to bring Ravin back when everything is ready. And Malakai loves a good show, so what better place to stage your death than in front of all his Ravinori supporters?"

"But if he's staging my death..." I started.

"You've met Kobel, right? Don't underestimate him. You may be *alive* by medical standards, but I wouldn't put it past him to let you be mortally wounded first. I've seen him do unthinkable things. You'd be surprised what the Ravinori will do to keep someone alive just long enough to get what they want out of them."

"How do you know all this?" I asked.

"I've been a fly on the wall with the Ravinori for years. It's a long story and I'm going to fill you in with as much of it as I can, but we don't have a lot of time. All I can tell you is that we're not safe here. Malakai's planning something big and whatever it is, I can guarantee it isn't good and it's going down at the Genesis Tournament. We have to get out of here before then."

I searched Terran's face. He was unmistakably the boy I'd seen in my visions. But I'd just met him and was now staking my life and the lives of my friends on his word.

"And we're just supposed to trust you?" I asked.

"Geneva, I get it. But you really don't have a choice. I'm your guy. Your friends can tell you about my wonderful upbringing that led me to work for these people later. Right now, we need to come up with a plan to get out of here."

"So Saturday?" Nova said already jumping into planning mode.

"What day is it today?" I whispered to Sparrow.

"Wednesday."

I swallowed hard. This wasn't good. We had three days to escape the Troian Academy and we were currently being held prisoner in the Locker. I'd successfully escaped once, but that had mostly been luck. I doubted I'd be so fortunate this time. The school was crawling with Luxors and I was still suffering from injuries and the lasting effects of whatever I'd been drugged with. Just the thought of running exhausted me. How was I supposed to be able to escape and lead my friends to safety?

"I think it's time we signal the Betos," Journey said interrupting my thoughts.

"It'll probably be two more days until everyone arrives,"

Nova said. "But Hollis and some of the Beto warriors should be to the edge of the rainforest by now."

"I don't think we can wait for them," Terran said. "We need to go at the first chance we get."

An image of Talon flashed into my mind. Without all of the Beto warriors, it would be a slaughter.

"No," I cried. "I will not risk more Beto lives to save my own. We need to find another way."

"Geneva," Remi said reaching for my hand through the bars. "We're running out of time."

"There is another way," Terran said.

"What are you talking about?" I asked.

"I know where the Soul Cell is," Terran said. "If I shut it down, you'll all be able to get your powers back and then we can blast our way out of here."

"What's a Soul Cell?" I asked.

"It's something that the Ravinori created after the Flood to harness the Truiet powers that were said to be lost. Malakai is using it here to harness your powers and use them against you. It's why you can't use your powers here. It powers the fence and makes it impossible to use magic inside its perimeters. The fence feeds off magic and Malakai feeds the fence by sucking magic from you through those cuffs," Terran said pointing to my wrist.

"I was right," Journey said triumphantly. "Told you guys it had something to do with the fence."

"The Orbiture?" I said.

"Precisely," Terran said. "The Orbiture is the Soul Cell. It was harvested from Cayo Cave, a sacred Beto cave in the Rainforest where it's said the highest concentration of magic powers are contained. That's where the ore used to create the cuffs and the fence was mined as well."

It clicked. The thoughts my mind had been circling around finally fit together. The shimmer of the cuffs had always looked familiar to me for a reason. They were made from the cave that Remi and I had fallen into. Perhaps that's why I'd been having the same visions here, as those my mother showed me while in the cave. And that final nightmarish one that haunted my sleepless nights, the one where Kai was standing over the lifeless bodies of my friends, it was in that cave. Everything was leading back to it. Something was pulling me back there.

"That's where we have to go," I said. "That's where we can finally end this."

Everyone was looking at me now. I couldn't explain it. I didn't know what exactly we were meant to do there, but I knew we were all meant to go there. There was a reason that my nightmares ended in that place. It had to be a way to end this. I just prayed that I could somehow make the ending happier than the one I had already seen.

"Why?" Sadie asked.

"I don't know yet. But I've been feeling a force pulling me toward it since I was first there. And anyway, aren't we getting a little ahead of ourselves? How are we supposed to get out of the Locker?" I asked.

Terran held up a ring of keys and jingled them.

"Pays to be friends with a Luxor," he said with a grin

46

We'd rapidly schemed our escape plan while Terran was with us on guard duty in the Locker. By the time he had to switch shifts we'd come up with a moderately solid plan. We decided to stay in the Locker as long as possible. At least here we were all together and safe from Malakai for the moment. Terran was nominated to destroy the Soul Cell, giving us our powers back, and then he'd sneak us out of the Locker to Hollis under Remi's invisibility power. Then Hollis could carry us to the safety of the forest.

I was concerned with how many variables there were. There seemed to be so many chances for things to go wrong. But we were running out of options and more importantly time. We needed to give Hollis a day to get into position, so Terran planned to send Niv with a message as soon as he was off duty and then he would destroy the Soul Cell the following night, so we'd at least have the cover of darkness on our side as we tried to make it to Hollis.

Terran squeezed my hand through the bars of the Locker before he left.

"We're gonna be okay, Geneva. We're all in this together now."

When we'd clasped hands, Terran had given me the same indescribable Pillar sensation, solidifying my trust in him. I did my best to return his smile, nodding my appreciation to him.

Now that a new guard was watching, our conversations lulled. I moved to join Sparrow. She stood staring at her feet, chewing on her fingers with worry. I grabbed her hands to save them from more abuse and her puffy amber eyes met mine. I knew she was thinking about her upcoming adoption. She had that faraway look in her eyes.

I couldn't help but wonder if she would be forced to compete in the Genesis Tournament or if she would be spared because of the adoption. Neither was an option I was prepared to let my friend face.

"We're gonna get out of here before Saturday," I whispered.

She squeezed my hand with appreciation and slumped down onto the floor. I was about to join her when I heard Nova calling my name. Or at least I thought I had.

When I turned around he was standing by the bars that separated our cells, staring at me, but it didn't appear that anyone else had heard him. The Luxor was still standing at the bottom of the steps looking unimpressed, so I strode over to Nova.

"I don't really want to talk to you right now," I whispered.

"You're the one that came over here," he replied.

"Because you called me."

He just stared at me, furrowing his handsome brow. He appeared to be mulling something over as he absently rubbed a red patch of skin on his chest that was barely visible through his open shirt collar. I blushed when he caught my gaze lingering too long. I tried to meet his penetrating stare but instead let my eyes settle on the tiny scar on his eyebrow and my finger itched to touch it. I angrily shook my mind clear.

"Whatever. I'm not in the mood for your games. Especially not after what you did to Kai!"

"Geneva – "

"Save it, Nova!"

"Hey! No talking!" the Luxor yelled, stopping our conversation.

I sighed and moved to the back of the cell, where the damp stone wall met the bars, and leaned my back against it. The coolness of the stone made me shiver as I slid down the wall to the floor. I leaned my head back and closed my eyes.

"Hey," Remi said sitting next to me and slipping his hand between the bars to grasp mine.

I let him weave his fingers between mine. The familiarity of it made my heart pang. When we were children, Remi would always hold my hand. We didn't have to talk; we'd just sit, hands clasped, for hours. Somehow, the silent connection would make everything better. I wished so badly that could be the case now. That I could hold Remi's hand with my eyes closed until everything was better.

I took a deep breath knowing it wasn't true and probably never would be again. Somewhere along the past year, we had crossed over into the unknown. Gone were the naïve days of childhood. Holding hands and hope weren't enough anymore.

~

"MASTER, forgive me, but I don't think that's wise," Kobel said. "You have her where you want her right now."

"Unless you've found out how to rip them from her mind, we're still two Pillars short!" Malakai fumed.

"But she's the *Ponte deorum*. You don't need the Pillars."

"Yes, but I *want* them! Do you know what kind of power that would give me? We can sacrifice the Eva to bring Ravin back and then with the four Pillars in our possession we would control the elements. We would be unstoppable! Can you imagine how pleased Ravin will be?" Malakai swooned. "Besides, she's not going anywhere. Did you see her? She could barely stand. I was merely toying with her in the Athlesium to show her I'm in charge. It still boggles my mind why the gods would give someone so unworthy so much power. Her sister seems much better suited for it."

"Perhaps that's why it's been so easy for you to convince her to help us."

"Yes, she has served us well," Malakai purred.

He stared out the tall stained glass window, momentarily lost in thought. His eyes took in the landscape, tinged orange through the colored panes. He was so close to fulfilling his life's ambition that he could taste it. Once he brought Ravin back to his rightful spot as leader of the Ravinori, they would rise to power and he would be handsomely rewarded. Sitting at Ravin's side would be the ultimate achievement. All the Ravinori who doubted him, would then bow to him. Malakai took a deep breath, closing his eyes for a brief moment to capture his vision and use it to fuel him forward.

"Have the arrangements been made to move up the Genesis Tournament?" Malakai asked when he turned back to face Kobel.

"Yes, the arena is being readied as we speak."

"And the dance?"

"I didn't think we were still contemplating hosting the dance with the accelerated agenda," Kobel said with mild annoyance.

"Of course we are. What's the Genesis Tournament without the preview gala and dance?" Malakai cried with mock sincerity. "Besides, wasn't it you who said it would be the perfect opportunity to observe them?"

"Yes, but Master – "

"Come Kobel, let's have some fun. It will be so amusing to

watch them struggle. Think of it as a farewell party for our fair Eva and her friends."

Kobel wanted to object, but he knew he wouldn't be able to change Malakai's mind.

"Yes, Master. I'll make the announcement today."

"Good. And send word to the Locker to release them. I can't wait to watch her squirm."

47

The clanking of metal against metal startled me from my sleep. I pulled my hand from Remi's and scrambled to my feet.

"Rise and shine! Your sentence is over."

"What do you mean?" I asked the Luxor who pulled our cell door ajar and was now starting on the boy's cell.

"Are you daft? It means you're free to go? So, march," he said gesturing to the stairs.

I glanced nervously at my friends, but hurried through the open door to the staircase. Something wasn't right. Why would they be letting us out? If what Terran had said was true, then Malakai should have been keeping us in the Locker until the Genesis Tournament on Saturday, where we couldn't cause any trouble or try to escape. Surely he knew that was our plan. He'd known my every move so far. This had to be some sort of trap, but I couldn't figure out how yet.

I rubbed warmth back into my stiff limbs as I climbed the stairs. The good news was that I felt better today. Much less dizzy. Perhaps the drugs had worked their way out of my system over night. The brightness of the early morning sun filtering in through the windows pained my eyes. A new day. Thursday. One day closer to the tournament; one day less to escape.

It took me a moment to adjust to the brightness in the room above the Locker. We stood huddled in a warm office filled with Luxors, while we waited for the guard who had freed us to make his way up the stairs. Terran was in the room standing near a stone wall where rows of gleaming weapons hung. I caught his eye. He looked distraught.

"Head to your rooms. Lessons have been canceled for today," Commander Gray said from behind his post. "Private, please escort them to their rooms."

"I'll help," Terran piped up. "This group has been causing trouble lately."

"Very well," agreed the commander.

We marched down the silent, deserted halls of the Troian Academy. My muscles were tense and my left eye was involuntarily twitching. Something wasn't right? Everything in me was telling me to stay alert. Why had Malakai let us out of the Locker and why were lessons canceled today?

Finally, the boys branched off toward their wing, following their Luxor, while Terran led us to our bunkroom. Once they were out of earshot I barraged him with questions.

"What's going on? Why are lessons canceled? Why are we out of the Locker? We need a new plan now!"

"Whoa, calm down. Let me give you an answer to one of your questions before you hit me with a dozen more. Geez."

"Sorry," I hissed. "But time isn't really on my side here in case you've forgotten."

Terran didn't stop walking, but he slowed his pace enough so I was by his side.

"Listen," he said in a hushed voice. "I know you don't know me and have no reason to trust me, but I need you to. I *am* who you've been looking for. I don't have time to explain it, but I need you just as much and you need me. If we work together we can get out of here, but you need to calm down. There's no doubt that Malakai is up to something and that he's watching us, so you need to keep calm."

"Okay, I'm sorry," I whispered. "Did you find out anything new since we last spoke?"

"Not really. They're definitely having the Genesis Tournament on Saturday. We've been ordered to prepare the Athlesium and security has been bumped up. Getting out of here is going to be more difficult than I originally thought, but I have an idea."

"Good," I whispered trying to keep the panic from my voice.

"Well, I don't think you're going to like it," he said.

"If it gets us out of here, I don't care what I have to do."

"I'm glad you feel that way," Terran said trying to hide a sideways grin.

We were just about to the door of the girls bunkroom and I could hear shrieks and giggles coming from inside.

"What's going on in there?" Sparrow asked from behind me.

"The dance is still happening. That's why lessons have been cancelled. It's so everyone has time to prepare," Terran said. "And you're all going."

"What?" I almost gasped. "This is hardly the time to be worrying about a stupid dance."

"That stupid dance is our best chance to get out of here. We'll all be together in one place and there will be so much going on that it'll be the perfect distraction we need for me to destroy the Soul Cell and for us to sneak out under Remi's... you know."

He was right. The dance was the perfect diversion. But Malakai had to know that too.

"It's too easy," I said. "I think it's a trap."

"Well we don't really have any other options. It's tomorrow, so find something pretty to wear and go along with the plan."

I swallowed hard. We were at the door.

"I won't see you until tomorrow. So keep your head down and good luck."

"What about the guys?" I asked as Terran turned to walk away.

"I'll make sure they know the plan," he said.

And with that he was gone. I watch as he clipped down the hall away from us in his shiny black Luxor boots until I couldn't see him anymore. I turned to Sparrow and Sadie and we collectively took a deep breath before pushing through the door and into our room.

"BUT, Father, she's the only one I want to ask to the dance."

"Kai. I'm sorry but that's my final answer," Malakai said without raising his head from the book he was poring over.

They were in their private wing, where Kai had found his father in his room. Everything inside the Headmaster's suite was grey; the velvet curtains, the thick blankets and furs adorning the four poster bed, the grey marble hearth of the fireplace. The entire room was dark and cold, like Malakai.

It was strange for Kai to be inside his father's personal space. He had only been inside the room once. It had been the first night after they'd moved into the Troian Academy. Kai had a bad dream and asked his father if he could stay in his room with him for the night and read a bit. His father had scoffed at him and sent him back to his room, telling him to think about if he wanted to be a man or a boy. Men were brave, boys were frightened. Kai shuddered, remembering the nightmare. He continued to have it, but never mentioned it to his father again, since he had made him feel like a coward. It was always the same nightmare that woke him. He was in a black cave, a girl was screaming and there were bodies--dead bodies--everywhere.

Kai shook himself from the haunting memory and looked back at his father, who continued to ignore him. He was determined not to give up. Just then, something Geneva had said popped into his mind. *'You've never seen him do anything suspicious?'*

"Father, what are you reading?"

Malakai immediately shut the book and covered it with the flowing black sleeves of his robe. "Kai, do not push me. You are not going to the dance with that girl. She is beneath you, son."

"Then why did you ask me to get close to her? I have done everything you've asked. I want to take her to the dance."

"Kai, she's a nobody, a charity case. Men of our pedigree cannot be seen courting a girl like her. The Genesis Ball is a place of prestige, where you flaunt your social status and reputation. Son, I realize you're becoming a man and there are things you want now. So be it Kai, I'm all for you being young and reckless, but choose another girl to do it with. Preferably one of higher social standing."

Kai hid his outrage and disappointment. He knew he wouldn't get his father to change his mind and pressing the matter further would only get him grounded from going to the dance all together.

"Yes, Sir," he said giving a small bow as he left the room.

48

When we staggered into our bunkroom, we were surrounded by a tidal wave of chaos. There were clothes flying out of wardrobes, some even hanging from the chandeliers where they'd landed. Girls piled before mirrors, brushing their hair and fussing with make-up. The scene would have been comical if our situation wasn't so dire. All the room was a blur of satin, lipstick and laughter, while we stood in the middle of it all, like sullen statues, not knowing where we belonged.

I finally spotted Jemma sitting in front of the mirror combing her hair without a care in the world. Of course, that's where she'd be. Something snapped as I watched her practice her flirtatious grin and bat her eyelashes, because I knew exactly who she intended to use them on and I was no longer going to sit by and let it happen. She'd taken too much from me already and I wasn't about to give her Nova. Not anymore. I had nothing left to lose.

I didn't care that she had saved me from the blood curse and said she was trying to be my sister or that she'd given me a birthday gift. Too little, too late. Actions spoke much louder than words and Jemma proved she didn't care time and time again. Her latest example, deserting us after the Luxor fight to make sure she didn't end up in the Locker. Jemma, always the self-preservationist. I was finally learning that nothing came without a price from her and the pain she forced me to cause Nova was too steep a price. Well, not anymore. It was time for me to get my powers back and end this.

I stalked across the room and shoved her hard on the shoulder to get her attention.

"Ouch! What's wrong with you?" she yelled.

"You're a liar!" I screamed.

"What are you talking about," Jemma cried, standing up and looking embarrassed now that all eyes were on her.

I moved in close so only she could hear me. "I'm through listening to you. Tell me how to get my powers back!"

"Not this again," she said feigning boredom.

"You truly don't know how to do it, do you?"

I waited for a response, but for once Jemma was speechless.

"Well you better figure it out, because tomorrow, I'm taking my powers back and we're getting out of here."

She glared at me and her eyes darkened to a black I had never seen before. She grabbed my wrist and wretched me away from the crowd of girls staring at us.

"Have you lost your mind?" she scathed. "You don't get to threaten me."

"Yes, I do. Because that seems to be the only way I can get through to you, Jemma."

"I'm not at your beck and call, Eva. I have my own plans."

"You're unbelievable. All this time, you've been telling me I can't even talk to Nova or go near him and that's not even true. You just jumped at the chance to keep me away from him so you could trick him into liking you, but that's never going to happen, Jemma. He loves me and he'll never fall for your tricks. Especially when he finds out what you've done." I whirled away from her. But she caught my arm and whispered viciously in my ear.

"Oh really, little sister? Are you sure about that? I know you saw us together in the Beto camp and you've been away for a while, sleeping in the infirmary. While you were dreaming of him, I was actually with him. A lot can happen in ten days, darling. Why don't you ask him about it?" She taunted wickedly.

My mind whipped back to that horrible image from the Beto camp that I couldn't forget. I'd hopelessly tried to erase those thoughts from my memory, but somehow visions of Jemma and Nova entwined in the hammock continued to haunt me.

Nova had hurt me so deeply in that moment, shattering the confidence I'd worked so hard to build. I'd been too hurt to come out and ask him about it directly, but I knew no matter how far we'd come, that tiny seed of doubt would always grow until I confronted it and dug it out for good. The problem was, Jemma seemed to be doing everything in her power to stop me.

As if reading my mind she asked, "Did Nova mention he's my date for the dance?"

"What?" I gasped. It couldn't be true. My heart was crumbling into a million tiny pieces again.

"Oh, you didn't know? Sorry, I guess he must have forgotten to mention it. He can be so forgetful sometimes." She laughed. "He asked me while you were in the infirmary," she said nonchalantly, like I had been there for a simple scrape. "Maybe he didn't think you were coming back," she added with a shrug. "Like I said, a lot has happened."

"Jemma, what did I ever do to you to deserve this? You're supposed to be my sister. You stole my powers and the only boy I've ever loved," I sobbed.

"You were born," she said. "It's as simple as that. You stole my birthright. If you weren't here then I'd have everything I've ever wanted. I'd be the chosen one, I'd have Nova, I'd be in control and I'd be good at it. All you ever do is whine and cry and waffle about your feelings. You're not worthy of being our Eva and I don't believe all that rubbish about your legacy in the *Book of Secrets*. I took your powers so I'd have some time to prove it."

"To prove what?" I asked in astonishment.

"That you're not my sister!"

My mouth fell open. Her words cut me like swift jabs from a dagger, each more painful than the last. I stumbled away from her in horror. I didn't know what to say. At first I was so shocked I couldn't speak. I had never anticipated the pain she could still inflict on me, but she did, by confirming my worst fears. That I wasn't good enough, that my own sister hated me and that everyone else would be better off without me around.

I tried to speak again, but no words would come out. The realization that my sister hated me was finally sinking in. My own flesh and blood. She truly despised me so much that she was consumed with madness at trying to disprove her relation to me.

I had been blind to think that just because the *Book of Secrets* said we were sisters it would make it so. We had never spent any real time together or bonded. And in Jemma's eyes I was nothing more than an undeserving thief. And maybe she was right. Maybe I was. Maybe if I had never been born, she would be the chosen one.

My mind was spinning and so many things were starting to make sense; Jemma's fickle moods, her constant competitiveness, her obsession with Nova, and her all too eager offer to help me veil my powers.

"Jemma, you know that's not true," Sparrow said. She must have overheard the end of our conversation as she walked up. I had been so absorbed in my thoughts that I didn't notice her approach. "Hollis told you that only you could save her from the poison that Kobel had infected her with. It had to be a blood relative."

"That doesn't make her my sister!" Jemma screamed, her eyes wild with hatred.

"That's exactly what it makes her," Sparrow argued.

"Jemma, I get it. I can see why you feel this way toward me. Everything you said is true, but I didn't ask for this. I never wanted to be the Eva or take anything away from you. You have to believe me," I pleaded.

"Oh please! Just admit it. You love the attention your powers give you. I could at least respect you if you'd own it," Jemma sneered.

Sparrow and Sadie were between us now and some of the nearby girls in our room where listening in.

"What the heck is going on here?" Sadie asked angry and confused.

"I don't love it, Jemma. I hate it. I never wanted this. I just wanted a family," I whispered, ignoring my friends.

"Well I don't! I wish we'd never opened that stupid *Book of Secrets*. Better yet I wish you were never born."

"Jemma!" Sparrow gasped in shock.

"Well that's not the case Jemma," Sadie retorted. "So we'll never know if you would have been anything other than the spoiled brat you're being right now, so drop it!"

Jemma laughed. "Ah, my sister's loyal friends. I can't wait until she drags you all down wither her." Then she turned and marched out of the room.

I was sitting numbly on Sparrow's bed where she had sat me after Jemma's cruel remarks. She and Sadie stared at me, neither one sure of what to say. They offered me kind words, but the damage was done. I now knew my own sister hated me.

"You can't let her get to you, Geneva," Sadie said after a while. "You're our Eva. We need you and we also need to find something to wear to this stupid dance tomorrow."

I wiped my nose on the back of my hand and nodded feebly. My heart had just been stabbed and cut out by my sister, but I couldn't think about that if I was going to pull it together and help get my friends out of here.

"Good. After we find dresses, we need to get dates."

49

"I think it'll work," Journey said between mouthfuls of creamed corn cakes.

Lessons were cancelled, but thankfully meals were not. It was our last chance to talk before the dance and get our plan straight. Terran had relayed the plan to the boys through Niv, apparently, who was now hiding out in his bunkroom. I tried not to feel too betrayed by that fact. All that mattered was that my little marmouse was safe.

"It has to work," I said desperately.

"It will," Nova said with confidence. "Terran will disable the Soul Cell one hour after the dance begins. We'll sneak out at that time and meet him in the Medicinal Horticulture room. It should be deserted and we can sneak out through the poison garden. It's the least reinforced part of the building."

"I suggest we test out our telepathy during the dance," Remi said. "It'll let us know if our powers are working and it's bound to draw less attention than any of our other powers."

"Good idea," Sparrow agreed.

"You guys can telepath?" Sadie asked.

"Yeah and you should be able to also," I said. "So don't freak out if you hear our voices in your head."

"Whoa. Thanks for the warning," Sadie, replied, her blue eyes wide and shining.

"So it's settled?" Sparrow asked. "Tomorrow's the day we break out of here?"

My friends silently stared at each other. I could tell they were all doing the same thing I was; taking everything in as if it were the last time, because it very well could be. I gazed at the apprehensive faces of my friends. Journey's tan, furrowed brow. Remi's darting, worried eyes. Sparrow's nervous twitching smile. Sadie, fretfully wringing and unwringing the hem of her uniform under the table. The way Jemma was chewing her pouty bottom lip. And Nova, the stern set of his perfectly structured jaw. I could see the muscles beneath the hallows of his cheekbones clenching, something he only did when he was worried. Even though the rest of him exuded confidence, I somehow took comfort knowing he was worried too. It made me feel more connected to him than I had in a long time.

"Now we have nothing to do but wait," Nova said.

"Can I actually talk to you about something?" I asked him. My voice came out more timidly than I'd expected and at first he didn't reply. I was awkwardly weighing my options of whether to clear my throat and ask him again when he stood up.

Nova strode to my side of the table and gestured toward the double doors of the dining hall.

"Shall we?" he said.

So he *had* heard me. What was the long pause for? Did he actually have to contemplate whether or not he wanted to talk to me? My heart squeezed in my chest. I truly had ruined everything.

"Sure," I said following after him.

We stood in the hallway just outside the dining hall. Nova

marched ahead, not bothering to wait for me to catch up. After a few paces he stopped and leaned against the wall next to a bold tapestry of two peacocks perched on a fountain.

Immortality, I thought, letting a history lesson slip into my scattered mind. How ironic that I was standing in front of a tapestry representing immortality when I felt so completely mortal at the moment.

"You said you wanted to talk, Geneva, so talk."

"I - " I didn't know where to start. For a moment I had forgotten what I even wanted to talk to him about. The constricting pain I felt in my heart whenever I was this close to Nova clouded my thoughts.

"Are you going to finally tell me what's really going on with you?" he asked before I could collect my thoughts.

I stared at him. His green eyes looked calm. For once he seemed like he was going to give me the opportunity to come clean without jumping down my throat. It was so tempting. He hadn't looked at me with this kind of hopefulness in so long that it was melting me. I felt as though I'd been transported, back to when I'd first met him and couldn't form a thought that didn't curl around his exquisite features. If only we could go back and start over.

"Geneva, you know you can tell me anything."

My heart sputtered. Could the truth really set us free or would it be one more wound adding to the chasm of scar tissue tearing us apart?

Nova leaned in and brushed a strand of my hair back, tucking it gently behind my ear. I shuddered at his touch and he misread my cue, pulling back.

"I'm sorry," he mumbled. A flush of red momentarily flooded his cheeks.

No. I couldn't tell him yet. Not here. We only had one more day to get through. No reason to put him amidst the anguish of knowing how we'd used and lied to him if I wasn't even going to live another day. Escaping Malakai and the Troian Academy would be no easy task and if I had to sacrifice myself to save my friends, I'd rather just have this last quiet moment with Nova.

"I wanted to ask you something," I finally said breaking our awkward silence. "About the dance..."

His cheeks flushed further still.

"Geneva, I already promised Jemma that I'd go with her."

So it was true? For once my deceitful sister was telling the truth. I should have known. She only tells the truth when it serves her and taking Nova as her date to the dance certainly qualified.

Somehow, I wasn't as stunned as I thought I'd be. Perhaps I was still in shock or just numb from everything I'd been through in the past few days.

"Oh - "

"I had to. She told me - "

"It doesn't matter," I interrupted.

I may have been keeping it together, but only barely, and I didn't need to hear the gory details of their romance. Jemma had already given me an earful.

"That's not what I wanted to ask you anyway."

"It's not?"

"No. I was going to ask you if you thought we could trust Terran. Everything hinges on him keeping his word and destroying the Soul Cell tomorrow. How well do you know him, Nova? What if he's not really on our side?"

"We can trust him, Geneva. He's a Pillar."

"I'm not trying to be difficult, Nova, but I'm going to need a little more to go on than your word."

Nova smirked, stifling a laugh. I crinkled my brow in confusion. I didn't see what was humorous about my question, but Nova clearly did. He leaned back against the wall and bowed his head in laughter.

"What's so funny?"

"Do you know you're infuriatingly cute when you're being a hypocrite?" he asked me with amusement.

Gods, why did he have to call me cute? And why did he have to be so beautiful when he smiled? It felt like the air was being squeezed from my lungs when Nova was happy and the only way I could breathe again was to be closer to him. It was a vicious intoxication that left me yearning for more. I could scarcely hold my scowl at him and I didn't have a retort. He was right. I always asked him and my friends to trust me and told him to take my word for things, but I didn't afford them the same courtesy. It didn't used to be that way. There was a time when my word was my bond and I trusted my friends completely. I felt my stomach twist with guilt. Perhaps all the secrets and lies were making me distrustful. Sometimes I felt like I didn't know where the lies stopped and the truth began anymore.

One more day, I reminded myself.

I let my shoulders slump as I too leaned against the cool stone wall next to Nova. It made my skin prickle to be so close to him. I could feel his warmth radiating toward me.

"You're right," I said glumly looking down at my feet.

"Hey," Nova said softly, nudging my foot with his own. The lightness was gone from his voice now. "I thought you knew me better, Geneva. I didn't just blindly trust him. I did some research. Terran's story checked out."

I looked up at him, my clear blue eyes dancing with questions.

Nova sighed deeply when he read my expression. He knew I wanted more. I needed to know what Terran's story was for myself.

"Come on," he said shoving off the wall.

~

Sparrow and Jemma sat in the dining hall as students merrily milled about them. The excitement of the dance was catching. From looking around, you'd never guess the Troian Academy was a horrible place run by a power hungry leader of a secret society. The large room was filled with laughter that echoed off the vaulted ceiling. The boys and Sadie had gone up for another helping of food, leaving Jemma and Sparrow alone at the center of the long table.

Jemma was anxiously reapplying another coat of gold nail polish to her slender fingers and looking over her shoulder. Nova and her sister had been gone from the dining hall for far too long. She worried he might be going back on his word to go to the dance with her. Finally she stood up, ready to find them and secure her date for the dance.

"Sit down!" Sparrow said, grabbing her wrist.

"Watch it!" Jemma said jerking her hand away from Sparrow. "You'll mess up my manicure!" Jemma fretfully examined her newly painted gold nails. "You're lucky they didn't smudge. This color suits me don't you think? It's called Drama Queen," she said with a smirk.

Sparrow shook her head.

"Don't look at me like that," Jemma spat.

"Like what?" Sparrow asked.

"Like you're above all of this. You know if you tried a little harder maybe you could get what you want."

"What I want is for our plan to work so that I don't have to go live with some family of strangers. This is my last shot, Jemma. If we fail tomorrow, you'll probably never see me again. Not that it will bother you any."

"Well, aren't you just a cheerful little thing? I was referring to the immediate future and the dance, but I guess you're not concerned with what he said about you."

"Who? What are you talking about?"

"Remi," she purred sitting back down at the table.

"Shut up, Jemma. Now really isn't the time."

"Now is precisely the time. You said so yourself. If we fail tomorrow, it's goodbye Sparrow. Why not have one night to cling to with the boy you like?" she shrugged.

"Jemma..." Sparrow said, afraid to hear what the selfish girl was alluding to.

"I know you like Remi and want to go to the dance with him, so I decided to talk to him and see what he thought of you."

"You did what?" Sparrow squeaked.

"Oh calm down, I was doing you a favor. I didn't want you to blindly stroll up to him and ask if he would go with you and then have you get turned down. That would be so embarrassing."

"Since when do you care about helping me?"

Jemma feigned shock and hurt, raising her eyebrows and putting her hand to her chest. She couldn't even fake her insincere concern for long before breaking into a grin, mischief gleaming in her dark eyes.

"Okay, fine. It's not so much that I care about you, Sparrow, but I *do* hate listening to you snivel about him all night. You know you talk about him in your sleep? I swear, between you and Eva it's like a regular romance novel haunting my dreams each night. *Remi, Nova, Remi, Nova,*" Jemma said turning her head from side to side dramatically in mockery.

Sparrow took a deep breath, composing herself. "So what did he say?"

"Not too much, really. He's not much of a talker. I'm not sure what you see in him."

"Jemma!"

"He said he didn't see there being much of a point in asking you to the dance."

"He said that?" Sparrow asked brokenheartedly. "Jemma, why did you have to say anything to him?"

"Whatever, it's not like you were ever going to get enough courage to ask him anyway. Just go with Journey, you know he wants to ask you."

"I don't want to go with Journey!"

"Fine, don't go with anyone. I really don't care," Jemma sneered. "I've already got my date."

"Who do you think you're going with?" Sparrow asked.

"I already told you. I'm going with Nova," Jemma replied confidently.

Sparrow laughed. "I'm pretty sure he's going to ask Geneva. That's probably what they're out there talking about right now."

"She can talk to him until she stops breathing for all I care. He made me a promise. He's my date."

"Jemma, how can you be so terrible to her? She's your sister!" Sparrow said incredulously. "Besides, anyone can see they're meant for each other. Stop trying to cause trouble."

"Oh that's a load of rubbish." Jemma hissed. "I'm so tired of Eva getting everything she wants. And I'm not an idiot. I know that Nova likes her. She's all he ever talks about. 'Tippy this, Tippy that, I'm so worried about poor Tippy, blah, blah blah.' But I know I'm better for him. Eva hurts everyone she gets close to. I don't want Nova to be one of her casualties. Besides, soon he'll see that I'm every bit as powerful as she is."

"What are you talking about, Jemma?"

"Oh, don't you worry about me. I've already got my dream date to the dance. You should really focus on yourself."

"It doesn't matter who I go with, Jemma. It's not a real dance. We're only going because it's our best chance of escape."

"If you don't think it's real than you're the one who's delusional. I only need one dance with Nova to get him to have real feelings for me. And if you'll excuse me, I'm going to go make sure my groveling sister isn't trying to take that opportunity away from me since she doesn't take a hint too well."

"What are you talking about?" Sparrow asked grabbing Jemma's wrist again.

Jemma slid in uncomfortably close to Sparrow, letting her hair fall in a dark curtain across her face, shadowing the cruelty in her narrowed eyes.

"That's why I had to make Nova the talisman for Geneva's powers. Genius, right?" Jemma whispered wickedly.

"You didn't!" Sparrow gasped. "It all makes sense now. That's why Geneva's been staying away from him and looking like she wants to run from Nova's sight every time he's around. You told her he's her talisman and she can't be near him, didn't you?"

"Duh?" Jemma said, delighted in her cruelty.

"Jemma, when he finds out what you've done he'll never forgive you."

"He's not going to find out Sparrow, because you're not going to tell anyone."

"He deserves to know."

"Fine tell him, but since we're sharing, I guess I'll just share with Journey how you'd rather go to the dance alone than go with him. It might break his heart, but he's a pretty tough guy, right? And I wonder what Remi would think of you telling Nova about being Geneva's talisman. You know it'll make him run to her, and undo all the work we did to protect her from the Ravinori. I'm sure Remi will appreciate you putting the girl he loves in danger and handing her to Nova at the same time. Look, here they come now. Should we tell them?"

"You're a horrible person, Jemma," Sparrow sobbed.

"Yeah, yeah, just keep your mouth shut and we'll both get what we want. You won't think I'm so horrible when you're at the dance with Remi. You just have to keep this one little secret and let me go with Nova."

50

"I think Terran does a much better job of telling it than I do, but I'll do my best," Nova said as we breezed down the busy hallways of the Troian Academy.

I hurried to keep up with him as he stalked through the crowds of students. All of them talked excitedly about the dance, gathered in clusters, passing notes and calling to each other. Their voices echoed through the stone hallway, filling it with an unusual commotion.

Nova rounded a corner and stopped. In a few more strides I'd caught up, stopping beside him. Suddenly aware of his close proximity, I took a step back. He didn't seem to notice. Instead, he stared ahead at a large tapestry hanging on the wall. It stretched from near the ceiling all the way to the floor. I looked at him, waiting for an explanation, but Nova kept staring. I focused my eyes on the tapestry and sighed. It was just another piece of art Malakai had brought with him from Lux. They were all over the Troian Academy boasting his wealth. What did a tapestry have to do with Terran?

"This one's his," Nova said, still staring at the art.

"Nova. I don't get it. What am I looking at?"

He finally tore his eyes away to look at me. He looked a bit bewildered as he sized me up, looking between me and the wall a few times.

"Take a few steps back," he said gesturing to the opposite wall. "You're a bit shorter than me, perhaps the angle is wrong."

I skeptically did as he said and stared back at the tapestry. It was the same as it was before. A large woven scene depicting a man with a dagger atop a mountain, the dark night sky above him dotted with stars. I was in the midst of raising my arms in frustration, when I saw it.

"Oh my gods," I whispered, as a hidden word materialized before my eyes. There, in the shadows between the stars, was a negative image. At first I hadn't seen it, but now it leapt off the wall at me, revealing it's concealed message.

"Nova," I whispered. "Is this what I think it is?"

He nodded and my breath caught in my throat. Could I actually be looking at a hidden message woven into a tapestry that revealed the name of a Pillar?

"But how?" I murmured.

How could anyone have known who the Pillars would be when this was woven? I thoroughly believed in magic and supernatural powers, but this was far beyond. This was a prediction of destiny that made my skin freckle with goose-flesh. I shivered as I tried to wrap my mind around the idea that our futures had been mapped out for us well before we were born.

"Is this the only one?" I asked when I found my voice.

"No."

"How many are there?" I choked out, my throat suddenly dry.

"Guess," he said flatly.

But I didn't have to. I knew there would be precisely four, depicting the four Pillars and my heart pounded. If Nova had found all four then he, and most likely all my friends, knew I had lied to them about being the wind Pillar. They would have seen Jovi's name written among the empty space in the stars instead of my own.

I turned to look at him and the moment my eyes met his cold jade stare, I knew I was right.

"Don't worry," he said coldly. "We figured it out without your help. You're not the only one who can act alone," he said bitterly.

"Nova – " I started, but he cut me off.

"Save it. I get why you did it. You were trying to protect her. That's always the reason you do all these foolish things. Like it or not I know you, Geneva, and no matter how much you pull away from me, that's not going to change. But I thought we were past all of this. I thought we agreed no more secrets, no more lies," he said, his eyes emerald slivers searching mine.

My heart twisted. He wasn't even mad and that made it worse. Why hadn't I just told him? I know I had been thinking that I was protecting Jovi, but in the end I never seemed to be able to protect anyone. My secrets always came back to haunt me, with far worse repercussions than I'd ever anticipated. The secret of Nova being the talisman for my powers weighed heavily upon me, but I still couldn't tell him. I swallowed hard, almost choking on the regretful taste of betrayal before I looked back at him.

"I'm sorry for not telling you about Jovi. You're right. I was trying to protect her and you. I thought if no one else knew who she was, that it would keep you all safe from being used to gain that information. These tapestries are perplexing, but they still don't make me trust Terran. He could be setting us up. He's a Luxor and they work directly for Malakai. What if Malakai planted the tapestries and told him to use them to gain our trust? I mean that seems more probable than our fates as Pillars being predestined, doesn't it?"

"I thought the same thing at first," Nova said with a hint of a proud smile. "But if that were true than Malakai would have already known who the Pillars were and wouldn't be after you to find them."

I frowned realizing Nova was right, but I still didn't buy it. Something felt off.

"Look at this tapestry. Does anything else look familiar to you?"

I stared at the stormy image of the man atop the mountain. Now that I looked closer, it wasn't just a mountain, it was a volcano, our volcano! I could see the familiar split down it's center, where the elder had struck his fabled weapon, tearing the earth open to swallow up Zophia and Kull, thus creating the four realms.

"There are 65 tapestries in total. Each one depicting a scene from the immortal war; the elder's deception, the creation of the four realms and then the four Pillars. Malakai is flaunting them right under our noses. Four of the tapestries have been woven with magic, revealing the Pillars names spelled out in the stars like this one. Terran, Sadie, Nova and Jovi; not Geneva. But I guess you already knew that," he added with a bit of deserved hostility. "Before I met Terran he had been searching for all of the tapestries, hoping to find the Pillars himself and unlock the ancient pathway."

"Ancient pathway?"

"Terran knows a great deal about the tapestries and he said legend has it that though they depict destruction, they deliver salvation."

"What do you mean?"

"If you follow them in order, they will lead you to a path of safety. Terran had been working on finding them all when we met him. We've been helping him figure out the order of the last few and we think they might point to a way out of here. But we were missing the last one until yesterday, when Terran came to visit us in the Locker."

My mind snapped back to the new accommodations in the Locker. The separate cells, the lights, the new squeaky set of stairs and the large tapestry that hung at the bottom of the staircase. I was so used to seeing them around the rest of the Troian Academy that I hadn't even paid attention to it. I hadn't paid attention to any of them apparently or I should have realized that the scenes were from the immortal war. But why would Malakai do that? Wasn't it an unnecessary risk to hang them in plain sight, practically screaming his allegiance to the Ravinori?

"We couldn't find the last one, the 65th tapestry, until we all ended up in the Locker, but now that we have, it solidifies my trust in Terran even more."

"Why? Because he guessed the number of tapestries in the Troian Academy? Finding the last one in the Locker doesn't prove Terran is trustworthy. If anything it proves he's lying. The Locker is a dead end, not a path to safety!"

Nova exhaled and ran his hand through his blond hair. It was slowly returning to its unruly waves.

"I don't have all the answers yet, Geneva. He said the last tapestry marks a pathway to safety. Maybe we're reading them wrong or something, but I know Terran is one of us. I can feel it. He's risked his neck to help us."

"He did?"

"When you were missing, I was desperate to find you. We all were," he added to hide his flushed cheeks. "Kai was even doing his part. He found Terran's name and we came up with a plan to meet him."

"How?"

"The details aren't important, but once I met Terran I instantly felt a connection to him. I was surprised he was a Luxor, for sure, but it proved to be helpful. We didn't have to waste time convincing him that the Ravinori exist. It turns out that the Luxors know about them and have to swear an oath to serve them."

"So the Luxor's are Ravinori?"

"Sort of. Let me finish," Nova added with mild annoyance. "Anyway, Terran was willing to work with us and he even told me that he knew where you were and what Malakai's plans were for you. Of course, I didn't trust him, but I was anxious for any news, so I made him convince me. He told me his whole life story, Geneva, the whole awful truth of it. Just because he grew up in Lux, doesn't mean he had it any easier than we did.

"Nova, you realize this sounds crazy, right?"

"Do you want to hear this or not?"

I crossed my arms, but nodded.

"Terran's ancestors had always been poor and worked as servants for the wealthy families in Lux. The women in his family were talented seamstresses and aside from mending clothes, they would weave rugs and tapestries to sell. It so happened that long ago, a young royal took a liking to one of these tapestries and bought it to take home. When his father, the King of Lux saw it, he was impressed. He sent his guards back to find the woman who had woven the tapestry and brought her back to his estate, the Tower of Lux. He commissioned her to weave a set of special tapestries, 65 in total, which would tell the true story of the creation of the world. They became know as the Tapestries of Truth."

While Nova spoke, I gaze at the enchanted tapestry.

"The entire set took thirty-three years to complete and the woman had requested that the King move her and her sisters into the tower so they could work on them together. They each possessed a special skill set needed to weave the truth into the tapestries. Their names were Devorha, Nephora, and Mortora, and each sister had a special gift. They were seers. And together, when all three of them wove, their hands would weave the truth of the past, present and future. The Tapestries of Truth became a valuable masterpiece that people from all over came to see. There were tales of magic being woven into the stitches, so naturally everyone wanted to see the work of the talented three sisters."

A foreboding feeling crept into my bones at the mention of the magical sisters and I shivered.

"Stories such as this were passed down through the ages and eventually drew the attention of Ravin, who stole the tapestries for himself. It was rumored that the rugs were all destroyed in the Flood. But Terran said that they could never be destroyed because of a spell that the three sisters created when they completed them. Supposedly the tapestries survived and were ultimately passed down from Ravin to the next Ravinori leader, Malakai."

"What does that have to do with trusting Terran?"

"I'm not done yet. Terran's great-grandmother was Devorah. That's how he knows so much about the tapestries. His family passed down their secrets through the generations. The King kept Devorah and her sisters at the Tower so he could brag of their skills and because he didn't want anyone else to have access to them. The sisters started lives for themselves within the King's estate. Years later, during Ravin's reign, it was said that he resided in secret at the Tower of Lux and that's where the Ravinori first formed. One of those first members was Lord Avery. That's where he met Terran's mother, Cleo. She was actually born in the castle. Cleo was very beautiful and many men pursued her, but she only had eyes for one, Lord Avery. He loved Cleo as well, but his family would never allow him to marry her because she was only a common lady and beneath his social status. But this didn't stop Lord Avery from trying to have both. He married another to appease his family, while still giving his heart to Cleo. But their affair didn't stay secret for long, especially when Cleo became pregnant. Lord Avery's wife found out about Cleo and was consumed with jealousy. She was unable to have children of her own so she made a plan to blackmail her husband. In exchange for letting Cleo keep her life, he would have to banish her from Lux, but not before stealing her child to raise as their own. That child was Terran."

"So Terran is not only a Luxor, but raised by a morally corrupt Ravinori family?" I gasped. "This is not helping his case, Nova."

"Just wait. Terran's father, knew that Terran was gifted from an early age. He could *see* things, just like his mother, and grandmother and great-grandmother. He was afraid that if the Ravinori found out about his son's powers he would become more valuable to them than Lord Avery himself, so he tried to beat the *sight* out of Terran. He whipped him, burned him and even broke his bones until Terran learned to lie and say that he no longer possessed his gift. Satisfied, Avery enlisted Terran in the Luxor militia and began grooming him to join the Ravinori when he was old enough."

"Nova, that's a horrible story and I'm so sorry that anyone would have to suffer through such things, but how do we know it's true?"

"Besides the fact that I've seen the scars with my own eyes, Terran told me where to find you and I knew he was telling me the truth because Sadie had confirmed it when she found you in the infirmary. Terran even knew the drug they were giving you and what they planned for it to do to you. He helped us get a message to Hollis so we could find out how to cure you. He knows the Ravinori's master plan and so far he's been right about all of it. Do you know how he knows all of this?"

I shook my head.

"His father was one of the Phantom mercenaries that attacked us on the bridge in the forest. I knew Terran looked familiar the moment I met him. He's the spitting image of his father and I'd never forget that face. It was the last one I saw before I morphed back to you. He's the one who killed Talon."

My blood ran cold as hate boiled up inside of me, and I assigned it to Terran. I couldn't help it. He may not have been the one who killed my friend, but it was someone related to him and that was too close to excuse.

"Terran was called up to take his father's place among the Ravinori so he has all the inside information we need and he's risking everything to share it with us, Geneva."

I had to admit, Terran's story had weight. I didn't want to believe it, but I could see his misfortunate life taking shape as it unfolded through Nova's hushed voice. Hadn't we all been dealt similar circumstances? Imprisoned with cruel caretakers, deprived of love and family. How could I judge Terran for just trying to get by, when I myself had done terrible things in order to stay alive?

"Why is his last name Clay and not Avery?"

"I'm not sure. We never really got into that," Nova replied.

I was so lost in thought that I hadn't noticed someone else had joined us. Nova's rigid stance was the first thing to clue me in. When I turned to see what had caused his unrest, I saw Kai standing next to him.

How long had Kai been there? How much did he know? From Nova's tense jaw, I was guessing that he had not shared the tapestry story with Kai. Although he may have worked with Kai to help find me, I knew Nova still didn't like him. Kai's broken collarbone was proof of that.

Kai grinned warmly at me. This was the first time I'd seen him since the terrible fencing display at the Athlesium. Kai's arm was still in a sling, strapped awkwardly to his chest, but he had more color in his cheeks now and seemed to move with less pain.

"Hello, Geneva," he said. "I've been looking for you. I was hoping we could talk."

"Is everything all right?" I asked.

"Oh, yes. I didn't mean to worry you, I just ..." he paused

and looked at Nova and then back at me. "Well I was hoping for a moment to talk with you, alone."

Nova gave me a questioning glance with his steady green eyes. When I nodded to him that I would be fine speaking to Kai alone, he glared at him, but retreated down the hall.

Kai and I stood in silence as we watched Nova walk away. Once he rounded the corner, Kai closed the space between us swiftly and wrapped me into a fierce embrace with his one good arm.

“Geneva, I’m so glad you’re all right. I’m so sorry about everything. My father... I thought...” he trailed off and pulled away slightly so he could look down at me. “You were right, Geneva. He’s not a good man.”

Kai’s dark eyes were glassy, and I could see the turmoil brewing within. It couldn’t have been easy for him to admit that his father, whom he’d admired, worshiped and loved, was not who he thought he was.

“I should have believed you sooner, Geneva and maybe we could’ve - ”

“Kai, please. It’s okay. You don’t owe me an apology. I know it’s a lot. Sometimes the truth is harder to swallow than the lies we often live.”

He nodded. A tiny grin, pulled at the corner of his pursed lips. He pushed his black hair back.

“I did enjoy watching you give him a haircut,” he smirked.

I couldn’t help but laugh myself.

“That was satisfying,” I beamed.

“Still. I’m sorry for the trouble he’s caused you and your friends. I know I can’t control him, but all I’ve ever wanted was to help you and I feel I’ve failed to do even that.”

The seriousness had returned to his voice now and he fidgeted with the strap of his sling.

“Kai, stop,” I said reaching to quiet his restless hand.

His hand was warm and he readily fitted his fingers

between mine for a moment, before he pulled me back into an embrace. I found it familiar, comfortable even. I'd only known Kai a short time, yet I found a part of me had grown to crave his affection. Kai was humble and honest, all warmth and kindness. I found myself wishing I could be the kind of girl that deserved a nice boy like him. But I wasn't. I was complicated, dark and twisted, lost within the layers of secrets and lies that I'd created. I felt like I was drowning in them and it was all my own doing. But when I was with Kai, he had this strange way of melting that feeling away. I felt like he was a tiny island in my sea of despair and I wanted to cling to him.

When Kai pulled away from me, he was grinning. He kept hold of my hand and knelt suddenly. He stared up at me, his dark eyes gleaming like the midnight sky. The way the light was hitting them, they almost looked an inky shade of blue; the ocean at night.

"Kai, what are you doing?" I said, feeling the blood creep up my neck to color my cheeks with embarrassment as a few nearby students started to take notice of us.

Kai cleared his throat and said, "Geneva Sommers, would you do me the honor of accompanying me to the Genesis Ball as my date?"

I was speechless. How had I not seen this coming? And how could I say no with all these people watching, not to mention without devastating Kai.

"Oh..." I said stalling. "Kai, are you sure you want to go with me?"

"Who else could I possible desire above you, Miss Sommers?" he asked with a gallant grin, bowing further still.

"Kai, I don't really know how to dance, and I don't have anything to wear."

"Your dress has already been taken care of and I doubt that you can't dance. I've seen you fence, remember?"

I stared dumbfounded at him.

"Do you have any more excuses?" he asked.

I shook my head.

"Great! Then I look forward to being your escort tomorrow evening," he said getting to his feet.

He bowed swiftly and kissed my hand. Then he smiled at me with the most joy I'd ever seen on a boy's face and clicked his heels in mock court, winking before turning to march away.

I couldn't help smiling after him. He was definitely standing a bit taller as he breezed passed the other students in the hall. They all stared wide-eyed as he sauntered by. I felt a bit of pride for him as I watched their astonished faces, until my gaze landed on Remi and Nova. They were standing at the far corner, staring past Kai, straight at me; shock and pain written on their faces.

51

I started toward Nova and Remi, but they both turned and stalked away from me. After they departed, I saw that the rest of my friends had been standing behind them. They at least waited for me to walk over.

"Geneva, what are you doing? We don't need to get close to Kai anymore. We already have a plan in place to get out of here," Sparrow said in disbelief.

"I know. It's just ... I thought..." I didn't know what to say. The whole thing had caught me off guard and I got swept up in the moment. I hadn't realized my friends had been watching. For a second I just wanted to be a girl being asked to a dance by a nice boy. But of course, nothing was ever that uncomplicated in my life.

"What? You actually like Kai too?" Jemma spat. "I know you think you're *sooo* special and the chosen one and everything, but you can't have a monopoly on all the boys in the Troian Academy, little sister."

"I'm not trying to do that," I yelled.

"Really? Seems to me that you are. Are you actually going to go to the dance with Kai or are you just stringing him along too?"

"I'm not stringing anyone along!"

"You kind of are," Journey said catching me off guard.

"Journey?" I whispered, hurt evident in my voice.

"Hey, I've been doing my best to keep Nova and Remi from fighting over you, and that's no easy job. I've been telling them that you're just using Kai to get us what we need to get out of here, but sometimes I think you push it too far. There's a line, Geneva," Journey said looking at me with disappointment.

"There's no point in going with Kai. It doesn't help to have him close tomorrow. He'll only be one more obstacle for us," Sadie added. "You should tell him you can't be his date."

"No. I can't do that now. Not after he asked me in front of everyone," I argued. "He'd be crushed."

"You're unbelievable," Jemma laughed. "I'm not allowed to go with Nova and Sparrow's not allowed to go with Remi because you can't make up your mind how you feel about them. But you're allowed to toy around with Kai?"

"Hold on," Journey interrupted before I could respond. "You want to go with Remi?" he asked looking at Sparrow.

Devastation danced across both of their faces as Sparrow struggled to find her voice. When she couldn't, Journey turned and punched the wall next to him, making us all jump. He shook off his hand, muttering to himself as he stalked away.

"Great," Sadie said. "That's just what we need. His hand is probably broken. I better go convince him to go to the infirmary."

I watched her trot down the hallway after Journey, who refused to stop despite her calls.

"Can we all just agree to get through the rest of this day without arguing about who's going with who to the stupid dance?" I sighed. "It doesn't even matter who our dates are."

"It matters to some of us," Sparrow said pushing past me.

I was now left alone in the hallway with my sister and a gaggle of onlookers. Jemma was grinning like a lunatic.

"Looks like I was right," Jemma said.

"About what, Jemma? That you're successfully ruining my life? Congratulations!"

"No, that you only care about yourself. I told them all that you'd only hurt them and I didn't even have to do anything to provoke you this time. You wounded them all on your own. And all in one day. Good job, *Eva*," she said, emphasizing my name with a bitterness that cut me to the core because I realized she was right as she sauntered away from me, leaving me standing all alone.

THE REST of the day was a blur. With lessons cancelled and all of my friends mad at me, I wandered the Troian Academy aimlessly and alone. I had no one to be angry with other than myself. I had made the decisions that led to this; to lie to my friends, to trust Jemma, to come back to this place and put them all in danger. Jemma was right. I was selfish. And I probably wasn't cut out to be the Eva. That had been my deepest doubt from the beginning. I was just a teenaged girl. A nobody. How was I supposed to lead an entire civilization out of the ashes of war and disaster and back to glory?

The weight of it all had been crushing me ever since I learned my destiny, but all at once it became too much and I slumped against the cool stone wall and slid to the floor putting my head on my knees and finally giving into the tears I'd been fighting back for months.

I had lost everything. My friends, my family, the boy I loved and any hope of a future. I'd had nothing before, but this was different, worse. Now I knew what it meant to have such things, and having them torn away was unbearable.

Why? Why had I been chosen? I wasn't fit to lead these people. I wasn't strong enough to stand up to the Ravinori and I was running out of time. I sobbed, praying for the strength to make the right decision. We only had one more day here and then we would attempt our escape back to the Betos in the forest, but then what? I didn't know what was next. I knew something was telling me to go back to the cave, but I had no idea what to do once we got there. I had never thought that far ahead, probably because I had little faith that we would actually succeed. Malakai was not Greeley. He would be ready for us and I couldn't shake the feeling that I was leading my friends into a trap tomorrow. Perhaps the best thing to do would be to turn myself over to Malakai. Maybe they'd stand a better chance of escaping if I was keeping him occupied. My chest constricted at the thought of never seeing them again, but I was desperate to finally do something right and save the people I cared about.

I heard footsteps marching toward me and lifted my head, wiping the tears from my bleary vision as two Luxors came into focus.

"On your feet!" one of them bellowed.

I scrambled to my feet and smoothed out my uniform as they approached. When they stopped before me I realized that Terran was among them. The Luxor with him checked his watch.

"You should be reporting to your bunkroom."

"Yes, Sir. I'm on my way," I replied starting away from them.

"I'll escort her," I overheard Terran say.

I kept my head down and continued walking as I heard his footsteps catching up to mine.

"Hey," he said once he was beside me. "Follow me, I want to show you something."

"No offense, Terran, but I kind of want to be alone right now."

"It can't be," he whispered to himself. "Geneva, where did you get that?" he asked, his hands moving toward my throat.

I instinctively batted him away, shooting daggers with my eyes.

"Don't touch me!" I yelled.

Terran put his hands up and took a step back.

"Sorry, let me try that again. Your necklace; do you know what that is?" he asked.

"It was a gift," I said. I'd almost forgotten about the stupid key necklace that Jemma gave me. No matter how much I hated her, I couldn't force myself to part with something that belonged to my mother.

"I don't know if it's safe to wear that here."

"What do you mean?"

Terran leaned close and whispered. "It's the Key to Salvation."

I shuddered. I had no idea what he was talking about. All I knew was that it looked similar to the scar I now bore on my chest, a parting gift from Kobel's blood curse. I was already suspicious of the key necklace Jemma had given me and having Terran say it wasn't safe didn't make me feel any better about it.

"Come, with me. I want to show you something," he said.

I stared at him, unmoving.

"Listen, I know you don't know me and you probably don't trust me, but I've been searching for you my whole life. I grew up hearing strange stories of our savior, the Pillars and mystical things like that key. Now that I've finally found you, there's something you need to see."

"How?" I asked. "How did you grow up hearing about me? Nova told me about you. I thought you were raised by Ravinori members? And why's your last name Clay. Shouldn't it be Avery, like your father?"

Terran smirked. "Well, they said you'd be feisty."

"Who?"

"The Believers, Eva. All of those who believed that our savior would come and restore this island, releasing us from the Ravinori's oppression. People have been whispering your name before you were even born. And don't tell me you think because the Ravinori raised me that I don't know anything about you. They probably speak of you more than anyone else. You're their biggest threat and the Ravinori are in the habit of knowing their enemy. As far as my last name, it's my real mother's. I wanted a part of her to stay with me. When you enlist in the Luxors, they're not particular about what your name is, as long as you sign the oath. Does that answer all your questions?"

We'd stopped walking and I was staring at Terran. His light hazel eyes were pleading. They made him look younger then he was. Or perhaps it was the rest of him that looked older. His thick brown curls were cropped short and his dark skin looked weathered from time spent outdoors. His grey uniform was tight against his muscular frame, concealing the scars I imagined from Nova's story. Terran carried himself as the rest of the Luxors did; tall, proud and with arrogance. It did little to put me at ease.

"This is important, Geneva," he urged.

"Fine," I said, sighing as I relented to follow him.

At this point, I didn't have anything to lose. After winding through the corridors of the Troian Academy, we were now in an area I hadn't been to before.

"These are our barracks," Terran said as we breezed through a hallway lined with oiled wooden doors. They all stood ajar and when I peaked inside, I saw bunk beds and desks, much more modest then the ones in our own bunkrooms.

The hallway came to an abrupt end, splitting off to the right or left. There were heavy doors guarding either direction.

"What's in there?" I asked.

"The armory and the chapel," Terran said, pointing to each door as he labeled it. "But that's not what you need to see. This is." He stood at the end of the deserted hallway in front of a large tapestry.

I followed his gaze and nearly stumbled backward as the image leapt off the wall. It was my nightmare from the cave, come to life. I'd recognize the faces of my friends anywhere. Their bodies lay crumpled and bloody on the ground as I crouched over them, facing a dark haired boy. Kai.

"But how?" I whispered.

"You recognize this?" Terran asked.

"I thought the Tapestries of Truth showed scenes from the immortal war?"

"They do," he said. "This is when Zophia realized that Kull had killed Aris. See, look at the blood moon and all the fallen bodies of the immortals that Kull slayed."

"Terran, I see this same vision in a nightmare that I've had every night since I've been here. This is me," I said pointing to Zophia, who bared an uncanny resemblance to me with her flaxen hair and clear blue eyes. "These are my friends," I said pointing to the pile of bodies.

It made me lose my breath, seeing the likeness of my friends in each of the twisted lifeless faces woven into the tapestry. A coldness ripped through me as I moved closer to the wall hanging.

"Look, this one is you," I said.

Terran was as close as I was to the tapestry now. I could see his eyes studying it. The figure I'd pointed to was even wearing grey clothing, his dark hair disheveled in death. Terran's eyes widened in disbelief.

"And this," I said pointing to the dark haired figure looming over the pile of bodies. "This isn't Kull... It's Kai," I said touching my finger to the haunting silhouette. *Kai is Kull, not Nova!*

As I made this realization, my fingers made contact with the tapestry. I felt a searing pain in my neck and chest. I tried to scream, but I was falling, fast. I had no voice as I plummeted. I was suddenly engulfed in icy water and struggled against it. I tried to scream again and sucked in water. Its sulfuric taste stabbed my memory. Swim! Swim, my mind reeled. And I did. Next, I was on the black sand shore of the cave. My friends were there with me, four of them standing in a familiar looking symbol, their hands joined in the center, chanting words I didn't know as a powerful ray of light arced from the center of their joined hands, lighting the entire cave. Wind howled and the earth shook around us. The water glowed, illuminating the faces of the others in the cave. Jaka, Vida, Mali, and so many other Betos. I followed their gaze to the cavernous lake. The water bubbled to a violent boil, alight with fire from somewhere deep below, reflecting tormented faces trapped just below the surface. They groaned and reached claw-like hands through the water, raking the air. I started chanting as well. The words were foreign to my ears, by my tongue formed them like I'd known them my entire life. I watched as the water began to freeze. A thick ice formed over the lake. I marched to its cold center, pulled a knife from my belt and held it high above my head while I continued to chant. The knife glinted to life as I slammed it downward and everything around me exploded.

I awoke on my back in a meadow, with ash floating silently above me. Birds were chirping and the sun shined warmly on my face. I was somewhere familiar. The forest? I heard my name being called, but I was in no rush to go to it. I was tired and just wanted to close my eyes and stay here in this peacefulness.

But the voice was persistent.

"Geneva. Geneva."

I felt myself being gently shaken and I when I opened my eyes again, it was Terran who I saw.

"What happened?" I asked as he helped me sit up.

I was on a bed in one of the bunkrooms we passed earlier.

"Oh thank the gods!" he said breathing as sigh of relief. He crouched in front of me, with worry creasing his face.

"What happened?" I asked again.

He sat on the bed next to me and looked at the floor, putting his elbows on his knees and rubbing the stress from his temples.

"I don't know. You touched the tapestry and started screaming and then you passed out. I didn't know what to do. I thought..." he shuddered. " I didn't know what to think. I brought you here and tried to wake you up."

We sat quietly on the edge of the squeaky bed, neither of us speaking. The rough grey blanket tightly tucked around it scratched at my legs.

"I think I had a vision," I whispered.

"Good or bad?" he asked.

"I'm not sure yet, but I know what we have to do when we get out of here," I said with renewed confidence as I got to my feet.

"What?"

"I can't explain it yet. But if we make it out of here alive we have to get to the cave. That's where we can defeat the Ravinori."

Terran stood and stared into my eyes. He was tall and had to bend to look directly at me. He put his large, warm hands on my shoulders and I felt an electric shock rush through me. It made my bones feel sturdier somehow, giving me energy and strength. His hazel eyes burned with conviction.

"We *will* make it out of here, Geneva. I will get you to that cave if it's the last thing I do."

I no longer held an ounce of doubt. Terran was a Pillar. I'd felt it in him, just as I had with Sadie, Jovi and Nova. There was no denying the inherent connection I felt to them. I finally had all the pieces I needed to defeat the Ravinori once and for all.

Just moments ago I had been ready to give up. But now, I had found a renewed strength from an ancient tapestry. If they indeed were Tapestries of Truth, then what I had seen gave me faith that I would fulfill my destiny and defeat the Ravinori. The three sisters had seen it and wove it into the fabric, knowing I would find it centuries later.

"Do you think there's time to get a message to the Betos before we leave tomorrow?"

"Yes, and I know exactly who can help us," Terran said with a grin before striding over to a chest near the end of his bunk. He flipped open the lid and pulled out a grumpy marmouse.

"Niv!" I squealed. "Oh you've gotten even fatter!" I laughed as Terran placed him in my arms.

"I've been smuggling him a lot of scraps," he said bashfully.

"Thank you, Terran ..." I said gazing at him around Niv's excited kisses. There was so much I wanted to thank him for. More than just taking care of Niv, but for helping my friends, for giving me time to trust him, for risking his neck to help us and for providing me a new determination to fulfill my destiny. I didn't know how to put it into words so I said, "...for everything."

Terran and I drafted a coded letter to Jaka telling him of my vision from the tapestry and that once we escaped the Troian Center we all had to go to the Cayo cave to preform a ritual. I hoped that Jaka would know what had to be done once we got there because I was sure there were preparations that would have to be arranged. But for now, I had to focus on our escape. I only had to make it through one more night here and then the dance.

"Thank you again," I said to Terran on my way out of his room.

"Anytime. Now, go get ready for the ball, Cinderella," he called after me.

I smiled to myself recalling the fairytale. I was no Cinderella. I wasn't waiting for a handsome prince to save me. I would make my own destiny.

52

"This is ridiculous," mumbled the boy crushing my fingers in his sweaty palms.

"Ouch!" I howled again. "You keep stepping on my feet!"

"Well you keep trying to lead! That's my job."

"One more time from the top," Professor Tremaine called exasperatedly over the rim of her wire framed glasses.

She had been charged with giving us a crash course on dance etiquette. Most of the students – the ones from Lux, at least – had been to a ball before, so this wasn't entirely new to them. But for me and any of the orphans from the Troian Center, dance wasn't a word in our vocabulary.

I had returned to my bunkroom just as everyone was heading to the courtyard for our one and only dance lesson. Sparrow was still giving me the silent treatment and Jemma was gloating, but at least Sadie was speaking to me.

"We're supposed to meet our partners in the courtyard for Genesis Ball etiquette and dance lessons," she said.

"Partners?"

"Dance partners. You know, our dates?"

Evidently Kai hadn't gotten the memo about the dance lesson or perhaps he had and changed his mind. For all I knew, Nova, Remi or Journey could have beaten him senseless and tied him up somewhere for asking me to the dance. If looks could kill, Kai would already be six feet under.

At first I'd been disappointed that he hadn't shown up. Jemma certainly was delighted to see I'd been stood up before even getting to the dance.

"See, that's what you get when you try to have it all, little sister."

I'd rolled my eyes and sat on a stone bench until Professor Tremaine spotted me hiding out and paired me with a massive boy named Gavin who was currently sweating on me and crushing my toes. I could see why he was dateless for the dance as I winced when my foot was caught beneath his.

"One, two, three. One, two, three..." sang Professor Tremaine's nasally voice.

As Gavin spun me around I caught glimpses of my friends; Sadie with Journey, Sparrow with Remi and Jemma with Nova. My heart sank. Everything was wrong. I knew it was just a stupid dance and it didn't mean anything – we were only going as a means to escape – but I couldn't help feeling a twinge of guilt. My friends had been looking forward to the dance. At least I knew the girls were. I'd heard them gossiping with the other girls in our bunkroom after we'd first learned about it. Going to a school dance with a dreamy boy was a rite of passage and even if it was under false pretenses, I wished my friends could have gone with who they truly desired, not just settled for where the pieces lay after my catastrophic dating folly with Kai.

Jemma was the only one who looked happy. A stupid smile was plastered across her perfect face as Nova lifted and spun her. Nova's face was blank. I tried to catch his eye and convey that I was sorry, but his eyes were glassed over, as he blankly moved through the motions like a handsome corpse that someone had cast a spell upon. His eyes were dead, his movements rigid, but accurate. Jemma didn't seem to notice or care. Her painted red lips were frozen in a dazzling white smile that whirled passed me to the rhythm of the music.

"Ouch!" The thud of my partner's foot on mine drew my attention back to him.

"You're not even trying," he said as he finally let my hands out of his sweaty grasp. "I demand a new partner!" Gavin shouted over the music to Professor Tremaine.

My cheeks flushed as everyone stared at me.

"Fine. Then you can dance with me," she said marching over to him.

"What? No, I – " he stuttered.

"You may sit this one out and observe, Miss Sommers," she said, nodding to the bench.

The music picked up again and I slinked away, knowing no one would miss me.

I headed back to my room feeling a bit sorry for myself. I tried to shake it off. It was only a dance. It didn't matter if I had a date or knew how to twirl around the dance floor. We'd hopefully only be there a short while anyway.

My heart stung when I tried to push the dance out of my mind. My thoughts always swam back to the last dance I'd been at; my Eva ceremony in the forest. It had been one of the happiest nights of my life. I swayed with Nova under petal brimmed trees. I could still remember the warmth, pressed against his shirtless chest, his muscles coiled rigidly under my touch.

"One more day," I whispered to myself.

It had become my new mantra. If I could get through one more day, I could tell Nova everything and maybe we could start over.

I pushed the door open to the girls bunkroom and strode to

my bed. Halfway to it, I noticed there was something on top of it. A large white box. I had to climb up the ladder to reach it. It was light and soundless as I shook it.

I pulled the box down with me and brought it to one of the tables in the center of the room. I awkwardly set it there, apprehensively examining it. It was a large white rectangular box made of stiff cardboard with a soft gold ribbon tied around the center. There was no name or note on the box, but it had been on my bed so it must have been for me. I had no idea who it was from or what it could be and was slightly frightened to find out. I looked around the room. No one else was there. What if there was something terrible inside and I was here alone with it? I leaned in closer and put my ear to the box. I didn't hear anything. I poked it and nothing happened. I felt slightly ridiculous. It was just a box, nothing to be frightened of.

I walked away from it and sat on the edge of the nearest bed staring at it. It sat where I'd left it on the table, innocently beckoning for me to open it.

"Oh, why not?" I said crossing the room and slipping off the gold satin ribbon.

Inside the box was a pile of soft, sheer white fabric and placed atop sat a stiff white card with elegant embossed lettering. The gold letters read:

Jacques & Gustav's Fine Gown Emporium

Under the large white card I found a small gold envelope with my name scrawled elegantly across. I picked it up and slipped out the white notecard from within.

Geneva,

Please accept my apologies for not attending the dance lesson with you tonight. I had to attend to the very important matter of this box. As for its contents, I hope you'll find it to your liking. I'm sure it will fit. No more excuses.

Truly,
Kai

MY HEART FLUTTERED. He hadn't stood me up after all! I peeled back the layers of soft white fabric until I reached a pale blue taffeta. I pulled it out to reveal the most beautiful dress I'd ever seen. I gasped and felt weak in the knees. This dress must have cost a fortune. It was layers upon layers of luxurious blue fabric. Gossamer, satin, lace, taffeta, tulle, all intricately embellished and embroidered. Beads cast sparkles across the delicate tiers of tulle the way the sun cast glitter across the ocean. The multiple hues of cerulean melted together effortlessly like the churning tides of the sea. The dress shimmered in the chandelier light, casting an array of tiny rainbows across my pale skin.

My hands shook. This was too much. I couldn't accept it. That wouldn't be fair to Kai. I would only be in this gorgeous gown for a few moments before we had to make our escape. It would most likely be ruined, a casualty of my destiny. No, a dress like this deserved more. Kai deserved more. I wasn't who he thought I was. I wasn't someone who deserved to wear such a beautiful thing. And no matter how much I was growing to care for Kai, I couldn't shake the feeling that he wasn't who I thought he was either. The terrifying vision from the tapestry still haunted me. Could a gift from him truly come with no strings attached?

Just as I was carefully folding the dress to put it back, I saw another gold envelope at the bottom of the box. It too had my name on it.

GENEVA,

You absolutely can and must accept this dress. Nothing will make me happier than to see you wear it. My father does not approve of me attending the dance with you as my date, and certainly would not approve of me adding this gown to his account in Lux. That said, it does make it seem all the more fun to be deceiving someone who has spent so much time deceiving me. I know we may only have one dance together before he puts and end to my evening, but I assure you, even one dance with you would last me a lifetime. You are worth it. I no longer seek my father's approval. I have the clarity to see him for who he truly is and the strength to stand up to him. I owe that all to you. Please accept the dress as a small token of my gratitude and nothing more.

Truly,
Kai.

"He really does think of everything," I said to myself as I folded the notes and tucked them back into the envelopes. I held the glittering blue dress up once more. The delicate layers of sheer fabric deepened in hue as they cascaded to the floor. I pressed it to me in front of the mirror and swayed back and forth watching the clear beads reflect a dancing array of lights as they shimmered. I wanted to put the dress on, but I couldn't risk it. If Jemma found me in it she'd probably steal it or destroy it out of spite. And I still hadn't decided if I should wear it. I took one last look and carefully placed it back in the box and slid it under her bed, pushing it as far back as I could, praying she wouldn't find it.

Just as I'd secured the box, I heard the bunkroom doors push open and excited voices filled the room. Apparently the dance lessons were over. I sat back at the table watching everyone flood inside. Girls collected in giddy groups, dancing and humming the tune from the hypnotic music we'd been waltzing to at the dance lesson. I envied their carefree musings. For a moment I found myself lost in thought, wondering if I could have been one of them if I had never learned the truth about myself.

Sadie interrupted my pondering when she pulled up a chair next to me. "So everything's still on for tomorrow, right?"

I nodded.

"Good, we need to get out of here as soon as possible," she said glaring at a group of spinning girls next to us.

"I'm sorry I ruined the dance for you," I said.

"Don't worry about it. It's not a real dance anyway, right?"

"Right," I said glumly.

"Besides, Journey's not so bad. His hand is so sore from punching that wall that he let me take the lead during dance lessons. It turns out I'm a pretty good dancer," she said with a shy smile.

"That's good," I said unable to muster much enthusiasm.

"I still can't believe he didn't break any bones. What is he made of stone?" she joked.

I managed a smirk. Sadie had no idea how close to the truth she actually was.

"Geneva, buck up. By this time tomorrow we'll be out of here. We can have as many dances as we want once we're free of this place."

"That's not it. I just feel bad that I upset all of my friends so much over this stupid dance. I wish we could leave right now and avoid the whole thing."

"Hey, they'll get over it. There will be time to mend friendships after we leave this place. The important thing is that we all make it out of here. Terran is right. The dance is our best chance to escape."

"That reminds me. I spoke to him today. I sort of had a vision about what we have to do once we leave the Troian Academy."

Sadie's big blue eyes widened with curiosity.

"We have to go to a special cave in the rainforest. It's at the base of the volcano. I've been there before. And in my vision, it's where we were able to destroy the *Ponte deorum* and defeat Malakai and the Ravinori once and for all. I've already sent word to the Betos so they can start preparations."

Sadie looked troubled.

"What is it?" I asked.

"Geneva, once we escape the Troian Academy I have to go help my sister. I can't go with you until I know Mala's safe."

"Sadie, once we defeat the Ravinori she *will* be safe. We can send in the Beto scouts to rescue her."

"What if it's too late? What if we fail? I can't risk anything happening to her. She's my sister. The only family I have left. She's taken care of me her whole life. Now it's my turn. I'll never forgive myself if something happens to her."

My gut twisted. I felt for Sadie, but we couldn't risk going to Lux to try to break Mala out of prison. Sadie especially couldn't go. She was a Pillar and my mission was to keep her safe and away from Malakai and the Ravinori.

"Sadie, I promised you I'd help you save your sister and I meant it. It won't do you any good to get yourself killed trying to save her. Once we escape, Malakai will suspect you as one of the Pillars or at the very least an accomplice to helping us escape. There will be a price on your head. You can't go marching into Lux to try to break Mala out."

"Don't you see? That's exactly why I have to get to her first. If Malakai knows what I am, he'll use Mala to try to get to me."

The worry painted across Sadie's face seared my heart. She was right. Malakai wasn't above torturing Mala if he thought it would help him control a Pillar. But my vision had been clear. I needed all four Pillars to complete the ritual that would seal the other side and destroy the Bridge of the Gods.

"You're right. I just need to think so we can come up with a plan."

"We don't have much time left to think," Sadie urged.

I didn't need reminding. I could feel each minute sliding by me at a reckless pace. Since the moment we arrived, the Troian Academy had seemed like a prison, with time trickling by so slowly that weeks felt like months, and months like years. Yet now, when I needed a moment to think, time was again my enemy. No matter how much I struggled to grasp it, it flowed through my fingers like water. My efforts were useless.

"Let's talk to everyone at breakfast tomorrow. It's our last chance to put our heads together," I said.

I SPENT the rest of the evening alone. Jemma had what she wanted and for once seemed happy enough to leave me be. Sparrow, on the other hand, was still giving me the silent treatment. I knew the threat of her impending adoption was probably adding to her mood. Even though I wanted desperately to speak to her, I'd followed Sadie's advice and decided to give her some space.

I used the time to think. I was going over every option in my mind of how we could rescue Mala without endangering Sadie. There was no way that I could let any of the Pillars go on a mission to Lux to try to break her out of prison. They were too valuable. Besides, I wanted to start the ritual I'd seen in my vision to destroy the Bridge of the Gods as soon as possible and I knew that would require all four Pillars. The only idea that I found myself circling back to was asking Journey and Remi to go to Lux while we escaped to the cave. I knew that Journey had the skill and bravery required and Remi could offer them the best chance of success with his invisibility power. But I felt a knot in my stomach even thinking about asking them. I didn't want to put my friends in danger, and I knew Sparrow would hate me even more for risking their lives, but if I didn't do something to save Mala, we would lose Sadie and possibly any chance at ever defeating Malakai.

When the lights finally went out, I knew my chances of sleep would be futile. I lay on my back staring at the tiny chandelier above my bed, letting thoughts of escape, battle and destruction dance across the surface of my mind. I must have eventually drifted off, because I awoke with a start. I was drenched in sweat and tangled in my mess of white sheets. My heart was pounding from the echo of my nightmares. I had once again been surrounded by flames, staring at the beautifully tortured faces of my friends. I could still hear Malakai screaming at me to "choose." The only difference this time was that Mala was there and I was wearing a beautiful blue dress.

The first light of dawn poked through the windows. I shivered as I waited for my heart to slow to a steady thump in my chest. I sat up, surprised to see that all the girls were already out of bed. They were flitting around fussing with their dresses for the ball. Hanging them to shake out the creases, taking in waists or up hems. All the girls from Lux had dresses sent to the Troian Academy from home. The walls of the girls bunkroom were now spattered with regal gowns in many different hues of red, the traditional color of the Genesis ball. I pushed back the thought that they made the walls look like they were dripping blood.

I slid out of bed and found Sadie and Sparrow helping each other iron the plain red dresses we'd been given. Anyone who didn't have a dress for the ball was issued one by the Troian Academy. They were exactly like the one shoulder white uniform dresses we all wore, except in a bright crimson hue.

"Morning," I mumbled as I rubbed the remaining sleep from my puffy eyes. "Why is everyone awake so early? The first bell hasn't even rung."

"Everyone's excited for the dance," Jemma called from a few feet away. "Lots to do!"

I hadn't noticed her at first because she was almost hidden behind a gigantic bolt of red fabric.

"What are you doing?" I asked.

"Oh don't you worry about me," she said with a mischievous grin.

I ignored her attempt to bait me into an argument. It was too early for that. Instead I sat down at the table with Sparrow and Sadie.

"Do you want help ironing your dress?" Sadie asked.

"Oh, I'm sure it's fine how it is," I said. "Besides, I think I've come up with a plan to help Mala. But not everyone's going to like it."

53

The entire dining room was ablaze with laughter and conversation, but our section of the table was silent. I studied the faces of each of my friends but they revealed nothing. I had just shared my vision from the tapestry, my latest nightmare and my plan to save Mala after we escaped. They'd been silent while I laid it all out and now I waited for them to say something. Anything. Especially Journey and Remi. They were the two most affected by this new plan. They sat next to each other, stoic and silent.

Sadie was the first to speak. "Listen, I feel terrible even having to ask you to entertain this idea. I should be the one going to save Mala."

"No," Journey said. "Geneva's right. It's too dangerous. You're not expendable. We are."

"Journey," I hissed in a low whisper. "You know I don't mean it like that."

"I know," he said with sincerity. "It's just how it is. It's a smart plan. If Remi's in, I'm in."

All eyes went to Remi. "Fine," he nodded.

Journey immediately jumped into planning mode.

"Someone needs to tell Terran."

"I can do that," Nova interjected.

"Good. We'll need him to get word to Hollis to meet us at Lux. That will be our best chance for escape," Journey said looking at Nova. "The old New Year Gala exit spot should work."

Nova nodded and Journey turned his attention to Remi.

"We should be able to get to Lux without being detected tonight. Everyone will be distracted by the dance and we'll have the cover of darkness on our side. If you can get us in and out of Lux we can have Hollis at the ready to get us safely back to the forest."

"I'll have Terran see if he can round up some Luxor uniforms for you both," Nova said. "Just as an extra precaution," he added, when Sparrow let out a tiny whimper.

"Thanks, mate," Journey said clasping Nova's hand.

The two boys shared a lingering look of understanding and mutual respect as they shook hands. Then Nova reached across Journey and offered his hand and approval to Remi as well.

"Then, it's decided?" I asked.

Everyone silently nodded.

"Tonight we take our lives back," I said.

When we returned to our bunkroom Sparrow went straight to her bed and buried her head in her pillow. I gave her a moment alone before sitting on the edge. She stiffened as soon as I sat down, but didn't tell me to leave. After a few minutes Sadie joined us. Sparrow sat up and pulled her knees to her chest and looped her thin arms around them, resting her chin on her knees. We sat silently for a while. I scanned the room; Jemma was nowhere to be found. I wondered where she had snuck off to as I watched the tornado of taffeta and satin twirl around us. We remained still, unmoved amid the chaos. Three tenacious girls determined to remain steadfast against the Ravinori. Tonight we would weather the storm, or die trying.

“She’s going to get her powers back during the dance. There’s nothing I can do to delay her any further, I’m sorry.”

“Don’t apologize. You’ve done well. Very well. We knew this day would come and we need the Eva to regain her powers back eventually if we are to use them for our cause. Knowing when it will happen has its advantages,” Malakai replied.

“And what about their plan to escape?”

“It will be taken care of.”

“I did what you wanted. Don’t forget what you promised me.”

“You will have my protection as promised,” Malakai purred. “You may be dismissed.”

Once alone in the room, Malakai beckoned Kobel to join him.

“I told you my informant would serve us well,” Malakai gloated.

“Yes, it seems you were correct. What do you plan to do about their escape plot?” Kobel asked.

“Let them continue their plans. I have a few of my own to prepare for.”

Everyone finished dressing and started heading to the courtyard where we’d all meet our dates to be escorted to the library. I stood in front of the mirror looking at my reflection as Sadie expertly applied my make-up. I barely recognized myself. Sadie had turned my pale hollow complexion into a delicate creamy glow, with peach kissed cheeks and pink glossy lips the color of a young rose petal.

“Are you sure you want to go with this eye shadow? It really doesn’t suit the red dress.”

"Yes," I said confidently.

Somewhere between when I'd first laid eyes on the dress from Kai and this morning, I'd made the subconscious decision to wear it to the Genesis Ball. I'd had Sadie apply a pale shade of shimmering blue shadow to my eyes. She highlighted it with flecks of gold like I'd asked and was now standing back to admire her work.

"Okay, then you're all set," she beamed. "You look beautiful."

"Thank you. You both look lovely," I said looking at her and Sparrow through the mirror.

"Not too bad," Jemma said coming into the reflection.

We all turned to look at her in person. She had somehow added a long flowing skirt to her standard issued red dress. The material swirled as she moved, showing one long tan leg through the high slit near her hip. The graceful skirt swept the floor with a soft rustle as she floated over to us. She pushed past us to get a full view of the mirror and adjusted a beaded gold belt that she'd obviously conned from another girl. She had braided her black hair into tight intricate rows. Her eyes were lined with coal shadow and her perfect lips and nails were painted red to match the color of her dress. She smacked her lips together and winked at her reflection.

"Perfect," she purred. Then she turned and gave us a slow judging glance, running her cruel eyes up and down us with disdain. "Well, good luck tonight," she said before flouncing past.

There was no denying that she looked beautiful, but I knew better. Deep down, Jemma was anything but beautiful. Something about the wicked gleam in her eye when she'd said 'good luck' made me think she actually hoped we'd fail.

I watched the back of her shiny black braids as she disappeared through the bunkroom door.

"We'd better get going too," Sparrow said.

"Go on without me," I said. "There's something I have to do."

They hesitated, looking at each other questioningly.

"I'll be there in a second. I promise."

Sparrow looked like she didn't want to leave, but Sadie shrugged and pulled her along.

"Don't take too long," she called over her shoulder. "Destiny awaits."

There was something I needed to do. I wanted to write everything down in a letter, just in case something went wrong tonight. I wanted Nova to know the truth no matter what happened. He deserved to know that I loved him and that Jemma had tricked me and used him. If things went badly, I was prepared to sacrifice myself to save my friends, but I also wanted to protect Nova from Jemma by telling him the truth. If I didn't survive tonight, who knew what lies she would fill his head with. I couldn't let that happen. I wouldn't let her trap him with her deceit. I wanted him to know the truth and have the freedom to make up his mind without her poisoning it.

When I was finally satisfied with my letter, I folded in into a tiny square and scribbled Nova's name across it. In a sudden rush of emotion, I impulsively kissed the tiny bundle of paper. When I pulled it away from my mouth there was a perfect pink imprint of my lips. I smiled with melancholy, knowing the note could be the closest I ever came to kissing Nova again. I tied it up with a long piece of twine and looked around the bunkroom. It was completely deserted. I was the only one left. I quickly darted to my bunk and pulled the white box out from under it. I slipped out of the red dress, my eyes settling for a moment on the nearly complete symbol of the four Pillars that remained on my chest. I had come so close to losing everything under the blood curse. I could feel it dissolving the veil and was terrified of what that meant for Nova, who was unknowingly housing my powers. I traced my fingers over the faint white scar and shuddered. I shook the terrifying thoughts away and stepped into the blue gown that I carefully unfolded from its hiding place under Jemma's bed. Kai had been right, it fit perfectly; from the fitted bodice to the sweeping neckline. I laced up the bodice and tied the elegant jeweled belt at my waist. I took a deep breath as I picked up the skirt and tiptoed over to the mirror.

My mouth hung open as I stared at my reflection. For a moment I thought that I was seeing Nesia in the mirror again, but as I watched the figure mimic my movements I knew it was actually my own reflection. The crystals on the bodice of the blue dress caught every fraction of light and made my skin look like it was glowing, while the soft full skirt seemed to float with my every measure. I felt like I was dreaming as I stared at the fairy princess that had taken over my body. The girl in the mirror couldn't be me. She looked solid, confident, graceful; where as I felt hallow and frail, like at any moment I would be pulled under and crushed by the weight of my destiny. I constantly felt moments away from drowning and seeing myself in a swirling sea of blue fabric made the feeling all too real. Tonight would make or break me. It would either be the beginning or the end. I would be victorious and start on the path to freedom for my people or I would watch that dream go down in flames, with Malakai and the Ravinori at the helm. I stared at my refection as I stood at the precipice of my destiny. I was shaking inside, but the girl in the mirror looked strong. She nodded and set her shoulders.

"It ends tonight."

I was halfway to the door when I heard a soft knock. I stopped moving and listened to the muffled voice calling my name on the other side.

"Geneva? Are you decent?"

It was Kai.

"You're not going to stand me up are you?" he asked, trying for sarcasm, but there was too much worry in his voice.

"Never," I said as I pulled the door open with a grin.

Kai was speechless when he caught sight of me. He stood in the doorway looking stunned, his jaw unhinged.

"What's wrong?" I asked subconsciously under his unwavering gaze. "Am I wearing it wrong?"

"You look like a dream," he said shaking himself back to reality. "Are you ready to go? We mustn't miss the selections."

I nodded. He was right. If I wasn't there for the tournament selections it would raise suspicion. The whole idea of the dance had originally started as a way for the athletes of the Genesis Tournament to have a place to parade around at the preview gala where the wealthy could take stock of them and place their bets for the event the following day. It was also the final chance to celebrate for many of the athletes who met their demise in the brutal tournament. Malakai was a traditionalist. Since he was determined to host his own Genesis Tournament, where I was sure he was planning to stage my death or worse, he was holding true to customs by also having the pre-tournament ball, where he would announce which event we'd be competing in. Perhaps he and the Luxors would be placing bets. I hadn't given it much thought since we'd originally planned to be long gone before the tournament actually happened.

"Just a moment," I said as I trotted back over to my bed where I'd stashed my letter for Nova.

I tucked it safely into the bodice of my dress and then strolled over to Kai. He grinned from ear to ear as he held his arm out for me to take. I draped my arm over his and smiled back at him. With any luck, both of us would show Malakai that we weren't afraid to stand up to him tonight.

"Ready?" he asked.

I nodded. "Destiny awaits."

54

"Where is she?" Nova asked quietly as he stood against the wall in the library.

"She said she would be right behind us," Sparrow replied with worry.

Sparrow, Remi, Nova, Jemma, Journey and Sadie were gathered in the library with all the other students awaiting the start of the dance. The library had been transformed into a beautiful ballroom. White floral garland hung from the chandeliers. The center of the room had been emptied of the research tables to make room for a white marble dance floor. Candelabras were scattered on nearly every surface, giving the dark room a warm glow. Moonlight shown through the stained glass windows, casting eerie shadows of color from the east wall. A small orchestra was playing a string melody as everyone patiently waited for Malakai to announce the Genesis Tournament selections. He'd entered the room a few moments earlier with some of the professors and about a dozen Luxors. He was gathering himself at the lectern, front and center.

Nova scanned the room once more and let out a sigh of relief when he realized that Terran wasn't among the group of

Luxors who'd accompanied Malakai. He was hopefully on his way to disable the Soul Cell so that they could all use their powers to aid them in their escape tonight.

After breakfast, while everyone was getting ready for the dance, Nova went to find Terran and update him on the newest addition to the plan.

"I can help by securing uniforms and sending another message to the Betos, but I already instructed Niv to remain in the forest after the last message Geneva sent. I'll have to find another way," Terran said.

"Is that going to be a problem?" Nova asked.

"No, it should be simple enough to get a carrier bird to send the message."

Even with Terran's assurances, Nova was starting to feel the pinpricks of doubt creeping up his spine. He pulled at the collar of his crisp black shirt he'd been issued. Journey and Remi wore their Cadet uniforms, but Nova had been stripped of his. He'd been put on probation after he broke Kai's collarbone and his fight with the Luxors had been the final straw. A small price to pay in order to find information about Geneva, he thought. The whole thing had actually been Kai's idea, although he doubted Geneva would believe him even if he did get the chance to explain himself. He'd seen the way she looked at Kai. Whether she knew it or not, she cared for him.

Her plan to get close to Kai in order to help them gather information about Malakai had caused her to develop real feelings for him. It hurt to see her have feelings for someone else, but that's part of what Nova loved so much about her. Geneva was so genuine. She didn't have a fake bone in her body. He should have known she wouldn't be able to help caring for Kai. Even Nova himself had started to trust the kid.

When he'd come to Nova with the plan for them to get into a scuffle that would send him to the infirmary to look for Geneva, he could tell Kai was genuinely worried for her. Nova hadn't needed much prodding to agree to Kai's scheme, though he did feel bad that he'd seriously injured him. The plan had only been to hurt him slightly so he could go to the infirmary, but Kai wasn't a trained fighter like Nova and perhaps he had gotten carried away. Either way, breaking his bones had been an accident.

Nova had never intended for Geneva to find out about his little pact with Kai. He knew she would only be angry with him for not trusting her to take care of herself. And with everything that Jemma had been telling him, Geneva was already fearful of Nova's violent tendencies linked to the Kull prophecy. He didn't want to add more fuel to the fire. Despite how their plan had turned out, Kai's commitment to it had solidified Nova's trust in him. But now, he noticed that Kai, as well as Geneva, were missing from the library.

Nova swallowed hard hoping he hadn't been wrong about Kai. At first he'd been out of his mind that Geneva was going to the dance with Kai, but then once he settled himself, he realized that she had to go with someone and Kai was probably the safest option, knowing that the boy would do anything to keep her safe. Still, he was growing impatient as he clenched and unclenched his fists. He watched as beads of sweat ran down Journey's neck and was glad he was only wearing the black dress shirt, rather than the heavy Cadet uniform. It was already too hot for his comfort in the library with all the candles burning and students giving off heat. It didn't help that Jemma was glued to his side. She was taking this dance thing way too seriously, Nova thought. He should have known better than to promise her a favor. But he knew he would have agreed to be her date a thousand times over if it meant Jemma would save Geneva. He would do anything for Geneva, including love her from afar if that was his only option.

Nova pulled at his collar again. It was getting hard to breathe in the stuffy library. He tried to shrug Jemma off his arm, but his attempts to ditch her were useless. Hopefully he would only have to endure it for a little longer. As soon as the Soul Cell was down, they were going to make a break for it. As long as Geneva showed up.

"Good evening, ladies and gentleman. Welcome to the first annual Troian Academy Genesis Ball. As you well know, the Genesis Ball and Tournament have been a long-standing and admired tradition in Lux. As the new Headmaster of the Troian Academy, I'm pleased to be able to bring that time-honored tradition here for you to be a part of. Tonight we will celebrate the bravery of the competing athletes and tomorrow we will hail their courageousness. The Genesis Tournament is where heroes are made. If your name is called tonight, you have been selected to compete in the tournament. Rejoice in your fate. Be fearless and revel in the knowledge that you will become an honored member of the Hall of Champions. Without further adieu, let the selection begin!"

Kai and I snuck into the library from a side corridor so as not to interrupt the selection ceremony. Even before we entered the room, I could here Malakai's booming voice calling out names. We slid in behind a group of students on the west wall. For once I was glad of my short stature. It was the only thing keeping me hidden among the sea of red and black that filled the library.

I watched as student after student marched stoically toward Malakai after they'd been selected. He assigned them their event, or in some cases, depending on their size and opponent, their death sentence. The opponents would shake hands and then bow to Professor Kobel, who placed a laurel crown atop their heads. After a round of applause they would join the line of competitors standing in the front of the library.

I was grateful the room was filled with constant applause. It allowed me and Kai to slip in unseen. I spotted my friends across the room, but they hadn't noticed us yet. I gave telepathing a try, hoping that Terran had been successful at disabling the Soul Cell.

"Over here. Nova? Remi? Sparrow?"

Nothing. It was worth a try. I'd figured my powers would still be veiled regardless of the Soul Cell blocking them. It bothered me that I wasn't sure how to get them back or if my backstabbing sister even knew how to do it. My only comfort was that we had a solid plan that didn't require me to have my powers to escape.

We just have to make it through the selection, then we're out of here, I pep talked myself.

I felt Kai squeeze my hand and it brought me back to reality.

"He'll be fine," Kai whispered.

"What?" I asked.

But when I looked through the crowd of students in front of me, I saw what Kai had meant.

Remi was marching hesitantly toward Malakai. His shoulders square and his fists balled tightly at his side. I knew it was likely that all of my friends would be chosen. After all, Malakai knew who we were by now and seemed to enjoy toying with us. My heart pounded as I waited to hear the selection of Remi's event.

"Grappling," Malakai purred with a sinister sneer.

Remi moved to the side and awaited his opponent. I knew who it would be even before the words came out of the headmaster's mouth, but my stomach still plummeted nonetheless.

"Nova Asher," he bellowed, his voice ringing clear through the library.

The crowd erupted with cheers and wild applause. Apparently his stunt with Kai had earned him a reputation with the students here. I watched with irrational fear as Nova marched forward, jaw set, fearless. I knew that we'd be gone before any of us actually had to battle each other, but it made my skin crawl to see my friends so close to Malakai. The way he smiled at them made my stomach churn.

"They'll be okay," Kai said squeezing my hand.

I hadn't realized I'd been gripping his so hard that my knuckles had turned white.

"They're both strong and smart. Nova will put on a good show and it'll be over quickly, just like he did with me," Kai said.

"What do you mean?" I asked tearing my eyes away from Nova and Remi for the first time.

"This," Kai said pointing to his sling. "This was my idea. Nova just helped me execute it."

"What?"

"When you were missing I was desperate to find you. I asked my father where you were everyday and he kept telling me that you were no longer my concern. That's when I knew you were right about him, so I went to Nova. We suspected you were in the infirmary so I asked him to injure me so I could go to there to look for you."

"Kai, he broke your collarbone."

"That part was my fault, really. Nova was coaching me the whole time, helping me, like he did when we were fencing. But I accidentally kicked one of his legs out from under him while we were in a hold. When he fell on top of me, the weight snapped my collarbone. It wasn't Nova's fault and I know that it won't happen with Remi. They're both good fighters."

I stared at Kai, astonished by the lengths he'd gone to in order to help me. I felt a deep pit of guilt for using him and not being able to tell him that I was leaving tonight. And then another for being so angry with Nova and thinking the worst of him. *Why hadn't Nova told me that it was all a scheme?*

"Sparrow Menders," Malakai called out.

My head snapped back to the center of the library, where Sparrow timidly moved toward the group of athletes who'd already been selected.

"Archery."

Applause.

"Sadira Calder."

More applause as Sadie assuredly marched up to join Sparrow. They clasped hands and received their laurel crowns. Journey was called up next, along with my dance lesson partner. He and Gavin the giant would be competing in flails, one of the most dangerous events in the Tournament, where they swung heavy spiked weapons on a chain at each other, hoping to gain points without getting bludgeoned to death.

"And now, for the final selection of the first annual Troian Center Genesis Tournament," Malakai said, pausing dramatically before looking back at his paper.

"Miss Jemma Sommers."

Jemma bowed graciously before making her way to the front of the room. She glided slowly in her floor length red gown, enjoying all eyes on her. She was smiling, reveling in the attention, as she stood tall before the rest of the students.

Malakai pulled the last slip of paper out of the crystal ball on the lectern and shouted, "Fencing!"

The room applauded and my heart thundered. I knew Malakai would call my name next. He had to. He'd been working to set this up since the day he met me. He'd seen me fence. He'd actually challenged me to a duel. He probably knew all of my weak spots and would make sure Jemma knew them too. Maybe he planned to give her a poison tipped saber to knock me out with. Something from Professor Kobel's poison garden, perhaps. I set my jaw and narrowed my eyes at him. I'd let him have this moment if that's what he wanted, but the joke would be on him when we escaped tonight.

I watched as he feigned surprise when he pulled the final name from the large metal challis on the lectern.

"It seems we shall have a familial duel," Malakai called. "Miss Geneva Sommers!"

I knew it was coming but I couldn't fight the shock and dread that took over my muscles. My legs locked, rooted to the safe space I occupied hidden behind a row of students. Kai's grip on my hand tightened as the students around us started to murmur. I saw the looks of concern wash the faces of my friends at the front of the room. Jemma was the only one still smiling. The room was silent. The little applause that I'd received had died down, leaving an uncomfortable echo of my name on everyone's lips.

"Geneva Sommers, please join us up here, won't you?" Malakai called again.

"No," Kai said, grabbing my arm as I tried to let go of his hand. "He can't make you do this."

I looked at his pleading eyes and smiled sadly at him.

"I don't have a choice, Kai. I'll be okay, but I need you to trust me."

He looked into my eyes, searching for something to hold on to. He must have found it because he finally let go of my hand and nodded.

I muttered a few excuses and the wall of students parted so I could make my way out of the shadows to the center of the room.

AFTER NOVA HEARD Malakai call Geneva's name, his heart was pounding so loudly he could hear the blood pulsing behind his eardrums, drowning out the applause, the whispers, and everything else. It took everything in him to stand still. He wanted to lunge for Malakai and kill him right then. How could the headmaster pit sisters against each other like this? He was pure evil and Nova felt sick with worry since he still hadn't spotted Geneva. Just as he thought he couldn't take another moment, he saw her.

It was like storm clouds parting and letting in a single ray of sunlight. Geneva stood in the center of the silent room wearing a pale blue gown. She was glowing, a beacon of light in a room of darkness. All the tension momentarily left his body. He'd never seen something so painfully beautiful in all his life.

Once, Nova had a dream that he was drowning. It had been so real that he imagined it was a memory from another life, rather than a dream. He'd been trapped in a tumbling blue abyss, not knowing which way was up until finally he saw the sun. He vividly remembered the way the sunlight had looked from underneath the water. It's magnetic pull on his very soul. It had been the only thing that guided him back to life. Nova felt that same pull staring at Geneva. He was inexplicable drawn to her, like he was to the sun. He needed her like he needed oxygen. He started to move before he even realized it, but suddenly he heard her.

"STOP!"

Her voice rang out loud and clear in his head and it startled him enough to stop his movement.

I MARCHED to the front of the room as swiftly as I could. I hated the feeling of everyone's eyes on me. I'd barely convinced Kai to let me go when I saw Nova about to do something rash.

STOP! I willed him and to my surprise he halted.

I gave a brief sigh of relief and picked up my pace. I just wanted to get this nightmare over with already.

I steeled myself as I shook my conniving sister's hand and allowed Kobel to place the laurel crown on my head. Finally, we all raised our hands and bowed as Malakai concluded the selection ceremony. I waited with baited breath for him to leave the room to the ceremonial music that the orchestra surged forth with after his short commencement speech. Once the doors shut behind him, I could finally breathe. Jemma was still smiling and I wanted to punch her, but my eyes went to the rest of my friends. Especially Nova, who was staring at me like I was from another planet.

"Geneva, you look stunning," Sadie said rushing over to me.

"Thank you."

"Where did you get that dress?" Jemma asked vehemently.

"I gave it to her," Kai said coming up behind me and looping his arm around my waist.

Nova's eyes followed Kai's hand, but he still didn't speak.

"May I have this dance?" Kai asked.

"Yes, but would you mind if I spoke to my friends quickly first?"

Kai looked a bit wounded but nodded. "Of course."

"Do we know if the Soul Cell's been disabled yet?" I asked in a hushed whisper as soon as Kai was out of earshot.

"No, I've been trying to telepath all night," Journey said. "I've got nothing."

"Me either," Remi said.

"We need to give Terran more time," Sadie said.

"I heard you," Nova said, speaking for the first time.

His eyes were locked on mine.

"What?" Jemma asked, wide eyed. "That's not possible."

"What do you mean?" Remi asked looking from Jemma to Nova, and then to me.

"I heard you," Nova continued. "Just as you were walking up to Malakai, you told me to stop. But it was different then telepathing somehow. It was like you were...were talking through me. I can't explain it."

I tried to ignore Jemma's glare. I didn't know how to explain what had happened. I hadn't been trying to telepath to Nova. I'd only known that I didn't want him to put himself in danger by trying to stop me from complying with the selection. Perhaps Terran was messing with the Soul Cell and the veil was finally crumbling.

"Maybe Terran's making progress with the Soul Cell," Journey offered coming to my rescue.

"Let's all try again?" Sparrow said.

Everyone's eyes widened around me and from the grins on their faces they must have been able to telepath. But I heard nothing.

"It's working," Sparrow squealed in excitement.

"That's so freaky!" Sadie said.

The poor girl looked rattled as she pulled her hands from her ears.

"It gets easier," Remi assured her.

"What's wrong?" Nova asked looking at me.

"I didn't hear anything," I said.

"You're powers must still be veiled," Jemma said. "Nothing we can do about that."

I glared at her, but knew she was right. I would deal with all of that once we were out of here.

"But I heard you," Nova said, still staring at me.

"I can't explain that, but as for the rest of us, it's good news," Journey said. "It means Terran succeeded. Now we need to wait for him to rendezvous at the main doors to tell us the coast is clear and then we're out of here."

Everyone took a collective breath. So far so good. Only a little bit longer. I could almost taste the freedom.

"Well since we have time to kill, we might as well try to blend in," Jemma said tugging Nova away from the group and toward the dance floor.

"Wait!" I said reaching for Nova. My hand grazed his shirt-sleeve and his eyes widened in surprise. Jemma shot me a livid glare, but I ignored her. “I need to tell you something,” I whispered moving closer to him.

“What is it?” he asked.

I was close enough to touch him now. I could feel his heat radiating toward me. “I just want to say ...” I started, but Jemma butted between us just as I thought she would.

“Come on. You promised me a dance, Nova” she whined but Nova held my stare.

“What did you want to tell me, Geneva?”

“Oh... um never mind. Good luck tonight. I think we’re all going to need it.”

Disappointment flickered across Nova’s green eyes and he shook his head, giving in to Jemma’s persistent tugs. I watched them merge with the colorful crowd swaying on dance floor. I envied their oblivious bliss. Kai emerged with his hand outstretched and I sighed. I owed him at least one dance as well.

55

"Perhaps this color wasn't the best choice," I murmured into Kai's warm shoulder as we danced.

"Why?" he asked.

"I don't exactly blend in. Everyone's staring at me," I said as we waltzed around the dizzying dance floor.

Kai grinned and tried to stifle a laugh.

"What's so funny?"

"That has nothing to do with the color of your dress."

"What do you mean?"

"You have no idea how captivating you are, Geneva. Everyone is staring because tonight there's no hiding it."

My cheeks blushed. How did Kai always have a way of stunning me with the most flattering words, without making me feel that he was saying anything but what he believed to be true?

We glided around the dance floor, me a flare of blue in a sea of red and black. I caught sight of my friends among the revolving faces. Remi and Sparrow actually seemed to be enjoying themselves, with smiles painted across their flushed faces as they swept passed us. But Nova and Journey looked miserable. Sadie seemed content enough to dance with Journey, but his eyes watchfully followed Sparrow around the room. Jemma was grinning obliviously as she pressed herself against Nova's tall frame, but his eyes were locked on me. It took the fun out of dancing with Kai.

"I do see what you mean, though," Kai said. "Nova has been staring at you all night."

"Perhaps you should have chosen a traditional red dress," I said with mild sarcasm. "This one is attracting a lot of attention and I'm sure that word will get back to your father that we're dancing together."

Kai sighed and pulled me toward his center so he could look at me while we danced.

"If you must know, I chose the blue because it reminded me of the color of your eyes. They're the most brilliant hue I've ever seen and as soon as I saw this dress, I knew no one would wear it better. And as for my father, I don't care what he thinks anymore. But you're probably right; he will surely be upset that I defied his orders. I don't want to cause you any trouble, so if our night is to be cut short by one of his Luxor lapdogs, then we'd better make every moment count."

"Kai, I don't want to get you into any more trouble than I already have. You've done so much for me and my friends and there's still things...things I haven't told you yet."

"Since when do you care about following the rules?" Kai joked. "We don't need to know all of each other's secrets at once, Geneva. I was hoping we'd have a long time to uncover them together," he said, driving guilt further into my flushed cheeks.

"But – "

"For tonight, lets forget ourselves and live in this moment," Kai interrupted. "I just want to be a boy dancing with the girl of his dreams."

I didn't get a chance to object. The music swelled and Kai firmly gripped my waist and pulled me into a swirling spin with the rhythm of the music. The rush was thrilling and I couldn't help but stifle a laugh as he whisked me around the dance floor. I'd never danced like that before and Kai was an incredible dance partner, even with one arm in a sling. He led me with ease, his firm hand at the small of my back, gently guiding me through each step. As the music quelled, he swooped me into a deep dip that caught me off guard. I lost my breath and my balance a bit, but his hold on me was steady. His face was so close to mine that when his curtain of dark hair came loose from its tie, it cascaded around my face, blocking out all the light. All I saw were his beautiful dark eyes, rimmed with impossibly long lashes. I felt a sudden urge to tuck his soft hair behind his ear so I could get a better look at his striking features. I could feel his breath, warm on my cheek. We were both breathing hard from the exertion of the dance. His mouth moved dangerously close to mine and I trembled. A barrage of applause broke our spellbound moment and Kai pulled me back to my feet. Both of our cheeks were flushed and Kai smiled warmly at me.

"Dancing with you has been worth every ounce of punishment my father will dole out, Miss Sommers," Kai said with a bow.

"Kai – " I started, but I didn't get to finish.

He must have seen them before I did. Three Luxors swarmed him from all directions. One grabbed his wrist and wrenched it behind his back.

"Your father would like a word with you," he said.

"Fine," Kai said through gritted teeth, trying to smile through the pain for my benefit.

Rage boiled inside of me. "Stop! Let him go!" I yelled at the Luxors. "You're hurting him!"

"What'd you say?" replied the one nearest me.

I recognized him instantly. He was the one from the Athlesium who'd been provoking Nova by harassing me. I knew I would only get us both in trouble if I said anything more, so I kept my mouth shut and turned my back from him, but there was another Luxor behind me.

"I think he asked you a question, darling," he said drawling out the last word with a rotten smirk.

I tried to push passed him, but he grabbed me by my shoulders.

"Don't touch her!" Kai screamed, but something inside of me snapped.

I ducked out of his grasp and slammed the palm of my hand straight up. It connected with the Luxor's nose in a sickening explosion of blood. He screamed and staggered around with his hands covering his face.

"You little wretch!" the other Luxor called lunging at me from behind.

I screamed as I dodged his advance, but he never had a chance. Nova was on top of him in a flash, knocking him off his feet. Kai struggled loose from the Luxor who was holding him just as a group of them rushed us. Before I knew it, the dance had erupted into a full on riot. Journey, Remi and a bunch of boys I didn't know were now in the mix. I recognized most of them as boys from the Troian Center. They had been waiting for any excuse to fight with the Pruxes from Lux.

I searched the swarm for my friends, but it was impossible to see anything. A table had been overturned and the candles had ignited the nearby curtains. The library was beginning to fill with smoke. Girls were screaming above the commotion. I dodged swinging limbs as I tried to fight off the brutal Luxors. I spotted Kai making his way to me. We silently fought back to back, inching our way out of the center of the battle. A boy charged Kai and slammed a chair over his head. I screamed as I watched him crumble to the floor, but before I could react my legs were swept out from under me. The Luxor whose nose I'd broken caught me by an ankle and jerked me to the floor. He pinned me down and spit in my face.

"I'm going to make you regret this," he hissed.

I closed my eyes to block out his bloody face and slammed my knee up as hard as I could. I knocked the wind out of him and rolled his wincing body off of me. Nova was by my side in an instant, as I scrambled to my feet.

"You okay?"

"Yes!"

"Get the girls and get out of here."

"Nova – "

"Just do it. We'll meet you. I promise," he said as he lunged toward another Luxor that advanced at us.

I didn't want to leave him or the boys, but I knew that I had to get Sadie and Sparrow out of here. The boys were strong. They knew the plan and I trusted they would meet us. I spotted Sparrow and Sadie and made my way to them.

"We've got to go!" I cried above the shouting.

They nodded and we tried to weave our way out of the smoke filled chaos.

We were nearly to the door when it burst open and a brigade of Luxors surged forward holding weapons I'd never seen before. A thick mist hissed from the strange weapons they carried and my vision swayed.

Blackness.

"THEY'VE BEEN SECURED, SIR," the Luxor reported.

"And my son?"

"Locked in his room as you directed, Sir."

"Splendid," Malakai replied, unable to hide his menacing sneer.

"What about the informant, Sir?"

"I've made arrangements," Malakai replied. "You have work to do."

56

I awoke groggy and sore on the hard stone floor of the Locker. My head pounded and I began to panic when I looked around the crowded cells. It seemed like the entire student body was down here. The last thing I remembered was holding Sparrow and Sadie's hands as a hissing mist filled the library.

I looked around and was flooded with relief when I saw them standing nearby. Remi, Journey, Nova and Jemma were with them as well.

"What the heck happened?" I asked as I sat up.

"Welcome back," Journey said pulling me to my feet.

I felt light-headed and had to steady myself against the damp stone wall.

"Nerve gas," Sadie said. "The Ravinori weapon of choice. We use it in the infirmary all the time. Professor Kobel perfected the mixture from the plants in his medicinal garden."

I was still trying to wrap my head around how we'd ended up here. Once my mind cleared, it balked at the grave reality of our situation. We were trapped in the Locker. Malakai was never going to let us escape now. We were doomed to fight to the death in the Genesis Tournament tomorrow. And Sparrow would be sent off to some strange adoptive family if she survived. I couldn't let that happen. I had to find a Luxor and get a message to Malakai that I would surrender if he would spare everyone else. I was trying to move through the crowd to get closer to the metal bars where the Luxors would surely be standing guard when a boy pushed me.

"This is all your fault, you know?"

"What?" I said stumbling, still feeling the effect of the nerve gas.

"Back off, Gavin. We're all in here together," Journey warned suddenly by my side.

He lightly pulled me back to the corner where the rest of my friends were huddled.

"Don't provoke anyone right now, Geneva," he said quietly. "We need to concentrate on how to get out of here and quickly."

"How?" Sparrow sobbed. "It's over. We're doomed. The Genesis Tournament is tomorrow. Malakai is going to kill us. I know it."

"Oh shut up, Sparrow. I'm going to kill you myself if I have to listen to another second of your whining," Jemma yelled.

"Don't talk to her like that," Journey said, shoving Jemma against the wall and holding her there.

Jemma's black eyes narrowed and she tore into Journey, shouting in his face.

"Just come clean already. Why don't you just tell her how you feel, you coward? Everyone knows you're in love with Sparrow, Journey. But if you want my advice, you should get over it. She thinks of you like a brother. She likes Remi, and if she makes it through tomorrow, she's going bye-bye to live with her new family, so it's never gonna happen, okay? Can you get that through your thick stone skull?" Jemma steamed.

Journey let go of Jemma like she was poison, his eyes wide

with shock. Sparrow's mouth hung open, but only for a moment before she turned on Jemma.

"If we're all being honest, why don't you tell everyone about Geneva's talisman," Sparrow seethed.

"I don't know what you're talking about," Jemma said nonchalantly.

"Yes, you do," Sparrow fumed.

"What's she talking about, Jemma?" Nova asked her.

"Please, she's delusional," she said rolling her eyes. "What's your problem?" Jemma called to the group of students gawking at us.

"Jemma, that's enough," Nova said pulling her focus back to our group. "Tell me what Sparrow's talking about. Now!"

"Why don't you ask my perfect little sister," she spat.

Now everyone was looking at me.

They all knew that Jemma had veiled my powers, but I had made sure none of them knew that she had used Nova as the talisman. But now it seemed useless to keep it from them. Despite my best efforts, Malakai knew everything and now he had the upper hand. What use was it to keep the lie going?

"It's a long story," I began, but Jemma cut me off by abruptly grabbing my arm and yanking me away from our friends.

"A word please, sister," she hissed.

She had a wild look in her dark eyes as she pulled me into a shadowed corner.

"Have you lost your mind?" she scathed.

"Apparently, I have, because I trusted you. There's no use lying anymore, Jemma. I'm going to tell them the truth."

"No. It's too soon."

"Too soon? Look around you. It's too late. Look where we are. We're in the Locker. I need you to unveil my powers now. It's our only chance to get out of here."

"You're such a disappointment," she sputtered.

"I don't care what you think of me anymore. This needs to

end now. I'm taking back my powers and I'm telling them the truth." I looked over at Nova and our friends who were growing impatient with our little sidebar.

Jemma stared at me with a mixture of loathing and fear. I shook my head in disgust. I was done wasting time on her.

"Go ahead. Tell you're precious Nova what you did. It's too late anyway. Nothing can save you now."

"What do you mean, Jemma?" I questioned.

"You'll see," she smirked.

"Jemma!" I screamed, lunging for her. I had my hands around her throat and I was pressing against her windpipe as she laughed in my face. "What did you do?"

Nova caught me around the waist and pulled my hands from her neck. I heard her laughing hysterically as he dragged me away. When he set me down, I flinched instinctively away from him, but when nothing happened I dissolved into his embrace.

"Okay, I think it's time for you to tell me exactly what's going on here," Nova prodded softly.

"It's her. She's a maniac. She hates me and she's done something to put us all in danger, I know it. She's trying to punish me for... for everything." I yelled. I was trembling with anger but was damned if I was going to let Jemma make me cry.

"Geneva, I heard her, but you have to be more specific so I can help. It's time to let me in, Geneva. Please?"

His eyes bore into mine pleadingly. His face was so close that I could feel the warmth of his breath. He was right, he deserved the truth. All these lies, no matter how good the intensions, were getting us nowhere.

"Okay," I whispered, nodding as I steadied myself.

He wasn't going to like this.

"Do you remember when Jemma veiled my powers?" I asked.

"Yes."

"Well she had to use a talisman to hide them."

"Okay..."

"Once the powers are veiled in the talisman, it's a place that I can't be near for fear of gaining the powers back."

He nodded.

"Jemma picked something that she didn't want me to go near. Something she wanted all for herself."

His eyes darkened and I saw an inkling of suspicion swim across his face.

"No," he whispered.

"You're the talisman, Nova."

"Me? But, that doesn't make any...."

I watched his face as he realized why she'd done it. Why she'd chosen him. His eyes narrowed and he closed his beautiful mouth, pressing his lips into a hard line while he took deep breaths through his nose trying to control his temper.

"So this is why you've been avoiding me like the plague since we left the forest?"

I nodded.

"And why you told me not to touch you when we were fencing and so many other times?"

I nodded again holding my breath. I was waiting for Nova to explode and yell at me for not trusting him enough to tell him what she'd done. Or I thought maybe he might try to wring Jemma's neck for using him as a tool in her little game of jealousy, but his calmness was unexpected. He stood before me, staring at where his hands were touching mine.

I couldn't stand the tension of silence between us so I started babbling. "I know you're going to say I should have told you, but I thought I was protecting you and I was afraid that if you knew, you'd try to give them back because you weren't happy I'd veiled them in the first place. And I know it wasn't fair not telling you why I couldn't touch you...I'm so sorry, Nova."

Why wasn't he saying anything?

I needed to make this right, so I continued my rambling.

"At first, Jemma told me that I couldn't be near you at all. She said even talking to you might jeopardize the veiling, but then I realized that wasn't true and she didn't know how I'd get my powers back. She was just trying to keep me away from you."

Nova was still stone silent.

"Nova, I wanted to tell you. I came close so many times. But every time she'd manipulate me with another lie. Jemma told me that you two..." My cheeks burned and my heart ached even as I formed the thoughts. "She told me that you two were together. That it started all the way back in the forest when you spent the night in the hammock and I thought... I didn't want to believe her, but I'd seen it with my own eyes, and then when you asked her to be your date for the dance..." My voice cracked. "I just want you to be happy, Nova. I never wanted anything but that."

Silence.

I couldn't take it. "Look," I said gently pulling one of my hands from his and touching his cheek. "We're touching right now. I think Jemma might have screwed it up somehow when she used you as the talisman. Or maybe the whole thing was a lie. I'm so sorry I didn't tell you. I was trying to protect you. You're always protecting me and for once I didn't want to put you or anyone else in danger. I was hoping if you didn't know where my powers were hidden then Malakai couldn't use you against me. You understand why I did it, right?" I pleaded.

Still he said nothing. He just kept staring at my hands.

"I guess none of this matters anyway," I said crestfallen. "Jemma doesn't even know how to give me my powers back and we're not going to be able to stop Malakai without them."

"It matters," he said finally looking up at me.

His eyes were a green sea of emotions. They seemed to be

glistening as if he were holding back a flood of feelings. I'd never seen him look so injured. His face twisted as though he was in physical pain. I had never intended for these lies to hurt him like this. I'd only wanted to protect him.

I didn't know what to say.

"Nova, I ..."

"It matters. All of it matters. I don't love Jemma. I can't stand her. She used me. She used all of us. And everything she told you was a lie! I never asked her to the dance. It was a condition of her healing you. I didn't have a choice. I would have agreed to anything to save you. And I don't know what she told you about the forest, but I never spent the night in the same hammock as her. And what matters most, is that I am the talisman and that you were acting like you hated me for a reason."

"Nova, I don't hate you! I could never, I – "

But I never got to finish that sentence. Before I could get the next word out, his lips were on mine, trembling and warm. He wrapped his arms around me and I felt enveloped in his safety instantly. It was like I was finally home, taking my first real breath since veiling my powers. I felt my lungs fill with hot air and happiness as I kissed him back. It felt like I was floating and I clung to him tighter, sighing as his strong arms crushed my body closer to his. Everything was bright and hot and my whole body felt like it was electrified, humming with life.

I spoke between breathless kisses as Nova entwined his fingers in my ruined dress.

"Nova... I'm... so... sorry. I..."

"Shut up and kiss me," he said breathlessly.

It felt like every cell in my body was going to burst. I tried to wrap my arms around Nova tighter to steady myself, but it was no use, my soul was already soaring, rejoicing that it was reunited with its match. All the months of convincing myself that I didn't love Nova evaporated the moment his lips touched mine. I knew I loved him; I always had and I always would. No matter who else came into my life, no matter what I felt for them, they would never be able to hold a candle to what I felt for Nova. There was something so natural yet surreal about our connection. It was almost indescribable the way I felt such sweet happiness, mirrored by a magnified fear. I guess that's what true love is; the feeling that comes with loving someone so entirely that the sheer thought of losing them terrifies you to the core. So much so, that you almost can't bear to risk it. Yet, at the same time, you know you couldn't survive without loving them. When we were together like this it was as if our hearts existed outside our bodies so they could beat as one; every breath, every heartbeat, every touch, mirrored by his.

I felt my eyes burning with tears, and Nova kissed them each away as they streamed down my face. I looked at him though my glittering eyelashes that cast ethereal prisms across his exquisite features.

"Geneva…" he whispered intoxicatingly, cupping my face in his large hands.

Just hearing him say my name was such sweet ecstasy. I felt like I could float away in this moment for all of eternity.

"Geneva," he said again. "No more lies. Promise me. Only truth."

"Only truth," I promised against his lips.

He exhaled my name again.

"Geneva?"

I didn't want to open my eyes and have this perfect moment end.

"Geneva! You're glowing!"

And just like that, my dream world evaporated.

57

When I opened my eyes, I saw that he was right. My whole body had an eerie orange glow to it. Perhaps that electrifying feeling wasn't Nova after all, my subconscious chided.

"What's happening?" Nova asked sounding worried.

"I don't know," I responded, trying to remain calm.

But something was definitely wrong. I could feel a powerful surge, heightening all of my senses. My heart was pounding; my pulse rushing and tiny beads of sweat were starting to form on my brow.

"You're burning up," Nova said, wiping at my forehead.

"Back away, Nova. I think I'm getting my powers back. It's not safe."

"Jemma wasn't lying then? Your powers were actually locked inside of me?"

I couldn't answer him. My breathing had quickened and I couldn't seem to stop it. I felt such a sharp pain sear through my head that I doubled over in agony and screamed.

"Geneva!" Sparrow cried rushing toward me. "You're bleeding."

"Stay back," I muttered through gritted teeth. "Keep them back, Nova!" I begged. "I can't control this!"

He nodded and pulled Sparrow back as he motioned for everyone to back away from me.

I pulled my hands from my pounding head and they were covered in blood. Sparrow was right, I was bleeding, but where was it coming from? I desperately tried to wipe the blood off on the fabric of my tattered dress. I doubled over again as a swift jolt of pain ripped through me. I screamed and squeezed my eyes shut, begging for this nightmare to stop. I wanted to go back to the bliss I had felt only moments before when I was wrapped in Nova's safe embrace. I could feel hot tears flowing uncontrollably and my face felt wet and sticky. As I wiped at it, my hands became blood stained once more.

I'm dying, the frightened voice inside my mind screamed.

I must have been bleeding from my nose and perhaps my ears. The front of my dress was drenched in a heady mixture of blood and sweat. I was trembling as I tried to control the insurmountable power surging through me.

No! No, I will not die, not like this, not now! Not once I finally have him back, I scolded myself. *You can do this. You're the Eva. Concentrate!*

I focused my seizing mind on one image, one image alone. It floated before me, first with an abstract resemblance, but then his features became sharper, more focused. His chiseled jaw, his furrowed brow, and the intense brilliance of his deep green eyes, shown like a beacon before me. Like my North Star, Nova grounded me. I was able to focus on his face long enough to think through the pain. Then suddenly Nova's face changed into Malakai's. He was inside of my mind and he was raging mad. His expression changed, like he suddenly realized I could see him, that I felt his presence trying to control me. I mustered all the hatred I had for him and funneled it into a single thought.

"Malakai will die!"

And like that it was over.

The storm had ended. I blocked him out. Malakai no longer held any power over me. I finally had all of my powers back and I was strong enough to shut my mind to him. I'd seen the fury plain on his face when he realized I was too strong and he couldn't control me.

I knew Malakai would never give up that easily. He'd anticipated me getting my powers back and was waiting for me. He was messing with my mind, turning my powers against me, while trying to read my thoughts and fish out the Pillars. I didn't know how much he'd seen. There wasn't a moment to lose.

"All of you listen to me now," I called addressing the shocked faces of my fellow students in the Locker.

"Malakai is evil. He can't be trusted. He's the leader of an elite secret society called the Ravinori. Take off your bracelets. They're not gifts. It's how he tracks you and steals your powers. Yes, I know some of you have powers. Some of you may not even know that you have powers yet, but you do. I know you all probably have a lot of questions and I hope that soon I will have time to answer them. But for right now, you need to trust me. Take off your bracelets and come with me. We're getting out of here."

"But they don't come off," a frightened looking girl said.

"They do now," I replied as I turned mine to stone and pulverized it.

I strode over to Journey and did the same to his. He nodded, immediately understanding what I wanted him to do. We moved through the crowd helping rid everyone of their bracelets just in case Malakai was able to reactivate the Soul Cell.

Nova, Sadie and Sparrow rushed to my side.

"Are you all right?" Sparrow asked, staring wide eyed at my bloody dress.

"I'm fine."

"What just happened?" Nova asked.

"It was Malakai. He must have been watching us. He was inside my head trying to read my mind. He was using my powers against me. Someone must've tipped him off that I would be getting them back tonight. He orchestrated this whole thing."

"Who?" Sadie asked in disbelief.

"I'll tell you who," I growled, already striding away from my friends in search of my traitorous sister.

"Help me find her," I said to Journey and Remi as I approached them.

"Jemma," I called. "Jemma where are you, you coward? I know it was you. I know you told him." I shouted.

"She's gone and so are all the Luxors," Journey said after completing a sweep of the Locker. "Must have slipped out while we were all watching you."

"I don't get it. How did she get out? Why would she do this?" Sparrow asked.

"Because she's jealous and vindictive and she's as power hungry as he is. If Jemma has teamed up with Malakai, we don't have any time to waste."

"She knows our whole escape plan," Sparrow said.

"I might have a new one for us," Nova said.

He quickly filled us in on Terran's story about the secret tunnel.

"But how are we going to get through it without Terran to navigate?" Remi asked.

"We'll have to figure it out," I said. "We're out of options and time. We need to get the Pillars and anyone else we can out of here right now, before they can regroup and mobilize an attack against us," I commanded.

Remi, Journey, Nova and the girls were staring at me like I had two heads.

"What?" I said.

"Nothing," Nova smirked. "You heard the Eva, lets go!"

"Journey, destroy all the cuffs. I don't want any left behind that Malakai can draw power from."

Journey smashed every cuff in the Locker while, I worked on breaking us out of it.

"Are you sure we can't wait for Terran? He's a Pillar," Remi said.

"There's no time Remi. Jemma's probably with Malakai by now. Who knows what she told him. Terran's smart. When he finds out we've broken out of the Locker, he'll know where to find us. He'll understand why we couldn't wait for him here. We'll telepath him our new plan on the way."

He stood next to me while I smashed through another lock on one of the cell doors. He was chewing his lip and I knew that meant he had more to say.

"Spit it out Remi," I said while I continued systematically from cell to cell, breaking each lock as I went.

"It's just... don't get mad, but how are you so sure Jemma is working with Malakai? Maybe someone else betrayed us."

"Don't you dare defend her, Remi. She stole my powers and hid them inside someone I deeply care for to torture me. Besides, she's the only one who knew where my powers were and when I might get them back."

"I'm not defending her, Geneva. It's just that you spent a lot of time with Kai, too. Maybe he figured it out. Look around you. He's not here either."

"Kai didn't betray us," I said impatiently as I worked on crushing the bars of another rusty cell door.

"Maybe he did without even knowing it. Maybe his father was reading his mind. He was just inside yours, we have no idea what his capabilities are."

"Remi! Give it a rest. It wasn't Kai. He wouldn't do that to me."

"Why? Because you made him believe you have feelings for him? You're really good at that," Remi said bitterly.

My heart plummeted because I knew Remi was right. I had used Kai, and Remi probably thought I had done the same thing to him. They both thought I had feelings for them, and I guess I did. I loved them each in their own way. Remi was my best friend. He'd been by my side my whole life. He'd been my friend when no one else would, and he didn't care if I was the Eva or not. He loved me and he had been honest with me about his feelings, even when I couldn't be honest about how I felt.

Kai was nothing but kind, sweet and generous. I knew he would give me the world if I asked him to. He was so loyal and open. He had bared his soul to me and he never asked for anything in return. He never pressured me or wanted anything from me, other than just to be by my side.

But Nova, Nova was the one my heart belonged too. I guess I had always known it somewhere deep inside, but I had been too terrified of what loving him would do to me. I thought it would destroy me or because I was the Eva I wouldn't get to be with the one I loved. I thought that loving someone would only put them in danger and make me weak. But I didn't care anymore. Everyone I loved was always in danger anyway and not loving them wouldn't change that. Being born on this forsaken island, surrounded by legends and mystical powers had doomed me from the start.

No, I wouldn't hide my feelings anymore. Now that I had my powers back, I had made up my mind that I'd rather die today than spend another moment pretending not to be madly in love with Nova. I hated that Remi had to witness me figuring all of that out firsthand. At least Kai had been spared since the Luxors didn't put him in the Locker with the rest of us. I'd have to tell him soon enough. But right now was not the time to rehash things with Remi. I had a war to end.

"Remi. It was Jemma, okay. I'm done talking about this."

Remi gave me a hurt look, but he dropped it and left me to work on the door. Finally the last one swung open and I grinned. I looked back at the confused faces of my classmates and friends, who were looking at me expectantly. I nodded to Journey and he started ordering everyone in line. Nova joined me as I headed to the tapestry that supposedly marked the entrance to the secret passageway that would lead us to salvation according to Terran's ancestors.

"Need a light?" Nova said with his familiar sarcasm.

"Why thank you, Sir," I said unable to stifle a laugh. "I forgot how handy you are."

"*We* are," he corrected me with a wink and a quick kiss.

"Really? Can we at least focus on getting out of here before you two make me vomit," Journey said interrupting us.

He was trying to suppress his grin as he shook his head at us, but I knew he was only joking. Journey had been rooting for us all along.

"Sorry," I apologized with a smile of my own. "According to Terran it should be right here."

We all looked apprehensively at the tapestry that hid the passageway to our freedom.

"Well, what are we waiting for?" Remi asked, striding up with Sparrow and Sadie.

I walked up to the ancient woven mural and took a deep breath. I touched it and an image flashed in my mind.

"There's a keyhole!" I said opening my eyes. "It unlocks a passage way that will take us to the Luxor prison."

Nova pushed the tapestry aside, revealing a stone wall that matched the rest of the Locker.

"There's nothing here," I said, unable to hide the panic in my voice.

"There!" Nova said as his flame wielding hand illuminated a tiny keyhole, hidden between two unimpressive stones.

"But we don't have a key," Sparrow said.

"I do," I replied.

I had it all along. I'd worn it around my neck since my birthday, when Jemma had given it to me. Terran said he recognized it when he saw me wearing it. He'd pointed out how the symbol was outlined in the Tapestries of Truth. It was the symbol of the four Pillars, one small diamond for each Pillar, surrounding a larger diamond that represented me; the Eva, the *Ponte deorum*. It was my symbol.

THE SAME SYMBOL from the hilt of the key had been forming on my chest when Jemma had stopped the blood curse. I hated that I thought of her whenever I looked at the thin white scar that permanently marked my chest.

I pulled the key from around my neck and held it up. It looked to be the right size.

Jemma's words from my mother echoed in my mind. *'Keep it close to your heart, someday it will bring you home.'*

This is too easy, I thought to myself. Something didn't feel right about it.

"This is a trap," I said turning to look at my friends. "Jemma gave me this key. She said it was from my mother, but what if she was setting us up the whole time?"

"We have to at least try it, Geneva. We're no safer here than we are if we try that tunnel."

I turned back to face the wall and felt a sudden uneasiness. I took a deep breath as I inserted the key into its barely visible hole. We were gambling our only chance for survival on Terran's word and a mystical tapestry. I didn't doubt that he was one of us. I knew he was a Pillar, just as I had known Sadie, Nova and Jovi were, but Terran always gave me a certain feeling of uneasiness because of his affiliation with the brutal Luxors and his closeness to Malakai.

"What's wrong?" Nova whispered sensing my hesitation.

"Nothing, I just wish Terran were here."

I looked around and the anxious faces of my friends and the others that had been thrown in the Locker with us.

"There are a lot of people counting on us," I whispered.

"You got this," Nova said laying a supportive hand on my shoulder.

I felt his confidence radiate through me and I tightened my hand around the cold steal of the skeleton key. With one more deep breath and a silent prayer, I twisted my wrist to the right.

Click

The wall shook and groaned before us as the large stones grinded away. They folded over each other magically, leaving puffs of dust in their wake. When the dust settled, it revealed an eerie dark opening, spilling cold air into the Locker.

"It worked," I whispered more to myself than the others.

They all had bewildered looks on their faces, confirming that they too had been skeptical that there actually was a secret tunnel behind this stone wall. But here it was, shadowy and mysterious, beckoning us to enter. It was now or never.

"All right," I said. "We head through the tunnel to Lux. Hollis should be there by now, waiting outside the city walls. Once we get there, Journey and Remi, you find Mala, like we planned. We'll meet you at the gate with Hollis."

"What about the others?" Sparrow asked looking at the group of shell-shocked students behind us.

I turned to address them. "As I said before, we are rising against Malakai's oppression. His promises are false. He's using all of us. He doesn't care about our education or well-being. We are merely a means of gaining power for him. We are leaving through this tunnel. Our hope is that it will take us inside the walls of Lux. I cannot guarantee that it will be a safe path, but it's our only option. What I can offer you is the freedom to choose, which is more than Malakai will give you. If we reach Lux, you are free to do what you please."

Everyone stared at me blankly.

"If you're with us, we're leaving now."

58

Remi led the charge, carrying one of my orbs for light. Sparrow and Sadie were right behind him. Nova and Journey flanked the group of students who'd decided to join us. All of the orphans had come and a surprising number of students from Lux.

I was bringing up the rear of the group. I tried to ignore the eerie image the orbs cast through the tunnel, silhouetting each head with a halo of blue light. Their footsteps echoed back loudly, adding to my restlessness.

"That's all of them," I said when I caught up to Nova and Journey.

"I didn't know we were taking hostages," Journey said. "I like it."

"They're not hostages. I meant what I said. They're free to go when we get to Lux."

"Still, it was a smart move. It's good to have leverage if we need it."

I shook my head at Journey and let Nova lace his fingers through mine. Being close to him gave me a sense of hope that we would make it through this day after all, and I needed that.

The march to Lux was grueling. The tunnel was long and dark. We trudged on, cold and wet. Sections of it narrowed so much that only one of us could fit through at a time. In some areas the ceiling dipped so low that we had to crawl on our hands and knees. We dodged stalactites and stalagmites the entire way.

"Well this is cozy," Journey added sarcastically as he squeezed through a narrow passage. "How the heck did anyone fit through here?"

"Duck," I shouted.

"Ouch!" Journey yelled as a section of stalactite cracked off on his head, clattering to pieces on the cavernous floor. "That's the third time I've done that. This is ridiculous."

"Better watch it, Journey, you're going to cause an avalanche," Nova joked patting him on the back.

"Avalanches happen on mountains, this would be a cave in," Remi corrected him bitterly.

He had hung back, waiting for us to catch up, leaving Sadie and Sparrow to lead the pack.

"Either way," Nova shrugged draping his arm over my shoulder smugly.

"Enough," I said shirking him off.

"You shouldn't have left the girls, Remi. I'm going to catch up to them."

"Wait, I came back here to see what your plan is when we get to Lux. We can't all pile into the streets. I think someone will notice a hundred kids dressed like battered gala patrons wandering around."

"I don't know, okay. I'll figure it out when we get there," I said striding away from him.

"How are you going to tell us when you figure it out? Are we supposed to read your mind?" Remi shouted after me.

"Yes!" I telepathed arrogantly.

"Oh yeah," Remi muttered.

"It's so nice being able to telepath again," Nova responded. *"I've missed having powers."*

"Great, now I get to listen to you two argue about who loves Geneva more out loud and in my head," Journey joked.

Nova laughed and jogged ahead of them to catch up to Geneva.

"Do you have a death wish?" Journey asked Remi when he realized it was only the two of them left bringing up the rear.

"Journey, listen. I'm not trying to get between you and Sparrow."

"Is that so?" Journey challenged.

"Yes. You of all people know that I have feelings for Geneva. It's clear she doesn't feel the same for me, but I swear, I wasn't trying to go after Sparrow. We're just friends."

Journey stopped walking and Remi collided with him. Journey pushed him up against the slimy, damp wall and kept his hands pressed firmly against Remi's chest.

"I know that Remi, but somehow Sparrow's gotten it into her head that she likes you as more than a friend. I don't know what she sees in you, but it's something. I love her, I always have and I always will, but I know she doesn't feel the same way about me. But that's fine because I'm still going to be right here watching out for her. That doesn't change the fact that it kills me watching her waste her feelings on you when you're never going to return them. She deserves more than that Remi, so you're going to stop leading her on, do you understand? She means everything to me and I'll be damned if I let you drag her into your messed up competition of catching Geneva. She's our Eva and she's trying to lead us and this whole island back from a decade of destruction. I'm pretty sure that's a hard enough task to handle without you and Nova and Kai all pulling her every which way. Did you ever stop to think about that?"

Remi was stunned. He'd never heard Journey speak so openly or so much, for that matter. He was normally more for action than words.

"Look I get it," Journey said. "Sometimes you can't help who you love. I'm not judging you for that and it's not up to me to say who Geneva should or shouldn't be with. But you all need to get your heads and hearts on the same page before one of you does something you can't take back. We're not kids anymore and this isn't a game. Love... all it does is fill your head with secrets and lies," Journey said shaking his head and letting his hands drop from Remi's chest. "People have died over far less."

"*You guys all right up there?*" I telepathed to Sparrow and Sadie.

Sadie jumped reaching out to clutch Sparrow's arm.

"I don't think I'll ever get used to that," Sadie said.

"It comes in handy," Sparrow replied grinning.

"I'm coming up to meet you. I just passed a narrow opening that I had to crawl through. How much further ahead are you?"

"Was it wet when you crawled?" asked Sparrow's voice.

"Yes."

"Okay we're only about fifty yards ahead of you. Want us to slow down?"

"No, keep going. We need to get out of here as fast as possible."

"See, it's a really useful power," Sparrow said squeezing Sadie's hand when she saw the worried look in her eyes.

"Yeah, I can see that," Sadie said sullenly.

"What's wrong?"

"Nothing. I'm just thinking about my sister. I haven't seen her in months. I hope she's where Geneva said she is and that she's all right. I don't know what I'll do if she's not okay."

"Hey, you can't think like that. We're so close."

"*That's right!*" I telepathed as I joined them.

"Geneva!" they both squealed, surprised and delighted to see me.

"Geneva, I didn't mean to question you. It's just – "

"It's okay, Sadie. I know you're worried about your sister. We'll get to Mala. I made you a promise."

We marched on silently until we came to a dead end. There was a stone wall, exactly like the one we had magically passed through in the Locker.

"How do we get out?" Sadie asked. "Is there another keyhole?"

"I don't know. Terran didn't say anything about this," I said.

"Guys, I think we're here. The path dead-ended into a stone wall. It's just like the one we came through in the Locker, but I don't see a keyhole. Can you come help me look?"

After what seemed like an eternity of fruitlessly searching the relenting stone wall, I was starting to lose hope.

"What's going on?" Nova asked as he, Remi and Journey broke through the pack of worried faces watching us.

"There's no keyhole," Sparrow gasped.

"Did Terran happen to mention how we get out of this secret tunnel?" I asked Nova.

"Maybe we took a wrong turn?" Journey offered.

"No, this is it," I said. "I can feel it."

Nova lit up the wall with his firelight. He stopped in front of a strange colored stone. It had a rough, puttied texture, much different from the rest of the smooth damp stones that made up the solid wall.

"It's been sealed shut," Nova said. "Here. This is where the keyhole was," he said pointing to the putty.

"It was a trap," I whispered, mentally cursing Jemma. "She set us up."

I was amazed that I could still feel pain from her unending

betrayals. Jemma had given me the key as a ploy to trap me down here.

"There has to be another way," Remi said.

I paced away from them, racking my brain.

Think, Geneva. There has to be a way.

I didn't come this far to turn back now and I couldn't let all these innocent students get stuck here with me. I tired of pacing and sat down with my back against the cold stone wall. It was impenetrable. I wiped the tears of frustration from my eyes and dried my hands on my ruined blue gown. The bottom of it was soaked from traipsing through the soggy tunnel for hours.

That was it! I jumped to my feet and stalked back over to my friends.

"Sadie, I think you can help us find a way out of here."

"Me? How?"

"This place is full of water. The wettest area seems to be here, near the wall. We must be near the aquifer. I think if you can call some water to you, from where the keyhole is sealed, it'll find a path to us through this wall. The water will choose the point of least resistance and that should be the keyhole."

"I don't know how to do that."

"Sure, you do. Sadie, you're a Pillar. You're much more powerful than you think you are."

"I don't know..." She remembered her experience with the well on her old farm.

"You can do this, Sadie," I encouraged.

She nodded apprehensively.

"You just need to wish for there to be water and the earth will respond. You have complete command over an extremely powerful element. Water is a life force. It can sustain us and it can also destroy us."

I saw her mind instantly go to the dark memories of The Flood.

"Sadie, you can do this. Think of Mala. You only need a tiny bit of water. Just call it to you. It'll come."

"Okay," she said taking a deep breath. "Where do I get it from?"

"Well, if my vision is correct, then the tunnel leads to the Luxor prison. They have to give the prisoners water, right? Try to picture a cup of water inside a cell on the other side of this wall."

"All right. I can do that."

"Close your eyes. Tell me when you can see it in your mind."

"I see it," she said breathlessly.

"Okay, now will it to come to you."

We waited. Everyone was silent.

"Nothing's happening. I don't know how to do this," Sadie cried in frustration.

"You have to really picture it, Sadie. Feel it, taste it, like you're dying of thirst and your life depends on it. Like it will carry Mala to you."

Suddenly we heard a faint hissing in the distance. Sadie's eye flew open.

"What was that? Am I doing that?"

"Yes! Keep concentrating!"

The hiss turned into a rumble.

"Sadie, can you still picture the water?" I asked.

"Yes," she said through gritted teeth.

Her brow was sweating and her eyes were squeezed shut in deep concentration.

"You remember I said we only need a little bit, right?"

"Uh, that doesn't sound like a little bit," Journey added.

"Sadie, are you listening to me?"

"Yes! I'm picturing it. I can see it, Geneva!"

"Nova you better get everyone back," I warned.

As soon as I turned back to face Sadie, I saw a small puddle pooling at the bottom of the wall. It hadn't been there before.

"Look!" I exclaimed

"Sadie! You did it!" Sparrow cried.

Water was streaming in from a small crack where the two stones had been puttied together. It had to be where the keyhole was.

"I did? I did!"

Sparrow and Sadie were jumping up and down in delight as the water continued to flow in faster and faster. Before I could get the key into the puttied hole, water burst forth from several other seams at the same time. Unexpectedly, it started spraying forcefully through every seam on the wall. The tunnel erupted with panicked screams that echoed into chaos.

"Sadie, you need to stop the water," I yelled.

"I can't. I don't know how."

"You control it Sadie. It responds to your will. Believe in yourself and concentrate on stopping it."

"But, I – "

"Sadie, just try," I barked. " I've got to try to find the keyhole."

As I tried to get close enough to jam the key into the hole, a stray jet struck me in the face, hard. It stung and someone bumped me from behind, knocking the key out of my hand!

"No!" I cried, frantically searching for the key in the rising water.

I looked down at my sodden feet. The water was knee deep and churning. There was no way I was going to find the key now. I scanned the frantic faces of my friends and the other students who had followed me through this secret tunnel. I couldn't let them all drown down here. I racked my brain for a fast solution to this flooding problem.

"Everybody stand back!" I screamed.

I summoned all my strength and drew on my powers. I

could feel them surge at my command, strength pulsing through my veins. It was so good to have them back. I didn't know if it was because they had been veiled for so long that perhaps I had forgotten how overwhelming they could be, but somehow my powers felt stronger than I remembered. I had to fight to focus them. I steadied my breathing and envisioned what I wanted to happen.

Here goes nothing, I thought as I slammed my fist down, through the swelling water and into the earth.

Just as I had commanded, the earth began to part beneath my feet. A small crevasse groaned open below me and the water rushed to fill it. I scrambled backward as the water swirled around me toward the widening hole. At first it slowly drained out, but as even more water rushed in on us, the crack in the ground shuddered and split even further. Screams of fright filled the tunnel as everyone crowded the dead end, clawing and pounding against the walls.

I had created and even bigger problem. I had to get us out of here and fast.

"Journey," I called through the panicked crowd. "I need your help."

Through the chaos, he emerged. I didn't even have to tell him what to do. He took one look at me and knew. That was one of the things I admired most about him. He was a man of few words and he was always calm under pressure. He nodded to me and cleared a path to the wall. I followed him and both of us laid our hands upon it.

I closed my eyes and concentrated again on drawing my powers. I heard creaks and groans and felt the cold wet wall start to dry up beneath my hands. I chanced a glance through one eye and was elated to see it was working. Journey and I were slowly fossilizing the wall. For a split second I was giddy, but just as I felt we could spare a moment of celebration, water busted through new areas of the wall.

"Now," I shouted to Journey and he retreated from the wall.

I held my hands firm against the stones that we fossilized. It took every ounce of concentration to keep the water from busting back through the wall. My strength was ebbing.

"Journey, NOW!"

As I felt myself fading, I saw Journey slam into the petrified wall to my left. There was an ear splitting sound and I was thrown away from the wall. I felt myself tumbling through stone and getting swept up in a mix of water and tangled limbs. I gulped a mouthful of water and came up sputtering and gasping for air.

When I caught my breath and regained focus I realized we were in new surroundings. We had done it. We'd made it through the tunnel and Journey had busted us through the wall into the Luxor prison. The water was draining away and so was my energy. I was exhausted.

"Is everyone okay?" I asked, breathlessly looking around.

We all looked a little worse for wear, but everyone was standing so that was a good sign.

"Geneva? Are you all right?" Nova asked, suddenly by my side.

"Yeah, I'm fine," I said smiling at him. "Just a little light-headed."

Using my powers like that had drained my energy. Nova softly laid his hand on my cheek and I thought he was going to kiss me and I let my eyes flutter closed in anticipation. But when he didn't, I opened them to see what was wrong. The hand he had pulled away from my face was covered in blood.

"Nova! What's wrong? Are you hurt?" I whispered in confusion.

"It's not mine."

"What?"

But before I got an answer, he swiftly scooped me up and started calling for Sparrow. His black shirt was soaking wet and tattered, but I still could feel the warmth in his strong arms around me and I clung to it.

"Sparrow! Sparrow!"

"I'm here. Oh my gods! What happened to her?"

"What's wrong?" I asked fighting off panic as Nova set me down gently.

"Geneva, did you hit your head?"

"I don't know. What's wrong? You're all freaking me out."

"You're bleeding from you're your nose and ears."

"I think she has a gash on her head too," Journey said looking at me with concern.

I reached up to my scalp and my hands came away red. What I thought was just wet from the water, was actually blood. How long had I been bleeding? What was wrong with me? I didn't feel injured, just tired. Was I in shock? I tried to wipe the sticky blood off on my disgraced dress and started shaking when it wouldn't come off.

"I hate blood," I whispered as I continued to tremble.

"You need to heal her," Nova said to Sparrow.

"Nova… I can't! I don't even know where she's hurt …"

"Sparrow, you can do this," Journey said by her side.

"But…"

"You've done it before, Sparrow. I believe in you."

"But the last time…" She trailed off looking at their matching scars.

Sparrow shuddered, the nightmare of her last healing incident still haunted her.

"You can do this," Journey said softly.

She swallowed hard but then took a deep breath and squared her shoulders.

"I'll need some space."

Remi and Journey, made the gathering crowd step back, while Sparrow tore off a section of her dress to use as a rag to wipe the blood away.

Sparrow looked deep in my eyes and I was happy to see them steeled with confidence.

"Promise you'll tell me if I'm hurting you?" she said.

"I Promise."

I felt her delicate hands on my temples. They felt cool, but I didn't feel anything else. No tingling feeling of healing power.

"It's not working," Sparrow said.

"Give it second," Nova encouraged.

She nodded and took a deep breath. She held my head a little more firmly this time.

"Nothing. It's not working," she said in a panic.

"Oh, I should have told you that your powers won't work here," came a haunting voice echoing through the speakers in the underground prison and startling us all. "I've outfitted my prison with some of the same precautions you were accustomed to at the Troian Academy."

"Malakai?" I whispered.

"Yes, good evening. I'm so pleased you arrived all in one piece. That was quite a grand entrance. And right on time. I'd be delighted if you would come join me in the square. We've all been waiting very patiently for you. And I think I have someone you've been looking for."

"Mala!" Sadie cried reappearing breathlessly. "She's not here. I've been up and down the row of cells twice. Malakai must have her!"

His laugh boomed through the loud speaker and echoed through the prison tunnels.

"The clock is ticking. Bring me the Eva and Mala will be spared."

We all looked at each other in horror.

"How did Malakai know we were here and that we planned to break Mala out?" Remi asked.

"Jemma," I groaned, my voice fading.

"It doesn't matter how Malakai found out. He knows

we're here now and he's expecting us to meet him in the square. We need to come up with a plan to get everyone out of here," Nova said gesturing to the group of disheveled students who'd followed us from the Troian Center.

"What about Mala?" Sadie pleaded.

"We can't go to the square Sadie. Malakai knew we were coming. It's a trap," Journey said.

"We have to do something," Remi interjected. "We can't use our powers and she's not in any condition to go anywhere," he said jutting his chin in my direction.

"I'm fine," I said using the scrap of Sparrow's dress to wipe the congealed blood from my face. "Just help me up." I felt woozy, but I didn't have time to rest.

My vision tunneled and I staggered as I got to my feet. A new stream of blood poured from the gash on my head. It streaked down my forehead and ran into my eye. I felt hot and cold all at the same time. Nova caught me in his arms and steadied me.

"We've got to close up that gash or you're not going anywhere," he said.

"I can sew," Sadie offered taking charge.

"With what?" Remi asked.

Sadie turned to the group of students watching us. "Do any of you girls have a hair pin I can borrow?"

There was no response.

"Please, our friend needs help. I need to stitch up her wound. My sister's life depends on it."

"Why should we help her?" one of the boys responded. "She nearly got us killed."

"Yeah, why shouldn't we just take you all to Malakai ourselves?" someone else shouted.

"She didn't almost kill you. That was Malakai," Remi yelled. "Those were his traps in the tunnel and he was probably the one flooding it since he knew we were coming. Geneva saved all of your lives."

"Remi, thank you," I said smiling at my vocal best friend before turning back to address the group of students. "But they're right. I'm going to turn myself in to Malakai to ensure your safety. No one else needs to get hurt because of me. I promised you your freedom, let me make good on that promise. If you involve yourself in whatever is going on between Malakai and myself I can't make you any promises of safety. He's unpredictable and he has an entire army working for him. He won't stop at anything to get at me and you'll all be expendable to him if he thinks you're in his way."

They stared back at me, unsure.

"I'm sorry I had to involve you in any of this in the first place. All I've ever wanted for you was safety and freedom. The choice is yours. You can turn me in if you think it is your best move or you can take my offer and let me turn myself in and buy you all some time and safe passage. I won't be a tyrant like Malakai. I will let you all make your own decisions."

The group of students were discussing whether or not to turn me in and it didn't sound like it was going in my favor. Then I heard a small voice above the rest.

"Well, I'm not going to let anyone die. I don't care who she is."

A small girl in a deep red dress emerged from the group. She ambled up to me and pulled a pin from her wet blonde hair, letting it fall down her back.

"Will this work?" she asked, handing Sadie a glittering broach that had been pinned in her hair.

"Yes, thank you," Sadie said quickly going to work. She ripped off her necklace, scattering tiny white pearls all over the dirty floor of the prison, while threading what was left of her necklace around the pin.

"Are you sure you can do this?" Nova asked nervously.

"Well, it's not going to be pretty, but it'll close up the wound."

"Do it," I said, bracing myself for the pain.

The blonde girl knelt down next to me. She had pale blue eyes like mine.

"I'm Lorelai," she said with a kind smile.

"Thank you for helping me, Lorelai," I said.

She nodded and gave me her hand. She instructed Nova to do the same.

"My mother was a healer. She said if you squeeze tight, it doesn't hurt so bad."

After what felt like an eternity of excruciating pain and screaming, Sadie was finally finished.

My head wound throbbed and I had thought I was going to pass out from the pain. At times I'd wished I had. But the blood had stopped leaking down my face so it seemed like Sadie knew what she was doing. She put six rudimentary stitches in my head and was now wrapping it with Nova's torn shirtsleeve.

"What are we going to do about them?" Journey asked looking at the agitated group of students we'd dragged on our suicide mission. They were watching us like hawks.

"It's me Malakai wants," I grumbled. "Just get me out of here so I can turn myself in."

"Are you crazy? You know we're not going to let you face him alone," Nova said.

"Nova, we can fight about this later, but right now I think we have a bigger problem," I said watching the three most vocal boys in the group approach us.

"Are you done with her?" one asked.

It was Gavin, my lovely dance lesson partner. He was truly starting to annoy me.

"Back off Gavin," Nova said on his feet now, blocking them from me.

"This is taking too long. She needs to turn herself over now before we all end up paying the price."

"But he'll kill her!" Nova pleaded.

"He didn't say that," Gavin replied.

"Yeah, well you're a little late to the party. You have no idea what's going on here," Nova quipped.

"Better her than us," another boy said.

"Just give us some time to come up with a plan," Nova argued.

"Sorry, Nova. We've waited long enough. She's coming with us," said a familiar looking boy in a soaking wet Cadet uniform.

I remembered fencing with him. His name was Luca. Apparently I hadn't made a good impression on him either.

Nova shot him a look of betrayal, while Sadie and Lorelai helped me to my feet.

The boys started to square their shoulders and I quickly stepped between them not wanting this to escalate.

"Guys. I'll go with you. I meant what I said and I'll honor my word. If you believe turning me in is your best option, then I'll go along with it."

"Geneva!" Nova argued.

I shook my head at him apologetically.

"Well, you can turn me in too then," Nova said.

"Your funeral," Luca replied.

59

As the boys organized the group of disheveled students, we prepared to move. Nova and I were at the front of the pack, followed by the three boys he knew. He informed me they had been in Cadets with him and their names were Luca, Aiden and Gavin. I'd already had the pleasure of meeting Luca and Gavin. I guess I hadn't made a great impression, because they were fine with turning me in. Nova was none too happy that they valued his friendship so little either and I listened to him grumble as we marched side by side.

Journey and Remi brought up the rear, while Sparrow and Sadie flanked the middle. We moved quickly through the damp, dark prison. We must have entered through an older abandoned section, but as we followed the twisting path upward, it led us to a densely populated area of Lux's prison. The stench was overpowering and the desperate moaning tore at my soul as we passed by the cells of rotting prisoners.

"Nova, look at them. These can't be deadly criminals. They're all emaciated and look like they can hardly walk. How can we just leave them here?"

"Geneva..." Nova warned as I slowed to stop by an overly packed cell.

I peered in at the small slumped shapes in the shadows. I was trying to make out how many were crammed into this dismal, filthy place when Gavin shoved me.

"Keep moving."

"Don't touch her," Nova growled pinning him up against the slimy stone wall.

They were about to come to blows when I heard a commotion a few cells back. One of the students who had fled the Troian Center with us, looked like she was being attacked. It was Lorelai. She was flailing and screaming as someone from inside of the prison cell clutched her.

I ran back to help Journey pull them apart, but when I got closer I realized that I had it all backward and bile rose from the pit of my stomach.

"Fallon! No! No!" Lorelai screamed as we pulled her away from the thrashing figure in the cell. "Stop! Stop it. That's my sister," she cried.

Journey let Lorelai go and she dropped to her knees and cradled the emaciated girl on the other side of the bars.

"Fallon," she sobbed as she stroked her sister's tear-streaked face.

I knelt next to her and stared at the girl. I strained to look through the pain and misery that encapsulated her features, but I recognized her from the Troian Center. She had been in my lessons.

"I remember you," I whispered.

Fallon and Lorelai looked at me, like they had just realized I was there.

"What happened to you?" I asked.

"I thought she was adopted," Lorelai answered.

But Fallon shook her head. "I wasn't adopted. I was sold," she whispered with her eyes wide with fear.

I nodded, encouraging her to continue.

"Malakai told me I was going to meet my new family but they weren't adopting me. They were buying me to be a servant in their home. I hated it there, so I tried to run away. But the Luxors caught me and dragged me back. There are others here," she said gesturing to the other cells.

"Others?" I asked.

"Others from the Troian Academy. Malakai tricked us all. None of us were adopted. He wanted to get rid of us when he found out we weren't useful to him. I've talked to the others I've met here and our stories are all the same. Malakai brought us each to his office and told us that there was a family interested in adopting us. He asked us a bunch of questions and took our cuffs and put them in the Orbiture and when it turned cloudy he looked disappointed at first, but then he said it turned out that we were a perfect match for some family after all."

"Then what happened?" I asked.

"That was it. He had two Luxors drag me out of there. I wasn't allowed to get my things or to say goodbye to my sister. They threw me in a carriage and delivered me to a man in Lux, and when he handed the Luxors a bunch of money, I knew I wasn't actually being adopted. I was being sold."

Lorelai sobbed and embraced her sister again through the bars and I turned back to Nova and Journey.

"We can't leave her here. We can't leave any of them here. Malakai was looking for *me*. He was testing those cuffs to try to see if they contained any powers so he could find me. When they didn't, he had no use for them and sold them into slavery. He's a monster!"

"Geneva, you're right, but if we don't get you out of here you won't be able to save anyone. You're going to bleed to death if Malakai doesn't find you first and finish the job himself," Nova said looking nervously at the bandage on my head.

I could feel that it was wet with my blood. The stitches had slowed the bleeding, but hadn't stopped it completely.

"He's right, Geneva. You're no use to any of us if you're dead," Remi said softly.

Nova stepped closer and put his hands gently on my cheeks, tilting my face up toward his. I could see the turmoil of emotions swimming in his sea green eyes.

"Please..." he whispered so only I could hear him. "I just got you back, Tippy. I can't lose you again."

I embraced Nova and felt my heart swelling with despair. He was right. We had only just come back to each other. I had wasted so much time denying my feelings for him. I could have spent that time with him and now we would be ripped away from each other again once Malakai got his hands on us. He would either imprison us, or worse.

I didn't know what to do and I was terrified. I let myself melt into Nova and held him tight, trembling with the thought that these might be our last moments together.

The others were milling about talking in panicked voices. I was trying to turn off my tired throbbing mind and drink in these final moments with Nova, but I couldn't block out the frightened voices of the students we'd brought with us to the prison.

Certain voices stood out, but soon they started melding together to sound as one. They were all saying the same thing.

"He did that to me too," said a small brunette girl I didn't recognize. "But my cuff made the Orbiture glow blue and he told me that I wasn't a good fit for the adoptive family."

"The same thing happened to me," another voice spoke up.

"And me," said another.

"Me too!"

Soon all the students were recounting their stories of Malakai questioning them and testing their cuffs. It was pandemonium. Everyone was talking and searching the cells for their friends and family.

I too, was remembering my session with Malakai and how furious he had looked when my cuff sent up grey smoke, revealing that I didn't have any powers. He had been so sure that he'd caught me. In that moment I had been grateful that my deceitful sister veiled my powers. Perhaps Malakai suspected we had done something of the sorts because he didn't offer to send me off under the guise of adoption. He was always a step ahead of us somehow.

Luca approached me, dissolving my memories of Malakai. "Geneva, what does this mean? Why was Malakai testing us?" he asked.

"I believe he was ultimately looking for me. But he was also keeping anyone around that had powers because he was collecting them for himself and his army."

"What powers?"

"Luca, I know this is a lot to take in right now, but all the legends we've learned, the childhood tales you've heard, they're not myths. They're true. Malakai and the Ravinori have fed us lies. Since the Flood, our entire existence has been an elaborate cover-up. Another civilization exists in the rainforest. Malakai doesn't want us to know about them, so they've been forced to live in hiding. But I've met them and I believe we're a part of them.

"I know you saw what I could do when we were in the Lockers. I've been chosen and gifted these powers so I could save you and lead our civilization back to peace and prosperity. Malakai doesn't want that. He wants all the power for himself and he doesn't care how he gets it. He thinks he can use us because until now, most of you didn't even know you possessed these powers. He masks his true agenda by distracting us with luxuries, but don't be fooled. He'll kill us if it benefits him and he won't rest until he has enough power to bring Ravin back from the dead."

I stopped talking when I realized that Luca wasn't the only one listening. Everyone was silently staring at me. They were looking to me expectantly and my heart ached, wishing I had an answer for them. Some chosen one I was. I could tell them who I was, but I could do nothing to protect them.

"So what do we do?" Luca asked.

I paused momentarily to look at my friends and then to the group of frightened students. I had to help them.

"We had a plan to escape Lux and get back to the safety of the forest. I can get you out of here the same way if you want to come with us."

"What's in the forest?"

"Others like us. You can trust them. They will protect you and can even teach you about our history and powers."

"You're talking about the Betos?" Gavin asked.

I nodded.

"They're savages and besides they were all wiped out by the Flood," someone shouted.

"That's what Malakai wants you to think," I said. "You're going to have to trust me for this plan to work."

Gavin looked skeptically at Luca and Aiden. They came to some unspoken agreement with a nod.

"What other choice do we have?" Luca asked rhetorically. "Tell us your plan, Geneva."

"If you let me, I'd like to leave ahead of you and go to the square. Give me a good head start so I can distract Malakai while you escape the prison."

They nodded, so far agreeing with my plan.

"In the meantime, free as many from the cells as you can. Once I'm gone you'll need to follow my friends out of the prison. We have transportation waiting for us right outside the gates."

"But there's so many of us," Aiden said.

"Don't worry about that part," I grinned thinking of Hollis's magic interior. "You'll need to focus on helping the sick and injured out of here. And make sure you avoid the square. Malakai is after me. If you all stay out of sight, and away from me you'll be safe. Can you do that?"

"We're from Lux, we know these streets like the back of our hands. We can get everyone to the gate, but how are we supposed to get out?" Luca challenged. "And even if we do get out where do we go from there. It's miles to the forest."

"We have the gate covered. You'll have to trust us on the rest."

Luca looked to his friends and they silently came to an agreement. He took two steps toward me and extended his hand. "Good luck, Geneva. I have a feeling you're going to need it."

"GENEVA, this wasn't part of the plan. Do you think Hollis can even fit this many?" Sadie asked.

"Hollis isn't the problem," Remi said. "How are we supposed to sneak this many people out? And Terran is nowhere to be found. He was supposed to secure the gate. Plus, we can't leave him here, he's one of us," he argued quietly.

"I telepathed Terran our plan. We just have to pray he'll meet up with us."

"I can help you take the gate, mate," Journey said cracking his knuckles.

"You're forgetting one very important thing, Geneva," Nova said. "We're not leaving you."

All of my friends nodded in agreement. I was always humbled by their loyalty and it cemented my need to sacrifice myself for them if that's what it was going to take.

"Guys, I'll be right behind you. I should be able to use my powers once I get out of the prison to buy you enough time. It's our best option," I said with confidence.

They looked like they were on the fence.

"Listen, I'm your Eva. I was chosen to lead you," I said searching each of my friends' faces. "It's time you let me."

They resigned themselves to nods.

"Malakai doesn't stand a chance," I grinned, adding a wink to try to sell that I actually believed what I was saying.

60

We were finally moving toward the entrance of the prison. The path angled steeply upward and fresh air breezed in, offering us encouragement that we were headed in the right direction.

We hadn't come to a unanimous agreement but we were running out of time. I had put the plan to a vote before the entire group, knowing that Nova and Remi would be out voted. They both paced by my side, silently brooding.

When sunlight started to filter in, I knew we were getting close to the entrance. Remi ran up ahead to scout it out. We hung back waiting for him to tell us when the coast was clear.

"I don't like this, Geneva. I don't want you going out there alone. Malakai is expecting you; who knows what he has planned."

"Nova, we've been over this..."

"And what if you can't use your powers or if you're too weak to?" he questioned, glancing again at my bandaged head. "You're just going to turn yourself over to that maniac?" Nova added

"Nova, if that's what it takes to ensure everyone's safety. It's my duty to protect my people. You know that."

"There has to be another way! I can't lose you," he said not caring who heard him.

"You won't. Nova, you won't ever lose me again," I said fiercely grabbing his hand and pulling it to my heart. "I love you, Nova. Believe in me. Believe in us."

He pulled me close and wrapped his arms around me so tightly I could feel him trembling slightly beneath his calm exterior. I rested my head against the rhythmic breathing of his chest and silently prayed that I was telling him the truth. I couldn't bear to lose him again, but I couldn't let him come with me to face Malakai either. My love for Nova was my Achilles heel and Malakai would see it as a weakness he could exploit.

"Promise me you'll come back to me," Nova breathed into the crook of my neck.

"I promise, Nova. I will do everything in my power to get back to you."

"Only truth?"

"Only truth," I nodded and I meant it. I wanted nothing more, than to escape with Nova back to the forest.

"Someone's coming," Luca called, breaking us apart.

He was right. Footsteps fell fast. They were coming toward us. I quickly ushered everyone back into the shadows while Nova, Journey, Luca and his friends held rank in front of us.

"Wait!" I called as the footsteps drew nearer. "It's Terran!"

"How do you know that?" Nova whispered.

"I can hear him. We must be close enough to the entrance that our powers are starting to come back. Listen."

It was faint but I could hear Terran's voice telepathing to us.

"Geneva.... Geneva..."

"Terran, we're here. Keep coming toward the sound of my voice."

In another ten seconds, Terran rounded the corner and the

group of students gasped and shrank away at the sight of him in his Luxor uniform.

"It's all right, he's with us," I said.

"Whoa! What's going on here?" he asked looking at the crowd of frightened students behind me.

"Slight change of plans," I said as he hugged me.

"What happened to you?" I asked. "We were starting to worry you weren't going to make it."

"I almost didn't. Someone tipped Malakai off on our plans. When I got to his office the place was deserted. It was too easy to get in, so I knew something was up. Sure enough once I got inside I found the Orbiture waiting for me. It was displaying my face in the center of the four Pillars symbol. They know I'm a Pillar. I smashed the Soul Cell and about a dozen Luxors jumped me."

"How did you get away?" Nova asked.

"I apparently owe that to you," Terran smirked. "Who started the fight?"

"It was a group effort," I grinned.

"Well it worked. Commander Gray called a code red and the Luxors holding me tore out of Malakai's office to deal with you rebels. But listen, we've got to get out of here now. Malakai's on a witch-hunt. He knows you're here and he's locking this place down fast. Where's Remi?" Terran asked looking around.

"You didn't pass him? He was scouting ahead," I said with concern.

"No, I came in the side entrance. That's the way we need to leave. There's Luxors stationed at the main entrance. You'll never get everyone out that way," he said pausing to telepath to me. *"I'm assuming that is your plan, right?"*

"Right." I grinned back at him.

Suddenly Remi came sprinting toward us.

"Guys we're in trouble. There's Luxors all over the exit."

"Hey, Remi." Terran beamed.

"Terran. It's about time," Remi said, giving his comrade a quick embrace. "You gonna get us out of here?"

"You know it," he beamed. "I brought you something," he said pulling his Luxor jacket off to reveal he was already wearing one underneath. He tossed it to Remi who shrugged it on over his stained Cadet jacket. "Looking good man," Terran said with a sarcastic wink. "Now let's get out of here."

"Let's go everyone; move out," I called quietly.

The group of frightened students behind me balked, but I motioned for them to move and Luca and his pals got them going.

We arrived at the side entrance to the prison much faster than I was ready for. My heart was pounding and reality suddenly set in. This could be the last moment I saw any of these faces again. I watched as they all marched past me single file, following Remi and Terran to an unused passageway. Terran said would serve as a safe hiding spot while I diverted Malakai's attention and they got rid of the Luxors at the gate.

Nova was suddenly by my side.

"Geneva, I – "

"I know," was all I let him say before I kissed him.

I didn't want to hear him say goodbye or that he was frightened for me. I was barely keeping it together and I knew if I let my emotions take hold of me I'd never be able to leave him. I put all my words and love for him into that kiss and it was like an electric charge. I felt my heart and spirit swell and I suddenly had a renewed faith in this plan. It would work. It had to work. I was going to make it work, because not getting another moment like this with Nova was not an option.

"In the forest," I said to him, staring into his stormy green eyes.

"In the forest," he said.

Turning to walk away from Nova was one of the hardest, yet most motivating things, I had ever done. Tearing myself away from him was excruciating, but with each step, I believed my path would lead me back to him; a path to fulfill my destiny and end Malakai's reign of terror.

I quickly padded back the way we had come and headed to the main entrance to the prison. As Terran and Remi had promised, it was full of activity. I crouched in the shadows behind the corner, listening to the commotion of guards shouting orders to each other. I needed to buy more time. I didn't want the Luxors to find me too quickly and not give my friends the time they needed to escape.

When I peeked around the corner, I could see the doors to the prison ahead of me. They were propped open, bright midday sun streaming in. After being in the darkness of the tunnel and prison for so long it was almost blinding.

"That's it," I whispered to myself.

I turned over my dirty palms and tested my powers. I felt them swell and surge readily. I must've been outside the bounds of the prison's Soul Cell. I stood up and marched around the corner quickly, letting loose a loud whistle to grab the Luxors' attention as I approached.

"Looking for me?"

61

"Now or never, man. You ready for this?" Terran asked, his adrenaline surging.

Remi nodded confidently and the two of them took off, running for the main gates of Lux. As they approached they started yelling and waving their arms to get the guards' attention.

"Hey! Hey, what are you two doing up there?" Terran called.

The two Luxors atop the gate tower looked at each other in confusion.

"Malakai ordered us all to the square," he continued. "They found her. They found the Eva and she's fighting back. We need reinforcements now."

The Luxors sprang into immediate action, each grabbing their weapons and disappearing down the spiraling gate tower stairs. Terran and Remi took their positions outside the doorway to each tower. They waited, anxiously counting each footstep, trying to time it perfectly.

Both Luxors burst through their doorways at the same time and Remi and Terran were ready. Remi swung hard and connected his helmet squarely with the jaw of his unsuspecting Luxor, knocking him out cold.

"I did it," Remi whispered in disbelief. "Holy crap, I did it."

"Great, how about a little help over here!" Terran called.

His Luxor was still conscious and fighting Terran as he tried to wrestle him to the ground.

"Right!" Remi called, running over to perform his same helmet to jaw move.

"Nice work, Remi. Way to use your head," Terran joked proudly as his Luxor crumbled to the floor.

"Thanks. It's effective," he grinned as they dragged the unconscious Luxors into the gate towers and barred the doors, locking them inside.

"Now, lets call this bird of yours."

Remi whistled a quick tune and they waited.

"You sure you did it right?"

"Yes," Remi grumbled, mentally begging the ornery bird to appear.

"Is that him?" Terran asked as a black and white blur glided into view.

"Yes!" Remi exclaimed. "I've never been so happy to see that cranky sack of feathers," he exclaimed signaling to Isby.

Isby glided lower and then started circling a section of the wall.

"Okay, that's where we're headed. Hollis will be waiting for us there."

"*Nova, we're ready to move,*" Remi telepathed.

Nova looked to the sky again and saw Isby circling low just ahead.

"Come on guys, we're almost there," he encouraged. He paused to let Luca and Gavin catch up. "I need you two to lead them to that bird. See it circling up ahead? There'll be a hidden break in the wall there and Remi and Terran have taken care of the gate guards. Our friend Hollis will be waiting on the other side of the wall to get you all to safety."

"Where are you going?"

"I'm going to hang back to make sure you all make it out."

"You sure you're not going to do something stupid like go after Geneva?" Journey questioned coming up behind Nova.

"I made her a promise. I'm not going to go back on it," Nova said sounding defeated.

"Good. She's no wallflower, Nova. She can take care of herself," Journey said putting his hand on Nova's shoulder. "She's going to be fine."

"That's what I'm counting on."

I BLASTED orb after orb of blinding blue light at the Luxors who charged at me. Just as I thought, they were temporarily blinded by the brightness and I edged my way to the door to make my escape. A few covered their eyes and ran blindly at me so I acted fast, bounding out of their way, springing off the slick stone walls. Two collided with the wall and knocked themselves out. I smiled briefly, and then I quickly turned my attention to a new batch flanking me.

"You guys just keep coming, huh?"

I called on Jovi's power and sent strong gusts of wind to push them tumbling down the hallway like fall leaves riding the breeze.

"Had enough?" I called, getting cocky.

More footsteps echoed toward me and I took my chance to run through the open doors while I had it. I commanded them to shut and sealed them with Journey's power. More Luxors shouted from above me and I narrowly ducked a spear chucked at my head.

"Hey! That's not nice," I called and sent a sudden gust of wind that bowled them over.

While they flailed about I morphed myself invisible, drawing on Remi's handy power. I went into hunter mode and crept through the deserted streets of Lux. It was eerie to see Lux so empty. Where had all the citizens gone? Had Malakai ordered them all inside or had he exiled them from their own homes? Perhaps he had imprisoned them too or made them join his secret society. Whatever he'd done, I knew it wasn't good. I could taste the fear in the air. The vibrant city that I had daydreamed about living in seemed like a fallen skeleton now. It's empty buildings like white bones, bare and picked over.

I heard a bird crow overhead and my heart leapt when I recognized it was Isby. He was circling near the North end of the wall. I stood still, straining to listen. I could hear my friends making commotion near Isby. I grinned and started to creep my way closer to the square, when the sound of boots on stone rang like thunder in my ears. I was horror struck when I saw a group of Luxors running atop the wall toward my friends.

"*Nova! The wall! Look up!*" I practically screamed telepathically.

The Luxors were moving so fast. I needed to attract their attention. I let my invisibility slip and sent up a crack of lightning. It ripped through the sky so loud that it sounded like the stone walls were crumbling around the empty city.

"I'm over here! It's me you're looking for!" I screamed.

The Luxors atop the wall stopped running. They were shouting and pointing at me as I gathered my powers, getting ready to strike, but I never got the chance. Suddenly pain ripped through me, leaving me breathless as I struggled against the object lodged in my back. Then I heard the feathers whistling through the air a fraction too late as even more arrows impaled me. My spine convulsed and I screamed in pain as they pierced my body and I fell to my knees.

Nova and Journey were helping the last two students through the tiny hole in the wall, when Nova heard Geneva's voice ring through his mind.

"*Nova! The wall! Look up!*"

He saw the Luxors charging at him, running along the top of the city wall. Then there was a sonic blast of thunder and lightning that ripped through the air, making the hair on his arms stand on end with an electric charge. The Luxors stopped their advance and redirected their attention, shouting and pointing at something Nova couldn't see.

"What the heck was that?" Luca asked poking his head back through the wall.

"Geneva," Nova whispered.

Then they all heard her scream. It rang out so clearly through the still air that it sounded like she was standing right next to them.

"Geneva!" Nova screamed.

Journey grabbed him as he tried to bolt toward the sound of her voice.

"Don't do it, mate," he said as he pinned his arms to his side and pushed him against the wall.

"Uh, guys? We need to go," Terran called to them.

"Journey, let me go! I don't want to hurt you."

"No. I'm not going to let you get yourself killed. You need to trust her. We need to go."

"What if it was Sparrow out there?" Nova appealed. "Could you leave her?"

When Journey said nothing, Nova had his answer.

"I didn't think so."

"Guys, this is a seriously bad moment for a heart to heart. We have to go right now," Terran yelled. "We've got company."

The Luxors on the wall had closed the gap quickly and were upon them, drawing their bows.

Terran helped pull Nova and Journey through the hole in the wall and they ran toward Hollis. There was still a group of frightened students making their way inside the giant rover Tortoise.

"We're never going to make it," Terran called.

"It'll be a slaughter if we don't draw them off Hollis," Journey yelled.

"Go! I'll hold them off. Just get everyone inside," Nova warned as he turned back to face the soldiers that were charging after them.

"Is he nuts?" Terran asked as he watched Nova run back into battle.

"No, just in love," Journey grumbled. "Get everyone out of here. I'm going to stay and help Nova."

62

The last thing I saw was the city walls aglow with flames. I heard the cries of battle and then a bag was sacked over my head and I was handcuffed and dragged away.

When the bag was finally removed I was shocked to see that I was in the middle of packed arena. So this is where all the citizens of Lux were. They came to see a show and I had a sinking feeling that I was the main attraction.

The purring laughter I heard behind me confirmed it.

"Ah, she has arrived. You certainly tested my patience, Miss Sommers," Malakai growled.

"Here she is, fair citizens of Lux. Your Eva, your chosen one!" Malakai bellowed as he angrily addressed the crowd.

"So good of you to join us, Geneva. Take a good look everyone. This is who you thought to be your savior. This child is whom you have put all your false hopes in. I'm here to show you she is nothing more than a cheap sorceress, an imposter. I am the one and only true ruler of this island," Malakai roared.

Every muscle in my body ached as I turned around to face him. What I saw knocked the wind out of me. There were three figures sitting with Malakai. The one to his right was no surprise, Professor Kobel. But the smaller dark figures on his left, left me gasping for breath; one was my sister and the other was Kai.

A fury and hurt I'd never felt before boiled through my body. I felt my powers surging underneath my skin. They were humming, eager to strike. I was actually grateful that Malakai had the Luxors restrain me with Cayo cuffs, stifling my powers, because I wouldn't have been able to control them through the blinding rage I felt for my traitorous sister and the excruciating betrayal I felt for having been so stupid and trusting Kai when everyone had warned me against it. I had even defended him!

I had suspected Jemma, but Kai? That was a blow that I hadn't expected.

"Geneva!" Kai called springing to his feet when he caught my eye. "Father! What are you doing? She's not a prisoner. She's my friend and she's hurt!"

Two Luxors grabbed Kai as he tried to spring over the wall down to the arena floor where I was being held. They dragged him back to his seat and forced him to sit.

Perhaps he hadn't sold me out after all, I thought as I watched him struggle.

"Sit down, Kai, or I'll have you removed. As usual you have no idea what's going on and you've severely underestimated your *friend.*"

Malakai smoothed his black robe and regained his composure. "Shall we begin?" he asked innocently looking at Jemma.

With a nod, the gates to the arena opened and six Luxors dragged in a hooded prisoner. They chained her to the post next to mine and when they unmasked her, I stifled a cry.

"Mala," I whispered.

"Hey, 65," she croaked through a raspy voice.

My old friend's face was so beaten and bruised I barely recognized her.

"I believe you were looking for her?" Malakai said with mock concern. "She's a criminal, you know? You really should keep better company, Geneva. You know we execute criminals and associating with known criminals is a crime in itself. "

"Who told you I was looking for her? My sister? You should know that she's a liar! I don't have any idea who this person is," I hissed, glaring at Jemma who wouldn't meet my stare.

"Oh come now. Your sister has proved to be quite a reliable source of information. Let's not lie to each other. You wear your heart on your sleeve. You're an open book." He laughed. "At least you are to me, since I've been privy to all the conversations you've had with my son."

Kai looked shocked as he stared open-mouthed at his father. Malakai waved away his hurt expression.

"Don't worry, he didn't betray you. He had no idea I was reading his mind. But that's neither here nor there. What is relevant is that it's obvious to all of us that you know this criminal. I didn't even need your sister's assistance in that matter. But she has told me a lot of things about you, Geneva."

"I bet she has. She's been jealous of me since the day I was born. She thinks I stole her rightful destiny and she'll say anything to get rid of me so she can have my powers for her own."

"Yes, she's a motivated creature, isn't she?" Malakai chuckled. "I admire her ambition, and I plan to reward her for it. See, unlike you, Geneva, I compensate my obedient servants. I don't expect blind loyalty and servitude. With me, Jemma will have everything she deserves. The powers and destiny you stole from her along with a place by my side in my new kingdom."

"Father, what's going on?" Kai questioned again. "What are you talking about?"

"Kai, it's about time I introduce you to who your friend truly is. You need to see this firsthand in order to believe it. This may be hard to watch at times, but believe me, I understand her in ways you can never truly comprehend. You are heir to the Ravinori throne and you will inherit the most coveted role in our society in a few short months. We are on the cusp of a new regime. Watch as it unfolds before you."

"Kai, don't listen to him. He's a power thirsty monster and he's been hiding things from you your entire life. And Jemma, you'll never be half the person I am! You're a traitor!" I screamed at her, losing my composure. "You're my sister! My own sister! That truly means nothing to you? How could you betray me, betray all of us this way? Malakai is using you! When you're no longer useful to him he'll discard you like he does everyone else. Do you know he has the prison full of our classmates? All the orphans he said were adopted...he sold them into servitude and if they stepped out of line they ended up in the prison, left to starve and rot. That's where you'll end up too!"

"Silence!" Malakai cried.

I felt a magic force crushing my throat, cutting off my voice. Malakai must have been demonstrating his powers on the citizens too because they instantly ceased their hushed conversations. I watched fear spread across their silent, distraught faces. Perhaps no one was here of their own free will.

"Is this true?" Kai questioned.

Malakai ignored his son's inquiry.

"Jemma, let's get on with this please," Malakai crooned in his silky voice.

My trembling sister stood, and started to move down the stairs toward me.

"Get on with what?" I whispered to Mala.

"This is an execution, Geneva. If you have any tricks up your sleeve you better use them now. I heard them talking while they were holding me captive. They plan to have your sister take your powers and give them all to Malakai."

"She can't do that!"

"Really? Because she sure has them convinced she can."

Jemma approached me timidly. She put her hand on my shoulder and I spit in her face.

"Get your hands off of me!"

"Just cooperate and make this easier on both of us."

"No! I'm not going to make it easy for you to kill me!"

"I'm not going to kill you, stupid. I need to veil your powers so I can give them to Malakai."

"He's going to kill me once you do. He's going to kill me and Mala, and what do you think he's going to do to you once you've given him what he wants?"

Jemma looked amused. "I know you don't think much of me, little sister, but I'm not a murderer. Which is more than I can say for you, or have you already forgotten about Greeley?"

"Jemma – " I sputtered, starting to defend myself.

"Oh shut up. Malakai's not going to kill anyone if you would be agreeable for once. He just needs your powers, so give him what he wants and everything will be fine."

"Jemma, I heard him talking. He's going to kill us both," Mala whispered.

This grabbed her attention.

"Well," she huffed. "I'll just veil your powers inside of me. That way I'll have them all and be in control, like I would've been if you'd never been born."

I stared at her in complete horror. She was acting like a brainwashed twit.

"Jemma, I don't know what Malakai's told you, but you're in over your head. You can't veil my powers into yourself. You know it doesn't work that way and even if it did, just because you're the talisman doesn't mean you have access to them. Nova had my powers veiled inside of him for months thanks to you and it did nothing for him."

"What's taking so long?" Malakai bellowed. "I'm not a patient man."

Jemma's face was pinched and red. I could tell she hadn't thought this through. As usual she was acting rashly and hadn't anticipated the consequences.

"Jemma, please. If you ever loved me, please don't do this. It's not too late to work together," I whispered. I could see her stubborn pride slipping away. Suddenly, she looked like a frightened little girl. "Just stall him," I coaxed. "I'll take care of the rest."

She nodded and trotted back to Malakai and whispered something to him. He barked orders and two Luxors approached me. They unceremoniously ripped the arrows from my back.

I screamed in pain and fought the wave of nausea that tore through me. I clutched the pole I was chained to for support, but it was a losing battle. I crashed to my knees.

"Stop! Father, stop this!"

Malakai ignored Kai's protests as usual, so he took the opportunity to duck the Luxors grasp and vault into the arena. He ran to my side dodging the Luxors in his way.

He stood between them and me, with only his words as his weapon, but they were powerful enough to get all of our attention.

"I'm in love with her, Father! If you kill Geneva, you will have to kill me!"

63

There was a stillness and silence that followed Kai's declaration.

Everyone looked to Malakai, who was stunned and speechless.

"Kai, you don't need to do this – " I started.

He turned around and helped me to my feet. "It's true, Geneva. I love you. I've been in love with you since the moment I met you. I don't know what's going on here but I'm not going to let anyone hurt you."

My heart swelled. This was all too much. I couldn't drag Kai down with me, but I didn't know what to say to him. "Kai, there are things about me that I haven't told you yet."

"I don't care, Geneva. I love you and you can't change that."

With that, he pressed his lips tenderly to mine and kissed me.

~

"WELL, THIS IS UNEXPECTED," Malakai said, interrupting us.

More like unfortunate, I thought smugly. Would Malakai

actually kill the love of his son's life in front of him? In front of everyone in Lux? There would be no coming back from that. Kai may be naïve but he wasn't stupid. He would never forgive him. I knew Malakai was a monster, but I still found myself desperate to believe that there was some small part of him that cared for his son and wouldn't make him witness my murder.

"Kai, I had no idea that you felt this way about Geneva. I don't think you truly understand who she is, son. She's not a good person, she has committed acts of treason against me and this fair city."

"I know who she is and I know how I feel about her. I think you are the one who is mistaken. She's not a criminal."

"Kai, she's not a normal girl. She possesses dark gifts and she's very dangerous."

Kai looked at me. "I know, Father, and I don't care!"

"Kai, you don't really understand," I whispered to him.

He turned back to face me again. "Yes, I do, Geneva. You already told me that we're alike."

"Yes, but its more than just having a photographic memory."

"Fine, show me. It won't change how I feel about you, Geneva."

"Kai, back away from her!" Malakai thundered, rising to his feet.

"I would never hurt him, Malakai. Unlike you I actually care about Kai. Just allow me to show him my powers and let him decide for himself if I'm still the person he thinks I am."

"Yes, Father. Let her show me."

He paced and threw his hands up at Kai's dramatic display.

"No! This has gone on long enough. Luxors, bring my son back to his seat."

They started toward Kai, but he picked up a bloody arrow from the ground and pointed it at them. They only sneered and kept advancing. But then Kai turned the arrow and pointed it at himself. The tip pressed firmly to his chest, directly above his heart.

"Stop!" Malakai bellowed.

Kobel pulled him aside and whispered something in his ear that softened the scowl on his face.

"FINE, SON," Malakai said after briefly conversing with Kobel. "No harm will come to Geneva. I give you my word. But only if you come back up here!"

I nodded to Kai and he kissed me one more time on the cheek before returning to his seat next to his father and my sister.

"Kai, I apologize. I didn't know you had these feelings. This changes things. Of course I won't hurt Geneva if she is important to you, but I think you need to see who she truly is before you make up your mind." Malakai turned to address me. "Jemma said she needs you to be healed in order for your powers to be intact when she veils them. Is this true?"

I nodded through my tear-blurred vision, appreciating Jemma's clever lie to stall for time.

"Then please do so. That should be sufficient enough to show my son your perverse power."

"I need to have my cuffs removed to heal," I called to him.

He looked to Jemma for confirmation and she nodded.

"Very well, but I think I'll need some insurance that you won't use your powers against us," Malakai said waving his boney hand toward Mala.

The Luxors behind her removed her cuffs and then stabbed her in the chest.

"NO!!!" I screamed.

"Tick tock, Geneva. I will let you heal her if you heal yourself first," Malakai said indifferently as a gasp of horror rippled through the crowd.

The Luxors removed my cuffs quickly and I ran toward Mala who lay gasping for breath on the ground. Before I could get to her they blocked my path with their gleaming swords.

"Yourself first, please," Malakai encouraged.

"You monster!" I screamed.

"Yes, well I needed to make sure you'd use your powers for healing and nothing else," he sneered. "You understand my need to be cautious. I too, have people to protect," he said gesturing to the panic stricken audience that packed the arena. "You're wasting precious time and Kai is waiting to see you in action."

I knelt in the sand of the arena and stared at Mala's gasping face, willing her to hold on while I concentrated on healing myself. I called on Sparrow's healing power and felt it surge through me. I felt the wounds on my back closing up as the warmth of renewed strength pulsed through me. Even my head wound was healing, and I felt my energy returning with a vengeance. I scrambled to my feet.

"I'm done, let me heal Mala!" I screeched as I tried to get around the Luxors who blocked my advances.

"Chain her back up," Malakai ordered.

"No! Mala!" I sobbed as they approached to cuff me.

I blasted them off their feet with a howling gust of wind and sprinted to Mala's side. I screamed and pounded my fists into the sand releasing a crack of thunder and blinding blue light. By the time the light dissipated, I had Mala and myself in the protective bubble of a fissure. I was cradling her head while I tried desperately to heal her. It was taking longer because I had to divide my power between the fissure and healing her, but it was working. Her breath wasn't gurgling anymore and her color was returning. I removed the blade that was lodged in her chest. It must have missed her heart or she'd already be dead.

Malakai had never intended to let me heal her. He was taunting me to use my powers to frighten Kai so he could still kill me without offending his son. I was all for scaring off Kai to protect him, but not at Mala's expense. I had taken the bait. But what other choice did I have? I didn't know how I was going to get us out of here but at least I had the upper hand now. I just needed some time to think. I could hear shouts of panic outside the fissure. Malakai was ordering his soldiers to surround us, but it didn't concern me. The Luxors were no match for my powers. As long as I could see them coming I knew they didn't stand a chance. I focused my rage and expanded my fissure, pushing them further and further back.

I had never tested the limits of my powers this far, but I had also never felt so strong. My hate for Malakai was fueling me with an endless supply of focus and strength.

"Mala, can you walk?"

"Yes, I think so," she answered looking at me in awe. "You saved my life."

"Not yet," I said. "I still have to get us out of here, but I think I can make us a path." I smiled.

"Who's that?" she asked looking past me.

I turned to look in the direction she was staring and my heart stopped as I watched two hulking Luxors drag a bloody figure into the arena.

"Nova!"

Behind him, the walls of the city were ablaze with bright orange flames, licking furiously skyward. The horizon wavered with thick black smoke. When his face came into focus, my heart splintered. It was just like my dream. I was in my tattered blue dress, with Mala and Nova. I knew what would happen next. Malakai would make me choose.

64

I watched in disbelief as the Luxors chained Nova to the post that I had been cuffed to a few moments ago. It seemed like it was happening in slow motion, which only prolonged the pain of watching him being mistreated.

"He's not supposed to be here!" I practically cried when I found my voice.

"You know him?" Mala asked.

"I love him," I whispered.

Checkmate. I knew my plans to escape had ended. There was no way I would leave Nova to suffer the same fate as Mala just had. She would have died if I didn't get to her with this fissure and I couldn't leave her unprotected to save him either.

Nova looked at me apologetically through a swollen black eye as two Luxors manhandled him into submission. The jagged end of an arrow shaft trickled blood down his muscular arm. I watched as he shook his head in disappointment. My heart was convulsing in my chest as the Luxors flogged him before the crowd.

"STOP! I'll surrender. Tell him I'll surrender!" I telepathed desperately to Jemma.

She leapt to Malakai's ear. One thing I did know to be true about Jemma was her feelings for Nova. She could no further watch him be beaten than I could. Malakai's hand went up, stopping the Luxors, and I caught my breath again. I hadn't realized I had been holding it.

Nova's head hung and blood dripped from his nose and mouth.

"Tell him, I'll give my life for theirs. Nova and Mala have to be set free and then I'm all his. I'll do anything he wants. He can have my powers, my life, anything he wants. I'll bow and serve Malakai and the Ravinori. He just has to let them go. And you have to be the one to lead them out of here."

"I'm so sorry Eva. I never meant for this to happen. I thought..."

"Just tell him what I said."

Jemma conveyed my message to Malakai.

"He said he doesn't need you because he has me."

"Did you tell him you're lying? I'm the Ponte deorum! That's what he really wants, isn't it? That's one power that you can't veil. No one else can possess that but me. I will help him get Ravin back. I'm the only one who can do it."

Jemma hesitated.

"Tell him!"

As she spoke, I saw a look of mixed emotions wash over him. Malakai conversed with Professor Kobel silently. I watched their animated discussion, while Jemma looked more vexed by the second. It was obvious from the Headmaster's reaction that Jemma hadn't told him everything after all.

KOBEL'S WRINKLED eyelids resisted as he widened them and a slow smile cracked its way across his bearded face like a fault line. A sinister idea sprouted in his twisted mind as he watched the bleeding hearts of the young lovers. He leaned over to Malakai and whispered his wicked plan into his ear.

Kobel didn't think Malakai could look more appalled than he did already, but he was wrong. "You can't be serious?" Malakai said incredulously. "Are you mad?"

"Master, we can use this to our benefit."

"How is my son's lovesick obsession with the Ravinori's prized possession a good thing? I don't need any more obstacles."

"Do you remember telling me how you employ me for my knowledge of dark magic and spells?"

"I'm not in the mood for your riddles, Kobel."

"Kai has given us a gift. I can't believe I didn't think of it before. I assure you that you will have everything you need. Complete control of the Eva and a way to access the *Ponte deorum* forever."

Malakai looked deep into the old professor's weathered face. His eyes were gleaming with youthful mischief. As much as he hated to admit it, he knew he should listen to his advisor. Kobel hadn't steered him wrong yet, but this seemed like an unnecessary distraction that would cater to his hopeless son's wants and delay their plans to resurrect Ravin.

"You're sure?"

Kobel nodded.

"What do you need me to do?"

Kobel leaned closer and whispered instructions rapidly into Malakai's ear.

Malakai sighed and turned back to face the crowd.

I WATCHED Malakai move away from Kobel and saw a slow sneer spread across his face and I knew he had accepted my terms. He had me exactly where he wanted me. He leaned over to Jemma's ear once more and her eyes bulged.

"He said he has one more request."

"Anything. I'll do anything if he lets you all go free."

"He said you have to agree to marry Kai," she said out loud for everyone to hear.

There was an audible gasp from the crowd.

"Father, no! I know I can't expect you to understand this, but you can't demand love. I want her to choose me, not be forced."

It amazed me that even when giving Kai what he wanted, Malakai was able to hurt him. How had a monster produced such a kind boy? I blinked my eyes to clear them and looked over at Nova through tear spattered lashes. This wasn't even a choice. I knew what decision I'd make before Malakai even asked me the question. I was prepared to do anything to save Nova. My heart wrenched as I looked over at him. His green eyes burned into mine.

He shook his head at me, pleading for me to save myself instead of him.

"I love you this much," I telepathed to him. *"Promise me you'll always remember that."*

And then I nodded to Jemma, letting my fissure drop.

"Tell him he has a deal. I'll marry his son."

65

"No! Geneva, don't do this!" Nova screamed as he fought against Mala and Jemma who were dragging him from the arena. I advised them to leave him cuffed so he couldn't fight back.

I swallowed back the burning lump in my throat. My heart was pounding, fighting me every step of the way even though I knew I was making the right decision. I was shaking from the pain I saw on Nova's face as my sister and Mala pulled him further and further from me. I bit down hard, grinding my teeth together and setting my jaw to keep from crying. I had finally made my choice.

"Geneva! Don't do this. We got everyone out. We got them all to Hollis. They're safe. Let me stay and we'll fight Malakai together. We can end this now. If we fight him together there's no way he wins. Believe in us. There's nothing we can't do together. You taught me that, remember?"

I couldn't look at him anymore. Every part of me was breaking, but I tried to turn it off; the pounding of my ruined heart, the bitter tears disgracing my cheeks, the words trapped by the lump in my throat, the screaming resistance in my mind.

"Geneva, I need you to fight," Nova begged. *"Fight for us! Please, Geneva!"*

"If I fight now it will start a war and the fighting will never stop. Look around you. All of these innocent people will be casualties. The Beto's, our friends and family. I would be selfish to condone that. I need to be the Eva now. I need to make this sacrifice so that others can live. One life is a fair price for many." I telepathed to him.

"No! You promised I wouldn't lose you again!"

"Trust me, Nova. I have a plan."

A lie never tasted so bitter...

NOTE FROM THE AUTHOR

I want to personally thank you for taking the time to seek out this great little indie series. Writing is truly my passion. I believe each of us can find a small part of ourselves in every book we read, and carry it with us, shaping our world, our adventures and our dreams.

Following my dream to write frees my soul, but knowing others find joy in my writing is indescribable. So thank you for your support and I hope your enjoyed your brief escape into the magic of these books.

If you enjoyed this story, don't worry, there's plenty more currently rattling around in my rambunctious imagination. Let me and others know your thoughts by sharing a review of this book. Reviews help shape my next writing projects. So if you want more books like this one be sure to shout it from the rooftops (or social media.) ;-)

- C.J. (Christina) Benjamin

PLEASE LEAVE A REVIEW HERE

Don't worry, this isn't the end of Geneva's story. You can start reading the next book now. ***Geneva Sommers and the Magic Destiny*** begins on the next page.

Or

Order The Complete Book 4 Now

-THE LEGEND OF HULLABEE ISLAND-

GENEVA SOMMERS

and the Magic Destiny

C.J. BENJAMIN

PROLOGUE

The walls crumbled, burning away all I believed to be true. Leaving nothing but a cold, dark, emptiness. Brick, by brick, I'd built my life on false hope, myths, lies. The truth is evident in how easily the walls crumbled. But after the darkness will come light. The dawn gives birth to an uncertain future, where greed and malice rule, but I know within me, a light shines bright enough to dissolve such darkness.

To stand at the helm of your own destiny is a heavy fate. And I miss you like the moon misses the sun, destined to chase it for all of eternity. But such thoughts must be cast aside for now. Destiny awaits.

1

Nova pulled the fragile bundle of paper from his pocket where he always kept it. He rubbed his thumb distractedly over the letters that penned his name and flipped the note over, staring at the trace of faded pink lipstick. He robotically put the note to his lips, matching the kiss stamped on the paper with his own. He squeezed his eyes closed tight, willing the pain to come. It was swift and all consuming, leaving him breathless. But Nova was desperate to cling to any proof that what he had with Geneva existed at all.

Gently unfolding the single sheet of delicate paper, Nova began scanning the words he'd already memorized. The folds were worn thin from the hundreds of times the note had been folded and unfolded since he first read it. Deep down, Nova knew the words wouldn't be any different than the first time he'd read them. He knew they wouldn't offer him any comfort, but that was partly why he wanted them. He needed to see Geneva's words, to hear that she had loved him, to know that he hadn't imagined it.

Little good it did him. They couldn't be together—not now. Knowing she still loved him was torture, but the searing pain that bit into his heart was the only proof left that he was still alive.

Ever since Nova had been dragged from the streets of Lux to the forest, he felt like he was in a nightmare that he couldn't wake from. Each morning painful memories flooded back to him. Geneva was gone. Nova was convinced that he'd died right there in Lux when he heard her agree to marry Kai in exchange for his life.

Geneva was his joy, his soul, his hope, and now it had all been taken away. He didn't know how much longer he could survive the memories that pulled him back to the painful mistakes that forced her unfortunate fate. Nova struggled for a moment with whether or not to read the letter again, but in the end he knew his heart would win out and he would surrender to her words. They were all he had left of her now.

Dear Nova,

You've said it yourself. We've never been good at just talking, but you already know that. So let me try to write it all out. Writing always helps me sort out my feelings. I don't know why I've waited so long to finally tell you the truth, because now that I have, I can't stop. The words flow from my heart with the strength of a thousand rivers. Perhaps it's because I've kept my feelings for you so dammed up lately. I guess a part of me has always been afraid of what loving you would mean. I knew if I ever had the courage to tell you everything, there would be no going back. But here we are. It's time for the truth. I promise you no more lies, only truth.

People can fall in love in so many mysterious ways, a touch, a glance, a word. But I fell in love with you before we ever met. You are a part of me, you are my soul. I found myself when I found you. I love you, Nova. I always have and always will. I love you with every breath, every heartbeat, every touch. You are my heart. You are my soul. You were a part of me before I even knew who I was. You knew me before I knew myself. You believe in me even when I cannot. Your existence sustains me. And trying to isolate myself from you has been torture. I love you and I can't hide it anymore. Whether we were destined to be together by some force of fate or if the madness that loving you has set upon my heart is completely from this world, I'm done fighting it. I love you.

Please know that everything I've done, I've done because I love you and I thought I was protecting you. If you take one thing from this note, let it be that.

I wish my love for you was all I needed to confess in this letter. But there's more.

First, I have to apologize. I hope you can forgive me, but I've made a horrible mistake. I trusted my sister. You were right, I shouldn't have let her veil my powers, because when she did, she did it with a motive—to get me away from you. Jemma deceived me. She used you as the talisman for my powers. It's why I've been avoiding you ever since we left the forest. Jemma told me I couldn't be near you, talk to you, touch you or I'd get my powers back. I know that was a lie now. She doesn't even know how or if I will ever get my powers back. It was all a ploy to get me to stay away from you so she could fill your head with lies about me and have you to herself. I don't doubt that she loves you in her own way, but she should never have put you in danger. I don't know what she's told you, but I promise you I didn't know she planned to use you as the talisman when she veiled my powers or I would have never agreed to it.

Second, I don't think we can trust her. I've tried so hard. I've tried for you and for my mother and for any shot at having a real family member in my life. But Jemma hurts me every time I give her a chance. And now I have a sinking feeling that she is working against us and may be leaking information to Malakai. Be careful what you share with her.

Last, I want you to be happy, Nova. Above all, that's what I've always wanted. We all deserve the freedom to follow our hearts. If yours should lead you to Jemma, so be it. But you deserve the truth so you can be free to make your own choices. Free to be the man you want to be. The man I always believed you to be. You are not Kull. You are Nova. We write our own destiny.

I love you, Nova. I will always love you. If tonight doesn't go our way, promise me you'll remember that. Tonight I can't simply be the girl who loves you. I must be the Eva. And if that means that I shall die so you can live, it will be worth it because I loved you and now you know.

Viamor ternis, (in this life and the next)

Tippy

TEARS STREAMED DOWN Nova's face as he stared at the fragile paper trembling in his hands. He concentrated on his breathing. If he didn't, he knew his powers would run wild with the anger that surged through him every time he read the note. The tiny burn marks on the edge of the paper were evidence enough.

THE FIRST TIME Nova read the letter from Geneva he hadn't been able to control himself. He'd woken up in a cave in the rainforest. When he sat up on his cot a dull pain stitched his side. He lifted his shirt to see the bandages covering his ribs. Fading bruises were all that remained beneath them. Someone had healed him. Suddenly the memories of what happened came rushing back—the dance, the Locker, their escape through the tunnel, the discoveries in the prison, leading everyone to Hollis, the whistle of arrows, Geneva's screams . . .

The last thing Nova remembered was being dragged from the square in Lux where Geneva had just agreed to marry Kai in exchange for the lives of her traitorous sister, along with Mala and himself. Nova shook his head trying to clear the heavy grogginess. This couldn't be right. He'd just gotten Geneva back. She'd finally told him the truth when they were in the Locker. She loved him. They'd torn down the unspoken barrier between them and found their way back to each other. He was convinced they could conquer anything together. It wasn't supposed to end this way, but the sinking feeling of despair in the pit of his stomach told him otherwise.

"Sorry, mate. They had to sedate you."

Nova looked up to see Journey approaching. "What happened?"

Journey knelt next to him and put a comforting hand on his shoulder. The mixture of kindness and sorrow in Journey's warm amber eyes told Nova what he recalled was true. But he had to ask anyway. "Where's Geneva?" he rasped trying to keep the fear from his voice.

Journey only shook his head. "Still in Lux."

"We have to go get her! Jaka has to have a plan, a way, something—"

"He does. He's been waiting to talk to you about it."

Nova moved to stand and Journey put a hand on his chest stopping him. He pushed him back down on the cot and sat next to him. "We need to talk first."

"About what?"

"You're sorta on lockdown at the moment, mate."

"Lockdown! What do you mean?"

Journey sighed, shaking his head. "I hate when they mess with our minds," he muttered under his breath. "What's the last thing you remember?"

"Geneva," Nova said instantly. "Being pulled away from her in the square. And . . ." His eyes glazed over, like he was searching for a memory beyond his grasp. "And Hollis."

"Yeah, figures you'd remember Hollis. Do you remember almost setting him on fire from the inside out?"

Nova rubbed his temples. "What?"

"You and Remi had quite the throw down over Geneva. It was all we could do to keep you two from killing each other. By the time we made it to the forest you'd set a few rooms inside Hollis on fire. Great news though, Sadie's gotten really good at controlling her powers squelching all your fires. But anyway, you're sort of public enemy numero uno around here after nearly choking everyone to death with smoke inhalation."

"That's why I'm on lockdown?" Nova asked.

"Partly."

"What's the other part?"

"Jaka doesn't want you running back to Lux first chance you get. It's not safe. Malakai issued an all out war against the Betos and anyone who's seen as a threat to his regime."

"Regime?"

"Yeah, he's declared himself the sovereign ruler of the whole island. He's had the Ravinori terrorizing the citizens for information about our whereabouts since we left. Jaka ordered everyone we smuggled from Lux to stay in the forest for fear that Malakai would think they're Beto spies if they returned to Lux. They're pretty pissed about it."

Nova scoffed. "We saved them from a filthy prison. What is there to be pissed about?"

"Not all of them. Some were students from the Troian Academy and they want to go back to their homes in Lux."

"Well maybe they can help us get into the city and get Geneva back," Nova said trying to get up again.

"I'm not finished." Journey pushed him back. "You tried to kill Remi when we first arrived. And Jemma—not that I blame you on that one. Anyway, Vida sedated you and put a block on your mind to calm you down. Then Jaka locked you in here once we got to the cave. There's an invisible perimeter around your cot. If you try to leave it won't feel pleasant."

"What?" Nova scratched his head in confusion. "How long have I been *locked up*?"

"About a week."

Nova winced at the idea of Geneva being trapped and alone with Malakai that long. This was all his fault and he couldn't live with himself if any harm came to her. Fuzzy memories of he and Remi pummeling each other came floating back. Along with a phantom ache in his jaw. "Did Remi hit me?" Nova asked massaging his face.

Journey chuckled. "Yeah. He's got an invisible right hook. It was kind of a cheap shot. You didn't even see it coming."

Nova shook his head with disappointment. "He has every right to hate me. I couldn't protect her." Nova rubbed his temples again as the haunting final images of Geneva standing alone in Lux seared his mind.

"Vida says the block will wear off soon. You'll start to get your memories back slowly," Journey said. "But a word of advice, mate? Try to keep calm or she'll do it again. That woman scares me. Plus we'll need you if we're going to get Geneva back."

"So we have a plan?"

"I'll tell Jaka you're awake," Journey said dodging the question. As he stood he pulled something from his pocket and handed it to Nova. "Found this in your pocket the day we arrived. Has your name on it, so I thought you should be the first to read it. Maybe it'll offer you some peace," he said before leaving.

All of Nova's memories came flooding back after he read the letter that first time. Geneva's confession of her true feelings for him lit a flame within his heart, and Jemma's betrayal set it loose. When Jaka came to the cave to see him, Nova was trembling. "Where is she?" he demanded.

"You know where she is, my son. Clear your mind and give the memories permission to come back to you."

"Not Geneva. Jemma," he spat waving the note at Jaka. "I need to see Jemma."

Jaka took the note and frowned as he scanned it.

"Your anger is misdirected. Jemma has realized her mistakes. Malakai exploited her weaknesses. She is committed to working with us against our common enemy, the Ravinori. We must all work together if we are to change the past."

Nova was shaking with rage. Jaka couldn't be serious. *He was holding Nova prisoner and coddling Jemma? She was the one who betrayed Geneva!*

"You once told me that you would do anything to save Geneva. Do you still feel this way?" Jaka asked.

"Of course I do," Nova replied.

"Then you need to put aside your differences and work with Jemma. Can you do that, son?"

Nova closed his eyes and pictured Geneva's face. A single tear streamed down his cheek as his disappointment swallowed him. He could hate Jemma all he wanted but it was his fault that Geneva had to surrender to Malakai. If he hadn't gone back for her, if he'd just trusted her like she'd asked . . . she would be here with him right now.

Nova bit his tongue and nodded to Jaka.

"Good, we have work to do. Come with me."

Nova followed Jaka out of the cave and into the green tinged sunlight of the forest. He searched the crowd of Betos, catching glimpses of his friends. But when his eyes locked on Jemma, he lost control.

Startled faces backed away in fear as Nova rifled through the crowd. He wasted no time closing the distance between himself and Jemma. He grabbed her by her throat—his body, molten hot with rage. "How? How could you do this? Did you really think that I could ever love someone who would do something like this to her own sister? She's your sister and you used her! You used me! You disgust me!"

Nova barely heard the voices of his friends screaming at him to get off of Jemma. They could do nothing to stop him. He was emanating a low glow of flames that kept them away. His image blurred, like heat wavering on the horizon. Nova stared at Jemma's dark frightened eyes waiting for some explanation. Somehow, she seemed immune to his scorching flames. After a moment the fear crept out of her eyes and it was replaced by her own rage.

"You're a fool just like she is! I can't believe I ever wasted my time caring about you. You two deserve each other. You and your precious, *Tippy*! She's not the chosen one. She's nothing. She can't even save herself."

Suddenly Nova's powers dulled, and then he was on fire! Jemma echoed his powers, rebounding them back at him in a powerful surge. *When had she learned to do that? Did she still have access to Geneva's powers?* He didn't understand how she was overpowering him. He could barely catch his breath as Jemma burned the oxygen from his lungs. Nova recoiled from her as she turned his flames against him, scorching his barely healed skin. He vaguely saw Sadie before they were dosed with a deluge of water. Jemma's hysterical laughter was the last thing Nova heard before Vida ordered him to be cuffed and sedated.

ACKNOWLEDGMENTS

A giant thank you to all who have added time, love, and support. Geneva would be nothing more than a fantastic musing of mine without you. Thank you for helping me bring the magic to life. Thank you to my parents for always feeding my imagination and love of creation. Thank you to my husband for literally molding the words of my heart into a book that launched a hundred more. To my team of editors, narrators, artists, all the love you've giving to Geneva is stamped in every page. And to the fans, your excitement is a flame that will burn within me and these characters forever. I hope you hold onto the magic between the pages and never stop seeking new adventures.

ALSO BY C.J. BENJAMIN

YOUNG ADULT FANTASY/DYSTOPIAN SERIES

Geneva Sommers and the Quest for Truth (Book 1)

Geneva Sommers and the Secret Legend (Book 2)

Geneva Sommers and the Myth of Lies (Book 3)

Geneva Sommers and the Magic Destiny (Book 4)

Geneva Sommers and the First Fairytales (Prequels)

ABOUT THE AUTHOR

Award-Winning author, C.J. Benjamin, lives in Florida with her husband, and character inspiring pets, where she spends her free time working on her books and speaking to inspire fellow writers.

Her best-selling novel, *Geneva Sommers and the Quest for Truth,* has won multiple awards and stolen the hearts of YA readers everywhere. Packed with magic and imagination, her epic tale of adventure hooks fans of mega-hit YA fiction like Harry Potter, The Hunger Games and Percy Jackson.

C.J. Benjamin loves to read and write across genres. She also writes YA contemporary romance under the name, Christina Benjamin.

For more information visit
www.crownatlanticpublishing.com

www.ingramcontent.com/pod-product-compliance
Lightning Source LLC
Chambersburg PA
CBHW030523310726
48979CB00010B/1783/J

* 9 7 8 1 7 3 2 6 1 2 3 7 2 *